# THE MASS INNOCENTS

### The continuing voyages of HMS SURPRISE

# ALAN LAWRENCE

*Huzza! Hodgson, we are going,*
*Our embargo's off at last;*
*Favourable breezes blowing*
*Bend the canvass o'er the mast.*
*From aloft the signal's streaming,*
*Hark! the farewell gun is fired;*
*Women screeching, tars blaspheming,*
*Tell us that our time's expired.*
*Here's a rascal*
*Come to task all,*
*Prying from the custom-house;*
*Trunks unpacking*
*Cases cracking,*
*Not a corner for a mouse*
*'Scapes unsearch'd amid the racket,*
*Ere we sail on board the Packet.*

*Now at length we're off for Turkey,*
*Lord knows when we shall come back!*
*Breezes foul and tempests murky*
*May unship us in a crack.*
*But, since life at most a jest is,*
*As philosophers allow,*
*Still to laugh by far the best is,*
*Then laugh on - as I do now.*
*Laugh at all things,*
*Great and small things,*
*Sick or well, at sea or shore;*
*While we're quaffing,*
*Let's have laughing -*
*Who the devil cares for more? -*
*Some good wine! and who would lack it,*
*Ev'n on board the Lisbon Packet?*

**Lines to Mr. Hodgson**
Lord Byron: on leaving Falmouth in 1809.

# THE MASSACRE OF INNOCENTS

## The continuing voyages of HMS SURPRISE

*The isles of Greece, the Isles of Greece!*
*Where burning Sappho loved and sung,*
*Where grew the arts of war and peace,*
*Where Delos rose, and Phoebus sprung!*
*Eternal summer gilds them yet,*
*But all, except their sun, is set.*

Lord Byron
*1788-1824*

**A tale of the struggle for Greek independence by**
**ALAN LAWRENCE**

Mainsail Voyages Press Ltd, Publishers,
Hartland Forest, Devonshire

https://alanlawrenceauthor.wordpress.com

# THE MASSACRE OF INNOCENTS

## The continuing voyages of HMS SURPRISE

This third edition is copyright (c) Alan Lawrence 2014, 2017 and 2022. Published by Mainsail Voyages Press Ltd, Hartland Forest Golf Club, Bideford, Devon, EX39 5RA. Alan Lawrence asserts the right to be identified as the author of this work in accordance with the Copyright, Designs and Patents Act 1988. The reader may note that this book is written by Alan Lawrence. It is not authorised, licensed or endorsed by Patrick O'Brian's family, agent or publishers. There is no association with any of those parties.

ISBN-13    978-0-9576698-1-9

Story text typeset in Times New Roman 11 point.

Cover painting by Ivan Aivazovsky:
'The Battle of Chesme at night'
Photograph courtesy of www.russianpaintings.net.
Cover comments by David Taylor, Cheshire; and
Steve Sutherland, Washington State.
The Reef Knot graphic in this book is courtesy of and
copyright (c) United States Power Squadrons 2006.

# The continuing voyages of HMS SURPRISE

## The series:

# THE MASSACRE OF INNOCENTS

## The continuing voyages of HMS SURPRISE

## A FOREWORD BY THE AUTHOR

This historical novel is founded upon the continuing voyages of HMS Surprise – not the 28-gun ship of 1796 (a ship design based on the captured French ship Unité) but the later 38-gun, Leda-class frigate of 1812 (also a design based on another captured French frigate, Hebé). This latter Surprise, though a relatively young ship, lay at Plymouth Dock in 1822, about to be reduced to a prison hulk. In this story her fate takes its fictional turn for the better. To our good fortune her sister ships, Trincomalee and Unicorn, remain preserved in Hartlepool and Dundee respectively.

For any novelist the writing of historical seafaring tales set in the early 19th century is to follow in the footsteps of and to strive for the literary heights reached by Patrick O'Brian, the author so appropriately described as "the greatest historical novelist of all time". It most certainly represents a challenge of the very first order. Who would honestly conceive that there could be two writers of his ilk? Not I. Consequently, the reader must be content with a historically detailed, seafaring tale of adventure, a story of battle and fascinating exchanges between all aboard ship, a tale which chronologically follows the enthralling Aubrey & Maturin novels and one which draws its inspiration of form and flavour from his genius; hence it is a story which might well have been conceived by O'Brian had he been blessed with more time to continue his stories.

The officers of the early nineteenth-century Royal Navy were drawn from every part of England, Scotland, Wales and Ireland (including the present Republic). It has been estimated that one in eight officers were Irish (though Catholics, if they had neither renounced nor concealed their faith, were not accepted) and that Scots represented a higher per capita ratio of officers to population origin than the Irish. The author therefore feels perfectly justified in enlisting a Scot as first lieutenant to serve alongside his Irish captain. Scots too were well represented as ships' surgeons in those times, and another has come aboard for this story.

This tale, a detailed and interwoven fabric of history and fiction, is set in the early nineteenth-century war of Greek independence. From the historical detail herein, I hope that the reader may find his or her own interest in the history of that period stimulated to find out more, as I did. The subject matter of this novel is seldom taught (except in Greece) and hence appears to be little known in any great detail outside the most narrow of academic interest. Yet it presents a most suitable subject for a work of historical naval fiction.

The conflict was a long one but this series must necessarily restrict itself to a very few of the significant and the minor naval engagements, detailed references to many of which are singularly few and hard to find even in these days of the facility of the web. Conversely, there are numerous contemporary books and reports from the Philhellenes themselves, the ones by Gordon and by Finlay being remarkably detailed. Two more modern accounts are well worth reading: *That Greece Might be Free* (1972) by William St. Clair, an excellent book and one which recounts the exploits of the Philhellenes of all nationalities; and the more general 2011 book by David Brewer, *The Greek War of Independence*.

Adding to the treasure trove of actual events that the historical novelist is blessed with are the real people of those times, many of whom grace this book. It is particularly pleasing to develop this rich mother lode into brief but colourful appearances within the story, the places and timing of which, if not the *actualité*, accord with the known detail of their lives. Lord Byron is one such person, and the author has taken the liberty of including a few words of simple yet sublime prose which Byron himself wrote within his journal for the 17th October 1823 describing his quietude in Cephalonia some weeks before he departed for his final destiny (and ultimate death) in Missilonghi.

A selected verse of Byron's famous poem (within a poem) The Isles of Greece (within Canto III of Don Juan) precedes each chapter. Lord Milton's stirring address to the formative London Greek Committee on 3rd May 1823 is similarly reproduced verbatim. The reader may also perceive the influence of that engaging wit Mark Twain gracing a few of these pages.

Notwithstanding that this is a work of fiction, the author has strived for the inclusion of many real historical events throughout the story. It is little realised, for example, that the phrase 'truth is stranger than fiction', now in commonplace use, actually originated from Lord Byron. The capture of Byron's companion, Count Gamba, by the Turks (which is described in this book) was a real event, and there surely cannot be anything stranger in fiction than the true tale of the Turk captain fortunately recognising his Greek captive counterpart, his own former rescuer, after an interval of fully fifteen years.

The historical researcher's task is made more difficult by the many and varied names which almost all the Greek, Turkish and other locations referred to within this story have possessed, not only since the early nineteenth century when these events occurred but from centuries beforehand when these lands and islands were within the grasp of a succession of colonial overlords, including Genoese, Venetians and Ottomans. For contemporary veracity many Greek places are referred to in this story principally by their then still widely used Venetian names, their Greek names generally only being used when mentioned by Greeks. These include, with today's name following:

Candia / Crete
Cape San Maria /Cape Mycale (Turkey)
Cerigo / Cythera
Cephalonia / Kefalonia
Colones / Pythagoras (Samos)
Leghorn / Livorno (Italy)
Modon / Methoni
The Morea / The Peloponnese
Nauplia / Nafplio
Scala Nova / Kusadasi (Turkey)
Thira / Santorini

The author would like to thank the following people, all experts on their subjects, for their courteous and helpful assistance: Hugh Ferguson on Paganini, Peter Cochran on Lord Byron, and the immensely helpful Elaine Vallianou on all aspects of Kefalonia. Thanks are also due to Edward Gaskell for encouragement in the early days, Don Fiander for consent to use the Reef Knot graphic, Ivan Gorshkov for the cover photograph, Paul Jones and Geoff Fisher for much help with the cover, Jackie Taft for early editing help, Helen Hardin for the final copy-editing; Anna Ravano, Anthony Gary Brown and Larry Finch for valuable comments on the emerging book; Don Seltzer and Mark Myers - both invaluable - for considerable ship- and sail-handling guidance; a very helpful David Lilley, HMS Trincomalee shipwright; Margaret Muir, David Hayes (webmaster at www.historicnavalfiction.com), my brother Geoff who long ago introduced me to the inspiring O'Brian novels, my son Alastair who managed to prise me away from prevarication disguised as continuing research for this book with a wholly appropriate "Just get on with it!" and last but far from least: heartfelt thanks are due to my love and greatest supporter, Sally.

With just a very little of artist's license, the first and third verses of the song in chapter four are the author's modest adaptation of the traditional song Mary of Dungloe, an Irish song originally penned in 1936 by a Donegal stonemason, Pádraig Mac Cumhaill. The second verse is from The Setting, a marvellous song from Ralph McTell. The two songs are customarily performed melded together by that musical treasure of the south-west of England: Show of Hands.

The beautiful poem in chapter six was written by Sally's mother, the late, much loved and missed Caroline Byron; bless her.

At the end of the book there is a glossary of contemporary words occurring within the story with which the reader new to the naval historical world may be unfamiliar.

This book is dedicated to all those who have served in the Royal Navy, past and present; to whom - lest we forget - our debt is immeasurable.

*Give you joy, shipmate! Come aboard! Voyage with HMS Surprise! Share her crew's reminiscences in familiar old haunts and revel too in their exciting new adventures. Come aboard! Swiftly now, there is not a moment to be lost!*

*Alan Lawrence          June 2022*

# PTSD

The modern world's greater understanding of "PTSD" (post-traumatic stress disorder) in large degree began during the First World War. It was remarked upon to a greater extent during the Second when the US Army conducted studies in 1944 of its infantry in North West Europe. Of course, medical understanding of the psychological mechanisms in play were little understood until much more recently; however, as long ago as the early nineteenth century, military commanders such as Clausewitz and Napoleon had at least a limited grasp of the susceptibilities of their men to the debilitating effects of observing and experiencing combat losses, both men always keeping the most careful dispositions of their reserves in mind during a battle.

Nineteenth century warfare was characterised by brief battles of one, two, or three days duration, and this facilitated the mental recovery of participants during the long periods between exposure to combat. However, the infantryman in the trenches, when wars became greatly more static, had far less opportunity to escape the constant strain of duty, usually under interminable artillery bombardment. Hence it was only these later, more cataclysmic and far lengthier wars which provided the surfeit of evidence with which to grasp that something, little understood, was happening in the minds of men who were exposed to hell on earth. Before this emerging plethora of material there was only a very incomplete picture and the most severely limited comprehension of what might be done to help the soldier who was afflicted; rest alone was helpful but did not 'cure' the patient.

The more complex detail of these effects on soldiers is beyond a book of fiction such as this; however, these issues rarely, if ever, make an appearance in fiction, and that hardly does justice to the story or delivers authenticity for the reader. In my own books I have strived to write with a degree of attention to these cruel realities.

*Alan Lawrence*                    *June 2022*

# THE MASSACRE OF INNOCENTS

## The continuing voyages of HMS SURPRISE
## HISTORICAL NOTE - THE CALENDAR

On the 24th of February 1582, Pope Gregory, by decree, determined that the Catholic world would abandon the Julian Calendar, introduced by Julius Caesar in 45BC, and change to the Gregorian Calendar after October 4th (of the Julian) when the date next day would be October 15th (of the Gregorian), ten days therefore being lost from that year's calendar. The two calendars differ only in the rule for leap years. The Julian has a leap year every fourth year while the Gregorian also has a leap year every fourth year except in century years not exactly divisible by 400. The Julian year therefore averages (over four years) 365 and one quarter days in length while the Gregorian year (averaged over 128 years) is 365 days exactly, and so after every 128 years (after 45BC) the date in the Julian calendar lags one further day behind the Gregorian.

Those regions of the early Americas, including lands now part of the United States and influenced by the colonising Catholic states of France and Spain, changed over in 1582 as per the Pope's edict, but the originally British-colonised States changed over when Britain did herself, in 1752, losing eleven days from that year's calendar. Greece however, not independent until 1829, did not make the change until as late as 1923. The reader of Greek history may therefore be presented with Julian dates differing from dates referred to by other sources using the Gregorian calendar, the same day having two dates twelve days apart. The sea battle off the Greek island of Samos, for example, is sometimes cited as having happened on 5th/17th August 1824. The battle did not take thirteen days! The Julian (Greek history) date being 5th August and the Gregorian (British history) date being 17th August, which was the date on which the climax of the six-day battle was fought, it having started on the 12th.

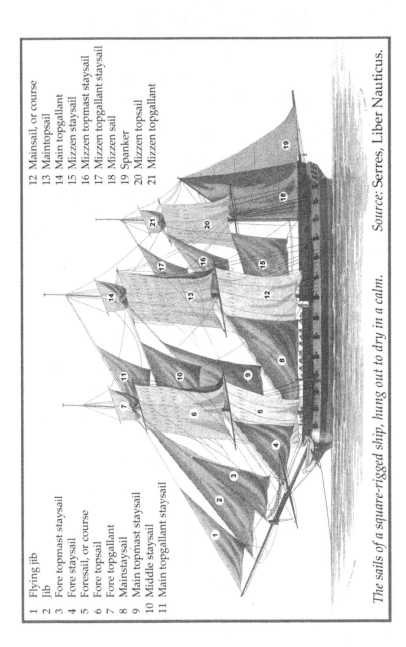

1 Flying jib
2 Jib
3 Fore topmast staysail
4 Fore staysail
5 Foresail, or course
6 Fore topsail
7 Fore topgallant
8 Mainstaysail
9 Main topmast staysail
10 Middle staysail
11 Main topgallant staysail

12 Mainsail, or course
13 Maintopsail
14 Main topgallant
15 Mizzen staysail
16 Mizzen topmast staysail
17 Mizzen topgallant staysail
18 Mizzen sail
19 Spanker
20 Mizzen topsail
21 Mizzen topgallant

*The sails of a square-rigged ship, hung out to dry in a calm.* *Source: Serres, Liber Nauticus.*

# Chapter One

*The mountains look on Marathon —*
*And Marathon looks on the sea;*
*And musing there an hour alone,*
*I dream'd that Greece might still be free;*
*For standing on the Persians' grave,*
*I could not deem myself a slave.*

*Thursday 1ˢᵗ May 1823*                    *Westminster, London*

The public saloon of The Feathers tavern, off the Strand and within the Liberty of Westminster, a very dimly illuminated room even approaching the top of the day, was filled with the drifting smoke from Mrs O'Donnell's faltering efforts to rejuvenate the smouldering logs on the stone flags of the hearth. Near to this in a much creased, green leather armchair sat a nondescript man of large stature and indeterminate age, dressed in even less determinate and somewhat crumpled attire, slumbering fitfully and coughing occasionally whilst embracing the fire's divine warmth, subsumed within its familar, pungent aroma, the meld of homely perceptions so sublimely comforting. With determined persistence he resisted the least inclination to fully wake - his state of deep somnolence so pleasing - despite the rising background clamour, the intrusive bustle of the growing preparations for the customary midday clientele.

The Feathers tavern, being a particularly convenient and welcoming hostelry for visitors to the nearby grand Offices of State, was oft frequented by actors and publishers, as well as politicians of several inclinations and generally fewer principles, but the man between sleeping and waking states in the chair was not of that ilk: Lieutenant Duncan Macleod - albeit a relatively seldom visitor, having been in near all the past twenty years more often than not to be found on board one or other of His Majesty's ships - was almost a member of the extended family of genial hosts, headed by Mrs O'Donnell, who served The Feathers clientele so personally. In fact, he was directly responsible for

1

the presence at The Feathers of the two attractive young ladies, Sandra and Emma, his twin nieces from the isle of Lewis, now busily serving the food, the aroma of which appetisingly permeated the room. However, it was the matronly presence of Mrs O'Donnell that tipped the scales in favour of waking, her optimistic if none too careful crashing deposit of a very large log sending the consequent explosion of sparks and crackling embers cascading out from the hearth towards the fireside armchair and its occupant.

'Ah, Mr Macleod; to be sure 'tis yourself, sir!' Mrs O'Donnell's matronly voice boomed out; 'A grand pleasure to see you this fine morning; indeed, it is. Would you care at all for coffee?'

The nondescript figure looked up, tired eyes blinking, 'Thank ye kindly, Mrs O'Donnell. A more welcome and roborative beverage I cannae think of at present. The stronger the better, if ye will... and perhaps a toasted muffin might be forthcoming.'

'Yes, sir; which the pot and butter have been a'waiting these five minutes past. How are you, may I ask?'

'I confess to a grand hunger, my dear... and the fatigue of the world.'

Mrs O'Donnell re-appeared with the coffee pot and a huge plate of hot, buttered muffins a few minutes later, fending off the keen interest of Sandra and Emma, neither of whom had previously realised it had been Macleod slumbering in the chair. 'Here you are, sir, and why ain't you a'sleeping in our best room?'

Macleod yawned, 'It was a long and most exhausting journey since Friday... aye, a most dreadful crossing on the packet from Stornoway - *the Minch at its worst* - to Glasgow, a tiring coach journey from there these past two days - *and cursed uncomfortable that was* - excuse me... and so I am brought here yesterday, long past midnight. Being so cold and damp I partook of just a bite of supper... grateful for this fire... with a wee dram of the proper malt, and then I fell asleep until just now.'

Mrs O'Donnell, who knew the lieutenant well of old, had the shrewd conviction that he had eaten nothing at all for his supper, certainly no breakfast since, and that he had simply fallen asleep in his clothes whilst warming in front of the fire, and likely very soon after his arrival.

'I will send Sandra to air you a room, sir, d'reckly.'

'Thank you again, my dear, but I must away at two o'clock for a most important assignation, and so I must keep one eye to the clock.'

'Ahhh, indeed, I am with you; lose an hour in the morning and you will be looking for it all day.'

Macleod stood up slowly, shook his head as if such would aid awakening, and he hugged the two girls for several minutes, kissing them on both cheeks before turning back to Mrs O'Donnell to hug her too. 'Bless this house and its treasure of a landlady; it is truly a pleasure to be here once again.'

'My home is ever your home, sir.'

'I take that very well, Mrs O'Donnell; aye, I do indeed; more than I can say.'

'Come along you two,' Mrs O'Donnell shooed the girls away. 'Leave the gentleman to his coffee, and see now to your duties. You can attend him later.'

The man in the chair yawned wide, smiled at Mrs O'Donnell, bit hungrily into the first muffin and munched with a divine contentment. In that awakening state between indistinct haze and sharp focus, his thoughts of hunger banished with some difficulty and rapid chewing, a weary Lieutenant Duncan Macleod contemplated the events of the recent few days and the brief letter he had received with uncomprehending astonishment from no less illustrious a person than Lord Melville, First Lord of the Admiralty. It was exceedingly fortunate that the letter had reached him, since for almost two weeks beforehand he had been contemplating leaving his Lewis croft, his half-pay of eighteen pounds fifteen shillings per quarter proving woefully inadequate to eke out even the most parsimonious existence on the windswept, bleak four acres of moor that represented his home on that northernmost Hebridean island.

He had previously determined to accept the offer he had long held in abeyance: command of the tiniest of merchant vessels, a Buckie-built scaffie, plying her trade, fishing, around the outlying Hebridean islands; a position to which was attached the princely pay of seven pounds a month. Her retiring master had long ago submitted his retirement resignation to MacDonald of Stornoway, her long-time owner; and Macleod's departure - so abruptly and unexpectedly presented after his initial and grateful acceptance of employment - had met with the stony faces of men in small places who held long memories. His interests were, he had discovered, more than life on Lewis could offer him. He had concluded during his ruminations through a cold, wet winter, huddled and often shivering in front of a smoky hearth fire for its meagre warmth – his peat stocks being so damp – that his interests lay in a much broader spectrum; but of how to realise such wider perspectives he had no notion. Although a keen participant in and a proponent of the traditional folk music of the Western Isles and of Scotland generally, and a Gaelic speaker, he held a passionate interest in the sketching and painting of landscapes; it was a pastime he had been able to indulge himself in during many voyages throughout the Mediterranean and across all the oceans. He now longed so dearly for the company of his shipmates of those long years serving in the Royal Navy during the testing times of struggle against the Corsican tyrant: his very good friends Captain Patrick O'Connor, a Galwayman, and Doctor Simon Ferguson, ship's surgeon and a fellow Scot who hailed from Mull.

For the four years from August 1815, after the end of the interminable strife to counter Napoleon, O'Connor had commanded and the three friends had served aboard *Tenedos*, a Chatham-built, 38-gun frigate of the *Leda* class. Post-war the Admiralty had designated Falmouth as her home port, and Pat and his veterans had transferred her from Chatham to the Cornish town. After a South Atlantic winter as Saint Helena guardship in the year 'sixteen, the Admiralty being tasked with ensuring that Bonaparte could not be rescued from his exile, she had patrolled in the Ottoman regions of the eastern Mediterranean until the summer of 'nineteen, when she had paid off from active service and gone into ordinary, laid up again at Chatham for extensive refit. The next two years until early in September 1821 had seen the three friends separated: O'Connor and Macleod had served as naval attachés to British consulates in different parts of the Ottoman Greek territories on account of their experience and knowledge of those waters and ports; whilst Ferguson, his meagre personal funds exhausted, had returned in 1819 to his adopted Plymouth Dock where employment was assured with a local doctor and fellow of the Royal College of Surgeons, Doctor Cornelius Tripe. The two medical men served the seafaring community founded on the Royal Navy base.

In that month of September of 1821, the situation in Greece had become exceptionally dangerous on account of the bloody insurrection against the Ottomans, mass killings of Turks becoming endemic, and O'Connor and Macleod were recalled to the safety of home.

Little seafaring was now called for by their Lordships as post-war budgets were severely trimmed, numerous ships decommissioned, experienced crews laid off, plus many captains and even admirals pensioned off. A reluctant Patrick O'Connor had consequently retired on a meagre stipend of half-pay (three and a half guineas a week) to try to scratch out a living on his smallholding: fifteen stony, windswept acres on the Atlantic coast near the village of Claddaghduff in Connemara, County Galway.

Macleod's wife, Kathleen, was the sister of O'Connor's wife, Sinéad; and so, at his wife's request and since late October of 1821, Duncan Macleod and Kathleen with their daughter Brodie had lived with the O'Connor family. However, after eighteen months in Ireland, they had subsequently returned to Lewis, to their neglected Hebridean croft, where Macleod was able to indulge himself with his hobby of drawing and painting, the wild and rugged landscapes of Harris and the Uists being his particular fascination.

A quarter hour passed by and Macleod began to feel a little more comfortable, the muffins doing their duty, when Mrs O'Donnell returned with more coffee. 'I hope I see you well, sir?'

'In the pink, I do assure you. We will have time this evening to catch up, I'm sure; and I look forward to it very much. Indeed, I am hoping that Captain O'Connor may join us too.'

'With the blessing!' Mrs O'Donnell smiled at the joyous thought of seeing her compatriot once more.

'Would you have the great kindness to prepare supper for eight o'clock, Mrs O'Donnell. His Majesty's captains dinnae care to eat later. Oh, here is a gold sovereign for you, my dear - *will that serve to cover our stay?* - and a gift of a silver sixpence each for the girls.'

'A flower on your head, Mr Macleod; to be sure it will; thank you and God bless you, sir!'

A tired and puzzled Macleod reflected at the fireside on his astonishing summons to London: although he had, in parallel with his duties as *Tenedos's* first lieutenant, sent periodic written reports on political developments and sentiments from some of the ports in Greece and Turkey that he had visited to a longstanding friend at the Admiralty, never before had he received a communication from such exalted heights. Why, he asked himself, had he - a lowly lieutenant - received such a letter from Lord Melville, requesting his earliest attendance in London and at Melville's home rather than at his office in the Admiralty? He had not the slightest clue to the purpose of the request. The message had, fortuitously, reached him by messenger on the final day of his preparation for departure from his tiny croft to Stornoway. His interest piqued, he had switched his journey to London rather than, as planned, assuming command of the sixty-three feet, oak on oak-built, herring lugger, *Monaco*; long past her prime but sound enough at least to ply her trade, fishing, during the summer months around the waters of the Hebrides.

Melville had hinted in his unexpected and mysterious letter that Pat O'Connor would also be summoned by the First Lord. It was therefore with rising joy and great expectation that Macleod looked forward to meeting again with his close friend and captain during the Napoleonic war years and afterwards.

The fire in the hearth now blazed vigorously, the smoke had cleared and the hubbub in the room had risen considerably as the number of patrons swelled. It was 2 p.m. and Macleod savoured the last of his coffee and determined to walk the short distance to Melville's house, and to gainfully use the blessing of a warm and sunny spring day to contemplate his unexpected summons from professional Royal Navy retirement – as life on half-pay had long seemed. His old uniform had been in his sea chest in his damp croft for several years and had been lost long ago to the mould, his wife's cleansing efforts not a success; and so he consoled himself that, as his invitation was seemingly of an unofficial nature to Lord Melville's private residence and the First Lord not being a commissioned Royal Navy officer, he might be forgiven its absence. Throwing on his old, still damp cape and donning a nondescript and very weather-beaten, even older hat, Macleod left The Feathers and stepped out purposefully along the Strand towards his mysterious appointment.

What he did not know or notice was that Captain Patrick O'Connor was strolling down the Strand a bare two hundred yards behind him. His friend, a man of modest height and stature with flame-red hair, had arrived in London early that morning and had all the time in the world before his own appointment. He was himself immersed in pondering his own recall from Connemara, summoned by George Canning, the Foreign Secretary, who was also his third cousin, a far-removed relative with whom he enjoyed only the most infrequent correspondence.

O'Connor walked west down the Strand, along the Mall, turned right into Constitution Hill and thence along Brompton Road, down Cromwell Road and so to Gloucester Lodge, a brisk walk of a pleasant hour and a half in the clement spring weather as he racked his brain to explain his cousin's unexpected call.

'What's afoot here?' O'Connor mused as he knocked twice and waited for the door to open, the tension within him rising.

The formally-attired porter, recognising Pat and forewarned of his arrival, responded immediately, 'Good morning, sir; I hope I see you well? Please do come in. Allow me to take your cape and hat.' He escorted an anxious and tongue-tied Pat, who nodded but could find no words, into the drawing room.

'Ah, O'Connor; how wonderful to see you again!' cried Canning, a gentleman in his early fifties, most distinguished in appearance and immaculately dressed, offering his outstretched hand, his genuine pleasure in welcoming his cousin plain to hear in the timbre of his voice.

'And yourself, indeed it is too, sir,' replied O'Connor, smiling broadly, much relieved that his former anxieties were somewhat cast aside. The distant relatives warmly shook hands and gazed for a few moments at each other. Their long-deceased fathers had been the firmest of friends for many years and distant cousins. In but an instant, with just that hint of warm inflection in their words, they achieved that cordiality customarily requiring years of friendship: the Irishman from remote Connemara and the respected statesman who considered himself to be an Irishman born in London, his family hailing from County Londonderry.

'Come in, come in,' enthused Canning, and closed the door. 'Come upstairs to the library. It is a rare day that I find I am here by myself. Mrs Malone is away to her sick daughter... and so there is only the porter to attend us. Do you remember Albert?'

'Most certainly I do, sir. I collect he was a veteran of the Peninsula war, if my memory serves me.'

'Indeed, he was... and long-serving with Sir John Moore... until that black day at Corunna. Colonel Anderson himself introduced him to my service. Please, take a seat; make yourself at home. I dare say Albert will attend with some tea shortly... but perhaps you will take a tint with me on this most memorable of occasions... our reunion.'

'I should like that of all things.' Slowly, Pat was beginning to relax.

'Splendid. I am so very pleased to see you again; it has been too long, far too long. I fear that a letter, welcome as it may be, is a poor substitute for a warm handshake and a spoken greeting in the flesh... but I am so sorry that I have been unable to travel to Ireland, to visit you. The affairs of State have never permitted me the luxury of an adequacy of time, much to my infinite regret.'

'I quite understand, sir; and never did I wish to intrude upon your most valuable services to the government, to take up your precious time... and my own, most modest of houses in far Connemara is hardly of a comfort such as yours.'

'Nonsense! You will allow me to say that you are to consider that my home is yours whenever you may be in London. Indeed, this house is of such a size that there will always be a vacant bedroom, and so I could not in good faith countenance you residing elsewhere when in town.'

'That is uncommon generous of you; I take that very well, sir,' mumbled an astonished Pat; the day was taking the most unexpected of turns.

Settling into an armchair in front of the coal fire, O'Connor was presented with a generous measure of fine old brandy before Canning sat in the other chair, gazing as if in inspection of his cousin, the sight so pleasurable after the long absence. Several minutes passed, both sipping their brandies, until finally he spoke, the warmth in his voice so very evident, 'Welcome, welcome again, dear cousin. It is so good to see you once more. When was the last time? So long ago, it escapes me. Was it five years? Perhaps six or even seven. I hope that you are keeping well.'

'Tolerably so, sir; and yourself? How is Mrs Canning?' O'Connor suppressed his curiosity as best he could whilst he keenly awaited Canning's expected revelations.

'Myself? Alas, whilst the mind is as vigorous as ever, one laments that the body is less so with advancing years. But I am still in relatively fine fettle. Mrs Canning is well, thank you.'

'And my nephews?'

'You may collect that George died but three years ago of the consumption. I grieve so much for him still. William is a lieutenant himself now, in His Majesty's service... aboard a frigate, *Venus*. Charles and Harriet are well, thank you. How are Sinéad and the children?'

*Thursday 1ˢᵗ May 1823, 15:00      Arlington Street, Westminster*

In his office at home a somewhat uncomfortable Lord Melville and a nervous Duncan Macleod had made their formal greetings and sat sipping tea, a grandfather clock ticking loudly in the background, each contemplating the other and passing a few moments in that expectant pause that frequently precedes the subject at hand. Eventually, the moment now pressing upon them, Melville, his silent considerations apparently satisfied, set down his tea cup, 'Lieutenant Macleod, my apologies for asking your presence here at such short notice. It is exceedingly good of you to come up from the Isles so swiftly. It is a matter of some urgency, my letter prompted by the Board... their Lordships making it plain that immediacy was to be the prime consideration. In fact,' he said in a low, significant voice, 'this is also a matter of interest to the Foreign Secretary, who particularly desires that I tell him the results of this interview when we dine this evening.'

Melville smiled broadly at his visitor as if seeking to prompt a favourable reception for his words and a satisfactory response from his guest, but Duncan gave this not the least credit, for he felt overwhelmed by the importance that Melville seemingly attached to his attendance, and he could say nothing. He began to perspire, just a little. His back itched unbearably but he did not dare scratch it, and his heartbeat seemed to pulse through his every thought. The First Lord, sensing his visitor's discomfort or perhaps his intimidation, continued in a more conversational, reassuring tone, 'I thank you again for your swift attendance... most courteous of you, and such a long journey in but a very few days. Doubtless you are wondering my purpose in requesting your presence?' Macleod simply stared at his host, nodding slowly as Melville continued, 'You will collect it was your most commendable report to their Lordships in respect of the Tucumán declaration of the United Provinces in the year 'sixteen which engaged my personal interest in your - *will I say - irregular* services... and may I say that your subsequent reports from the South Atlantic on the Falkland Islands' developments were of the greatest of interest to me?' Melville rang a little bell and looked closely at his visitor, 'Would you care for another cup of tea?'

Macleod mumbled his acceptance, conscious of but trying hard to avoid the appearance of simply staring at Melville, his mind whirring as he strived to think what conceivable further interest in him Melville might reveal. Eventually he found a reply, 'Sir, I am a mere ship's officer, a junior one - *for all love...* and... I... I cannae speak with the least authority on any matter likely to be of interest to yourself.'

'Perhaps, Macleod; but we now have need of you again in a most *personal* capacity. I will explain my letter... A most intriguing matter was recently expounded to me, one which His Majesty's Government has come to consider as worthy of the wholehearted endeavours of the Royal Navy. It is one for which I can perceive but two individuals suited to such aspirations. The first is Lord Cochrane, who has exhibited the most exemplary success in... in *similar* endeavours in the service of Chile... but any decision as to his present suitability must rest in the delicate deliberations of the highest political circles... Cochrane has exhibited a... a degree of - will I say - *interpretation* of orders in the past, and on that I will say no more. However, you will be acquainted with the second, an individual well known to yourself. Indeed, I am meeting with him tomorrow afternoon; yet I find myself uncomfortably reticent to postulate said matter to the officer in question in my capacity as First Lord, having only the slightest of personal acquaintance with the gentleman... and that many years ago... I find myself most uncomfortable indeed; and so my letter to you was ...' Melville paused briefly in his halting preamble as the servant entered with the teapot. He leafed through the file of papers on his desk for some minutes. After pouring the tea he pressed on in a somewhat uncertain tone whilst continuing to peruse the file with brief glances. 'Perhaps I am grasping at straws, but no better person than you yourself could guide me towards how best to broach a somewhat unusual proposition to your brother officer. Yet, perhaps too the task and the man may not be suited at the present time. He is a relatively young man still... and it may be too early in the career of ... of your friend to merit consideration... but I am talking in irritating riddles.'

'Not at all, sir; celerity is, I find, nae always the true friend of discourse. Pray take your time,' said Macleod cautiously, finding his tongue and successfully concealing his soaring curiosity.

Melville looked up from studying the file on his desk, his tone firming, 'I understand from your official service record that you have served for many years with Captain Patrick O'Connor?'

'Aye, sir. He is an officer I have been most pleased to serve with... for many years; indeed, he is a capital fellow and the very finest captain I have ever found; and in these years together he is now become my particular friend. I would most dearly wish to depart to sea with him on the first tide of the morrow, and I believe O'Connor himself would share my feelings about a ship again, my Lord.' Macleod nodded emphatically, as if in reinforcement of his affirmation, his mind striving to find the significance in Melville's words.

'That is indeed warm testimony to your captain... and your service with Captain O'Connor was for... for *fully fifteen* years, I note. Your own Royal Navy service record is quite unblemished, your conduct unassailable, and your occasional *covert* service in Greece was of considerable value to their Lordships. Your analytical reports from Hydra on the Arvanites and their shipping were of a particularly inestimable value... given the developments in those waters... and I am also aware that with O'Connor you have represented well their Lordships on more than one occasion when called upon for - will I say - matters more requiring of diplomacy in some of our more far-flung outposts on the Imperial periphery. Indeed, your friend has recommended and requested of their Lordships that your step be granted.'

'I was not aware, sir,' mumbled Macleod, his eyebrows rising.

'I note that *Tenedos,* Captain O'Connor in command and with your good self, peaceably resolved that aggravating little spat six or more years ago with the American sealers on Saunders Island. There's many as have received their promotion for less; and so I will therefore add my own recommendation for your step, late as you may consider it to be.'

'Why, thank you; you are very good, sir; that is most gracious of your Lordship,' a pleased and surprised Macleod exclaimed his thanks, the meeting taking the most unexpected but welcome turn; indeed, it seemed quite incredible.

'I will confide in you in this matter,' Melville lowered his voice to a whisper and pushed the file on his desk to one side. 'It is one on which I have recently been asked my opinion by the

12

Foreign Secretary. Your colleague, it has been mooted, may be suited to a role which is but recently emerging. You will be familiar with the ... the quite *independent* service of Lord Cochrane several years ago in Chile with the frigate *O'Higgins*. Their Lordships are considering whether such a similar scenario might arise in the near future, *the very near future*... and whether another officer, suited to a venture of that nature... a suitable ship too... might be forthcoming. His Majesty's Government has observed the developing deterioration in the Ottoman provinces of Greece. That is *our* area of interest... while political interest is also rising in all the states of Europe, most particularly directly across the Channel. Contingency planning it is, Macleod. I am looking to identify suitable officers with a deal of experience in those parts, and I was reminded when perusing this matter of a number of letters which you sent back to my office when you were in Greece two years ago. I noted with interest that you served in Patras, at our consulate there. One particular letter suggested to me that you are eminently suited to our imminent requirements... indeed, I am minded... and I trust you will bear with me... to quote from that specific letter.'

Macleod blinked and stared but could say nothing as unwelcome memories of Greece flooded into his mind to instantaneous and shocking effect: recollections of bloody events, visions of deaths by the score, even in the hundreds; the witnessing of the horrific massacres of many innocents, women and children included.

Melville began to read his long-forgotten letter aloud; 'Patras, 15th April, 1821. I send this brief letter in haste by the schooner *Pomona* which is departing today. I am attending Philip Green, British consul in Patras, in the capacity of military adviser with particular emphasis on naval matters, consequent to the rising throughout the Morea. The Turk military authorities are besieged here in the Citadel whilst the town has been overrun by Greeks who exhibit the utmost violence to their Turk neighbours; with the consequence that the prospects for civil stability have, in my humble opinion, been lost irretrievably; indeed, there is so much bloodshed and anarchy here which, together with an increasing number of reports reaching the consulate of mass killings throughout the rural parts, the Turk peasantry being massacred in every village, that I must conclude that the future will only be anarchy and a very bloody war...'

Macleod squirmed uncomfortably in his chair, he felt his temperature rising, his collar uncomfortable, and his mouth dry as Melville continued reading aloud, 'The outcome cannot be foreseen on account of the majority of the populace being Greek, whilst the only regular military force is Turk. In that respect, the Ottoman navy may be a potential saviour for at least some of the Turk population who are fleeing the countryside for safety within the larger towns; however, I fear that will not save the lives of the majority of them. If your Lordships are so minded, it would seem timely to consider the stationing of a squadron of Royal Navy vessels in these waters to prepare for all possible eventualities; every one of which I have no doubt will be unpleasant for the population of the Morea generally. I regret to say that the future may also present concerns for the safety and the standing of the Ionians. I am, sir, your obedient servant, Lieutenant Duncan Macleod.' Melville paused and stared directly at Macleod, awaiting a response.

Long seconds passed in silence, save for the clock ticking; a minute and more slipped by as Macleod struggled to gather some semblance of order amidst a veritable flood of unwilling thoughts, every one of them being an unwelcome intrusion into a mind inflamed to alarm; until the clock chimed the half-hour and registered its prompt, when he managed to speak, very quietly and with a discomfort which was plain for Melville to see and hear. 'I collect that particular day, sir,' Duncan declared eventually; 'It pains me very much *even now* to think of it. In the consulate we had received scores of reports of killings throughout the Morea, where Greek villagers were murdering their Turk neighbours *en masse*.' Macleod shuddered as unwanted, horrible memories scoured his mind. In more liberal company he might have described a plethora of vile horrors in the most graphic language, but he strived to confine himself to a more restrained account, 'In Patras the Greeks had risen to seize the town... and there were bloodied bodies strewn unburied throughout the streets... many of them mutilated and dismembered.' Macleod's heart turned over; his mind seemed sub-consciously to be blocking his recollections, so very unpleasant that they were, and he swallowed hard to hold back a rising tide of burning bile. After a few moments he resumed, 'Mr Green, the consul, feared for our lives and insisted that we stay inside the consulate, the doors remaining locked and barred for our safety. There was a most alarming - *indeed frightening* - fear that the massacre of many more innocents would be perpetuated. From our own observations in the prior two days... before we retreated to the security of the consulate... the Greeks were seemingly determined to kill every one of the Turks they could find.' Macleod swallowed hard and paused momentarily, Melville's staring silence prompting him to reluctantly continue, 'Neither women nor even children had been spared in most families, and their corpses were burned on the timbers of their ransacked and ruined homes, hundreds of them set afire throughout the town. The air stank of death... and a black, choking smoke from burning houses filled all the daylight, such that the sun's light could scarcely penetrate to the streets... and later... during the night... from the roof of the consulate, brightly burning fires were visible everywhere in the darkness; why, we could see scores of them burning even on the other side of the straits.' Macleod drained the dregs of his tea and sat in silence, the recollections an unwelcome and distressing burden upon him.

Melville, appalled and gripped by the dreadful tale, nodded and murmured, 'Please, do go on.'

'I believe it is acknowledged that during that spring near all of forty or even fifty thousand Turks living in the Morea perished; the more fortunate - *if, indeed, that is the correct term* - of them survived for a little longer as slaves... a woman would sell for forty piastres... *mere pennies!* Whenever I later asked of any Greek an explanation for these monstrous atrocities and solicited news of any survivors, the only reply I ever received - *ever evasive, for that is how it seemed* - was that *the moon had devoured them.*'

Melville blanched, 'Ghastly... terrible indeed; and, I am sure, so frightening to observe.' He looked up and stared at Macleod, 'I venture that in the light of developments, your letter has proven to be most prescient... indeed, the veracity of your concerns, your predictions even, cannot be faulted.' The First Lord paused with a deep breath as if evaluating how much to disclose to a lowly lieutenant, 'I regret to say, Macleod, that the situation has, if anything, greatly deteriorated even since those deeply disturbing beginnings of the insurrection, and His Majesty's Government much regrets its failure to consider and act upon your suggestion - *the advisability* - of sending vessels to those waters. Indeed, a squadron of five ships has of late been sent, Captain Hamilton with the frigate *Cambrian* in command. However, Hamilton has no license to challenge any Ottoman ship... *for political reasons which we need not dwell on.* This war and its ultimate outcome is a delicate matter in the highest political circles throughout all the European capitals.'

Macleod merely nodded; such sentiments, indeed any matter of state, went far beyond all comfortable thinking; but he tried to avoid any impression of disinterest, merely murmuring his consensus, 'Nae doubt, sir.' The First Lord remaining silent and seemingly awaiting his response, Macleod temporised, 'Sir, my own abilities lie more in the seafaring than the political line.'

'I shall come to that, Macleod,' Melville allowed a shade of testiness to creep into his voice. 'In the light of a perceived... *a general* sympathy for the furtherance of Greek aspirations for freedom from - *so it is believed by the public at large* - Ottoman oppression, the Admiralty has also been tasked by the Prime Minister with a pressing matter, as I shall seek to explain: the Royal Navy has been charged with the despatch of one further vessel... *a solitary frigate...* to aid the Greeks in any way that may be identified by its captain and senior officers at sea when in the region; hence, such officers must, most desirably, be familiar with those parts; that is to say with a deal of experience of past service there.' Melville paused and sighed, 'However, the Prime Minister is also mindful of the great potential for diplomatic frictions... and so advocates the utmost caution... the smallest of naval presence... *I am sure you grasp my drift...* '

Macleod, for the most part did not; but, shocked and speechless as he was with numerous, racing thoughts raising alarm in his mind, he nodded vacantly, a dawning perception of the possibility of returning to Greece inflicting upon him a maelstrom of near panic in a rising feeling of discomfort. Flashing recollections of dreadful experiences in Greece, one after another, were swiftly bringing about a complete change in his body temperature, from feeling overbearingly hot when Melville had begun reading his old letter to sensing a cold chill upon his chest; and he felt an uncomfortable patina of damp sweat under his arms and all down his back. A horrifying recall of dreadfully shocking events filled all his thinking to the exclusion of everything else, and in that chilling recollection, until now largely suppressed in his memory, he was once more back in the stifling hot, midday air within the consulate in Patras, all persons within the building extremely frightened and fearing for their lives as loud, rampant mobs surged up and down the street outside, the sound of many panic-stricken screams piercing the air. Very vividly he remembered his discovery of a crouching Greek servant at the second floor window: the man was pointing a rifle down to the street and aiming at a fast approaching Turk, the panicked man running in desperate haste, a barrage of loud curses pursuing him from wild beserkers no more than thirty yards behind. The memory was so very vivid, the shock inherent within it so powerful, that adrenalin was rising in alarming, powerful flushes throughout all his arteries and veins, his eyes were blinking rapidly and his heartbeat was racing frenetically: 'WHAT ARE YOU DOING?' Duncan Macleod recalled his strident, loud shout, almost a scream of panic; a reflection of the severe tension wholly gripping his mind and body. Without the least ado he fiercely seized and violently wrested the firearm away from the man's hands, bestowing a desperate stream of vehement Scots curses upon him in a hail of abuse, even as the Greek protested loudly that it was laudable to shoot the Turk. Macleod with a rare violence kicked him hard in those delicate parts with which only men are blessed, then kicked him again harder for good measure as the man writhed on the floor even as there came the most harrowing scream from the street below: the mob had caught up with the fleeing Turk and, as Macleod turned about and looked out of the window down to the street, he saw with abject horror that the victim was being viciously hacked to

17

pieces, a defending hand and other dismembered body parts strewn in a spreading red pool beneath his body as bloodied blades flashed in the sun's rays. But then, even as he gasped and shuddered, bile rising in his throat, another brief but welcome chime of the grandfather clock on the hour brought him back to the present and something of huge relief. He struggled repeatedly to swallow with the driest of mouth which felt increasingly constricted even as he stared and blinked at Melville whilst striving to recover from those most frightful memories of his life, searching for something of his composure.

Melville, mindful of the significance of the clock and feigning obliviousness of his visitor's visible discomfort - *perfectly plain to see* - resumed, 'Naturally, Macleod, His Majesty's Government cannot condone serving officers entering into such a venture... which would be quite contrary to the Foreign Enlistment Act; however, *retired* officers and other persons *quite outside* His Majesty's Service would be perfectly and properly entitled to serve. Macleod simply sat in silence, unmoving and wide-eyed in his incomprehension, as Melville pressed on, 'It is plain that their Lordships cannot order any serving officer to such a post were they minded to do so, and hence I find this a most uncomfortable task indeed... and you are therefore to consider our discussion is not of an official nature; it is for your private ear alone. Hence before my interview with Captain O'Connor on the morrow, when I intend to solicit his interest, I have asked you here to invite your opinion of his likely inclinations about such a proposal... This is entirely in confidence, of course, and our private conversation, most unorthodox as it is, must never be revealed to any person.'

The First Lord now staring pointedly at him and self-evidently awaiting his response, Macleod, his state of mind still in some disarray, strived to grasp the complex extent of what Melville had asked him; but, feeling well out of his depth, he struggled to reply, 'Sir, what ye say is of such import and substance that I cannae conceivably offer my own opinion of the likely interest of such a venture to O'Connor.' He continued cautiously, substantially taken aback by his violent memories and the gravity of what he had been listening to, 'From his recent letters, which are of course confidential and from which I cannae quote... excepting in only the most innocuous of generalities, I might conclude that life in Connemara with nae sea-going commission these past few years has nae sat well with him. He is a sailor through and through, certainly nae farmer, and so the economies of the fleet lie hard with him. He is surely the most temperate of men in his considerations, none more so, and I have nae doubt that such a proposal would receive the most considered reception.'

Melville seemed to be satisfied with Macleod's reply, and he resumed, 'It is pleasing to hear that O'Connor holds you in his confidence, and - *you will allow me to say* - perhaps therein lies the opportunity to ascertain any likelihood of his interest in a scheme such as this.' Melville spoke with less than complete conviction, though with his purpose now blindingly clear and his voice as close to plaintive as ever it might be, he pressed on, 'Would it not be too great an imposition to ask you to moot the idea... in the most cautious of terms... and to express the search - *the requirement* - for a senior naval officer... in terms of the third person? Would such allow O'Connor to avoid any answer which might be embarrassing to either of you?' His somewhat awkward request made, Melville relapsed into thoughtful silence, leaning back in his chair. He sipped the last of his tea, now cold, allowed his head to droop as if to leave his visitor a moment to ponder, to collect his thoughts. The mood of the meeting seemed to slip into uncertainty as he glanced surreptitiously towards the clock and then to his visitor, awaiting his response, the significance of his request so very important.

Macleod had gazed at his hands for several minutes, and the slow ticking of the clock, so loud, seemed brutally intrusive in the background even as his mind raced; he looked directly at the First Lord. He so much did not wish to disappoint with his answer. 'I am, fortuitously, taking supper with O'Connor this evening, sir. Perhaps it might be a timely moment to expound upon the subject.' This was said in a tone of some uncertainty, of caution, but with as much commitment as he could summon.

Melville brightened, 'Capital, capital, Macleod; that would be most obliging of you. Then there is but one other matter to speak of, and I will be brief if you are to be at your abode ere dusk; it is near five o'clock now. A new body of political interest has been formed, and this *Greek Committee - wild enthusiasts, no doubt* - is meeting on Saturday at noon at an inn in the Liberty of the Savoy... at the Crown and Anchor on the Strand. Should your discussion spark any interest with O'Connor... and failing any immediate arrangement with him whilst you are both here in London, it would seem to be an ideal moment to attend the Committee and gain a grasp of what these gentlemen are about: whether it be practical in substance or... or mere wind and hot air. In conclusion, Macleod, allow me to say that, were you also to accompany him to Greece, reports from that place with the proven veracity we came to expect of you from Greece in 'twenty-one would be of the utmost value to their Lordships. It would serve them well were you to associate yourself with the emerging Greek authorities, to gain and report some cognisance of their naval officers and capabilities.'

'Sir, I thank ye for your kind words and also your pledge to support my step. I will do all I can to help ye. I find myself likely late for supper already... aye... and must away speedily before the footpads and ne'er do well loiterers in the vicinity are emboldened by the dusk. I am very sensible of and I thank ye for sharing your confidences with me... and,' after a thoughtful pause, 'whilst I cannae speak for O'Connor, I believe I may see him supporting your proposal, and I assure ye that we shall both attend the Committee.'

'Thank you, Macleod; I will value your opinion on what is said tomorrow.' Melville rattled a small bell, stood up and vaguely indicated the door.

Macleod rose to his feet, gratefully took his cape and hat from the attendant porter, a degree of normality returning to his thoughts, to the timbre of his voice, the interview coming to its close, his spirits buoyant, indeed soaring; his step was now assured - well, almost. In his wildest of dreams, he could never have conceived the day this was proving to be: the most vile and horrific memories re-awakened, followed by astonishment and delight at rekindled hopes of long-abandoned dreams of promotion.

'I bid you good day, and please accept my thanks for your time and your earnest considerations,' said Melville in the most cordial of tone before the porter closed the door.

Macleod, his mind whirling in the most vivid maelstrom of thoughts and emotions, set off with a brisk step in order to overtake the approaching gloaming, in hope of reaching The Feathers in the last fading vestiges of twilight.

*Thursday 1ˢᵗ May 1823, 16:00*      *Gloucester Court, Brompton*

At Gloucester Court George Canning continued his somewhat rambling briefing, 'It seems only yesterday that we were rid of Bonaparte... and the prospects for more peaceable times were brightening; yet once again the French have crossed the Bidassoa and the Pyrenees into Spain... *Have they no shame?* But even that, cousin, is not the reason for my murmurings, as I will seek to reveal. No, much further away than Spain another spark has ignited and appears to be poised to burst into a flame which could have untold consequences for the interests of His Majesty's Government... most likely adverse ones. Such consequences remain unpredictable and the magnitude of them is uncertain. The likely celerity of the changes too is unknown... and yet it might have been reasonably foreseen that these changes have been long in coming and were surely destined to come about, notwithstanding the very substantial forces aligned to resist them.'

Patrick O'Connor, recalling his cousin of old and aware that any interjection would likely not be well received, simply sat and listened as Canning continued in full flow, 'The Ottoman Empire, I have no doubt, is creaking like an old and rusty hinge in need of oil. The Turks are under pressure from the Russians in respect of the Black Sea, their Egyptian fiefdom is subservient in title but increasingly less so in practical matters of control, the rising in their provinces in Wallachia has but recently been put down... and now their Greek subjects are revolting against the Turk yoke.' O'Connor simply nodded. 'The Turk economy has not been a success for some years and the Sultan has had recourse to print new money to fund his military apparatus, with

21

the consequent debasement of the piastre, and so his credit is no longer considered sound in London. He can consequently ill afford to lose his Greek provinces. Even the Janissaries have revolted and been put to death. As the frictions between Greek and Turk have been rising, the Greeks have resorted to outright piracy in the Aegean and the Ionian Sea... I receive a rising number of reports of such from consular and other officials. Indeed, Sir Frederick Stovin, the Resident on Zante, has long complained of trading vessels plying between the Ionians and Patras being intercepted by pirates; this happened so frequently that he felt obliged to conceal a detachment of the ninetieth regiment aboard a large merchant brig, a vessel well known to all in those waters. Sure enough, it was waylaid by pirates, when Lieutenant Wilson's soldiers fired upon and routed them.'

'I was serving on the island of Hydra in 'twenty-one, sir,' declared Pat with a sinking feeling, unwelcome recollections stirring in his mind; 'I was sent to assess the state of repair and the armaments of varied Greek vessels for the Admiralty; and I can only accord with the veracity of such stories. Indeed, I was uncommon relieved to depart that sorry place.'

'I don't doubt it, cousin; in fact, I collect that it was not many months after that when Sir Frederick Adam felt obliged to declare martial law in Zante, a Greek mob having fired upon our soldiers - killing one unfortunate - who were seeking to protect the crew of a stranded Turk vessel.'

'I regret to say that a mutual Greek and Turk hatred abounds everywhere, even within the relative safety of the Ionians.'

'At least the principal culprits were apprehended, court-martialled, and five of them hanged. That appears to have quieted any further hankerings for violence on the island.'

'I greatly fear that won't answer, sir, in the long term... not by a chalk as long as your arm.'

'Well, the Turk fleet has since instigated a blockade in the Gulf of Patras, and Ionian commerce is much reduced for fear of vessels being impounded... but we digress. Many more reports of brigands have also reached me, of bandits abounding in the mountainous terrain of all the Ottoman Greek territories... and the Turks are increasingly retaliating.' Canning swallowed a glass of water; 'Only last year the most extreme massacre of innocents... of a substantial part of the island population... was perpetrated on behalf of the Sultan on the Greek island of Chios.' Canning sighed deeply, studying his cousin's face, 'Reportedly tens of thousands of Christian women and children were taken away to slavery. Subsequently I have received reports of plague and pestilence arising from the unburied bodies of countless victims of both sides.'

Pat felt his stomach turn over, and he coughed as a most unwelcome feeling of nausea overcame him; a rising acid bile burned his throat: the discussion with his cousin was on a subject very far from his liking, and he began for the first time to regret attending.

Canning continued, 'It was not, however, an event that stirred His Majesty's Government to interest, let alone action, *until recently*. The Treasury is, as ever, urging restraint in case of the slightest thing arising which might call upon the most severely depleted coffers. Since Bonaparte drained us so very nearly dry the government debt is in consequence now large, very large indeed. No, the government will not be stirred to remonstrate with the Porte, let alone move to anything more - will I say - *militaristic*.' Canning paused, as if in expectation of comment or question.

O'Connor nodded slowly; he had nothing to offer, the subject was so far removed from his interests. He wondered: was this the Admiralty's purpose in calling him to London? Perhaps even to send him back to Greece. He cursed inwardly and strived to persuade himself without conviction that it was simply his cousin's political conversation. He sipped his brandy in silence, the liquor adding to the burning sensation he had felt for some minutes, as Canning resumed, 'Castlereagh, Metternich and even the Tsar have been resolutely opposed to any support for the Greeks. The official French position is unclear; whilst they favour some form of intervention this is concurrent with a stated belief in the inviolability of the Sultan's territorial integrity.'

'Sure, 'tis a pity they don't have the same opinions about Spain,' murmured O'Connor quietly under his breath, recollecting the long years of blockade in the war, many months on station, tossed about at sea in leaking ships, in all weathers and no prospect of leave.

Canning blinked, ignored his cousin's near inaudible aside, and continued in full flow, 'Unofficially, it is clear that France aspires to greater influence in any independent Greece as may come about and is covertly behind the scheme promoted by the Knights of Malta, who have offered a loan of ten millions of francs in return for the permanent sovereignty of Rhodes; though His Majesty's Government has recently blocked their loan promotion in London. It is plain that France is backing both horses in this race and has trained a modern army in Egypt for the Pasha. The Tsar, however, steadfastly ignores the injustices perpetrated against his co-religionists. Yet since the Sultan hanged the Patriarch of Constantinople from his cathedral gates - *poor fellow* - and the shocking massacre on Chios there is a deal of public opinion fomenting against the Turks, with a growing number demanding support of some nature for the Greeks... both here and in many European populaces. Since August last year when I succeeded Castlereagh …'

'The back of my hand to that blackguard, who none will miss; may he rot in hell,' thought O'Connor, his interest diverted to his Irish roots and sentiments, though he held his tongue, his concentration drifting. His Irish republican sympathies, never greatly strong, were dim; but neither were they wholly forgotten, and Castlereagh had been a brutal suppressor of the United Irishmen. His attention drifted back to Canning's somewhat tedious and discomfiting briefing.

'… as Foreign Secretary, it is no secret now that I am sympathetic to the Greek cause. As I declared but three weeks ago: *when a whole nation revolts against its conqueror, the nation cannot be considered as piratical but as a nation in a state of war.* His Majesty's Government has since made our friendly relations with the Porte conditional upon a respect for their Christian subjects. Further, I have instructed Maitland, colonial governor in the Ionians, to deprive the Turks of resupply from those islands.'

O'Connor sipped again from his brandy, but regretted it immediately as his mouth now seemed to be on fire. He refrained from comment, perceiving that his cousin was most unlikely to welcome interruption.

'Lately, as well as the Spanish Committee there has been formed a self-styled London *Greek* Committee... with a goodly leavening of Members of the House, perhaps a score or more. For the main it comprises of Whigs, Radicals and Liberals, but even some Tories; all postulating strong commitment and support for the Greek rebels... seeking supporters, proposing even to raise a loan for a provisional Greek government; though no doubt the more keenly mercenary proponents will have a vested pecuniary interest... as we will doubtless see in time. This committee also comprises military men and persons of some financial stature; there is even talk of enlisting Lord Byron to promote it.'

Canning paused once more as as if to compose his further thoughts, and O'Connor interjected at last, his brandy exhausted, his patience ebbing like a receding tide whilst he had politely endured his cousin's blather, for so it seemed; and his curiosity was now insistent; indeed, his cousin's focus on affairs in Greece screamed loud at his reluctant mind, vile memories of shocking horrors witnessed in Greece never far from the surface, 'It seems a near lifetime that I have spent fighting Boney's tyranny, for the most part afloat upon all the oceans in His Majesty's ships and service. Indeed, I have been at sea since I was thirteen, and I have seen brutal violence in many engagements and in far distant lands, some of which had even laid claim to be civilised...' Pat took a deep breath and wondered if his litany might not be appreciated by his cousin; nevertheless he continued, 'I abhor tyranny in all its guises, most particularly the slavery which is practised by the most odious of regimes. The Ottoman empire is surely one, oppressing Greece. Fellows more learned than I state it to be the historical font of civilisation; but - *it pains me to say* - that has long been a distant memory... and near forgotten in that particular place, for there is a want of the least civilisation there at all.' Pat's discomfort was rising to such an acute level that he decided he must stop and bring matters to a head, 'May I enquire, sir, why this has brought about your direct approach to myself?'

'Yes, yes, cousin; I will return to that subject in but a moment; please forgive my loquacious ramblings...' Canning for the first time sensed his cousin's impatience, '... which no doubt seem interminable and grow longer as I grow older; but as you will readily grasp and as I will seek to explain... the essence of the matter is twofold: in the first part the Greeks are perceived by many of His Majesty's Government to be mere brigands and pirates, disreputable characters all; and therefore unlikely to long forestall the Sultan's territorial recovery and consequent unpleasant retribution... at least without the assistance of more professional military officers to the Greeks being readily forthcoming. As to the second part, His Majesty's Government cannot and does not wish to be remarked by the Porte to be assisting the Greek rebels.' Canning reached the crux of the official British dilemma.

'In what form then, may I ask, sir, does His Majesty's Government envisage matters developing?' asked a puzzled O'Connor in a low voice, staring at his cousin, his mind dimly beginning to perceive the possibility but groping to establish the nature of some indistinct connection with himself.

'There is already a number of − will I use that rather indelicate term for want of another − *mercenaries* assisting the Greeks, including reputable former British officers. Latterly the Committee has enlisted a veteran fellow officer of yours from the war against Boney, a very able officer, Abney-Hastings, a proponent of some new kind of naval vessel. This *modus operandi* appears to offer the opportunity to His Majesty's Government to encourage limited and yet wholly deniable support... *covert support*. This has found favour with certain members of His Majesty's Government who are also aware − thanks to our Post Office friends in Abchurch Lane who have intercepted and deciphered the letters from several consulates to their governments − that there is an emerging European sympathy for the cause of Greek independence. Old Mr Willes, a capital man, has never been defeated by their ciphers; and his son is an expert *par excellence* with the repair of broken seals. But I digress: I now find myself sympathetic to such aspirations. However, this is far from the Government's official position, which is one of friendship with our ally the Ottomans.' Canning pressed on, perceiving his cousin's disinterest, 'It has been discreetly mooted to myself, very recently, that we should consider the possibility of a loan of an able British captain with appropriate experience, were the Admiralty Lords able to identify such a candidate officer. There is *of course* Lord Cochrane. The First Lord, when I pressed him, opined that there could be no finer fighting officer for such a venture than Lord Cochrane. However, their Lordships at the Admiralty have expressed certain reservations about his candidacy... his own leanings on *financial matters* being well known... but we need not go into that.'

'I can only concur with Lord Melville in that respect, sir... on the fighting abilities of Lord Cochrane, that is; though I am no more than an occasional acquaintance of his Lordship.' Curiosity now shrieked loud in Pat's mind - where was this leading? 'Sure, we have met in passing... when our ships shared the same port. I collect once enjoying dinner with him in Chatham in the year 'fifteen, after *Tenedos* had paid off for the first time, and for years later we exchanged the odd letter, one unemployed captain to another; I collect the most recent was late last year. Well, of course, he is in the Brazil since March.'

Canning managed a disinterested half-nod before he resumed, his voice lifting, 'To return to the present, I believe that you are meeting Melville tomorrow to discuss your prospects of a ship... and that he expects you to attend him in his private residence in the afternoon?'

'Why, yes, sir, that is the case. I hope that we may discuss my prospects for another command, however trifling they may be. I have long held hopes of a frigate; one of the new twenty-four-pounder ships would suit. In my dreams I conceive of a ship-of-the-line... *Hah! Hah!*' Pat joked. 'However, I am scarcely above half-way in the List and I must refrain from these fanciful notions until I speak with the First Lord on the morrow. Conceivably he may be more minded to speak of the Fencibles... or some receiving hulk. Either would be a bitter blow, to be sure; but perhaps I can't ask better than that.'

'Dear cousin, some moments ago I mentioned Cochrane as suited to such an unusual venture. However, it would seem to me that there is a further candidate, another fine officer, one whose career I have followed at some distance – *when time has permitted* – and whose occasional letters from precious Connemara and, indeed, the waters of many and various distant countries... I have much appreciated; and so I conceive that he is perfectly suited to such a task.'

'Sir?' Pat's heart began to thump as he sensed the very purpose of the meeting was upon him, a beat so strong that he felt even his cousin must hear it. He sensed a connection with an unpleasant past and he tried to close his mind to recollections of bloody events in Greece which had distressed him hugely and still did in his recall.

Canning looked directly at Pat, a goodly degree of affection wholly unconcealed in his gaze, 'Why, Captain Patrick O'Connor himself.'

'I am most gratified, most honoured... honoured indeed by your opinion of me, sir,' a shocked Pat replied, his voice barely a whisper. He sat bolt upright in his chair in some small state of alarm, his brandy glass rattling as it settled on the table. His mind was immediately plunged into a maelstrom of conflicting hopes and distressing thoughts, awash with vivid recollections of horrible events in Greece, and he could not answer further, as was apparent to his cousin.

'I venture you will require to consider of it most carefully,' Canning relented, cognisant of the undisguised and extreme dismay upon Pat's face.

It was fast approaching seven o'clock and the sunlight was beginning to fade when O'Connor reached The Feathers, his thoughts in turmoil.

Macleod had arrived an hour previously, and his mind too was spinning with the momentous matters which Melville had revealed. 'How best to raise such a delicate subject with Pat? Mercenary indeed!' pondered Macleod, the significance of the First Lord's request still pressing upon his mind. 'Yet perhaps Lord Cochrane's past Chilean venture was nae so very much different.'

No such hesitation subdued Pat's warm greeting for his friend. Upon entering the public bar, he immediately encountered a pacing Macleod who, smiling broadly, offered his hand even as Pat, with the same delight, disregarded it and seized his old and dear friend in a fierce bear hug. 'Duncan! Is it you? Give you joy! How are you? Why are you here? How long are you staying?' the questions poured from Pat's mind and lips in a swift stream whilst Duncan gasped for breath until his friend relinquished his embrace. 'I hope Kathleen and Brodie are keeping well.'

'Och, I am glad to see ye too, Pat. I am very well, aye, thankee. Kathleen and Brodie are in fine fettle, though Kathleen has been unwell this past winter. What of Sinéad? What of the bairns?'

Pat could hardly contain his enthusiasm for his old friend and his curiosity for news, 'All are well, thankee, and lamenting still your and Kathleen's departure, Brodie's too. What are you doing here, tell?'

Duncan hesitated for only a moment, putting aside all thoughts of his meeting with Melville for later before replying, 'Oh, that can wait. Let us proceed directly to supper and wet the swab; sure, there is plenty to talk about. Mrs O'Donnell has been a'fussing this past hour... and we are to settle in the snug. Come, let us share a bottle or twae with our news; so much to catch up. How long, tell, are ye here?'

'Why, 'tis but a brief visit; I am summoned by the First Lord. Likely I will be on the road and back to Ireland within a day or two. What of you?'

'Och, I have spoken with Melville myself this afternoon... and I will likely be off back to the Isles, to my wee croft on Monday, if nae before,' Duncan spoke as casually as he could, not wishing to raise the burning matter of his meeting with Melville so soon.

Pat was greatly taken aback; indeed, he was astonished that Duncan, a mere lieutenant, would be meeting the First Lord: such was unheard of. This most eventful day was proving to be the strangest he could recall, but he did not press his intensely burning curiosity. He forced his thoughts back to the joyous reunion. 'Oh, for you to come back to Connemara, to Claddaghduff with me... at least for a short spell,' he declared in hearty good spirits. 'Sinéad would dearly love to see you; I would enjoy walking the Twelve Bens with you; do you recall our intentions there on the mountains? That has been long in the planning.'

A little later, in the privacy and quietude of the snug, a more relaxed Pat and Duncan sat together enjoying supper with several of the best bottles from Mrs O'Donnell's cellar. Neither man cared to touch on the day's events, not least the subject of Greece, but they exchanged memorable recollections of other times, for the most part when they had served together aboard *Tenedos*; times and adventures which were recounted for several hours. Neither man was willing to let the slightest tidbit of bad news cloud their enjoyment of renewing a friendship built so solidly since a first meeting in Portsmouth in the year 'three. Subsequently, whilst serving on the gun-brig *Starling* together, they had discovered their mutual interest in playing musical instruments. The 'cello and playing of Irish traditional music was a passion of Pat's, and the flageolet or pennywhistle, that delightful feature of Gaelic music, was Duncan's personal joy. It was a pastime which had proved so valuable in cementing their solid friendship during many difficult voyages and hardships across all the oceans.

Time passed until, the food all consumed, the wine near gone and their reminiscences temporarily exhausted, they remained silent for a few minutes, each contemplating the other and wondering whether to raise the subject of more immediate matters. It was Duncan who eventually broke the somewhat glum silence; 'Ye seem in twae minds, brother,' he observed with searching inquiry in his voice; 'Contented and settled ashore after all our long years at sea, I fancy.'

'Oh no, no; 'tis the liquor... working upon me; no, I was contemplating on our days at sea... A landsman's life is not for me, old friend: such tedium, to be sure. These days, these *quiet* days at home, I oft collect our time serving together... sixteen long years it was,' Pat sighed, his voice dropping, 'Oh how I ache for a ship again... 'tis a long time now since we fetched home to Chatham and *Tenedos* paid off.' Try as he might, his overbearing mental hesitations and extremely grave apprehensions would not allow him to speak of the subsequent summer in Greece and the single, hugely distressing event which was the culmination of it; and nor did he care to mention his cousin's enquiries. He sighed as he asked himself if he was wasting his time in London, and a shard of melancholy came to his mind before he recalled his own hopes for his visit, the possibility of gaining a ship once again; but the doubtful prospect of that, notwithstanding what his cousin had said, loomed large; for in truth the various implications of Canning's discourse remained somewhat unclear to him; indeed, he consciously suppressed all thoughts of Greece.

'And is there nae some wee silver lining in that dismal grey cloud, Pat? Time ashore with Sinéad? Time with the bairns? Have ye nae enjoyed these past eighteen months?' Duncan asked, striving for encouragement in his voice.

'Eh? Oh, most certainly, and I would never look into the mouth of a gift horse... even if it be long in the tooth. That is, no... that ain't what I meant. These near two years past with Sinéad have been the greatest of pleasures... though with the swabs less so; but of late my dreams shift to standing astride a deck... nor even a *seventy-four*... a tight little frigate with a crack crew would make me the happiest sailor that ever served. Lord, I would be content with one of the horrible, leaky *Forty Thieves*; even the smallest brig would serve. To be at sea again is now my dearest wish.' Pat stopped, his thoughts shifting from his own aspirations. He poured out the last of the wine and gazed at Duncan, the warmth of long years of firm friendship lighting his face, his deep affection exuded in his voice, 'And you, tell: have you been happy in the Western Isles since you took your leave of us? You know you will always be welcome back. Sinéad misses you all so much, her sister particularly.'

Duncan smiled and nodded, 'I grant ye Connemara is splendid and nae so very different from the Isles, but Lewis is my home.'

'Well then, what news of Brodie and Kathleen? What report do you have for Sinéad? She is anxious to hear of her sister and niece; 'tis some months since the last letter.' Pat waved to a distant but attentive Mrs O'Donnell.

'Both are well... for sure they miss Claddaghduff... but they are simply happy to be with me in our wee croft; aye... 'tis in some disrepair, I grant ye, as a dwelling... and lacking a wee tait of comfort, but we have spent there many happy days together. Kathleen, being another of your Irish ilk...' Duncan joked, '... near fresh off the bog... she does nae find my aesthetic tastes too disagreeable; and so 'tis a marriage that works tolerably well. We oft stride together over the Harris hills in companionable fashion... and spend hours at the hearth in the most cordial of discourse. We have grown very much closer this past year, and know each other now so well. Brodie too oft accompanies us on our walks; we have a brace of Shetlands to carry our dunnage... the easel and paints... In the main they are a pleasantly docile breed, as ye know. Brodie is now a much more confident wench. She speaks the Gaelic, a wee French too... even she is learning the Latin; such a cannie lassie she is. We have passed many occasions in Edinburgh too... *such a splendid city.*' Duncan sighed, 'But now all is up... I nae longer possess of twenty pounds and I must return to sea with what employment that I might find. I had been near accepting MacDonald's offer of his scaffie... He is a Stornoway fisherman.'

'There you are, Mrs O'Donnell; a bottle of port if you will,' said Pat pleasantly, smiling at his hostess, his attention swiftly returning to his companion. 'But you will all be most welcome again in Connemara, old friend. The twins have repented their objectionable treatment of Brodie and now lament her leaving. Sinéad so dearly misses Kathleen... Murphy being no companion at all and hardly ever to be found when needed... and always frittering away his wages in beer *or poteen*. Like myself, this landsman's life sits ill with him, and I have had occasion to speak sharp these past months about his slacking off. The man is like a fish out of his depth, Duncan, quite unmanageable for Sinéad; yet the twins adore him. He can be both a pearl and a swine, and at the same time. Fergal and Caitlin, the swabs, become ever more a tribulation; sixteen going on twenty-six, spending all their time with the village lads, no efforts made for the household chores; daily routines hold no interest for them. They can cook neither a simple potato nor even burgoo, and what am I to do about it? I can't fathom it at all, 'tis impossible to choose the right course to steer...' This was said with a sigh of deep resignation, Pat's spirits dropping momentarily into gloom and despond.

'Och, I am sure of it, dear soul, yet persevere ye must. Kathleen and Brodie are in Minorca at present, in Port Mahon; aye, would ye believe it? They have been there these past three weeks. Kathleen is an accomplished artist, as ye know, but she has been unwell for much of the past winter... so terribly damp it is in the Isles. I greatly fear that it may be the onset of consumption, and so they are enjoying the Mediterranean warmth... whilst we still possess of a few pounds. Brodie too is painting now whilst Kathleen recuperates... for the next few months at least; but what news of Simon in these recent times?'

'Oh, he is still in Plymouth, I believe; with a local surgeon serving the fleet at the Dock; though I receive but scarce news from him... perhaps an occasional letter oft lamenting his long absence from his beloved Mull.'

After more enjoyable reminiscences had been shared, the port all consumed and the relatively recent events of the past year recounted once again, they settled to enjoy a wonderfully aromatic pot of coffee, being their particular favourite, brought without bidding by Emma.

Pat's mood began to sink a little. 'The fleet is much reduced, so my cousin in Portsmouth reports from the yard there; even those ships that remain are, in many cases, in such poor shape as could hardly put to sea in a breeze... let alone in a storm. Many are unfit to sail, much of their timbers devoured by the worm... and there is a want of crew - the Press now long gone. All ship's supplies are short, stores of foodstuffs rotten – *if they have not been stolen by some dishonest quartermaster*... Capperbar is rife, you know that. Powder is lacking and often damp; anyways, always insufficient for firing practice; ship's officers are frequently away, captains are at Westminster more often than aboard ship, shipyards merely feign their restorations, port admirals fail on their promises... and over all this lamentable debacle their Lordships claim lack of funds to do more... 'tis a pretty state of affairs. God help us were Boney to come back.'

Pat's reference in passing to the deceased Bonaparte had provided the opening for Duncan to introduce the subject still burning within his mind, Melville's request persisting through the wine and the convivial reminiscing of the long evening. 'I am fully persuaded of it. I dare say 'tis dismaying to ye and but wee consolation that Boney will ne'er come back. But there is one matter on which I might seek your opinion.' Duncan had been pondering for some time how best to broach such a delicate subject; indeed, he sensed that Pat was afflicted by the same reluctance to speak of Greece as himself, for no mention of their final months in that Godforsaken place had crossed either man's lips in all the hours they had been reminiscing. 'Do ye collect our times in the Aegean waters, when we were pursuing French ships amongst the many isles?'

'I do... but it seems a lifetime ago. No, it is those damnable, hellish years *later*... in 'twenty-one... and the bloody beginnings of the Greek rebellion... which I find fills all my recollections with dismay...' Pat stirred in his chair, his face sinking to display his utter despondence, his spirits sinking further.

'Aye, I am of a mind with ye there; since fetching home I have tried to cast it out of my mind. I collect we never spoke of it in all our time in Claddaghduff. It seems that troubles are still afoot there in many more places as the Greek rebellion strikes with increasing force against their Turk masters, and ever more bloodshed is being inflicted throughout the isles and in the Morea... as I imagine ye will have read in the press and - nae doubt - heard of even in the wilds of Connemara?'

'It is never far from my own mind... 'tis certain those events will never be forgotten... never in life,' murmured Pat, staring across the table, vehemence in his voice and a gleam rekindled in his eyes despite the fatigue now beginning to settle upon him. 'I have scarcely visited Dublin these past two years and returned to London not at all since the autumn of 'twenty-one. Excepting a very occasional visit to Galway town I have never left Connemara, and I have paid no attention to anything in London or elsewhere... save for my correspondence with their Lordships... The farm, of course, is something of a burden, I regret to say; a small place it is... after the sea... after the expanse of the oceans... astride a deck... the bow pitching into successive rollers... Oh dear, what a bore I am become!' declared Pat, still firmly of a mind to avoid mention of Greece, and to save what remained of his evening and his reunion with his friend. He endeavoured to change the subject, 'Now that you mention that... *that place*, I do recall some talk about a new form of warship for... *for the insurrectionists*. Yes, it comes back to me now: a steam-driven vessel, by God; and we have one in service too, *Comet*, and a second... *Lightning*, is on the stocks... 'tis sure they are the coming thing. I collect *Savannah* steamed across the Atlantic in the year 'nineteen in but twenty-four days... 'tis most assuredly a signal for what is yet to come.'

'Och, I am nae engineer, Pat; little do I know about this emerging form of motion or the construction of ships – such things are wholly outside my experience – but of one thing I am certain, progress is relentless in all of our activities and certainly therefore 'tis as sure for *political developments* as it is for the propulsion of ships.' Duncan was thinking now rather more nimbly as to the line that he might take with this particular subject. 'In fact, now that ye mention such a form of ship, I do collect it was spoken of only this afternoon in the discussion I had with Lord Melville.' He began to feel his way to surer ground, 'His Lordship referred to a most interesting dilemma which had arisen following the succession of Castlereagh by Canning as Foreign Secretary... and the emerging interest amongst the Whigs as well as the Radicals for the cause of an independent Greece... free of Turk suzerainty and with a generally Christian society... albeit of the Orthodox persuasion...' Duncan paused, Pat's interest was visibly waining.

Pat sighed inwardly, politics held not the least interest for him; indeed, he had never seen Duncan display any such interest either, and he wondered why on earth his friend was unexpectedly speaking of politics and where this was leading. He nodded without enthusiasm to Duncan. 'Please... do continue.'

'Apparently, a committee has been established to further this cause, to procure supplies and funds, military provisions too, so as to aid the Greek liberation. That is where I recall mention of this new form of ship... steam-driven, as ye say, and 'tis

35

propounded by a former naval colleague, Abney-Hastings, an officer whom I believe served with Lord Nelson at Trafalgar.'

Intrigued by mention of the new steam ship, Pat began to feel an emerging interest in Duncan's explanation and, as best he could after such prodigious consumption of alcohol, he sloughed off his fatigue somewhat, his tired mind recalling the name after a moment, 'Abney-Hastings was a youngster, a volunteer aboard *Neptune* at Trafalgar, aged but eleven; he later became a lieutenant and master of the survey vessel *Kangaroo* in Jamaica. I collect he left the service after some disagreement with the flag-captain at Port Royal, who bawled him out publicly, for he had overlaid his cable... Captain Parker shouting from his deck that his ship handling was not seamanlike. Did not Abney-Hastings offer him out... and so was dismissed the service, Melville refusing to hear his case? A thoroughly shabby affair.'

Duncan, sensing firmer ground approaching for Melville's proposal, continued, 'I am sure ye are right, but we digress. Those Members of Parliament and others who have declared support for the Greek cause will meet in committee at the *Crown and Anchor* on the Strand this Saturday. Their intention is to procure able military and naval officers to further the prospects for the formative Greek government. I have heard mention of Abney-Hastings in that respect... and indeed also Cochrane.'

'Cochrane! Cochrane, the Sea Wolf, the Old Dog!' exclaimed Pat, his voice rising. 'Well I never! His name was mentioned to me only today, this Greek committee too. My cousin, Canning, was sounding out my interest in some rum venture to Greek waters... I cannot fathom it. Certainly, Cochrane would be an excellent prize for the committee and the Greeks; but, as I collect, he was still in service for Chile when we quit the South Atlantic... and if my memory serves me well... yes... I do believe that he intends to return to service down there for the Brazil... and may be there already.'

Duncan was taken aback to find that Pat had already been introduced, to some degree, to the very same subject which he had been manoeuvring to broach for several hours, and he gazed with astonishment at his friend. A silent minute or more passed as he summoned with difficulty near-forgotten memories from a patchy recollection of a conversation with Cochrane himself during dinner many years previously, eventually relegating his recollections as irrelevant. 'I am sure ye are well informed and correct as to his whereabouts as well as his continuing responsibilities, and there can surely be nae certitude that Cochrane would return in response to any call from their Lordships at the Admiralty; indeed, I imagine that the friction with which Cochrane engages still with ministers might well be prejudicial to just such a proposal.'

Pat nodded, 'Of course Cochrane has lobbied hard these past years to secure his pardon... and also his knighthood restored in the face of the King's unwillingness to entertain his case... Aye, I venture 'tis surely unlikely that he could be persuaded by any pleas originating from anyone associated with His Majesty's Government. No, Cochrane will not do... and a further matter to be minded: any serving British officer... myself included for that matter (the thought struck him) is forbidden from engagement by the foreigner... which surely narrows the field considerably.'

This latter comment from Pat, being a fresh element in Duncan's exceedingly thin knowledge of the restrictions of the British state for its officers in foreign military servitude, stopped the tentative thoughts of his tired mind dead in their tracks, until he recalled that - as Melville had explained - any officer acting for the Greeks could not be a serving British officer in any event, for political reasons. The Foreign Secretary would only commit to participate in such an undertaking in support of Greece were the arrangement to have absolutely no overt link to His Majesty's Government whatsoever. Of what arrangement was Melville possibly thinking when he referred to O'Connor? How could he suggest Pat become a participant whilst being a serving captain of the Royal Navy? Deep fatigue began to overtake Duncan, for the continuation of a subject in which he was clearly foundering on the very limit of his experience was rapidly proving beyond him. Time to leave matters until the morrow, he thought. 'I cannae linger with ye longer; my eyes demand sleep and my bed beckons.'

Pat too, despite the more intriguing elements of their conversation, was flagging; and, mindful of his appointment the next day with Lord Melville, he resigned himself to his bed. Their eyes met as they rose from the table and Pat reached for Duncan's hand. 'Good night, brother; 'tis so very good to see you. I will surely sleep well tonight.'

'Good night, auld friend,' Duncan nodded, returning Pat's unwavering, fierce grip.

# Chapter Two

*The Scian and the Teian muse,*
*The hero's harp, the lover's lute,*
*Have found the fame your shores refuse;*
*Their place of birth alone is mute*
*To sounds which echo further west*
*Than your sires' 'Islands of the Blest'*

*Friday 2ⁿᵈ May 1823*                    *The Feathers Tavern, 2 a.m.*

Contrary to his expectations and despite the substantial volume of liquor which he had consumed throughout the enjoyable evening with his bosom friend, Pat did not sleep well at all; rather, as the alcohol burned through his blood flow and his body temperature rose to an uncomfortable high after several somnolent hours, he restlessly turned about in search of a deeper sleep. His mind hovered in a fluctuating state of discomfort between slumber and wakefulness until, eventually, it wandered into disturbing recollections of painfully distressing past times in Greece, his discussion with Canning perhaps preying on his subconscious mind. He most particularly recalled being stationed as an Admiralty observer on the island of Hydra in 1821 after *Tenedos* had been laid up in ordinary at Woolwich. Hydra was the home of the largest collection of Greek brigs serving as warships, and Pat was tasked with discussing the war at sea with the leading Hydriot leaders there who owned ships, the merchant Andreas Miaoulis being the most well known of them all. The Hydriots and their neighbouring Spetziots were often rivals at sea, and Pat had been charged with exploring the possibility of the organisation of a unified Greek naval authority; but to his dismay the command of fifty or more ships, the smaller ones being converted fishing boats and the larger ones merchant brigs, all with disparate collections of guns of many calibres, was little more than anarchical, or so it seemed to Pat's regular, Royal Navy mind; and after several months he despaired of achieving anything, the slightest thing. Indeed, with no Englishmen, no Irishmen, no Scots, or even a solitary Welshman to speak with; not a one with him on the island, Pat had become quite lonely, even despondent; for it was plain that none of the Greek captains paid him the slightest mind once they had determined that he had no access to funds to disburse to them; and so he reconciled himself to waiting each day for any Royal Navy vessel to call, or even any merchantman which was bound for England, Gibraltar, Mahon, Malta, or anywhere else at all, *anywhere*; and he intended that he would embark, and never mind the consequences even if they mandated an obligatory stay in the Marshalsea or the Fleet. He was past caring, he simply longed to return home, home to his family, to his hearth and peat fire, to even the plain meals of the despised potato, and to see the very precious foundations of life itself restored.

In his semi-conscious state of sleepless discomfort, in his turbulent mind, Pat's vivid dream once more returned to the most distressing day of his life, in May 1821: it had started well enough, in the late afternoon, where he was sitting at a table on the quayside of Hydra, despondently reflecting on the evident futility of his efforts and abstractedly considering the relative merits of warm, sunny Hydra in comparison with his cold home in windswept, wet Connemara. In the quietude of his relaxation, a delightfully agreeable recall entered his thoughts: he was sitting on a tree stump in the smallest, most ramshackle of shebeens, and the homespun scene was wholly, vividly real to him: a familiar excursion into the Roundstone Bog, familiar faces before him around the smoky peat fire as he sipped a rough - *the roughest* - of bootleg poteen; even now, thirty years and more later, he was sure he could still taste it - the delightful memory that it was - and he was equally convinced that he could feel the burning sensation of his throat as he swallowed; and in that brief moment it exerted the most delightful appeal to his senses, a warm glow of nostalgia coming upon him as he dreamily reflected on those distant days of his youth. Oh, to repeat them... if only such was possible. He sighed, the rude realisation that some things would always remain beyond the most determined of grasps, that such memorable - indeed precious - times would never return, brought him back to earth with another and more sobering sigh of dismay. He blinked in the bright sunlight and looked across the harbour waters as his eyes caught the approaching topsails of the Hydriot brigs returning to port. He raised his telescope to study the flotilla, a dozen vessels at least, and his eye followed them closely until they anchored, when a profusion of small boats were filled with their disembarking crews, and all were rowed ashore. He wandered in pleasant fashion down to where Greek crews were stepping up to the quay where his gaze caught sight of two score and more of Turks, whom he presumed were a captured crew, all cowering in a huddle on the beach, frequently lashed by a Greek with a stick. All the arriving Greeks ignored Pat as they passed him by and went to seek refreshment in several nearby tavernas on the waterfront. He stepped down to the sand and walked across to the captive Turks, the most dejected and frightened group of people he had ever seen, and so visibly crushed in spirit. He had no Turkish language with which to speak with anyone present but he learned from an English-speaking Greek that the Turkish merchant brig had been caught by an overpowering number of Greeks and they had consequently surrendered.

Pat determined to speak with Admiral Tombazes and he set off in search of the Greek, believing he had gone ashore with his men, but an hour exploring the quay taverns and he was nowhere to be found. The sun was fast sinking as Pat walked slowly along the quay, and with a rising feeling of alarm he saw the Turk prisoners being hastened along the stony beach towards the west, a loud and cursing mob beating them with staves and batons. He wondered, with a most disquieting sense of premonition, what was going on; and he strived to reassure himself that the Turk captives were being driven to a place of confinement, even as they rounded the prominent spur of the coast. The low sun began to dip behind the island horizon and a disconsolate Pat stared for a half-hour into a sky filled with a radiant backcloth array of reds and purples until the sun's rays were gone and a diffuse twilight lingered upon the scene. Resigned to another day passing with nothing achieved, or so it seemed, he returned to sit outside his favourite taverna for a late supper, from where he could overlook the harbour and watch the world go by until the light was finally gone. He chewed slowly on an uninspiring flat bread, reflecting on his unwelcome feelings of exile, and he sipped a poor wine from a pewter goblet without a deal of taste registering from either, even as his mind strived to figure out how much longer he would be marooned in this backwater, wholly bereft of influence or interest; until his nose caught the sharp scent of burning wood, probably driftwood, as it blew in from the west, from beyond the coast promontory; and he wondered why on earth anyone would light a fire in that location. His food arrived, a stewed beef stifado with a most appealing aroma, his table illuminated by a lantern, and he began to eat at last with relish. Fifteen minutes gone and almost all was consumed, when he heard distant loud screams and squeals of people who were undoubtedly enduring the most excruciating agonies. Greatly alarmed, he downed his knife and fork, and he rushed from the taverna and hastened across to a cluster of locals; he seized by his shirt a familiar man who he knew had at least a smattering of English. 'What's that screaming?' he screamed himself, his mind racing with an alarm which ripped through all his thoughts to the exclusion of everything, the brutal sounds so absolutely frightening and so extremely incongruous in a place he had believed an oasis of tranquillity; the shock absolutely destroying the usual placidity of his day.

'Pay that no mind,' replied the Greek offhandedly, 'the Turk prisoners are being burned alive.'

Pat was utterly overwhelmed by a body blow of shock in an instant, his very being submerged within a huge flood of distress, both mental and physical; in scarcely a second he vomited, not the least control available to him as his throat convulsed in spasms and convulsions, the whole of his undigested dinner sprayed upon the ground as the Greek leaped backwards. The acute screams, scores of them, seemed louder than ever and violently assaulted his ears; it felt as if his heart was physically turning over within him, and it raced like never before, strong beating pulses assailing all efforts at control, at restraint ; and as his mind scrambled to regain some form of grip over the fierce

42

fury of the tumult of his thoughts, he realised that he was more grateful than he had ever felt at any time of his life that he could see nothing of the murderous massacre. 'WHAT AM I DOING IN THIS GODFORSAKEN PLACE?' he cried out at the top of his voice in unconstrained despair; to the consternation of his Greek acquaintance and all others nearby.

Several painful minutes of the most extreme anxiety went by as if carrying him on a mental flood tide whilst his mind was racked by extremely painful and bloody recollections until, in huge distress and with his body shaking violently, he woke up. He sat up in a bed, much of which was soaked wet in sweat, with his whole frame pulsating with severe palpitations, so extreme that he felt sure he could hear his heart beating; his chest and back were stuck to his sodden nightshirt which was rapidly cooling in the cold, unheated room. Several more greatly uncomfortable minutes elapsed as the panic slowly subsided and Pat, sloughing off the mental confusion as his mind made the transition to consciousness, finally recognised the dismal bedroom all about him in the darkness. The realisation that he was no longer in Hydra but in London and the massacre was long in the past brought a tidal wave of relief. He lay back but he could not bring himself in his still considerable angst to try again for sleep, so profoundly disturbed that he was by the unwanted recurrence of unwelcome thoughts: black memories which he had tried hard to put out of mind ever since the event itself but only ever with limited success; for the nightmare had recurred on several occasions, and it always left him hugely set back in a paroxysm of distress verging on panic. More cooling minutes passed as he shifted to sit on the side of his bed and strived to gather more of his senses, his body's enduring physical tremors an unwelcome reminder of his tormenting recollections. He rose from his bed eventually, shivered violently in the cold air, his sweat now a chilly film all about his upper body. He slung his overcoat over his soaked nightshirt and he stepped, his gait unsteady, down the stairs to the great bar of the tavern where the welcome fire still burned brightly. He slumped into the fireside chair, grateful for the warmth of the flames, and he tried to gather some better semblance of control over his thoughts even as he found himself quite choked and with tears streaking his cheeks, and he felt sure that his thumping heart - pounding harder than that of a hound closing on its prey, for so it seemed - would burst even as his breathing slowly subsided. Slow, silent minutes went by as he sat all alone at the hearth, only the crackling and spitting noises of the burning logs scarcely intruding into an absolute quietude as he tried to think of anything, the least thing, save his dreadful experience in Greece, on Hydra island; and he resolved - swore to himself - that he would never return to that bloody conflict, never! Even if it condemned him to paupery for evermore and an unremarkable life of small routine on his cold, bleak and rainswept croft on the peat bog.

A concerned young voice sounded quietly in his ear, 'Can I be of assistance, sir?' It was young Emma approaching, and Pat, much startled, turned around. 'Beg pardon, sir,' she spoke with a solicitous air, 'I am the night porter.'

'Oh... no, no; thank you my dear,' exclaimed Pat, the small reminder of a present normality so welcome, a tidal wave of relief flooding his confused thoughts to the exclusion of all else; until his thinking processes had slowed, and he began to embrace a gradual and most welcome return to more comfortable considerations; 'Well, perhaps a cup of coffee... if that is possible at this hour.'

'Of course, sir; just a few minutes, if you please.'

Ten minutes later and Pat sipped the most welcome cup of coffee of his entire life; the gloriously strong, black beverage flowed pleasurably through his every fibre, or so it seemed in his deep fatigue, and the tiny dawnings of small relaxation began to settle upon his racing, despairing mind; his distressing recollections of Hydra were, thankfully, slowly fading; and he strived to gather his thoughts in some semblance of preparation for the new day, until Duncan stepped through the door a few minutes later and came over towards the fire with a smile.

'Duncan, what are you doing up at this unearthly hour?'

'Aye, well, I could say the same about you, save that I heard your shouts from the next bedroom.' Duncan sat down in the near chair and waved to Emma, 'More coffee if ye will, lass.' He turned back to Pat, 'Greece again? Hydra? The Turk prisoners?'

'Oh... yes, but we will pay that no mind?' said Pat; 'We are military men and must bear that particular cross; it is our lot, I regret to say.'

'Aye, military men for sure, but nae murderers,' Duncan spoke in a low voice, not wishing Emma to hear anything of such a horrible event; 'Melville spoke with me of Greece only yesterday... and I didnae have the courage to tell him I would never return to that dreadful place... that vile pit of human suffering... never... even were I to become a beggar in Stornoway's streets. No, the only islands I am minded to visit are all north of the border, the glorious Hebrides... cold, wet and windy that they are.' Duncan grinned broadly in an effort to cheer his friend, and Pat managed the weakest of smiles in return.

'I could not hold back in my dreams from another vivid return to Hydra,' said Pat with quiet reluctance, 'I ran foul of those horrible memories again, and that was the end of all comfort in my sleep... and - *I blush to say it* - when I awoke my cheeks were running tears.'

'I am with ye there, auld friend, but I dare say that Melville will raise the subject - *Greece* - when ye see him today...'

'And I am of a mind with you,' declared Pat emphatically, 'I will never return to that vexatious hell.' He became increasingly aware of the uncomfortable, cold and wet sweat that still bathed his chest and back despite the warmth of the fire, and he shivered. He gratefully drank the remainder of his coffee and readily accepted a returning Emma's refill. 'We are... all these years... accustomed to death, fighting aboard ship,' continued Pat in quiet voice, 'indeed, I do not have to tell you that... It is to be expected when serving aboard a frigate, for that is our very purpose... as Simon would surely remind me... but to murder the defenceless... civilian mariners, all of them... is sickening, and I would ever be grateful were I to receive no further reminders of it.'

'I am, of course, long familiar with your principles and scruples, brother; indeed, I honour them,' said Duncan gently, 'and I am of a one with your thoughts on the merits - *or otherwise* - of a return to Greece... but I wonder, I do, if we can afford such a sure but likely parsimonious stance. It is the sad day when a man has to count his farthings, and I dinnae much care for my present state of near poverty.' To which Pat had no reply.

At nine o'clock in the morning, Duncan and Pat were back in the parlour enjoying Mrs O'Donnell's breakfast; neither had slept particularly well after they had returned to bed at 4 a.m. Breakfast was a meal that Pat favoured over all others, whether ashore or at sea. In Connemara his breakfasts were prepared by his second steward, Freeman, and were often just the uncomplicated, sea-going dishes of burgoo or skillygalee, which meals were at the very limit of his steward's culinary abilities. Pat employed two men to serve him: one was Freeman, an ebony-black former slave from West Africa who was his butler and cook for Pat's simplest of meals: ones such as toad-in-a-hole, the meal that Pat and Duncan generally shared for supper when at sea, the cooking of which had been taught him by Wilkins, Pat's personal cook aboard *Tenedos*. The second was Murphy, who had been Pat's principal servant and valet for as long as he could remember. Hailing from Galway Town, he had been serving on Pat's first command in Portsmouth in the year 'three and had miraculously ingrained himself into Pat's life, the Galway connection perhaps one of the doubtful reasons he had persisted.

Freeman had been liberated seven years previously when *Tenedos*, passing through the Atlantic en route to Saint Helena, had stopped and impounded a Bristol slaver running her cargo of misery long after the prohibition. Freeman and scores of others had been thrown over her side by her captain. Freeman had swum to *Tenedos* and hidden away in the for'ard locker until the slave ship had departed, in fear of being shackled once again. The *Tenedos* crew, and later the officers, had all warmed to his gentle nature and good humour, Pat bestowing his new name upon him and the crew teaching him his limited English. A reluctant Murphy had been ordered by Pat to take Freeman under his wing as assistant steward, and - in this capacity - he had excelled, to the point where Murphy - one of life's inveterate grumblers - had long ago become anxious about his own position.

Duncan, still wondering precisely what Canning might have said to his friend on the matter of service for Greece, determined upon a cautious exploration as he returned to the previous night's subject, 'Pat, ye will forgive me for expounding last night upon matters of which I know not the least... or at the most just a wee tait, but it crossed my mind that perhaps Melville may have something worthwhile to discuss with us to benefit his own ends. Indeed, his Lordship might conceivably offer some suggestions which could be delivered to the Greek Committee on Saturday. Melville suggested ye may care to accompany me... and we will find out what these gentlemen are about?'

'Certainly, it is a matter of some interest to me, and I would be pleased to do so,' Pat lied in agreeable voice, pouring the coffee, the welcome smell of which was so invigorating. 'Though to be sure nothing worth tuppence e'er came out of any committee. It will likely be stuffed with self-important, arrogant, narrow-minded prigs, ever parsimonious if it will save them tuppence, and full of ignorance and hot air...'

'They have their attributes then,' murmured Duncan as Pat paused for breath, and more than a little surprised by Pat's vehemence.

Pat continued with a passion, 'Committees, bah! I will give them no countenance whatsoever. In my experience they are shallow men, utterly lacking in integrity... and always pressing anyone who will extend the least interest to endure their ill-considered, self-promoting and pompous blather; and what is worse - *if indeed such is possible* - is the plethora of mindless sycophant followers that attaches to such whoreson popinjays!'

'Ye have quite the affinity for committees, I see!' Duncan interjected at last before laughing aloud.

'You forget that I have attended the House in my capacity as a member for Galway county,' Pat spoke in acerbic voice; 'Not often, as I have generally been at sea these twenty years and more, but plenty enough to remark what the conceited windbags

47

are about.' A pause for reflection. 'I beg your pardon; here I am again, prating like some fishwife.'

Conversation passed by pleasantly enough for some hours, much of it a return to the subjects of the prior evening, no conclusions being reached in the prevailing background of fundamental uncertainty in the matter in hand - the potential for a return to sea, until Pat concluded, 'I am meeting Melville at his private house at two o'clock, and I suppose we will speak again about Greece. I will ask him about the specific difficulty we identified... Royal Navy officers not lawfully able to serve the foreigner.'

At one o'clock Pat O'Connor departed for his appointment with the First Lord. For Duncan Macleod it was his first opportunity to speak with his twin nieces, Sandra and Emma. Their mother, Macleod's sister, had died giving birth, and their father, a fisherman, had been lost at sea several years ago. Consequently, Macleod had brought them to London where they were assured of a warm abode and a friendly upbringing during his absence at sea. The twins had since become quite beautiful and also the most wonderful of cooks, turning out meals of a quality renowned throughout the Liberties of Westminster and the Savoy.

'Are ye joyful my bonnies?' ventured Macleod.

'Yes sir,' chorused the twins.

'Learning well your writing?'

'Yes sir,' trilled their reply.

'And your Gaelic?'

At that only a few giggles came back.

'Bless ye, weans,' Macleod was delighted to see them happy.

As the St. James's clock struck 2 p.m. Pat O'Connor knocked on Lord Melville's door in Arlington Street. The servant led him into Melville's study where the First Lord, a man in his early fifties but looking older in his rather dour tweed attire, was seated behind his desk. 'Welcome, Captain O'Connor,' said Melville in a loud but cordial voice, rising and extending his hand to Pat with a genuine air of welcome. 'I am most pleased to see you. I hope I see you well. It has been some years, some long years indeed, since we last met.'

'Thank you kindly, my Lord,' Pat murmured; his mouth being dry in anticipation, he could say no more.

'Please be seated. Make yourself comfortable. May I offer you tea?' Lord Melville was indeed particularly pleased to greet his guest and, as his porter disappeared for the tea, he bestowed his warmest smile, 'Thank you for your swift passage from far Galway; I am in your debt.'

'Not at all, sir,' Pat gathered his thoughts, swallowed hard and launched directly into his plea. 'I have been ashore these four years past, the last two in Connemara, and hence I am most solicitous of your interest in myself. To be sure, I had begun to despair of ever going to sea again in His Majesty's service...' his mind began to race but the words, frustratingly, would not come.

Pat's nervousness was plainly apparent to Melville; scores of officers had become tongue-tied in similar circumstances in every prior year in his office. His eyes widened as he immediately smiled and interjected to preclude any embarrassing pause developing, his voice maintaining a low, encouraging tone. 'You were saying... please take your time.' The servant returned with a tray. 'Will I pour you some tea?' asked the First Lord.

Pat, encouraged, looked Melville squarely in the face, nodded and resumed, his voice rising with his confidence returning. 'Sir, my only sea time these past two years has been fishing aboard a Galway hooker. The command of even the smallest sloop holds an appeal. Indeed, I would happily return to the tedium of a blockade, were one in the offing, and even, dare I say it, a Revenue cutter begins to exhibit an attraction. I cannot stay longer on my farm without I forget which is the bow and which is the stern. My Lord, if I may? Since I have been recalled from the Mediterranean, I have sat cooling my heels in Connemara. It pains me to hear from my cousin in Portsmouth, who writes often of ships in fine fettle reduced to store hulks and - *I can scarcely believe it* - new ships off the stocks going straight into ordinary... and he reports nine hundred dockyard men were laid off last year... *nine hundred!... and five hundred and fifty the year before!* It is all very dismaying.' Pat's ire

49

quickly deflated as he realised that the First Lord was unlikely to take it well. Surprised that Melville had not interrupted his tirade, he pressed on in a more subdued tone, 'I have sat like a stone these past four years... certainly gathered a great deal of moss... and when is it to end? Have I any prospect of ever returning to sea?'

Melville looked sternly at Pat for a few moments before replying, 'O'Connor, you speak very plainly, and I understand you well, but you must collect the public purse has been exhausted these past ten years or more. Boney did more damage to the Treasury than ever he did to the Fleet. Our resources are much down these days... since Addington repealed Pitt's income tax...' Melville paused for reflection, 'Indeed, the government insists we make do and mend with a mere 30% of our financial allocation of ten years ago - *how could an honest man countenance such as that, eh?...* It does not sit well with my conscience - *not in the least!* - and worse, after the doldrums of last year, the damnable costs of everything are rising everywhere once more. I believe that the money men in the City refer to these soaring increases as *inflation...* as if such is akin to a swelling balloon... *inflation indeed, bah!*' Melville growled his expression of deep disapprobation before resuming without pause, 'Yes, *inflation...* I am minded that it will ever be with us, with its damnable cost increases in every respect since the government has made recourse to printing paper money - *paper money be damned!* Where will it all end, eh? Must I contemplate some future time when I must make use of a wheelbarrow with which to draw my paper salary and carry it home? Yes, the damnable inflation is consuming a significant part of our Admiralty budget these days... so much so that we lack for a great deal of money; and now - *will you believe it?* - ministers - *the damnable pinchfarts that they are* - are minded to *further reduce* the naval estimates, and they postulate that the navy will be adequately served with but forty-four ships - *forty-four!*' Melville was much annoyed, his face reddening; that was plain for Pat to see. Pat coughed politely and Melville continued, 'It is a quite preposterous notion, O'Connor, when one hundred might conceivably be no more than adequate... You will know as well as I that many ships of the fleet are old and rotten with the worm, and I dare say you grasp perfectly well that such ships cannot endure much longer and are fit only for the breaker's yard and scrapping!' Melville sighed, a deep sigh of despair, 'At least we have seen the end of Boney, but who knows when the yankees may cause trouble once again?' The First Lord checked himself as he stared at Pat's despondent face, his guest staring in bleak incomprehension; 'However, I do assure you that sound ships we have aplenty. Assuredly and regrettably many fewer ships than previously... for the economies forced upon us by the Treasury have no end in prospect... but new ships are also on the stocks. There is, for example, *Asia*, in build now at Bombay... plentiful timber supplies there... and shipbuilders - *the Wadia family* - who do not charge an arm and a leg... and, *furthermore, do not put back rotten timbers*; there is *Hastings*, was built in Calcutta back in the year 'nineteen; there is *Unicorn*, in build now at Chatham; there's *Prince Regent* and *Britannia,* launched at Plymouth Dock... both first rates. I venture that these new vessels may not all be known in Galway... or indeed even in Portsmouth...'

'No doubt, sir,' Pat interjected at last; 'But may I beg you to speak of the particulars so far as they relate to me?' Pat spoke quietly, his curiosity overcoming his natural reticence in the presence of the First Lord and he not greatly following Melville's train of explanation.

Melville frowned and stared closely at Pat's face, as if considering how best to continue, before resuming. 'I was speaking of economies, sir... *economies!* It is most unlikely that we will see the fleets of Boney's era afloat this year or next, nor for quite some time for that matter.' Pat did not dare to interrupt again, and so gratefully he sipped his tea. The First Lord rose from his chair and paced towards the window. He looked out for a long minute, as if gathering his thoughts, before turning around to contemplate his visitor. He gazed at Pat for a moment before his stern face at last broke into a slow smile as he resumed, 'O'Connor, I have the conviction that you do prize fortitude and that you will not be shaken by disagreeable news, however bitter it may come.'

'I hope I can bear it, my Lord.'

'You may not know that when I became First Lord there were one hundred and eighty-eight officers appointed admiral, though but few were serving with any squadron. Whilst there still remain nine officers appointed to fleet commands, these appointments have become, in the present lamentable diminution of the fleet... somewhat... *hypothetical*. It is far worse for captains... and as for lieutenants... well, I will say no more. You are to remember that - *whilst you are made post* - you are – will I say – *with little influence*, and so you can expect to be ashore these next few years... pending perhaps the unfortunate death of several or even a score or more of your fellow captains.'

'Most dismaying, sir, bitter news indeed,' was all a shocked Pat could mutter, his discomfit starkly plain, and his hopes draining away as if akin to an ebb tide leaving exposed all its hidden detritus, for his prospects seemed no better than such.

Melville resumed, his voice rising, 'I have been in discussion with the Foreign Secretary on a matter requiring of the utmost discretion. He has pressed me to expedite matters... and so I will speak candidly with you. Doubtless you are familiar with the events occurring in the Ottoman Greek provinces... which His Majesty's Government deeply laments, particularly as it represents an opportunity for the advancement of Russian – their *Orthodox* brethren – or even *French* interests in the region... interests which one might easily conceive as being not necessarily wholly coincidental with our own. A great number of Philhellenes - adventurers for the most part - have left for Greece these two years past from many countries on the continent. These men have been ineffective... fighting and dying on land; and the survivors are now reportedly starving, bereft of any commissary. The Greeks have no regular forces, no artillery and hence no prospect of reducing the Turk fortresses, which are resupplied by sea. Hence, it has become plain to all professional military men that thwarting Turk resupply *by sea* presents the most propitious means of assisting the Greeks...'

Pat nodded; 'No doubt, sir,' he mumbled with a deal of caution in his voice, not wishing to open unwelcome doors, a rapid re-evaluation of his mundane recent life in Connemara bringing a quite unexpected but substantial appeal.

Melville directed a frosty glance at his visitor's visibly waning attention, 'I am reliably informed, O'Connor, that substantial funds are being raised in certain circles to purchase proper ships of war for the provisional Greek government. Their Lordships are aware of intentions to procure a small fleet of steam-driven sloops or corvettes... and even heavy frigates: ships which would not disgrace a post-captain, nor any admiral for that matter. For the moment the Greeks have only ships of such small size which can hardly stand against the Turks - *were it not for the considerable ineptitude of the Turk officers and crew*; yet stand the Greeks do, and they have achieved surprising victories. I am reliably informed that were the Greeks to be assisted by even the most modest of warships... *with competent officers...* then considerable success could well be achieved. In fact, even the smallest frigate, well-founded and manned by a competent crew, would be perfectly capable of dealing heavy blows to the Turk fleet.'

A momentary assessment of a silent Pat's interest or lack of such - Melville could not gauge, he could not be sure - and he resumed, '*Captain O'Connor*, the Foreign Secretary has pressed me to find one or more officers of the measure and experience of such as yourself to join such a venture. However, such officers *cannot* be serving Royal Navy officers. Whilst some subterfuge may be necessary at the present time because of that, any officers on such a secondment - if I might use that term - would be highly regarded by their Lordships, by many Members of the House and, indeed, by the country at large. Need I say more?'

Pat, his mind in greater turmoil than he had ever experienced before, his blood pumping, his curiosity searing his every thought, tried vainly to interject, 'Sir, pray tell me... am I to believe that you wish me to resign the Service and... and return to Greece... as captain of a... a... *a privateer,* for all love?'

There was no reply, the First Lord was once more in full flow and disregarded Pat's look of abject shock and his exasperated tone of voice. 'I wish to speak with you about a prospective command. I do not say that it is one which will suit your interests... that is for your own consideration. The Foreign Secretary did, as you may collect, strive to preclude any French interest developing in the new South American states. He is similarly minded to do the same for any new *Greek* state. Canning is therefore inclined to do everything within his power to ensure His Majesty's amity for any emerging Greek government is recognised there by their nascent leaders. But assuredly, at this indeterminate stage of potential developments, we cannot be known to be a participant in the current turmoil. However, His Majesty's Government is not averse to the activities of Members of the House seeking to promote independence for Greece... and notes the emerging activities of the so-called London Greek Committee... of its efforts to procure competent military officers in the service of the provisional Greek government. Do you follow my drift O'Connor?' Melville, seeing Pat's self-evident exasperation, paused.

'My Lord, I have not been to sea these four years since fetching home to Chatham,' Pat seized his moment, his voice loud, all care cast aside, his indignation exploding. 'I had thought I am come here to discuss my next ship... *or lack of one*. Since arriving in town I find I hear little else but constant mention of the Greek war - *Greece*, the piddling periphery of the Porte's realm - and from all corners... and I confess I am astonished that I find it at the forefront of your own interest too. If I deduce rightly what your Lordship is suggesting, am I now to choose between my rank - with few prospects of active command - or resignation and serving with a country with no navy to speak of – save perhaps for a few fishing smacks... *am I next to command a sardine boat?*' Pat spluttered to a halt, almost in disbelief that it was he himself uttering such words to the First Lord, a being considered by Royal Navy officers to be higher than God in the celestial firmament.

Melville was taken aback, irked by Pat's candour, 'That is coming it a trifle high...'

'I beg your pardon, sir.' His outburst exhausted, Pat sat back, his hand reaching to scratch his head, now drooping with some little embarrassment as his fervour cooled.

The First Lord resumed in conciliatory voice and in haste so as not to brook any further interruption, 'You will forgive me for perhaps not explaining matters as best I might. No, it is not suggested that you irrevocably discard your well-earned rank - *far from it* - and even your worst enemy would hardly deny what a well-earned rank it is, indeed. No, the Foreign Secretary has proposed a rather similar scheme to Cochrane's Chilean adventure, albeit different; actually, *rather* different on consideration, if I might explain...'

Pat was speechless and quite unable to interject as the First Lord continued. 'Certain senior persons in the Foreign Office have devised a scheme which, so they believe, would allow His Majesty's Government to deny any - will I say - *unorthodox* participation in such a venture, as I will seek to describe. You will be aware that we have far more post-captains than ships, and so for the majority of them a life ashore on half-pay is all that they may reasonably contemplate. Some of them are politically well-connected... and have expressed their grievances most candidly, several resigning to take up *foreign* service; Cochrane is a perfect example of such a process, O'Connor; well... perhaps not a *perfect* example, but you will grasp the general notion. Indeed, in your own case your service in the Eastern Mediterranean was considered somewhat unorthodox in certain circles... *I collect the movement of refugees aboard His Majesty's vessels was spoken of in the House.* Yet in such unconventional arrangements... that is to say *when notable success is achieved...* I have always been minded that it would be churlish indeed to refuse credit for such an initiative... and perhaps at a more convenient and later time... to bestow official reinstatement to post... and with full seniority. In similar circumstances... *I speak of this Greek venture...* one might easily conceive of such a possibility... a vessel, rising seniority and... and...'

At this last point of Melville's, Pat, recovering himself and beginning to embrace the attractive prospect of a ship again, thawed very slightly, even at the prospect of Greek waters. 'My Lord, I am sorry. I expressed myself badly. I see now that there is something in what you say. If I do not mistake you, your Lordship is suggesting having two bites of the cake and eating the cherry.'

'Exactly! Quite so!' replied the First Lord after a momentary pause and concealing well his inability to grasp the precise provenance of O'Connor's phrase. 'I am heartily sorry for your embarrassment. It would be extraordinary... *indeed, it would be downright incredible...* were a *serving* captain of the Royal Navy to enter service with a provisional government... in command of no more of a fleet than a frigate - *I dare say it would be a frigate, O'Connor* - and a collection of Greek brigs. His Majesty's Government could hardly expect to credibly deny any allegations of the Porte that such an arrangement was merely a convenient subterfuge to conceal their interest in such a venture. No, such an obvious provocation most certainly cannot be countenanced... *Resignation*, O'Connor, is plainly a necessity. I venture that this is all highly irregular and quite beyond any scheme that their Lordships could conceive of... and could only come from a branch of service more familiar with subterfuge and deception, if you catch my drift. I will add that His Majesty's Government can suffer no record of any such arrangement to be made... *were such a scheme to find favour with you*. Of course, I will personally assure you of restoration to the List... and with no seniority lost.'

At last, Pat found a moment to speak, but he floundered as the words were still formulating in his mind; 'Sir, you put the matter very well, and perhaps I was in haste earlier. The scheme has merit, no doubt. Indeed, I am most sensible of this mark of confidence; it is most certainly an honour to be described in such terms and to receive this opportunity... a ship once again; 'tis such a welcome and a... *an unexpected* prospect. To be sure, I find myself taken aback, without wind in my sails. You spoke of a frigate; what ship will you have me command?'

'Our requirement is for imminence, and so I find I have few choices left to me, the fleet now so much reduced. A frigate would suit our purpose tolerably well. I have considered of *Unicorn*; she is but recently launched at Chatham... though to equip and ready her for service will take several months at best, perhaps a year before she will swim... No, she will not do. Also at Chatham is *Shannon*. I collect you served on her if my memory serves me well.'

'Only for the shortest of spells, sir,' murmured Pat.

'The yard believes it would require of at least four months to bring her out of ordinary, though I am minded she may follow you later. In similar condition at Portsmouth there is *Trincomalee;* she too would require of several more months to bring her to readiness. No, there is but one ship which appears to be eminently suitable, particularly in view of your former command, and which can be spared. Admiral Sir Alexander Cochrane from Plymouth Dock has informed me this past hour by telegraph that down there in the south-west, within his province, he has this past month completed the refitting of a fifth rate, a frigate of thirty-eight guns. She is much the same ship as your former *Tenedos,* eleven hundred tons. She is now seaworthy and awaiting her crew. She had been sent there from Milford Dockyard for hulking to a prison ship, but on inspection the shipwrights were amazed at her condition. She was one of the original Leda class and built with the very best of oak... and so has survived both Boney and the worm. She is presently about to come out of ordinary and back to service. Ain't that the most amazing thing?'

'Indeed, it is, sir... and what ship is she?' Pat racked his brain to recall the whereabouts of all the frigates in service and in ordinary.

'She is *HMS Surprise*, a sister ship of your former *Tenedos*,' Melville announced, gratification plain in his voice, as if announcing some naval victory to his premier.

'My Lord, at the first I am greatly amazed to hear such an unexpected proposal,' Pat replied, 'and such a fine ship...' The mystery resolved, deep satisfaction was expressed in Pat's tone, his relief overflowing his every thought, '... and - *I collect* - thankfully, she is not one of her rotten, fir-built sisters.'

'Indeed; she is English oak through and through,' remarked Melville, adding, 'We will curse Boney for a hundred years and more for the shortage of oak, so many ships did we build to see off the villain.'

'A splendid ship she is, to be sure,' said Pat with a feeling of rising contentment. 'Sir, I doubt I can long further endure the tedium of life ashore, sitting idle on my Connemara farm. These past three years have not been kind for the potato crop, and a return to sea and on a ship such as her is the most welcome of prospects.'

'Very good, O'Connor. We will continue... and I must apprise you of a more - will I say - *unorthodox* arrangement; let me say this, for I have it on the most impeccable authority; I will not enlarge on that: you will be purchasing *HMS Surprise,* for she cannot credibly remain a Royal Navy ship.'

Pat gasped; he had thus far in the interview experienced a veritable assault on his mind, though he had since rebuilt his equilibrium, yet he reeled with this latest shock, leaving him speechless for a few moments until he spoke at last, his disbelief plain in his tone, his mental processes recovering, '*Hah! Hah!* You jest, sir! It is a delightful thought, I confess... though my precious small capital is tied up in stock. Certainly, I am in funds, yes, but precious little. Such a modest sum as I possess is such that I could scarcely buy an Inishturk curragh. *A frigate!* It is far more than I could ever afford.' No sign of mirth from the First Lord, who stared blank-faced, it dawned on Pat that he had intended no joke. 'But, sir, where is the money to come from?'

Melville smiled at last in the realisation that he had not explained himself at all well. 'I beg your pardon, O'Connor; I have not made things plain. Whatever may be the cost of this venture, sufficient will be pledged from the secret fund for you to ostensibly pay for her and to bring all remaining restorations about... *and at best speed.*' Melville brought matters to a head, 'Should you find my proposal of interest, please inform me at the earliest opportunity. If such is the case then I will be most grateful if you would put in hand immediately such arrangements as you think necessary to bring *Surprise* to readiness, and in any yard that you care to choose, from where I will look forward to hearing from you with such progress reports as you can offer as her readying proceeds. *Speed is of the essence*, O'Connor; and so I will await your decision... and - *I must stress* - at the earliest moment; there is no time to be lost dilly-dallying.'

'Of course not, sir.' It had been some considerable minutes in which Pat had been striving to grasp the totality of Melville's incredible briefing, and he could not shake off his state of utter astonishment; indeed, his amazement; nothing like it had he ever heard before. He could barely whisper his reply, 'Perhaps my Lord would allow me to contemplate your proposal for the very briefest of delay before reaching any decision... I find myself, unexpectedly, attending that same Greek Committee on Saturday with Lieutenant Macleod. With your permission, sir, I intend to discuss this with him after the committee meeting and before reaching any conclusion. If your Lordship would graciously allow me a little more than twenty-four hours then I will deliver my decision to you in person.'

'That is perfectly proper,' Melville nodded. 'I will be at the Admiralty tomorrow and I will expect you at 5 p.m.' pronounced the First Lord with a degree of finality, almost relief, rather vaguely indicating the door. 'Thank you kindly, and I bid you good day; I look forward to seeing you on the morrow,' Melville concluded. Rising, he shook a still shocked Pat's hand as the porter entered to escort him out.

'Until tomorrow, and good day, sir,' was all that a stunned O'Connor could mutter, exiting the study.

The servant showed him out to the street. The walk back to The Feathers was slow, and Pat, his mind all awhirl, pondered his future: if he turned down the First Lord's offer of a command, however rum it seemed to be, then was that the end of his career, his life reduced to an abject failure, to a destiny of potato-growing on the cold, wet and windswept peninula which was Connemara. Was that all he had to look forward to? He was wholly engrossed in his ruminations when he was almost run over by a carriage and four on the Strand, leaping aside only at the shrill and abusive shouts of the enraged driver.

It was approaching seven o'clock when a hungry O'Connor arrived back at The Feathers, long after his customary dinner time when at sea, although the thought had not crossed his pre-occupied mind in the slightest until the aromas of the public room restored his attention. 'Duncan, there you are!' Macleod was seated again in his favourite armchair by the fire. 'A glass with you... and perhaps then we will eat something of Mrs O'Donnell's splendid mutton, eh?'

'Sure, I would like that of all things. Will ye tell me about your meeting?' asked a most curious Duncan, setting down his own cup and staring intently at his friend.

'Upon my word and honour, Duncan, I am all at sea! Yes, I must tell you of my meeting with the First Lord... I am dismasted, rudderless, quite brought by the lee. Where will I begin?' A clearly consternated Pat began to recount his meeting, 'It started well enough, Melville welcoming me. He was pleased to see me, and that ain't happened afore, cordiality generally being in pretty short supply from all the First Lords I ever served. The pleasantries did not linger, and I began to see my prospects swiftly foundering until Melville offered me some rum command... *a privateer! Indeed, it was!* I could not believe my ears... *in foreign service...* Would you believe it? My heart churned over. The devil to that! Will we ask Mrs O'Donnell for a jug of ale? A man could pass out in here... it is so damn hot. I had hoped, *prayed* he would give me a frigate again, even were it to be in the West Indies... that festering, vile station of yellow pestilence. I would have snatched his hand off, I would have departed on the morning tide; but no, I am asked to resign... *resign!* I have been offered a *letter of marque... a privateer!* Brother, tell me: have I ever laid myself athwart his hawse, fouled his cable? What have I done to deserve that? My mind is all ahoo since that moment.'

'Did ye decline his proposal?' The blunt question was asked in some trepidation, Duncan most anxious for the answer, his own mind also a confusion of daunting concerns.

'Eh? I may seem a whit slow alongside you learned types; indeed, such has been voiced before by Simon... but no, it would never do to turn down the First Lord... to bite the mouth that feeds you; no, no, no; that ain't likely to ever secure you another command... That is a sure way to remain on the beach, half-pay forever, your card marked... of that there is no doubt... no doubt at all, and I could not countenance that... I said I would consider his proposal. Note, I am not committed, though I am minded that a bird in the hand is surely worth two sitting afar on the fence. I am to meet with him again on Saturday... that is *tomorrow.*'

Long before Pat's return to The Feathers a grasp of the likely well-developed and close association between Canning and Melville had dawned on Duncan, mulling matters over, as Canning's careful scheme had become clear. Much of what Pat had recounted therefore came as little surprise. 'A privateer, ye say; in whose service? Would I be far astray in thinking of Greece? I am sure ye ken that they are still in revolt against the Turk... have kept fighting since we departed in the year 'twenty-one.'

'Greece... yes. It has been near two years since we were in that infernal place, and yet, as you know, the memories... *the nightmares* linger still. Later, he mentioned a frigate, the sister of our old *Tenedos: HMS Surprise*. A fine ship she is... aye... and it seems that she is now near restored... to be sold... *sold to me*. Am I dreaming, tell?' Pat shook his head, his dolorous face exhibiting his confusion.

'Pat, I see now that Melville is the instrument of Canning, and the scheme has been some time in the making. I consider that - *Lord Cochrane aside* - there cudnae have been many worthy candidates for such a venture. Yet Cochrane is now serving in the Brazil, is still in bad odour with many at the Admiralty, and so I cannae conceivably imagine why they would consider him undertaking such a scheme. Ye are surely... there cannae be any doubt... the man they seek.'

'Why, to be sure, 'tis back to sea. Admittedly in foreign service and in command of some disparate flotilla of small vessels... brigs most likely, anyways likely scarcely bigger than fishing smacks for the most part... *and Greeks too...* but I will be restored to post and seniority at the end. I wonder how long is this enterprise likely to last? God's my life, will I be too old on my return to hoist Royal Navy colours ever again? Forgive me, I have yet to hear your considerations on this rum proposal: will you tell me your thoughts?'

'Och, I will nae. I cannae say... I beg your pardon... my capacity in service with ye was as your First. Little understanding of the Admiralty and its workings do I have, let alone the high political circles such that ye now appear to find yourself in. There are days when I flounder with a particular difficulty, a curious predicament perhaps, and I feel as if I am fresh from bonnie Lewis, just off the peat bog; but my grasp of the politic in this Greek business falls far, far short of offering any opinion worthy of more than a Brummagem farthing. Let us,

I venture, attend tomorrow this Greek Committee... and we will ponder further as we look for our course.'

'Mrs O'Donnell!' Pat hailed, 'Will you kindly put dinner in hand? Please to find us a splendid leg of mutton and a brace of ducks. I am mortal hungry; horses ain't in it!'

'The mutton to be sure, sir, but we have no ducks. We do have a lovely side of venison, slow roasted with fresh herbs, and we have fresh soda bread, baked this past half-hour.'

'Capital, capital... my dear; do put in hand the venison if you will; and please bring us a pair of red, *first rate* bottles of red... burgundy perhaps,' urged Pat, adding with a laugh, 'There's nothing of that ilk to be found in Connemara!' An emerging inkling of his customary good cheer was returning, 'And, Mrs O'Donnell, a fine plum pudding to finish if you please!'

'Yes, sir; d'reckly.' Mrs O'Donnell hastened away.

The boiled leg of mutton was sublime, with hot buttered mashed turnips and carrots, served with caper sauce; the venison came roasted with young red onions and was served with steaming bright yellow rice; and the dinner finished with the sweetest, fruitiest, richest plum pudding Pat had ever eaten, with liberal sprinklings of cinnamon, the whole amidst plentiful hot custard. 'A magnificent dinner, Mrs O'Donnell; thank you kindly, and please be sure to pass these two sixpences, one each, to Emma and Sandra,' insisted a now very happy Pat, 'and a bottle of port to see us into port - and sleep. Hah! Hah! *Into port*, did you smoke it?'

At 10 p.m. another bottle of port having followed the way of its fellow and two pots of coffee having been finished, Pat peered rather vacantly into the distance with an uncertain gaze and a furrowed brow as he rose to retire to his room. 'Duncan, a ship and a command again is a powerful sauce for a gander,' Pat steadied himself; 'Yet were I to return from Greek service and their Lordships not recall me to post... my goose would be... *surely would be...* quite roasted to a crisp.'

'Not at all, dear soul; the public clamour for the Greek cause will make a hero of ye, and on your return I have nae doubt that ye would be restored to post,' Duncan ventured, a little more optimistically than he felt. 'Your position would be unassailable.'

Pat, standing now, paused, supporting himself upon the table edge before speaking very softly to his longstanding friend, 'I am minded 'tis the long road we have trod together these past years since Portsmouth... All the world's oceans we have crossed... ships sunk under us, aye... and good shipmates lost aplenty... I oft think of many of them. In my dreams I speak with some of them still. Through all these years... in those many black moments... I have been most sensible of your enduring friendship... most precious it be. Thank you kindly for what you have told me these two days past... your words have touched upon my heart, so they have... but now I find I must go directly to my bed.'

'Aye, pray sleep well... and good night,' mumbled Duncan, his own head drooping.

*Saturday 3rd May 1823*                    *Westminster, London*

'Good morning,' said Duncan to an obviously still tired Pat as they settled for a late breakfast. 'Ye will forgive my curiosity, a deplorable vice for sure, but have ye considered further Lord Melville's proposal?'

'All night. I have scarcely slept a wink considering the pros and cons; indeed, my dreams... *my nightmares...* of Greece were never out of my mind; or so it seemed as I lay awake for hours. At the present there are no prospects of hoisting any colours and no ship; indeed, Melville made it plain that this tedious and thankless time ashore could endure for years. So, should I enter into this Greek scheme indefinitely? If I do not, will I miss my tide? Should I leave Sinéad in Connemara alone for some years longer? And, were I to accept, what would she think? I don't speak the Greek. And are good men still to be found for a crew, officers too, to join me on such an enterprise? All my life I have been at sea... since I first put on long trousers. The sea is all I know since time out of mind... Four long years now with no ship... *four years and no ship!* I had always thought of Fergal at sea with me, beginning his long road to become made post. I despair, I do. I collect you are away directly to Stornoway; will you fly off, abandon me? Will you see me depart for Greece without you?'

'Never in life,' replied Duncan, reaching for the bacon; 'Am I nae telling ye for ever that I am always with ye?'

'I am heartily pleased to hear it,' Pat looked at Duncan with glowing affection in his gaze; 'Indeed, that puts me into a better way of thinking.'

'There is, to be sure, a tide in the affairs of men, as the Bard said, brother; and will I deduce that ye conceive that yours has been at its ebb these twae years past. Such a decision must be taken in the round, with an honest acknowledgment of all your circumstances. I allude to your family in that respect. Another egg, if ye would pass that pan, please. Is there a wee drop of coffee left?'

'What a capital shipmate you are,' Pat smiled, 'More than anything I have a hankering to return to sea, master of my own ship and with a crack crew. But in damnable Greek service? Is it the sensible thing to stay on the beach these years to come, awaiting a ship and my squadron? I wonder... am I beating about the wrong tree...' adding after a moment's hesitation, 'barking up the wrong bush?'

'Dinnae suppose I am unaware of your eagerness to set foot aboard ship at the earliest moment. As your friend I must also be concerned with Sinéad's happiness. Ye will be a great way off, near twae thousand miles or more... and she is nae longer a young lassie. Your presence at the hearth will doubtless weigh more with the lass than some escapade in foreign service, for that is how she will see things. Ye may therefore consider how to reconcile that. D'ye suppose Sinéad might be persuaded... were she to accompany ye to some nearer place, some safe haven... out of peril but with the prospect of your company more frequently than she has previously found in these past years at sea?'

'You are very good; 'tis a notion, sure... and I am most sensible of your advice,' replied Pat, grasping at the straw.

'Perhaps I can remind you that after the Corsican tyrant had finally been defeated, the Congress of Vienna established yet more of His Majesty's far realm in that very location. It is familiar to both of us... the protectorate of wee isles... the Ionians. A safe abode for your family might be established there, facilitating contact with a frequency we never afore enjoyed.'

'I catch your drift, I do;' Pat smiled, 'The Ionian isles... *a capital notion!* Thank you. I will speak of it with Sinéad.'

As the twins cleared away after breakfast Mrs O'Donnell announced in a whispering voice plainly filled with awe, 'Mr Canning, His Highness the Foreign Secretary, is here to see you, sirs, if you are at leisure.'

George Canning had arrived, in evident good humour. He nodded pleasantly to Duncan and Pat. 'Macleod, it is a great pleasure to see you after all these years. It has been an age...'

'Indeed, aye, 'tis ten years at least. Captain O'Connor's visit to ye in the year 'twelve... or perhaps it was 'thirteen. Och, 'thirteen it was - after *Shannon* took *Chesapeake*! How could I forget? Well, 'tis a pleasure to see ye again, sir.' Duncan proffered his hand with undisguised warmth and cordiality, shaking Canning's hand vigorously.

'And you too,' Canning graciously replied before turning to his cousin. 'O'Connor, I have decided I will accompany Lieutenant Macleod to the Greek Committee this morning, and I will look upon it as a most particular favour were you to join us. It will surely prove most interesting.'

'You are very good, sir; I would like it of all things. Macleod has already suggested I might come along, and I will be most happy to join you. I am particularly interested in hearing of the prospects for new ships of war for the Greeks, which only yesterday were mentioned to me by the First Lord, and also the opportunity, perchance, to meet with one of the proponents of the new steam-driven ships... not vessels with which I have been acquainted at all. The name Abney-Hastings has been mentioned, and I recall he is a veteran of Lord Nelson's victory at Trafalgar, and it would be a particular pleasure were I to meet with him today.'

'Well, let us be away; 'tis but a short walk,' said Canning, collecting his stick and hat.

In the growing warmth of another fine spring day, walking east through the bustle that was the Strand, it was just a few minutes to reach the Crown and Anchor, located on the corner of Arundel Street and almost opposite the church of St Clement Danes. At the door the arrivals were directed to the committee room on the first floor where a hubbub of conversation filled the room from approaching thirty gentlemen including many MPs; largely Whigs, many of whom were known vaguely in passing to Pat from his occasional attendances as an Irish Member in the House.

'Here,' said Canning to Pat as they bumped shoulders with another individual in the crush, 'is one of the more vocal proponents of support for the Greek cause in the House.' The man had recoiled from his jolt and turned to face them. Canning spoke up, 'Burdett, may I present my cousin, Captain Patrick O'Connor, who has a deal of experience of the Greek provinces, the matter of today.'

'Aaahh... O'Connor, welcome to our small gathering,' Burdett proffered his hand to Pat.

The rather uncharacteristically friendly greeting from Sir Francis Burdett, an outspoken Whig MP, somewhat surprised Pat, an occasional visitor to the House as an Irish Member. 'Thank you kindly, Burdett.' Not wishing to engage in dialogue about Greece, Pat swiftly changed the subject, 'Allow me to introduce Lieutenant Duncan Macleod, my particular friend.'

'Macleod; my pleasure, sir. Are you a Philhellene?' asked Burdett in a conversational tone.

'I am, sir, a friend of freedom in every sphere,' Duncan replied cautiously.

'O'Connor, Burdett is a supporter of the Papists... as you may know, a particular friend of Cochrane too,' Canning spoke up, sensing Pat and Duncan's confusion, 'though he is also one of those promoters of wild ideas, like Tom Paine: revolutionary ideas, democracy and a general benignity for all. Bah! Such puerile notions would surely lead us to a pretty state of affairs.'

'Och, he has sound qualities then,' remarked Duncan, the comment prompting raised eyebrows all round.

'What have we come to here? Whigs a'plenty and ne'er a Tory can I see? 'tis a hotbed of Radicals,' said Canning, still smiling.

'I am reliably informed that the Committee has at least one Tory, sir: The Reverend Thomas Hughes. Are you acquainted with the gentleman?' asked Burdett, pursing his lips.

'No sir,' Canning scowled.

'A thoroughly ghastly man; no doubt he has missed his true calling. I understand that he advocates the extermination of all the Turks in Greece... Such is hardly the tolerably benevolent approach which we have come to expect from our - will I say - *more enlightened* clergy. Let us hope the Radicals might serve Greece better!' The hint of triumph was plain in Burdett's voice. Pat and Duncan found their interest wavering; Canning too was visibly tiring of Burdett.

'Macleod!' came a familiar voice from the nearby throng; 'What brings you here? How do you find yourself? Tolerably spry, I hope. So good to see you again.' It was a welcome distraction for all. 'You remember me?'

Duncan brightened. 'Why sure, my friend, never forgotten! Pat, allow me to introduce John Lempriere, scholar and long an acquaintance of mine. Lempriere, Captain Patrick O'Connor.'

'Your servant, sir,' nodded Pat respectfully, shaking hands.

Duncan was plainly relieved to find an attendee at the meeting who was not a politician, and gladly entered into a discussion with Lempriere about the classical ancient history of Greece. Meanwhile, Canning had disappeared into the far corner of the room and was engrossed in conversation with a trio of distinguished-looking gentlemen. Pat had begun to feel a little detached from the gathering, political matters never holding great interest for him, and so he looked around, rather hesitantly, to search for a fellow military man. Although his gaze fell upon one or two of conceivably military bearing, he could not identify any.

Shortly after, nearing 1 p.m., there came a strident shout from the corner, 'Gentlemen! Gentlemen! May I bid you all heartily welcome. The meeting is about to convene. Please be seated. Thank you.' The hubbub of conversation died as the assembly sat down and the announcer resumed, 'Thank you for coming today to this meeting of the London Greek Committee. My name is Bowring and I am Secretary of this new body, which was formed only in March, so we are young in our standing and young in our achievements. However, our aspirations are strong, our support is growing, and we are determined to effect everything we can to further the worthy cause of freedom for the

67

valiant Greeks, striving to shake off their Turk oppressors.' He paused to assess the murmured reception of his words before continuing. 'Today I have great pleasure in welcoming our esteemed new Chairman and distinguished Member of the House... who will give the address. Please welcome, gentlemen... Lord Milton!'

There was a polite ripple of applause. Lord Milton stood up and began to speak, his voice a little stiff and formal, but without the false excitability and exaggeration customarily employed by the auctioneer, though carrying that conviction of purpose in somewhat stentorian tone, so convincing to the listener, most particularly so to the gullible; 'Thank you kindly, gentlemen. I am exceedingly honoured and pleased to be here today as Chairman of this most admirable cause, one which is truly worthy of the support of all parties of the House and all outside; as can be vouched today from your attendance.' Whilst looking round the room he continued, his voice very low, 'Through our efforts and those of our valiant soldiers and sailors we have seen off one tyrant, Bonaparte, and it is surely within our collective desire to help liberate Greece from another, the Porte.' There was a general murmur of assent from the room. Milton resumed, 'Under the most disheartening circumstances the Greeks strive to achieve the independence they have long aspired to, but they are failing. To all friends of humanity and civilisation this insufferable Turk yoke presents intolerable anxiety. Throughout Europe societies have raised considerable sums to support our holy Christian brethren, yet in England little money thus far has been raised. And so, it is to this committee and to all friends of the Greeks... formerly a free and enlightened people...'

'Perhaps some of the time,' thought Pat, failing to suppress painful memories of less enlightened people.

'... that the obligation falls to make public appeal to provide support and funds for the Greeks to throw off the Ottoman tyranny. The Turks have signally failed to put down the early insurrection...'

'Oh dear, will I return to Connemara on the morrow?' mused Pat, his attention wholly lost, his mind rebelling, proactively refusing to admit intrusive memories of Greece, very confusing feelings which threatened to cast down his spirits generally. Never before had Connemara, despite its associated - indeed, its near assured - impecunity, seemed so appealing. Duncan reappeared at his side, smiled and winked, a greatly welcome and cheering signal for Pat in that bleak instant of profound doubt.

'... and it is clear that the struggle can now end only with independence. It will likely be beneficial to England and the world that the Greeks establish a government in the Morea, and in that we will assist. We must also strive to help prevent further Turk butchery, as has taken place on Chios. This committee will henceforth seek the most effective means to do so. We will be seeking donations. We will be seeking also the assistance of military officers of Christian principle to help the Greeks. Gentlemen, your support is sorely needed. These endeavours will be communicated to the provisional Greek government after our next public meeting on the fifteenth of May. Thank you!'

There was warm, vigorous applause for the speech and many shouts of 'Hear him! Hear him!' as the formal meeting dissolved into numerous informal and voluble discussions which filled the room, the babble vibrant, busy, enthusiastic.

Canning returned to stand with Pat and Duncan. 'Cousin, I regret I am unable to introduce you to Abney-Hastings. I am informed that he is at present in Hydra...' Pat's stomach turned over at the mention of the word. '... in Greece and in the service of the provisional government there. However, may I introduce, from the shipbuilder's company, Mr Daniel Brent, who will describe his proposed new ship?'

'Very pleased, sir; I have heard but little of this new steam propulsion and greatly aspire to know more,' said Pat, turning and offering a hearty handshake to Brent, warm pleasure in his voice, any alternative to thoughts of Hydra a precious sanctuary.

'If you please, Captain O'Connor; let us repair to the quietude of the saloon downstairs where we can speak further.'

'Most happy,' Pat replied. They left together, engaged already in animated conversation.

'Will O'Connor support the proposal, the return to Greece, Macleod?' Canning asked, the tinge of nervousness, apprehension and uncertainty all plain in his voice.

'I dare say he is turning over the situation in his mind. We have spoken of it at some length...' Duncan replied, striving to place confidence in his reply, '... and we will probably know very shortly, sir; likely on the morrow... perhaps later today.'

'Macleod, how did you receive the address?' Burdett had returned and was standing alongside Duncan, leaning on his stick.

'Admirable words and worthy sentiments, sir; 'tis to be hoped that such a campaign can be concluded rather more quickly than it took to put Bonaparte down.'

'Yes, indeed so,' said Burdett sharply, ill-concealing a sympathy for the early republican aspirations of Bonaparte's regime.

By now, it being after 4 p.m., Pat had cause to make haste in order to fulfil his promise to the First Lord, and he double-timed down the Strand, no carriage for hire to be had at all. His lack of fitness let him down after fifteen minutes, but he struggled on even as he gazed about him for a coach. It was fortunate that he was able to hail a Hackney carriage, and he urged the driver to haste. He was growing anxious as twenty minutes later, as 5 p.m. pealed from the church bells of St. Martin-in-the-Fields, the coach arrived at the Admiralty, to Pat's great relief. He gratefully pressed a half-crown, hastily retrieved from his pocket, into the delighted coachman's hand and hastened over the cobblestones into the Admiralty courtyard and thence to the main waiting-room, at that time quite deserted save for a solitary porter. With a nod he passed through to the tiny room adjacent, termed by visiting captains immemorial "the Bosun's Chair" and reserved for appointments solely with the First Lord. The room was warm despite the high ceiling. Though it was the height of summer, the customary fire was lit and exhibited a welcoming cheer in a room in which generally the occupants sat nervously, awaiting their moment with their ultimate superior; moments which for many had been the make or break of their career. Pat did not sit down, rather he paced slowly up and down the room whilst glancing through the little window from which could be seen the Whitehall Arch. Anxiously, he inspected his uniform coat and brushed off two or three specks which caught his roving eye. He smoothed imaginary creases in his sleeves, his gaze then falling upon his shoes, which he briefly considered buffing with his handkerchief. He dismissed the thought and gazed through the window, passers-by under the Arch catching his gaze though not his attention. He mused that he recognised one or two of the officers, though at that distance he could not be sure. His nerves were on edge. Had he come to the right decision? He could not waver with the First Lord. He was staring again through the window and started when the summons came, the porter's tone quiet, neutral but not unfriendly.

'Captain O'Connor, sir, you are expected. If you are in the way, His Lordship will see you now.'

'Thankee, Tom, much obliged,' murmured Pat, his pulse instantly racing. He smiled weakly to a familiar old face of many years service at the Admiralty, a man who he had known since his days as a young lieutenant. With some anxiety he paced the corridor, following the porter, constraining his step behind Old Tom on the stairs, and so to Melville's office.

'Good afternoon, O'Connor; welcome; be seated if you please. Can I offer you tea? How has your day been? Did you find the Greek Committee of interest?' said the First Lord, coming straight to the point, a thin smile offered as he shook Pat's hand.

'I thank you most heartily, sir; tea would be most welcome.' The porter disappeared. 'As to the Committee, they were all gentlemen who were more in the political line than anyone I could be comfortable with... not a one a military man at all. I was but a bystander. No, I will never be successful in political circles, to be sure.'

'Pray tell, did you consider my proposal?' Melville pressed, raising an eyebrow at Pat's hesitation, a flurry of it passing fleetingly through a mind made up but in momentary turmoil, anxiety showing plain in his face.

'My Lord,' said Pat, suppressing the nervous anxiety he felt and speaking with as much authority as he could summon, 'I would give my hearth and home away today for a plum ship, one on any station of His Majesty's realm. It would give me joy to consider anything which will float; even a receiving hulk begins to exhibit an attraction which I never would have conceived of. I have served their Lordships o'er all the oceans... and so to contemplate a ship in... in *foreign* service is something I have never been accustomed to. I have been quite despairing of ever going to sea again.' Pat hesitated only momentarily as the porter deposited the tea tray, 'Sir, may I say that I have found these past three days particularly stirring; I have encountered my dearest friend, Lieutenant Macleod, after an absence of near two years; I have attended a committee formulating proposals for a fledgling new fleet; I have heard explained the mechanicals of the new steam propulsion, for ships only just now coming of age; and I have reflected on the likelihood of several more years on the beach, which is not something I am sensible of... far from it, as you are aware. My absence from command, I reflect, gives me great concern; I have only this past day considered your Lordship's proposal for a return to sea... *in foreign service*... and giving up my cherished post.' He paused, searching for the best way to further explain his own turmoil of thoughts, and sipped repeatedly from his cup.

'Yes, yes, but does this... this *undoubtedly sensible* consideration... pray, lead you to any conclusion?' prompted Lord Melville, striving to avoid the audible hint of impatience in his voice.

Pat stared, unblinking, at Melville for a long moment before he swallowed to clear his throat, which even now, after the tea, seemed so uncomfortably dry; he nodded and made his commitment, stated with a firm voice, the words coming as if from afar, even to Pat's own ears. 'Your Lordship will be pleased to know that I will be most uncommon happy and I have decided to accept your proposal.' He exhaled deeply with the release of tension; his pledge was made.

'Well done! Excellent! Capital! I am most heartily pleased to hear it,' said Melville, rising to offer his hand.

'I have one question of the first significance, my Lord,' said Pat quickly, sensing that the remainder of his appointment would be short.

'Please to continue, O'Connor.'

'I must necessarily require officers of the very first rate for this enterprise,' Pat spoke in firm voice, 'and so I must be assured of your Lordship's commitment – your *personal commitment,* sir – to restore any that join me to the List when this venture is concluded.'

'Of course, on that you have my word,' Melville replied unhesitatingly and with some relief, shifting quickly to conclude the interview. 'Well... I have an eight o'clock appointment with the Foreign Secretary himself, so away ye go now... 'til we meet again to make the necessary arrangements... and perhaps Lieutenant Macleod might join us next time. Good evening to you... and thank you.'

As they approached each other to shake hands Melville rang a little bell whilst edging towards his inner door. Pat, his heart racing still and his mouth dry, gulped down the remnant of his lukewarm tea, shook hands firmly with the First Lord, nodding as he replied, 'Your servant, sir.' He was shown out by the long-serving porter, who handed over his hat and coat in the reception room downstairs. He looked hopefully at a not unhappy Pat, who paused in the hall, standing stock still in reflection, the gravity of his commitment coming home to him.

'Something Bristol fashion, sir?' enquired Old Tom gently. He knew almost every officer in the Navy, and by longstanding tradition was perfectly entitled to a tip if something had come up to the satisfaction of the visiting officer.

'Indeed, Tom; thankee,' whispered Pat absently, his mind whirling. He pressed the only coin he could find in his pocket, his last one, another half-crown, into the porter's hand.

A delighted Old Tom rushed ahead to open the door whilst gabbling on with pronounced gratitude, 'Thank you, thank you most kindly, sir!'

But Pat was already marching across the cobbles and deep in deliberation now that he was committed, his mind whirring frantically with a myriad matters to organise, until came the alarming thought which quite stopped him physically in his tracks, 'On my life, how am I to explain this to Sinéad?'

Pat and Duncan arrived by carriage in the late evening at Sinéad's aunt's Truro home, their temporary abode, and they settled before the fire, a brace of fine port wine bottles bestowing relaxing contentment upon them after their dinner. They intended a speedy return to The Feathers and the Admiralty, planning only the briefest of interlude at Truro and allowing for just enough time to alert Murphy to proceed with all haste to raise a crew for *Surprise* from former *Tenedos* crewmen, many of whom lived in Falmouth; and, with luck, for Pat to persuade Sinéad of the merits of the scheme. She had accompanied him from Connemara, her mind filled with trepidation at what she might find the purpose of Pat's invitation to be, her acerbic tongue exhibiting the greatest truculence, shrill and unceasing for the whole of a most uncomfortable journey, the coach drivers all coaxing their teams to go too fast. At least that was how it had seemed for mile after mile to a subdued Pat, the Truro arrival coming not a minute too soon, his nerves at breaking point. After some minutes of reflection, he lifted his gaze from a contemplative stare into the fire's flames and looked across to his longstanding friend. 'Duncan, I dare say Murphy will raise a good many men for *Surprise* in Falmouth these next few days... and the rogue will assuredly enjoy his time spending my shillings... *indeed, as much of my money as the grasping rogue can get his hands on...* in the taverns... and most likely in doubtful company; but we must go ourselves and recruit the best of our old shipmates. We cannot offer them any prizes since Boney has long gone and our American cousins no longer truckle with our commerce, but Falmouth has been hit hard since so many of our fleet were struck off and so many more vessels laid up in ordinary. With commerce being so down these past few years 'tis sure we will have our pick of the best seamen of the town.'

'There is nae doubt, nae doubt at all, brother,' murmured Duncan quietly, most pleasantly surprised to find a glow of enthusiasm for a ship, a feeling lost for four years, rekindling deep within his heart.

'I must speak of this with Sinéad afore she hears of it from Murphy or anyone else,' Pat spoke with a slight tremor of audible anxiety.

'Gently, I beg ye; given time to consider it she may come round... though I beseech ye, please dinnae press her.'

Sinéad was no different from any other naval wife, accustomed to the lengthy absences of her husband at sea but dearly enjoying his company during the interludes at home. After the unprecedented near two years of being in Connemara, it was all the more an unwelcome shock when Pat broke the news of his aspiration, indeed his intention, to go to sea again. Her reaction was one of the utmost vexation, followed by many hours of sobs, her contentment and accumulation of peaceful quietude in having her husband at home now proving so fragile and temporary that it was more than she could cope with. She had made the journey from distant Connemara to London and thence to Truro most uncomfortable; that she was much put out made perfectly plain to Pat; and now that a new commission seemed imminent, her dismay and truculence knew no bounds.

In vain did Duncan too consider how best he might help comfort and convince Sinéad. Pleas in support of Pat's career seemed wholly inappropriate given the proposed changes in Pat's circumstances. 'He has been offered a command; he is going to sea. Is such so very disagreeable to ye, my dear?'

Sinéad's withering scowl gave him his answer, her vehement reply scarcely necessary, 'I have endured many long years of his absence. Indeed, until the year 'nineteen the twins did not know him. Did you know, our farm is now strewn with dross, with mounds aplenty across all our small fields? But no precious metals have we ever found; and our potato crop has failed these past three years. Home... *home* is where we need him.'

'Ye spoke of dross, my dear, of precious metals?' Duncan was puzzled, such extraordinary ventures had never before been mentioned to him.

'Indeed! Vile promoters from Dublin it was,' Sinéad's reply was despairing. 'Gold aplenty assured, of that there was no doubt; *so they said.*'

At that an astonished Duncan, blinking, could find no words at all for some minutes. 'How little I know of commerce,' came his eventual and rather inadequate reply.

Later that day, Pat himself tried desperately to convince his angry wife to accept his looming return to sea. 'My dear Sinéad, for all these last eighteen months I have fretted ashore, ne'er commanding more than a Galway hooker, my uniform collecting dust, and all the officers and crew of *Tenedos* long thrown on the beach. The fact of the matter is... the fact is... plain: the fleet continues to be paid off... You are also to consider that my friend Duncan... *and your sister, Kathleen,* will remain far, far away on Lewis, in Stornoway... and my other dear friend - Simon Ferguson - I have never seen these near two years gone.' Pat sensed his failure but persevered, 'The twins become ever more feckless, Murphy is more than ever a mumping nuisance... our cow is dry... we ain't seen a pint o'milk these two months gone, and... and - *God's my life* - I swear even my horse tires of me! Now, here... 'tis a chance to be at sea again, with a ship, with Duncan... and - *we may hope* - Simon too... Murphy and the crew afloat once more... *with full pay restored*, and - *my dear* - I don't ask better than that... It will surely make our life easier... ' Pat played his final card with a heated passion, 'My dear, the Ionian isles are a pleasant enough place for you and the twins to spend a summer.' It was Pat's last throw, a quite desperate plea to recover a losing position, which was obviously the case as he readily saw, all this to a distinctly frosty Sinéad.

'No, Pat, I will not have this,' Sinéad spoke with a boiling anger; 'The twins are in need of your presence, your guidance. The farm is failing; we have ne'er seen a glimmer of the promised gold and even the potato crop has not been worth tuppence these three summers gone, and I will not stay there without you for more years, I will not!' With that she dissolved into tears but steadfastly refused Pat's embrace.

Despite Pat's most persuasive and heartfelt efforts, with Duncan maintaining a most diplomatic silence, it was an unexpected and wholly coincidental letter from Sinéad's sister, Kathleen, written and posted many weeks before from Stornoway, that ultimately swayed her. The letter expounded on the prospects for the twins to travel, perhaps to visit her in Stornoway or even further afield. She wrote of an imminent visit to Port Mahon and suggested that the twins might gain a little worldly experience, might more rapidly mature, in mutually reinforcing new and unfamiliar family surroundings, and yet stay close to and see more of their father were he to accompany them. She urged Sinéad to embrace wider prospects for the twins in comparison with the recent years wholly spent in Connemara. In short, Kathleen had suggested that the twins would, in travel, grow up and out of their adolescence and their petty jealousies of Brodie, and would develop into the young adults that they so nearly had become. Sinéad could not deny these points and, at the end, after several days, had quite accepted them as the benevolent advice that she had become accustomed to hearing from her older sister.

After this changed conviction had finally been embraced by Sinéad, preparations for departure were adopted with a bustle and enthusiasm Pat could scarcely have imagined: copious orders were issued by the lady of the household, Sinéad's aunt Nora – a wealthy and greatly excited old woman – with letters to a myriad local tradesmen: for clothing which he could hardly credit as suitable but to which he made not a whisper of protest, and for foodstuffs by the wagon, ordered for delivery to Plymouth Dock where *Surprise* was being refitted. All this was despite Pat's attempted but wholly disregarded protests that a crew was yet to be found and there must be some doubt about how far the caulking had progressed, never mind the restoration of the hull's copper-plating.

'I congratulate ye, brother. Never did I think for a moment that it would be Kathleen that would bring her round,' said a delighted Duncan, a warm satisfaction flowing throughout his very being.

'She had pressed me to consider command of the old seventy-four, the Plymouth receiving-ship... full pay assured... To be sure there's a great deal to be said for that... and all my nights ashore ... but 'tis no ship for a proper captain, and I would surely be yellowed in time. To be sure, we have the blessing this day,' murmured Pat quietly, a conviction firming despite his reservations, great relief in his voice, and a little understood form of satisfaction coursing through his fibres.

# Chapter Three

*And where are they? and where art thou,*
*My country? On thy voiceless shore*
*The heroic lay is tuneless now —*
*The heroic bosom beats no more!*
*And must thy lyre, so long divine,*
*Degenerate into hands like mine?*

*Wednesday 7<sup>th</sup> May 1823*　　　　　　　　*Falmouth, Cornwall*

It was with great anticipation mixed with rising joy that Pat and Duncan had mounted their horses early in the morning to ride down to Falmouth on a very fine spring day so as to assess the likely crew numbers to be engaged there. Not more than two hours of gentle riding brought them into the town where they had taken rooms for the night at the Royal Hotel. Time enough remained during the day and on the morrow to interview applicants, of which Murphy had gleefully reported to Pat a plentiful number had presented themselves.

'How many men would that be, Murphy?' asked Pat, seeking something more specific; 'A hundred or more?'

'Well, sorr, there is plenty enough, even were we a seventy-four!'

'Very good,' Pat sighed, remembering that neither his steward's numerical competencies nor any of his utterings customarily stretched very far towards exactitude, most particularly when accounting for the wine stocks; truth and certitude both being unnecessary burdens that Murphy could not comfortably countenance.

The port's population of ship owners and mariners generally had been much concerned in recent years by rumours and fears of unemployment. The near neighbouring and long-established port of Plymouth Dock hosted much of the Royal Navy, and hence the town's particular fear had been losing the packet trade entirely to the navy in that place. It had been well known for some time that the Admiralty were looking to replace the older packet ships with navy vessels. It had now happened, in April, and the takeover of the service had only served to heighten fears generally within all the Falmouth seafarers and merchants. The end of the French war had meant the loss of any sure and significant opportunities for the few remaining local fishermen, demand from the fleet greatly reduced, leaving many to engage in smuggling. The Revenue watchpost on Pendennis Point was a successful deterrent to this, save when the weather in the Channel was inclement and no shore watcher could see the slightest movement through the fog or discover landings on nearby Maenporth Beach. Even so, the economy of the town was not prospering, the pilchard catches being so much down, and many seamen were idle for want of a job.

Pat had posted letters to several of his former officers, and whilst no replies had yet actually reached Falmouth - let alone any of the men - he was determined to press on in the meantime and personally engage the crew. The fame of Pat O'Connor as a fighting captain and *Tenedos* as a lucky ship was well known by all the locals. No crew member had ever returned without a sizeable purse from her cruises in the French war, and so there was no lack of volunteers to the call, which Murphy had spread throughout the popular and well patronised public houses of the town for several days beforehand, diligently speaking at length over necessary refreshment, as he saw things, with many ladies of less certain repute he found within them. Pat and Duncan therefore had the greatest difficulty passing through the thick crowd awaiting their arrival. The ostler at the Royal Hotel having taken their mounts, the two old friends walked down to the Fish Strand Quay, cheerfully recognising many familiar faces and greeting with pleasure old hands, veterans of prior voyages, prime seamen by the score presenting themselves; both shaking so many hands that the flesh became sore and the bones ached. At the end of the quay some ten yards away Pat, Duncan and Murphy were astonished but delighted to see a most unexpected figure, a man of between forty and fifty, being dressed in somewhat dishevelled attire and unshaven; he was a man of medium but wiry stature, but radiating an energy, a *joie de vivre,* all about him, the composite of the man's attributes exuding a familiarity and a feeling of well-being which was captured and immediately reciprocated most volubly by the excited, chattering throng of seamen in whose midst he stood. A gathering of old *Tenedos* men stood all about Doctor Simon Ferguson, boisterous and loud in their shouted exchanges.

'Simon!' shouted Pat as joy spread throughout his every fibre, not having seen the other of his two closest friends in all the world for several years. He quickened his step and gently pushed through the throng of seamen, accepting the briefest of handshakes from a dozen or more old salts pressing him, the men keen to greet their former captain; all were now laughing and gabbling with great joy at this unexpected reunion. Pat nodded to many more, and a very few words were swiftly exchanged with others until he finally reached his dear friend amidst the joyful crowd, both his arms outstretched, his face radiant with pleasure. 'How wonderful to see you, my dear, dear friend! How are you?'

'Greetings, brother,' Simon smiled broadly, and the two hugged, their arms thrown about each other in tight embrace, no words approaching adequacy to be found in the immediacy and warmth of their reunion.

'Joy be with you!' exclaimed Pat after some moments in great exuberance; 'It makes me so very happy to see you again.'

'*Ceud mìle fàilte*'[i] Duncan pronounced, pumping Simon's hand even before he could extract himself from Pat's embrace.

'*Tapadh leat, ciamar a tha thu?*'[ii] was all that Simon could reply before Pat released him from his grip and seized his hand immediately upon Duncan's release of it in his enthusiasm to perpetuate the warmth and physical greeting of his dear friend.

From inauspicious beginnings when the trio had first met in Portsmouth in the year 'three, a deep and enduring friendship had grown and blossomed during all the years afterwards whilst they had served together aboard His Majesty's ships.

'We will speak the Gaelic then!' Pat interjected. 'Splendid! *Gabh mo leiscéal, Duncan! Ní fhaca mé le fada thu.*'[iii]

[i] *'A hundred thousand welcomes'*  [ii] *'Thank you. How are you?'*
[iii] *'Excuse me, Duncan! Long time no see.'*

'Och, ye have the Gaelic. I would never - in all these years - have thought it,' said Duncan in mild surprise.

'Oh, I speak it so little... occasionally with the older villagers at Claddaghduff. A very few of them speak no English, and so it lingers there still, in the hamlets of the bog and on the islands. It is so very close to the tongue of the Western Isles that I imagine that your Hebrideans would understand my neighbours. You may collect that aboard *Tenedos* I would hear it occasionally spoken by some of the hands, men of Clare and of Galway, sometimes speaking with our jollies who hailed from the Uists - the dialects are tolerably close; and it would always bring a little cheer and remind me of home.' Pat turned back to Simon, 'We have a ship, a ship again! Ain't that the wonderful news of the world - eh?'

'Why certainly it is a capital development; there is no doubt, no doubt at all.'

A fleeting anxiety filled Pat's mind, 'Sinéad and the twins are here; they are so much looking forward to seeing you. How have you been? You *are* with us... eh? Simon?'

'I received your letter only yesterday and I came immediately. I had long ceased to contemplate going to sea again, and so your letter was welcome indeed.' Simon, smiling, pointed to his companion, 'Mr Tizard here, ship's carpenter and a native of Falmouth, is with me. He is a veteran of the old *Surprise,* and so has gladly shifted to this successor ship.'

'My duty and best respects sir, if you please. Stuart Tizard, carpenter, in the old *Surprise*, Captain Aubrey commanding.'

'A pleasure to meet you, Mr Tizard,' said Pat loudly, delight frozen on his face, proffering his hand and shaking the carpenter's vigorously. 'Why, you served with Lucky Jack Aubrey, the legend himself! Well, that is all I need to know. I am greatly pleased to have you in my crew, and I look forward to hearing all your tales about Aubrey, I do so very much indeed.'

'My pleasure, sir.'

'Murphy!' exclaimed Simon, seeing Pat's compatriot for the first time. Not even Murphy's reputation as a sour curmudgeon, an habitual grumbler, could cast a shadow over Simon's greeting, 'How are you keeping? Tolerably well, I hope?' He enthusiastically seized and pumped the steward's hand.

Murphy was revelling in his role of bringing about the reunion of so many old shipmates; his gap-toothed smile, usually seen only on rare - the very rarest - of occasions, was never absent this day, and he exhibited not the least indication of his usual shrewish, suspicious nature. 'All fine and dandy, sorr! And you look spry, if I may say so,' Murphy hesitated only momentarily, the vision of disorder, of generally unkempt dress before him pressing hard upon his natural leanings, a discernible lack of conviction in his voice; at least until he resumed, 'That is to say saving that your coat could stand a grand clean... *the grandest!*' The steward relented, for Simon was speechless in his momentary instant of diverted self-inspection; 'Well, ain't it glorious to be going back to a barky?' said Murphy with genuine feeling, great pleasure evident in his face, in complete contrast to his customary bearing of the most pinched, put-upon and miserable man aboard ship.

'Indeed, it is; for sure,' replied Simon, not offended in the least, the pleasant prospect becoming more real to him by the minute.

'Well, the whole town is all fired up, sorr; no better news has been heard these four years past. I ne'er knew so many in Falmouth afore these few days, prime seamen aplenty all pressing me for news, old *Tenedos* lads and many others, wives too. Well, I was ne'er so popular with the ladies, your honour.'

'Take no liberties, Murphy,' Simon laughed; 'The ship is a small place to share with any husband with a grudge... I collect you had a wife - in Pompey was it?'

'Well, only in the roving kind, sorr; if you know what I mean,' Murphy laughed aloud now, in high good spirits; 'but only for a few months there.' His old shipmates stared, open-mouthed, for such was an exceedingly rare event, one which some of them had never seen.

'She was no Cleopatra then?' declared Duncan.'

'Eh? No, no; that was Peggy.'

'You lecherous dog!' exclaimed Pat in good humour.

'And was there a wife in Mahon too?' this was asked quietly with a whiff of suspicion but none of reprobation in Simon's voice.

Murphy laughed again and his shipmates looked shocked, 'Well, I had wives in Wapping Dock and in Plymouth Dock as well, though only when we was in port like.'

'Trollops all no doubt, Murphy; you shameless whoremonger,' said Pat, though with nothing of acerbity or condemnation in his voice.

'I venture that you have surely loved not wisely but too well, eh?' offered a smiling Simon, adding, to Murphy's puzzled face, 'The Bard.'

'Browster wives all, Murphy; a crabbit auld laidron ye are,' said Duncan, standing alongside Simon, the exchange catching his ear.

'To be sure, there's a deal of sense outside your head, Murphy,' added Pat, smiling.

'Well, sorr, it stands to reason that empty and cold is the house without a woman.'

Simon shivered momentarily, but nodded in grim acknowledgement; his own wife, Agnes, had been lost to him five long and painful years before.

Pat stared all about him at a great press of happy faces. Amongst the Falmouth seamen, Pat's reputation for his ship handling, his plentiful and profitable victories – tactically so well managed as to be won generally at very little cost to his own men – and his kindly and considerate crew management meant that *Tenedos* under his command had always been filled with willing Falmouth hands and only rarely a pressed man; and her crew embarked not solely for financial gain but also in a spirit of adventure. The seamen were long accustomed to the often poor standards of food and accommodation aboard a fifth rate, but Pat O'Connor offered a harmonious regime without the starting or hazing customarily found on many Royal Navy vessels, and so, for the old *Tenedos* crew, the self-imposed mutual discipline of professional seamen was a great part of their keen interest in joining up again. As most of the former *Tenedos* men were well known to them all, Murphy had already, with the aid of a clerk, constituted the prospective crew list for approval. Pat spent the day meeting many of his former shipmates and others brought along by them, every potential crew member vouched for by veteran shipmates; until, by 8 p.m. when they stopped for supper, over one hundred and fifty had been interviewed; albeit very briefly in the case of those particularly familiar to Pat, and over one hundred and thirty men had been engaged; only the old and infirm had been turned away in kindly fashion and with the most gentle words of reluctance. Simon Ferguson, meanwhile, was consulted by several old shipmates with minor ailments and one or two with social diseases, which he was able to treat, having brought with him the basics of his medical chest in anticipation of just such a necessity.

*Thursday 8th May 1823*                            *Falmouth, Cornwall*

By eight o'clock in the morning there was gathered a further queue of hopeful applicants to complete the crew of *Surprise*, all keen and filling the public room of the Royal Hotel to capacity. Scores more waited outside; for the most part they were former shipmates from *Tenedos's* years in His Majesty's service, particularly from her last voyage to East Mediterranean waters. More men had gathered than had been present to welcome Pat on the quay the previous day; hence, Pat, Simon and Duncan, with Murphy leading, struggled with difficulty through the loud crush at the public bar and out again to the street outside, the bar proving wholly inadequate in size for all the boisterous seamen gathered within and without, all of them anxious in every case to know whether they could make the crew roster.

'I will tell you what: we will have no want of shipmates, Duncan; the line since this past hour is a hundred yards if an inch,' remarked Pat.

'There is a deal of prime seamen like myself - hungry and with nae work - since so many ships were paid off.'

'We will have no need of the Press then?' asked a fascinated Simon.

'There ain't any Press,' Pat smiled, ''tis gone these eight years, but with so many men seeking a berth we shall have no need of any scrovies in our crew; we will have no froward troublemakers; *we will take none but prime seamen*... the pick of Falmouth's tars.'

Murphy, glorying in his role as recruiting sergeant, stepped up on a bench brought out to the quay and, at Pat's nod, commenced calling out the roll of men in the line which had been prepared by the attendant clerk, 'Adams, Bailey, Bartlett, Benson, Bluett, Bolitho, Boscowen... Boswell... Bower... Bodrugan, Brompton...'

'Capital gunners,' said Pat, with a wide smile, recognising many old hands; 'Welcome Boswell, welcome Brompton.'

'Thankee, sir,' the excited replies came back with huge grins.

Murphy resumed with gusto, 'Beer, Belker, Boulderson, Bown, Bowen, Braithwaite, Browne, Bull, Carne, Clies, Collins, Corker, Courtney, Currie T, Currie W - *Tom's younger brother*, sorr.'

'Do you vouch for him, Tom?' demanded Pat of one of his *Tenedos* veterans.

'Aye, your honour. He is right masterly on the yards, sir... a grand man to have aloft. He came d'reckly all the way from Pompey as soon as he heard you was recruiting.'

'I will take him. Murphy, enter young Currie as able, topman.'

'Aye, aye, sorr. Daniels...'

'Daniels! Welcome back,' cried Pat to his captain of the maintop of long ago, 'Grand it is to see ye.'

'Thankee, sir,' came the cheerful reply.

'Dalby,' continued Murphy, shouting loud, trying to make himself heard above the general babble.

'There you are, Dalby. Welcome back!' shouted Pat with just a shred more enthusiasm than he felt.

'An honour, sir,' bawled "Clumsy" Dalby: probably Pat's most devoted crew member of many voyages, but a man with a fully deserved nickname. He looked very pleased to be acknowledged by his captain and touched his knuckle to his forehead.

Murphy pressed on, 'Horsey, Jelbert...'

Pat glanced momentarily at a young man whom he did not recognise, yet the name was familiar to him: an older Jelbert had been his master gunner on *Tenedos*, an able and most valued shipmate; indeed, he had very much been considered the father figure of the people.

'James...'

Pat shouted across the throng to several of the men who had customarily served two of his great guns. 'Abel James, William Horsey! Welcome to our new barky. We will be well with our guns now, lads!' His greeting raised a great cheer from the throng.

Another veteran, Maclean, pushed forward, 'Douglas Maclean, gunner and topman on our auld *Tenedos*, your honour. I hope I see ye well, sir?'

'For sure 'tis a pleasure to see ye, Maclean; that it is.'

'Marder, Millett, Mould, Mumford,' Murphy battled on, valiantly persevering for a full two hours, his voice cracking, his mouth dry despite his plentiful swigs from a quart flagon of ale kept nearby, until the end of his list of more than one hundred and fifty names approached, with Pat greeting many more old shipmates with a kindly word or two until, his own throat now sore, he shouted once more over the hubbub, 'Welcome, Mr Wagstaff; I trust you are all shipshape and Bristol fashion?'

'Prime, sir!' came back the enthusiastic reply.

'Ah... Wilkins! Grand to have *you* back,' said a smiling Pat to his personal cook of *Tenedos* days. 'Praise the Lord, we will not have to count on Murphy for my dinner!' A delighted Wilkins grinned and touched his forehead with his knuckle as Pat laughed loud and long, and Murphy scowled.

'Zabinski... sorr, 'tis the last,' croaked Murphy with considerable relief, his voice beginning to fail him.

'Make your mark, here, Zabinski,' croaked Pat amiably to another *Tenedos* veteran, 'and welcome back.'

'Thankee, sir; a happy day this is, so it is.'

'There is no man here happier than me, Zabinski. Deeply pleased I am to see so many old shipmates... men of *Tenedos* aplenty. Will you wait on 'til we are finished here? I have a few words to say to all our lads.'

'Aye sir, for sure I will. We all will... obliged, sir, obliged.'

The second day had now passed with barely any pause. Early evening was near upon them by the time all one hundred and fifty candidates had been interviewed to select the final hundred and ten or so needed to make up his crew of some two hundred and forty men in all, plus warrant officers. At the end Pat was very satisfied. 'Well done Murphy! Well done indeed! A capital job!' Pat tried to shout across the street but his voice failed him.

'Lads!' Duncan shouted, 'Pipe down!' The hubbub faded away in a few seconds and all the hands stood in silence. There was an expectant air amongst the Surprises, all of whom exhibited a perfectly discernible satisfaction, holding to an air of visible self-assurance, a conviction even, that their lot was about to change for the better, *for the substantially better*, and they were happy men.

'Lads,' Pat resumed in a quieter voice, 'We cannot be sure of any prizes on this voyage, Boney being dead these two years gone.' A great cheer arose, fading after a minute. 'We will not start in the thick of any French war... and our particular circumstances will be for us to discover... but I can assure ye of timely wages...' another huge cheer, '...good commons, safe lying...' Pat, his mouth feeling drier than ever and desperately painful, seized Murphy's flagon and took a deep draught. 'I can... I can assure ye of the companionship of a sound crew, kindly officers and an adventure for sure. What say ye, lads?'

The cheering resumed, tumultuous for several minutes, reverberating along Market Street, the atmosphere of the gathering jubilant, all standing in the warm evening air; women were staring out of all the opened quayside windows, waving, laughing. Very gradually the roar abated as Pat raised his hand in happy acknowledgement, in joy, his face radiating happiness.

From the back of the crowd, from Wright, a very stout former Tenedos and a prime gunner whom Pat had been particularly pleased to re-enlist, there came a loud shout of 'OFF HATS!'

The street filled again with resounding cheering, continuing for some minutes, blissful to all present, until Pat slowly raised his hand once again and waited for the din to subside. In a low voice, for that was all he could manage, he whispered, 'The bar is open this evening, lads, on my purse for all the crew.'

This brought further cheers from the contented assembly and loud shouts of, 'Hurrah! Hurrah! Hear the captain! Hear him!' interspersed with scores of whistles. All shipmates, for that is what the gathering all now felt themselves to be, were most vigorously clapping. The cacophony diminished only after several minutes more when an obviously tired and emotionally moved Pat raised and waved his hat in salute to them all.

'That is most benevolent of you,' declared Simon.

'Does it not lift your spirits mighty high, Simon, our old *Tenedos* shipmates here again, a prime crew, not a landsman amongst them... all - *to a man* - rated able... the barky being readied for sea?'

Simon hesitated only momentarily as recollections of prior times in a bloody cockpit flickered to brutal flames within his mind, but then he remembered a cold and empty home, lifeless in spirit, in Tobermory, and he nodded in emphatic embrace of what could only be a change for the better, a reunion with his two closest friends in all the world, 'And we will have no hallions; we will have none of the sad gomerels inflicted upon us in *Tenedos* by the Press.'

'No, not a one; no landsmen at all; no sea-lawyers and no awkward buggers! I venture we will not need the lash. Their fellows will keep every man strictly in countenance. Is this not our happiest day for many a year, Duncan?' observed Pat with evident feeling.

'I wholly share your sentiment, brother; nae brighter day e'er arose in all my time in the Isles.'

By 6 p.m. a very tired Pat prepared to leave for Truro with Duncan. An extra horse had been procured for Simon. Murphy, being no rider - for that was his own clear statement and expressed with great emphasis - was to settle the bar account next day and follow on by coach.

'A prime set of lads, Duncan, prime. So many Falmouth men are competent sailors... and many of them navigators too; we will not want for anything from this crew,' declared Pat with satisfaction as they mounted their horses.

'Never in doubt, my friend,' Duncan replied, pleased to see the deep satisfaction so evident on Pat's face.

The sun was sinking beyond the higher town behind them, quietude beginning to descend over the quay as the gulls settled for the night, the masts and rigging of the smaller ships tied alongside the quay still just illuminated by the sun's fading rays; dark shadows reached out from the walls of the buildings, vapours now forming everywhere on the water's surface, rising into the cooling evening air, the more distant and larger ships in the Carrick Roads disappearing within the dense mists save for their masts which resembled ghostly, ethereal protrusions.

Nearly two hours of wearying, slow riding through the sunset, the twilight, dusk and eventual darkness brought the now deeply fatigued trio back to Truro where they sat in front of the blazing log fire, the later hours of the early spring evenings still cooling quickly. Within a short time they were delighted to enjoy their favourite supper of toad-in-a-hole, prepared by Freeman, and washed down with a bottle of excellent Madeira from the wonderful vintage of 'seventy-five, which Pat eked out from his travelling dunnage and brought out from his private cellar only on the most particular of occasions. He explained recent events to Simon: the call from his cousin, Canning; his interview with the First Lord; and the offer of *Surprise* for the Greek venture. 'Tomorrow, I must be away to Plymouth Dock and see what, if anything, can be done to speed the refitting. Would you both care to join me?'

'I should like it of all things. Is there much yet to be done, pray tell?' inquired Simon, who had not heard much about the venture.

Pat set down his glass and recounted the refit progress, the minutiae of it all so clear in his mind. 'The hull caulking and sheathing fixing must be nearly finished by now; the rotten keel bolts may not all be out and replaced yet; new sailcloth has come but recently from Pompey; and the yard are making new mainsails and jibs...' Duncan was listening closely, Simon's attention wavering as Pat continued, 'Some cordage is to be replaced... the rats having inflicted grave damage on it whilst she has been lying up, and there remains the decking to be recaulked in some few places; some netting is very old and will need replacing ...'

Duncan interjected, 'Och, 'tis all in good hands at Plymouth Dock, nor any other place would scarcely do better?'

'Oh yes, *Surprise* is in the best possible place, and in very good hands for her refit, dear friend; be assured of it,' Pat replied with an undisguised tremor of growing enthusiasm in his voice. 'On the whole she is not far from being shipshape and all Bristol fashion. She is a prime ship; I dare say she may be the very finest fifth rate afloat. Perhaps another week or two will serve...' Pat paused and smiled.

'I am most heartily glad. What better prospects could we see, auld friend, eh?' said Duncan, sharing his enthusiasm.

Pat resumed, 'The report I have received from the Master Attendant explains her state as she was and as she lies now. The yard in her refitting has installed strong cross bracing within the hull and even new knees... that is, where there has been any doubt of the originals.'

'She has knees then?' asked Simon, his wavering attention recaptured.

Pat paused, as if deliberating on how best to reply to his revered friend's plainly absurd question. He stared at him with sincere kindness and affection. 'Of course, she has knees! Have I never explained ships' structure to you afore?'

'Oh, I dare say you may have mentioned it.'

'For all love, not above a score of times!'

Duncan replenished the glasses with whisky, 'Auld Scotland wants nae skinking ware; but, if ye wish her grateful prayer... to our dear *Surprise*, aye!' He raised his glass. Pat and Simon, both looking puzzled, he followed up, 'A wee tait from Robbie Burns.' Drinks were downed in one and all sat back in utter contentment, the pleasure so much more in all being together for the first time in years.

'I have never doubted the Plymouth men,' said Simon in sincere voice, sipping a fresh measure of a gentler Madeira, the pleasing, warm glow of satisfaction spreading within him; 'Though there be many shifty rascallions in that yard, as I have found these two years gone, there can be no doubt at all of their abilities... not in the least.'

With the warm and fine spring weather persisting, the trio of friends had set off from Truro after a very early breakfast, all in good cheer, and ridden the Friday to Liskeard, resting there overnight before riding through the bright morning at a gentle pace to reach the Hamoaze at noon the next day. With a rising sense of anticipation they stared across the grand, sheltered river where three seventy-fours and two frigates were anchored, gazing for long minutes in the bright sunshine to take in the satisfying sight of the familiar naval ships, something about them so reassuringly strong and substantial even as they rocked so very gently on the calm, sparkling waters. They sniffed the scent of salt air in the gentlest of breeze and revelled in the familar smell of tidewrack, and within their hearts and minds they silently delighted. Within a few minutes they crossed over via the New Horse Ferry from Torpoint and walked the horses through the New Passage fort gates, passed by the barracks and on to the Dock gate at the top of Fore Street. They were directed along the length of the rope-houses, past the mast pond and so to the waterside, the yard busy with many men moving all about it. Carefully they picked their way through timbers, ropes and materials of all forms, strolling amidst the aroma of boiling hot tar, staring about them as if to drink in the pleasure of being amongst ships once again. They walked slowly a hundred paces further in their excitement, all the while staring everywhere about them, until they came to *Surprise,* propped majestically on the slip and quite resplendent even though her masts were absent. They stared in silence for some minutes, each in private contemplation, the pleasure within running so very deep.

'Look, Duncan, Simon... ain't she the prettiest sight of the world?' exclaimed Pat eventually in a low voice, the ship so significant, his excited thoughts formulating only with difficulty into his words.

'Och, there is a sure resemblance to our auld *Tenedos*. Indeed, I venture she is practically indistinguishable,' said Duncan quietly, finding the moment so uplifting, a return to sea after long years now so imminent, so real.

'Magnificent, nothing finer could we behold,' Simon added, finding his own spirits soaring; for the ship before his eyes exhibited a presence upon his perceptions, a thoroughly powerful impact upon his thinking, his mind immediately setting all prior concerns aside and embracing something indefinable but unexpectedly so welcome, tangible, and warming his very being.

'Let us find the Master Shipwright, Edward Churchill. Simon, *mind that yard!*' shouted Pat when they moved off after some minutes towards the ship. 'Step carefully now.'

They scaled the ladder to gain the deck amidships and slowly paced aft, gazing at a hive of activity all about them, staring at everything in view in perfect fettle, the sight of which delighted Pat. They stepped up to gain the quarterdeck, and Pat and Duncan saluted, as was the custom; and they rejoiced with a deeply satisfying pleasure, a delight in being aboard a splendid ship once again, a homecoming of sorts, one of which they had long despaired. They looked to the wheel where they found a grizzled old man approaching seventy, still with a plethora of white hair, wrinkled hands and the florid, wind-burnt face so customary to those engaged in outdoor working. He was inspecting the new deck caulking, and introduced himself as they approached, 'Good day, sirs. I am Edward Churchill, Master Shipwright.'

'Mr Churchill,' Pat replied in effusive voice, crushing the shipwright's hand, 'How very pleased I am to meet you. My name is O'Connor, shortly to be captain of this fine vessel. May I introduce my First, Mr Macleod; and my ship's surgeon, Dr Ferguson?'

'A pleasure to meet you, Mr Macleod. I am acquainted with Dr Ferguson; indeed, he has attended a number of my lads here in Dock.'

'Mr Churchill, I rejoice to see you again,' said Simon, offering his hand. Duncan followed with a hearty handshake.

When they asked of the progress of the works Churchill pronounced himself delighted with progress, declaring with enthusiasm, 'The ship's hull is as sound as the strongest bell.' Having also expertly assessed the bracing he deemed it 'as firm as the day it was installed.' In the preceding week he had scrutinised the keel on the slip with the utmost care, and so assured Pat that every single keel bolt had been changed so as to hold not the slightest doubt about the hull strength; even the seemingly sound bolts having been pulled out and replaced. 'To be sure, 'tis the iron of the bolts and the copper of the sheathing, and they don't get along. Best change 'em all whilst she is out of the water. She be good for at least another five years now,' he pronounced with unfaltering confidence. 'Her masts are in good order, and my lads will begin to refit them on the morrow. All her sails will be ready next week - every one of 'em fashioned new here in my yard... only the freshest bolts of number one canvas for the leech and the best number three for the centre - *every one so!* The new Riga cordage will be here come Monday... and fitted too by Friday - *we will have no twice-laid, rotten rubbish.* Just you be leaving us to it, Captain O'Connor, sir, and we will see all is finished, timely like, afore Whit.'

'That is very welcome news, Mr Churchill, and I thank you kindly for your progress thus far,' said Pat gratefully, trying hard to keep his face turned towards Churchill, everything about the ship, *his* ship, demanding his eyes. 'Sir,' he added, 'it is our intention to be away to sea on the Tuesday after Whit, as we will find few crew happy to sail on the holiday.'

'No sir, neither will any of my lads be here in this yard 'til the Tuesday,' the Master Shipwright replied.

'Duncan, we must fetch her crew here afore Whit Monday to ready her for the passage to Falmouth,' declared Pat, 'and that means at least forty men. We will use *Eleanor;* we can accommodate them aboard *Surprise...* she will be off the slip and in the water by then. It will be no bad thing to have them here by the Friday so as to check and tighten rigging, and to load the casks of salt pork and beef. She will receive her stores from the victuallers here, for we have none of significance in Falmouth.'

Satisfied that *Surprise* was in good hands and the refit proceeding admirably, Pat, Duncan and Simon left the yard for dinner, the horses resting and being fed at the yard's own stable. A pleasant stroll past the New Basin and the drydocks brought them to the Steam Packet public house. 'It ain't Fladong's, I'm sure,' remarked Pat, '... but they will serve beer and pies.'

'Have you missed the sea, Pat?' asked Simon as they sat waiting for the food they had ordered and enjoying their ale.

'Sure, I have,' Pat smiled, 'for the landsman's life is not for me.'

'But I collect that there were the most unpleasant experiences when you were last in Greece. You have never spoken of them at length, and your letters to me merely hinted at your distress. Were those months so greatly disquieting, and... and does that not give cause for a degree of anxiety... our return there?'

Pat's spirits sank like the lead line; his face reflected such, 'I did not care to burden you with the gory details... *the specifics* of the horrors that I saw... no... I could scarcely believe that one man could inflict such upon another.'

'To what do you refer?' Simon pressed even as he studied the distressed face of his friend carefully; 'I would be exceedingly interested to hear of this affliction; that is to say, in my capacity as a medical man. You are to recall that I am your particular servant in that respect, and there is no doubt that it would be beneficial for the mind - *your mind* - were you to expound upon your recollections to some further extent... to a confidant.'

Pat sighed, 'Well, if you must insist... in April of 'twenty-one, it was; I was in the Morea, on the mainland and - armed with Smyth's charts - looking to the harbours - *their depths particularly* - along the coast, when I saw the black smoke of fires rising above the hilltops further along the road ahead. Naturally, I coaxed my horse and my servant on his mule towards the scene...' Pat took a large draught of his ale, hesitating to continue; 'Lord, I could do with a bite. Will we look to the host and see what has happened to our pie?'

'I most certainly share your cravings for comestibles, I do so,' said Stephen, 'but, for the moment, are you not straying a trifle from your tale before we arrive at its conclusion?'

'Eh?' Pat looked doubtful. He wrung his hands during a long pause before he resumed, 'Yes, I suppose I am... After an hour we came upon a small village of perfectly ramshackle abodes - *I will not term them houses for they were scarcely more than*

95

*thatched huts* - and near a quarter of them were afire. For the most part they were burnt out, and what remained was little more than smouldering, charred timbers... but the horrible smell - *the stench* - was... was not solely of the ash, blowing in the wind, nor indeed the blackened wood...' Pat sighed again and took another draught of his ale, his reluctance to continue perfectly plain to his friends. A minute passed and the Landlord deposited the hot pie upon the table, hugely appealing to hungry eyes as steam rose to waft a divine aroma up from the plate. However, it remained untouched as Pat continued in a low, halting voice, his friends fascinated, 'Upon the first fire we came to there were bodies... a dozen of them or more... It was a pyre of corpses... several of them burned most severely... and the Greek villagers were bringing another to the fire... a slain boy it was, no more than ten years old... carrying him right before my eyes. I could see that his throat was slashed. More villagers were coming... and all those bodies that they carried were bloodied, mutilated, their vestments torn away... the bloody cuts and piercings of blades plain to see...' Pat swallowed from his glass, his throat dry. 'The bodies were infested with ticks, swarms of them feeding on the flesh... greatly more than ever the plentiful number of bargemen which was customary on the biscuit in the hold.' Pat coughed, he picked up, stared at and set down his now empty glass; he took a deep breath, his anxiety rising, his voice in audible difficulty, 'The hair of dead children was matted with blood... and dogs scavenged everywhere amongst the ruins, fighting over and gorging on severed limbs.' Pat waved to the Landlord and shouted in loud voice, 'More ale, if you will! Thank you!' The pie was cooling as he resumed, his friends silent and staring, 'May God, Mary and Saint Patrick help me,' exclaimed Pat with feeling, 'I have seen men killed before, aboard ship; of course I have, a deal of them... but this was horror... *Hell* itself. In that moment I could scarcely move another step... I instructed my servant to ask for an explanation...' Pat halted; the story was plainly so painful to recount. He lifted his empty glass and set it down again, 'Where is the damnable ale?' The landlord arrived within seconds; Pat gulped another draught and resumed, 'The bodies were the Turks who had lived in the village... innocent

96

people... and their Greek neighbours - *their neighbours!* - had... had slaughtered every one of them.' Pat was in difficulties himself, 'God rest their souls! I was told that some of the younger women had survived, shackled and carried away, to be transported to Constantinople and sold as slaves.' A horrified Simon was sitting immobile, and Duncan was cutting the pie into slices, saying nothing. Pat was reduced to scarcely more than a whisper, 'Damnable Greece... it has never been out of my thoughts all these last few years gone... and now - *have I lost my senses, tell?* - now we are about to return... *to return to Hell.*'

Simon spoke at last, 'Dear God, I do most humbly beg your pardon, my dear friend; I hope you will forgive me for precipitating such acute anguish in your mind... plainly a veritable Gehenna. Your story... those dreadful events... would surely trouble a saint. Your memories of such tribulations... do they often greatly oppress you, tell? Does your recall frequently intercede in the peace and tranquillity of your sleep?'

*'Tranquillity?'* exclaimed Pat with surprising vehemence; he swallowed hard, his throat dry and gripped by the sensation of constriction, 'I rarely find tranquillity in my sleep; no, 'tis a rare night when I sleep all through to the dawn; nightmares are more the norm, I regret to say...' A long pause, 'Until I draw my last breath on God's earth, I will never forget those sights... dead women and children... covered in blood... the Turk corpses afire on pyres... that black day.'

'Pat, you are in a passion, soul,' declared Simon with feeling.

'Here, don't let this go to waste; take a piece of the pie while 'tis almost still hot; I beg you will,' declared Duncan, proffering the plate whilst seeking to divert minds elsewhere.

'Have I acted in haste, Duncan... Simon... this new venture decided upon out of my own frustration, not being at sea these four years past?' asked Pat, selecting a slice with some hesitation and pausing before his first bite, his thoughts all ahoo, a maelstrom of fresh indecision and doubt raging in his mind.

'Nae, my friend, I dinnae suppose ye have,' replied Duncan in encouraging voice; 'It seems very much akin to Lord Cochrane's voyages for Chile, and ye are to consider we will be accompanied for the most part by our close friends and family. What more could ye ask? Give ye joy with all my heart.'

'I will be very happy; thank you,' whispered Pat, more in hope than conviction.

*Friday 16ᵗʰ May 1823*                    *Falmouth, Cornwall*

Early on the Friday morning before Whit, the sun emerging, weak and low in the sky, the three friends were once more at Falmouth with their dunnage already loaded aboard *Eleanor,* a Garmouth, Geddie-built, two-masted topsail schooner belonging to Pat. Bought on Duncan's personal recommendation and a fast sailer even when close-hauled, for she could sail closer to the wind than Pat might ever have believed, she had served as tender to *Tenedos* in her latter years under Pat's command. With *Eleanor's* small crew were a forty-strong nucleus of *Tenedos* veterans, many of whom were members of the Wesleyans of Falmouth, an ecclesiastical movement, recent in origin but not the only one in the town, which was also home to many other nonconformist congregations. Men from most of these chapels had been represented in the crew of *Tenedos* on prior voyages.

Whilst the last of *Eleanor's* stores were loading, Simon engaged the master in conversation. He was a cautious and scrupulous man, a Wesleyan elder. They sat on small kegs - water butts for the boats - along the Custom House Quay, 'Mr Prosser, good morning to you. I venture the crew seem to be in prodigious fine spirits this morning, very pleased to be serving again... and with Captain O'Connor.'

Jeremiah Prosser was old in comparison to the average seaman; a veteran of many voyages aboard *Tenedos*, his face and arms burned brown by long years of exposure to the sun; deep wrinkles covered every visible area of his skin and his hands were large and muscular. From his eyes, still bright blue, shone an energy, a spirit, which radiated confidence to all men aboard the ships in which he served. 'Why to be sure, Doctor, there is no doubt. We have all of us given thanks to Our Lord every day in our chapel since Murphy brought news of the captain returning and *Surprise* coming out of ordinary to go to sea again. These past four years have brought hard times to this town. After the French were beaten most of us were turned ashore; even our kin working away in Plymouth and far Pompey dockyards have been laid off, precious little work to be had and our families all long since on short commons... little or no fishing left any more... no privateering these days, no money hardly at all and no brandy smuggling worth a candle this past year since them new Revenue cutters were built in Poole. Very swift indeed they be, Doctor... and then the rumour in the town which all have long feared - *that the packets would be handed over to the navy* - has come true... at least for the older vessels. No, we all gave praise to Our Lord when we heard that the barky was coming out again, to Falmouth, and the captain seeking a crew for a year or two; 'tis a chance again for pay and to put some bread on the table.'

'Mr Prosser, did Murphy explain to you and the lads that this was not to be another surveying voyage? *Surprise* is no longer a Royal Navy ship and we are to be privateers; that is to say *mercenaries,* in the service of the new Greece,' Simon enquired cautiously.

The master's smile stretched all the way from one luxuriant sideburn to the other, unkempt sideburns being common to the Wesleyan seafarers of Falmouth. 'Oh, yes, sir, 'tis clear... and nobody cared, nobody cared at all. Even were we to be sailing against the French, against the Yankees... or even the Spanish, sir... just as long as we could get back to sea. The same pay as our brothers still serving on His Majesty's ships and the prospect of some prize monies as well... it answers amazingly. It seemed too good to be true. We thanked Our Lord.' There were nods all round from the hands coiling away *Eleanor's* cords, and Prosser continued. 'We all hurried to make our preparations, to tell our wives, mothers and fathers. Off to sea again... Praise Our Lord and be thankful.'

'We are all thankful of that, Mr Prosser,' Simon said warmly.

'When the captain himself arrived, sir, it was all that many of us had hoped for... and for a very long time... and then *Eleanor* came into the harbour. When she came alongside the quay there were already more than a score of us to help tie her up, and a goodly cheer was raised when the job was done. Young Mr Reeve, her skipper, is a Falmouth lad, sir, born and bred. A grand day it was, indeed. Plentiful ale was drunk in the King's Arms later... and the chapel was full that evening, Doctor, I can tell you.'

'I am sure of it,' Simon replied, heartily pleased to hear of the good spirits pervading Pat's new crew.

At last *Eleanor* was ready and the tide was high, just past slack water; she was set fair for the ebb current. Pat was perfectly at ease leaving master's mate William Reeve to take her out. The lines were cast off and - with just her topsail and jibs to drive her, the schooner's men standing ready to hoist her fore and main sails - with only the faintest of north-westerly zephyr acting upon her, *Eleanor* slipped gracefully away from the quay, shifting away from the inner harbour towards the Carrick Roads. The Falmouth men were all waving to their families, a happy multitude still thronging the waterside, all of them still waving back to *Eleanor* as she tided a mile distant into the Roads, many anxious hearts and happy faces left far astern in her wake.

The master hovered at Reeve's elbow in a schoolmasterly fashion, not wanting to utter a single word of guidance unless it became absolutely necessary; not that he thought it would be. The Falmouth men, the Surprises, some forty or so now aboard, lined *Eleanor's* sides, as if in a kind of wonder, all striving to savour the realisation, that fleeting moment of joy: they were at sea again, on a respectable venture and departing in the full glare of daylight. Several still gazed back for long, thoughtful minutes to their now distant family and friends; most simply savoured the moment, basking in the pleasure of being aboard a vessel once more. Once *Eleanor* was in mid-channel and Pendennis Castle off her starboard beam, Reeve ordered the fore and main to be hoisted, the Eleanors aided by the Surprises making light work of the sail handling: *Eleanor* was now bearing for Falmouth Bay.

Pat was watching events with the utmost delight from the taffrail, and not a word passed his lips until he spoke to Duncan as they passed the Black Rock to starboard, 'William is a splendid man to have with us. Ne'er a better master could we ever have for *Eleanor*.'

'Nae doubt at all,' said Duncan, pleasantly engrossed with the spectacle of their departure.

'I should take it very kindly if you will join me for dinner, Mr Reeve,' said Pat with a broad smile, 'when she is set fair on her course.'

'Oh, with great pleasure, sir; thank you.'

Both fore and main sails were now full and *Eleanor* swiftly picked up speed. 'Nicely done, Mr Reeve, most uncommon neat,' pronounced Pat as she passed St Anthony Head. With a strengthening north-westerly wind behind her and a very pleasant sea state *Eleanor* made short shrift of the bay crossing to Plymouth. By early afternoon she approached the emerging new breakwater and sailed on past Saint Nicholas's Island, past Devil's Point and so to the shelter of Mutton Cove, tying alongside. Neither Reeve nor the master were greatly familiar with the Hamoaze, and both were anxious not to foul any ship's cables by approaching the higher Devonport anchorage.

It was a brief walk for the Surprises, a short half-mile from *Eleanor's* berth to where *Surprise* had previously been on the slip. She was now anchored within the Hamoaze, still very near the New Basin. The men shuffled along the quay and through the yard, chatting away in prime good humour; every man was eager to go aboard the frigate, one so nearly identical to *Tenedos,* which for most of them had been their home afloat for many a year. Their rising excitement was palpable as they were rowed out to *Surprise* in the yard's boats, revelling in the day; their loud, jocular comments and good-natured banter was endemic. Pat could not bring himself to call them to order, feeling precisely the same himself. He was the first to climb aboard. There was no formal, welcoming guard of marines; nor would there be on this *unofficial* voyage, but he cared not a jot. He gazed slowly all about him, subsumed in his happiness, his mind swiftly registering the yard's restorations. Her guns, masts and spars were all restored and half a dozen yard workers were still aboard, making final touches to deck caulking. The Master Shipwright himself, Edward Churchill, was there, keeping a wholly unnecessary eye on his team, of whose workmanship Pat had never seen the equal.

'Upon my word, Mr Churchill, she does look prime!'

'Thank you, sir.'

Pat gazed about him, noting the masts and spars all a-tanto, the rigging restored and the deck all freshly caulked; only in a very few places was it yet to be holystoned to remove the little surfeit of pitch, a task for the Surprises on the morrow. The new sails were for the most part all loosely hung and strapped from the yards; not in any ways that any other than a yard crew would be happy with, but hung nevertheless. The cordage was everywhere new, nicely coiled where it lay on the deck. All the old tars were immensely gratified to see that the men of the yard – knowing that *Surprise* was bound for Greece, the Royal Navy grapevine being what it was – had hung a long, blue pennant at the mizzen, now fluttering proudly in the strong breeze. It was not a pennant that could be considered official, of course, and it was one that would be swiftly struck down as soon as *Surprise* left the yard, but it was a visible and generous token of the esteem in which Captain O'Connor was held in all the West Country ports, Devonport most particularly.

'I am infinitely obliged to you, Mr Churchill. A finer and faster refit no other yard could have accomplished in the time. Thank you kindly; she is a beautiful sight to behold,' said a delighted Pat.

'The task has been a great pleasure for us all here in the yard, sir. Indeed, my lads all think of her as *their* ship... since she has been their largest job in this yard in all these recent years, and 'twas my lads, bless 'em, that fitted her new knees. I venture no other ship has ever given them so much pride in their work,' offered a deeply moved Churchill, so obviously and genuinely pleased to see a ship returned to active service rather than the now far more customary work of his yard of hulking ships, ships that in many cases had many more years of useful life left in them. He was visibly extremely delighted and relieved that *Surprise* was preserved from that particular and ignominious fate, and proud too that she had been saved by *his* yard and by *his* lads.

'Allow me to say that she is a credit to you and your men, Mr Churchill. There is no doubt, no doubt at all.'

The Surprises, for that is how they all immediately felt themselves to be, were now swarming over the quarterdeck, the gun deck and the rigging. Some were already preparing to shave and holystone the new deck caulking, prominent in its seams. The cook had gone below to light the galley fire; others hands were checking the water butts, inspecting the bilges, testing the pumps and generally busying themselves in every conceivable task, all to a man delighted to be aboard a ship once more.

It was gratifying to Pat to see all the activity happening, all wholly unbidden. 'Simon, old friend, ain't it very like a homecoming?' he whispered, feeling quite emotional. 'And how are you yourself? I have not asked how you are; forgive me for being so remiss these past days... and the fact of the matter is... *the fact is* that it has been something of a... a...' Pat paused, searching for the right words but finding his feelings rising to the fore, so powerful and overtaking his train of thought.

'A risorgimento?'

'Eh? There you go again with the Latin.'

'A renaissance, if you will... of the spirits.' Simon continued, 'You are of my way of thinking entirely, soul. I do not believe I had expected this... this *deep satisfaction*.' Simon too seemed genuinely overcome, his words came slowly as if gathering his thoughts, 'Although Dr Tripe at the Dock is a fascinating man... and too a member of the Royal College... I have oft enjoyed the most cordial of hours with him in examination of his collections, his stuffed birds most particularly... and his wife, Mary, is the most kindly treasure... I admit I have long tired of this place.' He sighed and gazed all about him at the ship. 'She is remarkably beautiful, for sure... and never before did I have the same pleasure in simply stepping aboard a ship... but is she not now an auld lady, so many years out of service? I only float out the enquiry; I beg you will forgive me if I am in error.'

'Old?' Pat stared at his friend, surprised and mildly affronted, 'Old? She ain't old, Simon. Only a scrub would say such a thing. You must never say that. Sure, there are some who would say she may be old-fashioned, long past mark of mouth and too puny to engage with her modern sisters, forty-fours and the like... and that she is too small for the current age. These opinions have credence for the most part in those lubbers who have ne'er found themselves spitting out the salt stream, wiping their eyes of the powder smoke when the shot is flying... or firing three broadsides in five minutes. She is but thirteen years old... and has been looked after tenderly, like a maiden aunt... handled gently like a risen pudding afore it reaches the table... since ever afore she was laid up for so long. You are to consider that Nelson took *Victory* into battle at Trafalgar forty years after she was built... *forty years!* No, she has a long life in her yet, our dear *Surprise*. I am cast down... quite put out... mortified to hear you say such things, I am; shame on you.'

Simon looked anxiously into Pat's face. 'I am so sorry, brother; I use the term only as an endearment... akin to making the acquaintance of a long lost, auld friend... a dearly beloved friend... one who had been thought lost and was found again, the pleasure being so much more in the finding. Doubtless you are correct as to her longevity.'

'In the matter of age, I assure you that a man and a ship are far, far from the same ilk,' declared Pat in acerbic voice; 'Indeed, they are quite different kettles of fish... *quite different!*'

'I have heard it remarked.'

'Why, the ship - *with proper maintenance and refitting, of course* - will long outlast the man.'

'Would that we might dream the converse was the case,' this in melancholy voice.

'Eh?'

'Forgive me, Pat; I meant no other implication. I find I love the ship as much as you, and there you have my confession, coming from a mind of a generally scientific persuasion... though assuredly I find that our dear *Surprise* now brings the nature of a philosopher to the fore.'

'Well, I am sorry I spoke chuff to you.'

'I did not take the least offence, never in life; and I give you joy of our shipboard homecoming, brother... and a precious event it is.'

At that moment Pat, smiling broadly once more, was distracted by Murphy, struggling by himself and with loud mutterings of indignation to hoist Pat's two bags up from the boat; loud cursing evidencing the steward's return to his customary form. 'Murphy! Belay that whingeing! Stow 'em away in the cabin; handsomely does it!' He looked round for helpers. 'Hartley! Currie!' he shouted to two of the crew who were engaged already in chipping away peeling black paint from a gun, the equivalent gun to the one on their former *Tenedos - their gun*, as they now considered it to be, and scraping away just a little crusted salt from the carriage woodwork. 'Bear a hand! Bring the Doctor's dunnage aboard. No need to pay any attention to the great guns just yet, lads.' He turned back to his steward, 'Murphy! Pass the word for the cook: plenty of bacon and soft tack for the crew in half an hour... and grog to wash it down. Freeman! Light along there and see about some coffee and kedgeree, if you will.' His orders were expressed rather more politely than his customarily more formal manner with his servants, for nothing would be allowed to intrude upon his enjoyment of this particular day.

'Well, just aboard and no bleeding peace already!' grumbled Murphy with audible discontent, standing with Freeman to recover from his exertions hauling up the baggage before going to the cabin, all the time awaiting Pat's further rebuke.

''tis coming, massa!' shouted Freeman.

'Waites! Fisher! See how much water is in the well.' Pat was once again in his natural element.

'She's nicely tight and dry, sir; barely an inch or two,' came back the report within minutes.

'Very good. Get yourselves some grog, lads.'

After a further two hours had passed with a myriad checks completed and as the crew were sitting on the deck with their grog and finishing up their bowls of burgoo, Pat, standing amidships on the gun deck and, as was plain to all, marvelling at his good fortune, called them all together. 'Lads, we will be taking on stores tomorrow. We will hold church on Sunday. On Monday we will bring aboard our water and livestock, and load powder and shot from the hoy. We will leave on Tuesday's ebb, over to Falmouth. Let us have no riotous drinking here in Plymouth Dock. Any hand who is drunk will be left ashore. There's five shillings each for all hands for your needs until we depart on Tuesday. Anderton! Belker! You will keep those lines just fine and dandy... be sure to look to the tide.'

'Aye aye, sir,' they acknowledged, grinning happily.

All day preparations continued to take *Surprise* to sea. The forty or so Falmouth seamen - the majority of them Wesleyans - worked from sun up, several of them nursing thick heads from over-indulging in the taverns of Morice Town the prior evening, but not a man missed the early start. Mr Tizard, the veteran ship's carpenter, checked the yard's workmanship with an experienced eye. Deck holystoning went on incessantly; the great guns were cleaned and oiled, several men continuing to chip away at their lingering remnants of peeling black paint. Below deck was aired, the deck gratings all lifted away. The galley was cleaned and the fire relit, bilges were freshened with salt water and pumped dry, and so it went on; the crew paused only for water, grog and the cook's burgoo, a great pot of which was maintained steaming on the galley, repeatedly fed with fresh milk and more oats.

From nine o'clock onwards a constant stream of coaches and wagons arrived on the quay with stores from the Plymouth victuallers, brought onboard by *Surprise's* boats: casks of salt pork and salt beef – every man entitled to six pounds of meat a week, gristled, bony and fat that it usually was; bread - whilst fresh for the few days after leaving port; beer, similarly; suet, oatmeal, oil, ship's biscuit - one pound a day per man, customary worms and all; dried peas, flour, salt, onions, carrots, turnips, sugar, twelve ounces of cheese - a favourite delicacy of all the hands and Pat himself when toasted for his supper, the last residues of which were always consumed in great haste when the blue mould could no longer profitably be pared away and all remnants were given to the ship's goat; great barrels of lime and lemon juices, kegs of vinegar and rum; and the hands' cherished favourite, two pounds of tobacco, the smoking of which represented the only pleasure between ports, if - that is - the grog was taken as plain rations, for the men considered it as such.

Amidst the bedlam which was the bosun cursing the loading of the stores, much of the captain's personal baggage came aboard in quantities which Pat could scarcely comprehend but to which he protested not a word. This had been sent down by Sinéad from Truro, anticipating *Surprise* being in Falmouth for the very shortest of stays and likely leaving little time to take the family's necessaries, as she deemed them, aboard. There were many and varied outfits of clothing, boots, wet-weather gear, hats of all sorts, woollen gloves, leather gloves, calfskin gloves, belts, crockery, even a silver dinner service. From the local vintners there were cases of good burgundy, fine French brandy, malt whisky for Pat's Scots companions. Pat's 'cello, Simon's viola, music stands, rugs, blankets, many and varied chests with Sinéad's accoutrements, clothing for Fergal and Caitlin, further clothing for Kathleen and Brodie; all came aboard; and so it went on for many an hour, all Pat's family's chests being manhandled by a disgruntled Murphy.

'Well, I ain't ne'er seen so much bleeding dunnage afore, and where is it all to be stowed?' declared an exasperated Murphy to his helper, Clumsy Dalby. 'A dozen o' shirts for the captain! Well, all will need pressing, and we ain't ne'er had more'n six aboard afore. We ain't some dandy Indiaman! Dalby, stop your blathering! Get your nose and paws out o' that chest, you grasping sod!' he grumbled in his irritating, high-pitched, nasal whine.

'Pipe down, Murphy!' exclaimed Pat in passing; nothing could be allowed to dim his pleasure in the day.

'Well, sorr, if you please, now here is your second-best breeches,' said Murphy later in the morning when unpacking clothing in the cabin. Murphy had served with Pat for many years; never a master mariner but originally a passable foremast hand, his very few abilities and perpetually complaining, shrewish attitude as the captain's servant left absolutely everything to be desired. Yet, with his old-maidish skills for sewing, silver-polishing and pressing Pat's clothes, with his trait for order in the cabin and an often vexatious approach to ensuring it, he had inexplicably overcome all rational selection processes to become Pat's valet and servant, performing the same service for Simon. Since he had been apprised of the imminent return to sea aboard *Surprise,* Murphy was a new man – almost; he had taken on the task of rousing out the former *Tenedos* veterans in Falmouth with an enthusiasm never before seen by Pat or Simon. Such stores of wine and brandy that had so far come aboard had, inexplicably, not suffered from any accidental breakages. Even Murphy's disagreeable, righteous whingeing had gone by the board for the most part, greatly to the astonishment of Pat and Simon. Still, Murphy could not quite rein in his matronly concern for his captain as he stepped up to the busy quarterdeck, distress mixed with anger as he cried, 'Mind your breeches on that hot tar! Oh bejabers, your honour has sat on it and you'se ruined 'em! Your best bloody breeches, for shame. Ne'er will it come out nor I spend a week a'washing. Ain't I for ever telling 'ee your sleeve is in the soup, and that takes a deal of scrubbing, and now hot tar on your breeches. Ruined, quite ruined they be. Well, I laid out them very old breeches this morning, and they be still there. Well, what your wife would say - *were she here* - the Lord only knows…' The steward offered a proper apology, 'Oh, beg pardon, sorr,' after a moment, adding a grovelling signal of attrition within moments, 'Coffee's up, sorr.'

'Thank you, Murphy. Now clap a stopper over your cross-grained blathering - *you insufferable blatteroon* - and bear a hand... Pass the word for the master,' replied Pat as patiently as he could, long accustomed to Murphy's irritating idiosyncrasies. The steward left and within moments Prosser appeared with a knock on the door. He had been listening behind it with barely contained pleasure to Pat's exchange with his steward and had strived diligently to avoid laughing aloud. 'Mr Prosser, the lads are working uncommon well these two days. You are familiar with all of 'em and the new lads. You would favour me most deeply by proposing one of them as my cox'n.'

The master paused momentarily, staring for several seconds as if weighing his reply carefully. It seemed to all the onlookers as if wisdom was radiating from his wizened face as he replied, 'Aye, sir; there is but one man I would favour as cox'n.'

'Who is this man, Mr Prosser?'

'He be coming from Pompey on the mail coach today and will be here presently. I took the liberty, sir, of sending for him when we was in Falmouth.'

'Pray send him in directly, as soon as he arrives, and we will ask his mettle,' said Pat, concealing well his curiosity. His deep respect for Prosser, a veteran of many voyages together, bestowed unquestioned confidence in his selection. 'Murphy, where is Doctor Ferguson?' he shouted, unnecessarily as Murphy was in his customary position whenever Pat conducted an interview in the great cabin: behind the door, his ear close to it.

'Below, sorr, in his store,' Murphy's face appeared.

'Perhaps it is a timely moment for an inspection of the lower and orlop decks?' said Pat to himself, and he paced out of the cabin and stepped down the companionway into the gloom of the lower deck. He looked about him: there were no men below, all were working above, and he was about to descend the steps to the orlop when Simon stepped up from below. Both were crouching in the low space afforded them, scarcely more than five and a half feet on the lower deck.

'Ah, Simon, there you are. Will you come up to the cabin and take second breakfast with me?'

'It is a benevolent offer, but not now; I am engrossed at present, I am mixing my stock of Paré's digestive.' Seeing Pat's blank look he continued, 'It is an ointment, a most excellent remedy in the case of gunshot wounds; but I am in need of fresh egg yolks - would you think the cook will spare some?'

'I hope you will leave Wilkins at least a brace to accompany my bacon; it ain't the same without eggs,' Pat laughed. 'The crew have done tolerably well and the ship nears readiness for sea. We will load our powder from the hoy on Monday and be away with the tide for Falmouth on Tuesday for the rest of our men - should we have any room left that is for the crew and family; never did we ever see so much in the way of stores loaded aboard. The master has proposed a cox'n, and I expect him directly. After that we will repair ashore for supper at the *Steam Packet*. Tell, eggs and ointment aside, are you now prepared with your customary medical supplies for our voyage? Is there anything you lack?'

Before Simon could answer there came a voice from the top of the companionway and Murphy's shrewish visage appeared, but instead of his customary high shrilling nasal whine it was almost a whisper, a reservation or an astonishment in his voice, Pat could not tell; 'Beg pardon, sorr, your visitor... he has arrived... Mr Prosser's cox'n be here.'

'Send him down, Murphy. At once, if you please,' Pat's voice boomed out imperiously. He wished for no distractions and remained intent on continuing with at least some small survey of the hold. However, the sight of the man who stepped down from the companionway, in the instant that he turned towards them, stopped Pat and Simon in their thoughts in a flash: the effect was overwhelming, heartbeats were missed, eyes widened, words were left unformed. For the first time ever in his ship, in the moment of the profound shock, Pat instinctively straightened bolt upright. He cracked his head on the low deckhead beam, shouted in some pain and fell back into a crouch against the gun-room door, nursing a sore and bleeding head. He gasped in astonished disbelief; he could not believe what he was seeing, for his thoughts had simply halted in the conflict of what his eyes were seeing and what his mind was telling him what could not be. He stared for a long moment before he could find any words at all, finally uttering, 'By God, 'tis Barton himself here before us,' his voice barely more than the quietest of whispers.

Murphy, further words failing even him, scrambled in haste down the steps even as Pat recovered himself and stood staring, open-mouthed at this so shocking sight. Pat's coxswain of ten long years, Brannan Barton, had been killed alongside him in the year 'thirteen in the boarding of *Chesapeake,* and Pat simply could not believe his eyes, was in total shock. Murphy stood there in dumb show, unable to shift or speak: never before had anything like it happened aboard.

Simon hastened round to Pat's side, wiping the blood trail away from above Pat's eye on his shirt sleeve, all the while staring at this apparition and whispering to himself, 'Oh, my Lord.'

Before them the unassuming seaman spoke up, 'Barton, sir; George Barton, cousin of Brannan. Mr Prosser sent for me.'

'Barton! 'pon my word, ne'er did two peas more resemble the same pod,' whispered Pat, struggling to find suitable words and trying unsuccessfully to come to terms with the sight of a man so utterly indistinguishable from his former coxswain.

Barton bravely resumed, 'Well, sir, Brannan Barton was my twin, but I was placed with my aunt when aged one on account of my mum having no breadwinner, our father having died afore I was born. She could not afford the upbringing of both of us, and so I have always been called cousin, even as we grew up not half a league apart in Falmouth.' Seeing that Pat was still agape, Barton pressed on with the details of his naval career, 'I started at sea in the time of his Lordship, Admiral Jervis, in the year 'ninety-seven, sir... I was a powder monkey for him at Cape St. Vincent on *Victory*. I was promoted able when serving on *Royal Sovereign* at Trafalgar... I was standing alongside Admiral Collingwood when *Santa Ana* struck to her, sir. The next year I was promoted to captain's barge crew... and I served with the Admiral until the year 'ten when his Lordship passed. Later, I was tiemate with William Mindham, gun captain on *Shannon,* in the year 'thirteen when we captured *Chesapeake*. Bill opened the firing on *Chesapeake* that day, sir, and we boarded her together, Brannan alongside o' me.'

'I collect the day uncommon well,' declared Pat with feeling; 'Admirable... admirable...'

'My brother was serving on *Tenedos* when Captain Broke sent her away, and she left him and a score of others aboard *Shannon;* her Second and Third were there too. We was rushing to help the cap'n who was downed when the prisoners broke out. Bill and one of the officers from *Tenedos* saved the cap'n, sir. I ne'er knew who he was. Bill and he reached the cap'n when he went down, one or t'other struck down the Yankee about to kill the cap'n... Bill I think it was, and we stood over him together 'til our marines came. It was a bloody business, sir...'

'No doubt, no doubt at all,' a fascinated Pat was reduced to a whisper; 'It was that, for sure.'

'When the cap'n led the boarding, he was followed by Mr Dunn - his clerk - and Mr Aldham, the purser. Can you believe it, sir? The clerk and the purser, near first over the bulwark! 'I am sorry to say that both were shot down dead behind the cap'n even afore they reached *Chesapeake's* deck.'

'I would have been with them, save that in the grand rush I tripped over a severed backstay, all ahoo around a gun truck... and I knocked my head on the barrel - *I was all ahoo myself for half a minute* until I was hauled up by Mr Macleod, and we boarded Chesapeake together.'

'You was one of the *Tenedos* officers; yes... yes,' exclaimed Barton; 'I collect the *Tenedos* people staying aboard.'

'We was shipmates then!' declared Pat, enthralled; 'At least for a week or so! How did you fare in the boarding, tell?'

'It was a right proper bloody mess... Tom Stevens, the bosun, had his hand hacked right off while he was lashing us alongside, though he carried on with his other hand 'til he was struck down by a musket ball, bless him. I have ne'er seen his like since... a great man, the pride of all hands he was, aye. Poor Tom lingered for near three weeks, sir, and died in Halifax.'

'And yourself?' Pat prompted gently, hardly daring to interrupt.'

'Oh, I was wounded dragging the cap'n back to *Shannon* - a ball from the tops - and two mates and my brother Brannan were killed alongside of me. I spent three weeks laid up afterwards... below in the sick bay and later in the Halifax hospital. I am glad I was able to give old Tom some little comfort there, sir, afore he passed. I was promoted bosun by Lieutenant Wallis on *Shannon* after I recovered, to replace old Tom. After *Shannon* went into ordinary, sir, I joined *Spartan,* and I served on her as cox'n until the year 'twenty when she also went into ordinary.' Barton's voice dropped from excitable to a lower octave, almost one of despondency, 'I ain't found a berth these past three years, sir. I've been working at the Pompey dockyards on ship refitting since.' With something of a plaintive look on his face, Barton concluded his truly exceptional record of service.

'Amazing... amazing!' exclaimed Pat. 'Well, you will allow me to tell you plain: you have found a berth now... you most certainly have! Barton, that is the most worthy of records... quite splendid! he declared, still in a state of some wondrous disbelief and nodding to Duncan. 'Mr Macleod here and I came aboard

*Shannon* from *Tenedos* just a day or so afore *Chesapeake* struck to her, your brother Brannan with us. I was Second and Mr Macleod was Third on *Tenedos*. Captain Hyde Parker sent us aboard with twenty men to assist *Shannon* before Broke sent *Tenedos* away... and Lucky Jack Aubrey was with us... I doubt you have forgotten him!'

'Not at all, sir; never in life!'

'And 'twas Jack Aubrey with your gun captain - Bill Mindham - that saved Captain Broke. Mr Macleod and I were but a yard behind Aubrey. And you were there with us! Simon, did you hear that? Upon my honour I have five guineas in my dunnage for you, Barton. Mighty pleased I was to have half a dozen good fellows with me when I reached Captain Broke; 'twas a desperate moment … a very bloody business indeed. And you were wounded in the boarding? Alas, I never saw you, nor anyone else I would recall after Broke was cut down; 'twas every man for himself for a few minutes there. As you say, we lost your brother Brannan that day; it was a painful loss to all of us on *Tenedos,* good man that he was. Lieutenant Macleod and I shifted to Halifax after the battle. And you served with Old Jarvie himself! Well, 'pon my word, that is a prodigious fine record, Barton, a handsome record indeed. The master speaks well of you; I need ask no more. You would favour me most deeply by shifting aboard directly as our new cox'n,' pronounced Pat, seizing and shaking Barton's hand in a vice-like grip. 'Murphy, lend a hand there, trundle Barton's dunnage aboard, cut along now. Take him to the galley for a pint of grog - *strong and fresh, mind; no four-water leavings!* - and then show him all around the barky.'

'Thankee kindly; I will not let you down, sir.' Barton touched his forehead and left in the company of a still dumbstruck Murphy.

'You seem greatly taken aback, brother,' said Simon, who had heard the story with interest.

'I should scarcely have thought it possible... Barton standing there in the flesh, and hard to believe 'twas not really him,' Pat heard himself whispering, remaining still in some small state of shock.

'To be sure, the twin's resemblance was assuredly so completely indistinguishable from that of our old shipmate, but it is not as rare as you might think. Perhaps one in three hundred births are identical twins,' replied Simon. 'I do not mean to urge you towards celerity, but if I may venture a suggestion, my dear... that is to say *if we are now at leisure*: would it be improper to suggest we get off this venerable vessel and step out for our supper?'

# Chapter Four

*'tis something, in the dearth of fame,*
*Though link'd among a fetter'd race,*
*To feel at least a patriot's shame,*
*Even as I sing, suffuse my face;*
*For what is left the poet here?*
*For Greeks a blush — for Greece a tear.*

*Sunday 18<sup>th</sup> May 1823*                *Plymouth Dock, Devon*

At first light Pat roused himself, dunked his head in the washbowl, and applied just a very little of Number Six cologne, it being Whit Sunday and no work was intended. The perfume was a present which had been given to him many years before by a particularly friendly, local young lady in Halifax, Nova Scotia; one which had remained unremarked upon by Sinéad in the intervening years, being secure in his shipboard dunnage. 'That will have to go to the deep six afore Sinéad comes aboard,' he thought absently. He dressed swiftly, his best coat and breeches having been pressed and left out the night before by Murphy. 'Freeman!' Pat shouted. 'Light along a pot of coffee... and do we have bacon left?'

Freeman appeared immediately, muttering, 'Pot 'im ready this five minutes, massa.'

Some little time later Duncan entered the cabin, sniffing the twin scents of coffee and bacon with undisguised delight.

'There is a whole pile of bacon, eggs too, in that pan, Duncan; Simon has spared us a few.'

'A most handsome prospect, for sure; I will gladly share your breakfast with the utmost pleasure.' Duncan settled at Pat's table, swiftly piling his plate with the most generous of helpings.

'Freeman! Bring some more soft tack for Mr Macleod... and pass the word for... for Murphy.' Pat remained still in some disbelief and confusion at Barton's arrival of yesterday, his thinking since oft slipping into small muddle. 'Will you not regret staying in the Hebrides, Duncan?'

Duncan paused from his obvious satisfaction with the fried breakfast and looked up. 'Och, I am sure they have their charms, but how greatly pleased I am that we are back here, aboard our new home, at sea again, aboard the barky, our dear *Surprise*. How agreeably homely it is; aye, there isnae doubt.' Deep conviction resonated plain in his voice.

'As you say, *there is no doubt*... so long ashore now I had near forgotten.' Pat looked wistfully into Duncan's face. 'A ship... once again. Oh, how I have longed these past three years for this moment to come, my hopes near dashed, and here we are.' Duncan merely smiled and nodded, chewing with great satisfaction, his mouth full. Pat sat down again in his chair and poured himself more coffee. 'Allow me to help you to a few more rashers; would you care for another egg or two?'

'Most certainly; I will finish the last three in the pan, if ye will. Would there be another wee drop of coffee left, at all?'

'Murphy! There you are. More coffee for Mr Macleod... and then we will rig church; I believe we will hoist the church pennant... if it is in the locker? Rouse out all the men, if you will. We are too few to muster to divisions, though it being Sunday I am minded to speak to the lads when we hold church. I fancy I will preach the sermon.'

'What? Ye will preach the sermon?' Duncan could not conceal his astonishment and laughed aloud. He slapped his coffee down on the table and clapped three times in merriment, as if in applause.

Pat glared at him. 'What a rattle you endeavour to be... and - *let me tell you* - without the least success. We have no chaplain and we ain't at war these days... *officially at least*... and the Articles... that is to say *without a prayer*... don't seem right. I have long had a copy of The Good Book in my dunnage all these years, and there are plentiful things in it which will suit when you trouble to look. It was plainly written by some honest fellows... fishermen and the like; doubtless many others were mariners too.'

'Aye and was Jonah one of 'em, Pat? I collect he spent much time asleep. I doubt ye should mention him to the men,' retorted Duncan, followed again by his hearty laugh.

'You do set up for a wit today, I see,' said Pat, peeved, 'and pray do not mention that particular name again if you please.'

Rather than below in the customary lower deck location, church was rigged on the gun deck, the morning being pleasantly dry and sunny; indeed, it was also unusually warm, with only the mildest of breeze rippling the reefed sails and the rigging. With so few crew aboard and no chaplain either - *Surprise* not ostensibly being a Royal Navy ship - and the weather promising to hold to its clement warmth, Pat felt a more informal occasion was called for. The ship's bell struck four bells.

'Murphy! My best scraper if you will.'

Murphy, looking unusually spry himself, was there in an instant. 'Well, 'tis on your table already, sorr.'

On stepping out from his cabin Pat gazed quickly, by instinct, across the Hamoaze which exhibited scarcely a ripple upon its placid surface, a scene of absolute tranquillity disturbed only by the gull, a hundred and more seemingly content to simply float and call to each other. He and Duncan were greeted by the Wesleyans, three dozen and more of them all lined up near the capstan, all scrubbed up, pigtails all newly plaited, broad-brimmed sennit hats atop every head (although the purser had yet to obtain the *Surprise* bands), every man wearing their best duck trousers, and - mystifyingly - all were garbed in a myriad shades of red; evidently all were prepared and awaiting the service. Self-evidently they had taken all possible steps to present themselves as tidy as tidy might be. The other crew members, tailing back towards the galley stove, were all also looking particularly prime.

'What's afoot? Has the fleet adopted a new uniform since we were last at sea... and forgotten to tell us?' joked Pat, laughing aloud.

'It is the Biblical colour for Pentecost, brother; and the Wesleyans are particular about the auld traditions, as ye may collect,' declared Duncan.

'I do not believe I have ever heard it remarked upon before. Very creditable in them, indeed,' said Pat pleasantly, being something of a traditionalist himself. The skeleton crew, barely four dozen men including the Eleanors, assembled in front of a sea-chest over which was draped an ensign to serve as a makeshift lectern. Pat's gaze ranged down the expectant lines, lingering momentarily on faces, brief appraisals coming to mind on the attributes of each of them: enthusiasts, competent tops men, skilful gunners, experienced riggers, a few exceptionally well-sighted with the glass; and not a one could he find who he would label as a skiver or a sea-lawyer; although there were certainly one or two who had a tendency to overly enjoy a generous libation when in port; but in all of them he saw the attribute which he shared with them: a dedication to the community which was the ship's crew, and a common purpose; indeed, there was something quite indefinable about them, an air of experience, of fortitude, which Pat found deeply warming; and none of them, he was sure, would ever let him down.

Pat was not a conventionally religious man but he was a pious traditionalist by nature. Lacking deep familiarity with the scriptures, he generally contented himself when required to give the sermon at sea with reading the Articles of War, which had become almost a venerable substitute for an appropriate ecclesiastical script. On this occasion however, *Surprise* not really being - officially at least - in His Majesty's Service, he considered that he should not read the Articles but expound on their particular circumstances before they sang the hymns. As Pat stepped to the sea-chest, the bosun's pipe shrilled and from the front came the shout, 'OFF HATS!' Pat paused long enough to take a sweeping look around; he inhaled a deep draught of the salt air carried on the warming morning breeze, and he gazed up as if towards the heavens, searching for the right words, the correct message for his people; for that is how he considered them: his people. Finally, his thoughts gathered as everyone present stared intently at him, he tucked his hat under his arm and began to speak, quite softly as there were so few present in comparison with a full crew. 'Good morning, lads. As we are so very few today and not quite yet in commission, I am minded to speak just a short piece to you. I ain't one for speeches, as you know, but allow me to share a trifle of my private thoughts from these past few days with you. Here we be, aboard our new home... the barky... our dear *Surprise*. It does my heart good to be aboard ship once again ...'

'Hear hear,' came the softly spoken murmur from the crew.

'Lads... most of you have been with me through the dam... *the gravest* of hard times, fighting Boney's ships and others too. We have been around the world together, through storms and the vilest of seas... We have shared hard tack and short commons...' Pat was speaking very slowly and with deliberation, as if still searching for the right words, the proper sentiments. 'We have lost some fine shipmates along the way...' He paused for a minute or two, looking round at all his crew, briefly studying each of their faces and remembering most of them from long voyages in years gone by, until his gaze alighted on his new cox'n, standing to the fore, and his mind painfully flashed back, recalling one lost comrade in particular; and in that instant his heart moved within him, a huge physical tremor rising from deep down, and his throat dried in an instant as his mind filled with a vision of Brannon Barton, a powerful recollection, one which utterly overwhelmed him, to the exclusion of all other thoughts. A long further minute passed, every man of the crew respectfully holding their silence, their captain's difficulty there to see, Pat plainly unable to speak again in the bleak moment of distress. Finally, he swallowed hard and forced his mind to focus; and quietly he resumed, 'I am minded of one lost shipmate... Brannan Barton was with me – *with us* – since my very first command, the gun-brig *Starling* in Portsmouth in the year 'three. In the year 'four I will never forget boarding *El Valiente* with him alongside of me, and when I was felled by a pike he saved my life, pistolling the Spaniard ere he could stick me again. Brannan Barton in those years became my friend... *our* friend... and served with us until he was killed in the year 'thirteen. I have oft thought of him these ten years gone.' It was obvious to all the assembly that their captain was struggling, in considerable difficulty as he resumed; his words, still very quiet, hardly more than a whisper, wafted across, so gentle, so kindly, as if borne by a magical breeze to reach them. His head lifted, he swallowed hard once more in a vain attempt to ameliorate his dry mouth, and he spoke again, the very few words revealing his thoughts with brutal clarity, 'I miss him greatly.' He paused again amidst a soft echoing of accord from the crew. 'Today, as you know, 'tis the day of Pentecost, the day our Lord Jesus returned to us...' Pat faltered once more, his knowledge of the scriptures was more than a little hazy. With only the familiar, shrilling noise of gulls in the background and an occasional rustling from the rigging, the crew, bluff seamen all, their whispered exchanges subsiding to a total silence after his words, he continued, '... and perhaps we too have seen someone come back to us yesterday; 'tis Barton here who reminds us that from our tragedy, out of that ache of our despair... will always come hope afresh.'

Not even the quietest murmur now disturbed the moment, all present listening intently, utterly unaccustomed as they were to words of such poignancy from their captain; the Wesleyans all stood with bowed heads. Another long pause, a minute or more, followed as Pat again gathered his thoughts and, as if realising that he had been speaking so very quietly, he swallowed again, silently damned his dry mouth, and continued, finding a more resolute voice, 'Afore we venture out again, lads... aboard our new home at sea, our dear *Surprise...* let us welcome aboard *George* Barton... our new shipmate... our cox'n... *our brother.'*

Pat concluded his address to hearty cheering from his men, 'HURRAH! HURRAH! Hear the captain! HURRAH!' As he looked all around him to survey his crew, the calm of the air having developed into a topsail breeze and having shifted round to the exposed south-west since the start of church and the sky having become progressively darker, unexpectedly a fine drizzle, hardly rain, began to set in, quickly wetting the faces of the assembly: a minor inconvenience, for which Pat found himself profoundly grateful, and obscuring, or so he thought, the tears trickling down his cheeks.

All hands had noticed that in the lattermost of Pat's address his voice had taken on a halting, softer tone than was usual on these occasions, one much more so than the very firm tone he customarily adopted for reading such as the Articles of War, and despite the fine rain no one could miss their captain's distress, visible tears, as he blinked repeatedly to clear his eyes and wiped his face with his hand. Mr Prosser, the master and elder of the Wesleyans, stepped up to the makeshift lectern – quite unbidden but understanding perfectly the moment – and waved the now chattering crew to silence once more. 'We thank you most kindly, sir, for your very handsome words.'

'Carry on, Mr Prosser,' said Pat in scarcely more than a whisper. After two hymns had been sung and the briefest of church sermon concluded, read by the master, the bosun piped the hands to dinner and the crew returned to the lower deck for the customary Sunday pork followed by plum duff: the culinary highlight of the week aboard His Majesty's ships. It was a tradition that Pat would never change. Shortly thereafter Dalby beat a loud, emphatic *Roast Beef of Old England* on the drum to signal readiness of the officers' dinner.

Back in the great cabin, Pat patiently awaited his dinner with Duncan and Simon, attended intermittently by Freeman. 'Allow me to fill your glasses, gentlemen. This is rather better than our ordinary, I believe?' Pat offered, pouring from a bottle of his dwindling private stock of the Madeira 'seventy-five.

'I am entirely of your way of thinking,' Simon replied, 'An exceptional wine it is. What are your present thoughts, brother; tell?'

'What butter or whiskey does not cure cannot be cured,' declared Pat rather obliquely, not quite ignoring his friend's question but not caring to expound on his profound uncertainties.

'What things you tell me!' exclaimed Simon, laughing. 'Perhaps they will serve for the moon pall and the marthambles... and the hockogrockle too!'

'So said my grandma,' Pat protested with an audible gesture towards indignance.

'That is quite worthy of Dr Tufts!' Simon laughed again. 'And an eminent quack he was indeed. Would that such pleasant placebos might truly function as panaceas,' he murmured absently; 'It is a most appealing notion, sure.'

'It will stand in Connemara,' exclaimed Pat, a little wearily, 'because there is precious little else, and not a one of doctors - save travelling to Dublin city. Oh, we have the salves, the leeches, hog's lard... and ever the old wives' remedies... but I never gave them much countenance.'

'I would not care to opine on the eccentric beliefs of the denizens of Ireland, the furthest remote parts most particularly;

for it seems to me that they hold to the strangest of notions; indeed, even the boggarts are believed to thrive there. However,' Simon continued with a degree of contrition, 'I will concede that the ancient folklore of medicine is not entirely to be despised, for we must consider that its essential roots are yet to be more greatly understood... but I doubt that the illuminati of the medical world would share your grandmother's conviction.'

Pat hesitated, twenty minutes having elapsed with nothing to eat in sight, 'I wonder if there *is* any pork left or whether Murphy has eaten it all up?'

Just at that moment Freeman appeared at the cabin door with a large and overburdened silver tray. 'Vittles is up, massa, if you please. Cook 'im sending best underside for dinner; here 'tis.'

'Thankee, Freeman; my compliments to Wilkins, if you will. I am sure we will do it justice!'

After Freeman had busied himself piling the most generous of portions on silver plates, he left the cabin. No one started on their food, all present aware of an unspoken hiatus, a reservation. Simon broke the silence, 'I heartily commend you, Pat; those were very fine words today, most commendable words. None finer have I ever heard uttered afore aboard this or any other vessel, and particularly well received it was indeed. Nothing like it have we ever heard before, and... forgive me, brother... I should scarcely have thought it of you... but, allow me to ask... I have a certain... *perhaps unfounded* impression... pray tell, dear soul, is there some uneasiness on your mind... a concern in respect of our return to Greece, that blood-soaked locus of death and despair?'

'If the sky falls, we shall catch larks,' declared Pat, followed by a long, long sigh.

'I do not quite follow you,' replied Simon; 'The precise significance is not clear to me.'

'We will not worry about things which may never happen. Will I help you to some stuffing?'

'Excuse me... if I might be permitted another observation... You were tolerably eloquent today, using very fair expressions which I do not generally expect to hear from you; indeed, I doubt I could say better myself.'

'Sure, I never was one for speeches,' replied Pat, smiling a little more broadly now, 'though I can bring something out now and then, given time.' And nothing more could Simon or Duncan extract from him.

*Tuesday 20ᵗʰ May 1823*                    *Plymouth Dock, Devon*

The fair weather of the weekend had deteriorated into a mid-grey sky with a diffuse dawn sky bringing a prevalent westerly light wind accompanied by broken cloud and soft steady rain, all so typical of the south-west of England at virtually any time of the year, but moderated, as is so often the case in those climes, by a warm temperature. The crew themselves, all cognisant of and familiar with the Channel weather in all its forms, were assured that all was well for the bay crossing to Falmouth, though it would be hard work were the wind to strengthen exceptionally with a crew of just four dozen, capable hands though they were. The Admiralty had denied *Surprise* any serving Royal Navy seamen from Plymouth, maintaining their official separation from the covert venture, and so, for the very short voyage, Pat had decided to rely on those few Falmouth volunteers who had come to Plymouth aboard *Eleanor*. As four bells struck, signifying the master's choice of time for departure just after high water, a few of the yard shipwrights were still onboard, though finishing up and removing their tools from about the deck as the Master Shipwright, Edward Churchill, accompanied by the Master Attendant, George Sidley, climbed aboard from the Yard's cutter and stepped up to Pat's quarterdeck to bid their farewells. They shook hands solemnly with both Pat and Duncan before looking about the decks and gazing at the masts and rigging as if in final inspection, and then Churchill spoke up, pride so very evident in his face and voice, 'Just you be very careful with her, sir, and be sure to bring her back to us in good order.'

'Never in doubt, Mr Churchill, never in doubt. My thanks to you again, sir.' Pat smiled broadly; his pleasure was irrepressible.

'I bid you all safe passage, Captain O'Connor. Goodbye, sir,' said the Master Attendant.

'Thank you, Mr Sidley. Goodbye.'

Pat watched his visitors disembark, and then with the deepest sense of satisfaction he gazed all about his ship. He allowed himself a few minutes to study those faces of his crew nearby, competency and experience so very evident in all of them; he studied the remainder as they busied themselves with final preparations, some glancing occasionally to the quarterdeck in anticipation of the imminent commands for departure.

The shipwrights were now all departed, rowing towards where the yard crew, many scores of men, all lined the quay. From the cutter, Churchill and Sidley gazed back, not wishing to miss any part of the spectacle of *Surprise's* farewell. Barton, with two of the Wesleyans, was at the wheel; Mr Prosser, the master, was alongside them. Simon stood at Pat's side on the quarterdeck, gazing at the final preparations. Despite witnessing many such departures, the nautical nomenclature had never rooted in his mind and the ship handling procedures still left him largely mystified. 'To be sure, we are particularly few, Pat, in comparison of our customary numbers; short-handed, I dare say? Will this present any difficulties for our leave-taking, would you think? I only throw out the remark.'

'Why certainly it will. Be a good fellow for once and lend a hand there on the capstan... and push hard when I give the word, will you?' replied Pat with a suppressed smile. The old hands at the wheel looked at each other, barely concealing their astonishment.

'Certainly, brother. I have oft heard you mention that particular device, but be so good as to remind me: where *is* the capstan? My familiarity is lacking a trifle in these nautical, these *mechanical* devices, as you may have noticed.'

'No, not at all.'

'Pray point it out if you will,' said Simon, falling wholly into Pat's little trap. The helmsmen tittered, stopping only when Barton kicked them. 'I see you practise upon me.'

'You are a hoot,' laughed Pat, his good humour plain.

'I am no navigator... no authority in mariner's matters.'

Pat gazed with deep affection at his friend. 'Oh, I should never say that. For sure you're an odd one: none finer in the philosophical line... a capital man with the Latin... and no doubt the only sight all aboard the barky would pray to see were they ever carried down to the cockpit; yet for all these years at sea you scarcely have any notion of the bow from the stern or your larboard from your starboard. If you will, pray see if that rascal Murphy might find us a pot of tea in about ten minutes.'

'I find you in tolerably better humour this morning, brother,' replied Simon, in good spirits himself.

'I am uncommon happy. Afloat again... aboard a fine ship and with a goodly set of hands; aye, I am as proud as a lord's bastard. Falmouth bound we are... and with a prospect of some proper seafaring ahead. Aye, 'tis a fine day, none better.'

Simon left the quarterdeck, and Pat turned to Duncan and the master, both waiting patiently alongside him. 'Our time is come to depart, Mr Macleod.'

'ALL HANDS, PREPARE TO MAKE SAIL!' shouted Duncan.

'LAY ALOFT!' shouted Prosser, and the men scrambled up to the yards. 'Rig capstan bars and bring to the messenger,' he bawled, and within a few minutes, 'MAN THE BARS!'

*Surprise* was anchored larboard side on her best bower, the cable hove short, her starboard side towards the quay as she was beginning to be drawn by the current, the tide beginning its ebb. The wind too seemed ready to assist the frigate's departure, veering to a north-westerly, fine on her larboard bow.

'BREAST THE CAPSTAN!' shouted the master.

'Up anchor!' ordered Pat.

'UP ANCHOR FOR HOME!' Prosser echoed, jubilation in his voice.

'Heave and a-weigh!' cried Duncan.

The cable began to be wound in on the capstan, announced by the familiar click-click of its pawls as it rotated, and accompanied by the sounds of Maclean's fife and a shanty coming from the men, '*Walk her round and round she goes, way oh, way oh.*' It was a vociferous departure from Royal Navy practices and one to which Pat paid no heed, for nothing short of King George himself stepping aboard could possibly impinge on his genial and deep satisfaction this day. Even the old salts of *Tenedos* had departed from their customary, restrained standard shouts of '*two-six, two-six,*' all swept up in the enthusiastic fervour. The capstan men, their singing now general, ran the cable in just fast enough for the few tierers present to keep up.

'Up and down!' came the shout from the bow.

'Thick and dry for weighing!' shouted Duncan.

The topmen meanwhile had shifted out on to the yards and had cast off the gaskets, the lines that held the sails tight furled to the yards. They gathered the canvas under their arms and waited. The tierers were coaxing in the remaining cable until all was swiftly stowed, and the best bower appeared, just hauled out of the water.

'Standby aloft, let fall!' ordered Duncan, and with his shout came the howling *peep-peep, peep-peep* whistle from the bosun alone, no mates available whilst so short-handed.

'Let fall! Sheet home, sheet home, hoist away!' the master shouted. The topmen standing ready at her topsails let fall the sails: down they tumbled, unfurling, loosely flapping, the men hauling on the braces. *Surprise's* afteryards were already braced ready for the tack to turn her gently to face downstream in the ebb tide, the headyards abox, headsheets hauled to larboard. She would come round gradually but would be afforded little steerage for the first few minutes.

'Hard a-lee!' Duncan commanded the two helmsmen.

*Surprise* now backed slowly, her stern coming round to larboard as she gained sternway, her bow coming round to starboard, turning faster now without the anchor constraint, her fore topsail pushing her, back, back, the main and mizzen flapping until she came further round and they filled.

'Helm up!' shouted Duncan when her bow faced the yard and she was beginning to be driven forward.

The combined wind and ebb tide were pushing her now with greater momentum, and the rudder was kept hard over until she was fully turned about and facing down the Hamoaze.

'Helm amidships!' The wind and current now combining to give her speed, she swiftly moved away downstream, whilst on the quay a hundred men or more waved their farewells. The deck crew heaved the remainder of the cable in and the anchor was quickly catted. Within a very few minutes *Surprise* was well underway in the fairway, the Hamoaze, and all along her sides there creamed a ribbon of white water.

'That was handsomely executed... and with just two score hands... 'pon my word we have some prime seamen aboard, Barton,' Pat shouted across to the wheel, slipping without thinking into the easy manner of past times with his old cox'n, Brannon Barton.

'Aye, sir,' George Barton shouted back, mightily pleased to hear his captain's compliment.

The master kept *Surprise* firmly in the deepwater channel and well within the half-hour she came out through the Narrows, the small crew making good work of the sail handling tasks. *Surprise* came swiftly out into the Sound, making a south-south-westerly course, sailing close-hauled with the south-westerly wind, passing the emerging breakwater and so to Penlee Point.

'Will we see what she can do when put to her shifts?' asked Pat of Duncan who nodded, smiling; 'Aye aye, sir.'

'Mr Pickering,' Duncan announced, 'I am minded that she will enjoy more sail aloft; royals, topgallants and fore topsail.'

'Aye aye, sir,' Pickering turned towards the bosun, standing near the bell, and bellowed out, 'Stand by to make sail! Aloft topgallant and royal yardmen!'

The bosun's pipe shrilled out a long, long note before his shout, 'Lay aloft!' and within minutes as the men readied atop the yards, and after another long ululating whistle, he cried out, 'Man the royal halliards and sheets! Weather royal braces! Haul taut! Sheet home! Hoist away royals!' The exercise was repeated with the topgallants and the fore topsail, and *Surprise* noticeably gained a knot in short order as she fairly cut a white swathe of foam through the moderate waves and trailed a long wake astern, all the while to the joyful, reassuring chorus of creaking, stretching rigging and new canvas coming under strain for the first time, the sounds an utter delight to an enraptured crew.

'Brace in the top yards a half-point, Mr Pickering,' added Pat with a careful eye on the sails, 'and a full point for the topgallants.' Finally, Pat decided that the yard bracing was as perfect as ever it would be, and he nodded to Pickering and the bosun, his face a joyful picture of pleasure.

'Lay in, lay down from aloft!' bawled the bosun after another long blast on his whistle.

The high sail additions pushed the ship further over on her lee heel and the resultant extreme pendulum-like roll as she tacked for the first time under her press of sail was quite exhilarating to Pat, to his officers and all his old tarpaulins, but less so for Simon who appeared on deck within minutes of her coming about. 'There is an uncommon severe tilt about this higher floor,' declared Simon in slightly vexatious voice to Pat as he struggled with his balance to keep his feet.

'Not at all... not at all,' Pat smiled as he replied, 'Here, clap on to the belaying pin rail.'

'Pray point it out.'

'Here, grasp it tight; *not the pins, the rail*. Why, the barky is simply finding her feet after being laid up so long in ordinary... Indeed, we might consider that she is akin to a thoroughbred at the off in the Two-thousand Guineas.'

'I am fully persuaded of it,' said Simon without the least conviction, 'but, speaking as a mariner of some *not inconsiderable* experience...' Eyebrows were raised generally on deck, faces everywhere looked down, and men bit hard on lips to avoid laughter, '... perhaps a more moderate velocity would better suit until all her parts are proven to be wholly in harmony? And... *to continue the analogy*... it would not serve us well were she to throw a shoe. Do you follow?'

'I do know a thing about horses, you know... and - with all due modesty - *about ships*; and if you do not mind my saying so,' Pat himself struggled to avoid laughing, '... you were no doubt forgetting that we endeavour to fetch home to Falmouth in the broad daylight.'

As Rame Head came up on the starboard beam the ship's bell rang eight bells and half the crew disappeared below for dinner. The rain had ceased and the sun broke through the clouds, bringing welcome warmth and good cheer to the hard-working crew.

Pat turned to his long-serving companion and First, 'At sea again, a frigate of the very first order and our old crew aboard. Don't it give you a shiver down your back, Duncan?'

'Aye, for sure it does, there is nae doubt at all,' whispered Duncan with emotion. 'I dinnae collect a bonnier day for many a year, and I widnae exchange it for a barrel of gold pieces.'

Later, in the great cabin, Pat, Duncan and Simon shared a pot of tea with sizzling-hot white pudding, brought aboard fresh that morning. '*Eleanor* is to follow us tomorrow,' declared Pat, 'and William will bring her over to join us in Falmouth with his small crew. We are still short of officers... but even with the fleet so reduced I have but small hope of serving officers quitting their commands to join us... and we don't possess even a single squeaker, *not a one*. No, our best prospects lie with those of our old friends who have been these past years a'fretting on the beach: lieutenants on their paltry half-pay with no prospects of a ship and no hope of being made post. I have hopes that James Mower may join us yet. I have written to him - his family has long lived in Falmouth - and to Tom Pickering also. Do you collect what a wit that man has? I venture 'tis likely the merchant service may have taken one or t'other of 'em. Do you collect them both on our first cruise together? Midshipmen they were... on our old *Starling*... my first command, back in the year 'three. Happy times... eh? Happy times they surely were.'

'Aye, I collect the twae, brother; but we were poor, widnae a dollar between us,' said Duncan.

'To be sure, yet I collect that sense of adventure, so long now lacking. Dear God, how good it was to be alive in those years... All of Boney's ships against us and fleets afloat that we shall ne'er see the likes of again.' A nostalgic Pat turned to the other side of his table, 'Do you miss those days, Simon?'

'The sentiments of adventure - *yes* - and, *much later*, of anticipation of profound political change that came about... but which was so sadly snuffed out in Scot... that is to say in *Spain*.' Simon suppressed distressing recollections of Hardie, Baird and Wilson, all hung and beheaded after the failed rising a mere three years previously. 'Those feelings I miss most dearly. Since Agnes's death...' A tremor surged through Simon's very being as he uttered his late wife's name, and he was sure that his heart was racing beyond the least control, '... I have felt only the cold

129

chill of disappointment in my bones and melancholia in my bosom.'

'I am most heartily sorry to hear that,' murmured Pat gently.

'This new expedition comes with great hopes for me, even a rekindling of purpose. These are aspirations and feelings which I had long thought dead these five years past. For sure it would also be a pleasure to see as many as may be of our auld friends again.'

'I have no doubt that will be the case. All have been laid up ashore for some years, and with none having any connections they are unlikely to find any berth. It has also reached my ears that William Codrington is hiding from his creditors and near bankrupt this past year. I gather that allegations of his severe gambling losses are well founded. He has been losing badly, as so many sailors do when ashore with a pocket full of guineas, and might well relish an absence from home; doubtless some foreign service would be particularly welcome,' said Pat, adding, 'We are to meet with the First Lord on Friday and sail on Sunday week, come what may.'

'I do not like to sound froward, brother,' Simon ventured, 'but might I trouble you and suggest it may be useful to our expedition were we to engage a proficient surgeon's assistant? One would hardly be a supernumerary. You are to consider that I am but one man alone in this capacity; I have no loblolly boy... nor even a horse-knacker to assist.'

'Horse-knacker did you say?' gasped Pat with something of a meld of astonishment and dismay.

'Indeed, I collect several occasions when I was a medical student in Edinburgh and the knacker had procured a most useful corpse for research... fifteen shillings each they were - *when one could be afforded.* The old hands that they were, they usually had the wherewithal for quietly finding something in the resurrection line... and they were ever prepared to assist the dissection... and that after faithfully sharpening the surgeon's knives to a whisker-like edge.'

'Dear Lord preserve me!' exclaimed Pat, aghast.

'And so, if you are in contemplation of an action where the extent of the bloodshed might most severely test my... my *solitary capacities...* then a second physician will certainly serve us well.' Simon shuddered with that particular thought and he paused to assess whether his plea had registered, but seeing no expression on Pat's face he resumed, 'Have you, perchance, also considered engaging a member of the cloth?'

Pat looked doubtful, 'To tell you the truth... to tell you the truth, old Simon, I have often wondered if a warship is a proper place for a priest; we may likely be going hammer and tongs to blow some other fellow's head off... and what are our people to think about that when the same man gives the Sunday prayer the next day and preaches looking after our fellow man, eh? I never thought it went down very well aboard *Tenedos,* and so I had set my face against it this time. Do you see what I mean?'

'That is perfectly true; but blowing the other fellow's head off is our very purpose *in extremis...* but the other fellow will likely have his own, similar intentions in the matter of *our* heads; and he may have some success; and that is why the crew will welcome a second surgeon... I most certainly shall... and...' Simon was reaching into his mind for the least idea, '... it is most firmly advocated by the Sick and Hurt.'

Pat reflected even as he frowned; plainly he had lost the argument, and so for the moment he determined to hedge, 'There you have me... and I believe there is something in what you say; but our time away is uncertain and our particular efforts may not signify for a long time... yet there ain't room enough in the gun-room for all these extra fellows... should we find all our officers awaiting us in Falmouth.'

'Allow me to raise the possibility, the very slight possibility, dear, of finding one single person to fit the bill for both these capacities. I have received a letter from Michael Marston... you recall him, an auld shipmate of ours?' If Pat's memory served him, he did not care to admit it, and he remained silent as Simon persevered. 'He is a gentleman and no quacksalver, I do assure you; indeed, he has admirable leanings in the direction of natural philosophy... but perhaps that is to be expected in a man of the cloth...' Simon's glance was rewarded only with Pat's face remaining immobile save for the merest indication of a frown. 'He also has a deal of experience in drawing teeth...'

Pat's interest in drawing teeth was insufficient to merit consideration of Marston's skills in the matter; indeed, he rejoiced momentarily that he still possessed all of his own, and that after several brutal ship boardings which had left others of his crew missing several molars; most of a mouthful, in fact, in one or two cases; nevertheless, he managed a civil nod of his head and a most noncommital murmur.

Simon was grasping for straws if not exactly clutching them with a firm grip, '... and he makes a decent attempt upon the violin...'

'I collect that his talents when last aboard did not lie in that direction,' remarked Pat eventually and somewhat acerbically, remembering Marston's indifferent skill as a musician. 'Indeed, if my memory serves me, I collect he had an affinity for prating... *excessively... and certainly one for untimely interruption.*'

Pat's doubtful visage shifting more towards condemnation, prating known to be one of the greater sins in his firmament, and interruption much, much worse, Simon pressed on in a vein which he hoped was more likely to strike a chord with his friend, 'He has been fretting to find some means of employment these four or more years... for he possesses no livings, being a clergyman of the Wesleyan persuasion. He is most diligent in his application in all matters... ' A hesitation, 'Would you consider of him... Pat?' The appeal was asked a little apprehensively; Marston's presence on board *Tenedos* had not been an unqualified success, Pat not greatly warming to Marston as an individual nor indeed in his role as a chaplain aboard ship; and the crew had considered it unlucky to have a cleric aboard despite their leaning towards the routine of a regular Sunday church service. Previously, Pat had admitted him for a short voyage only in his capacity as Simon's assistant surgeon.

'Allow me to mull it over.' Pat's scowl betrayed his thinking. 'We will speak further about it at supper,' he added without conviction, still temporising. Simon was content at that moment to ignore the evasion, plain as it was.

The afternoon passed pleasantly, the sun staying to warm and cheer them as *Surprise* made long tacks, close-hauled, through

Whitsand Bay in a south-westerly Topsail breeze; she passed Dodman Point and left Gull Rock in her wake, coming up to the approach to Falmouth. Seven bells struck as Pendennis Point came into sight directly off the bow. The master was back in his home port and carefully brought *Surprise* past the Black Rock to larboard and into the Carrick Roads. The wind was now south-westerly, abeam, the frigate's double-reefed topsails alone driving her on a north-westerly tack, her courses long since furled before her approach to the inner harbour. Pat had decided to bring her as close as the master thought fit to the town, and the topmen, skilled as they were and needing no bidding, gradually checked her braces to deaden her topsails, so slowing her momentum to a snail's pace; her course shifting closer to westerly, she could not get closer to the wind. Simon stood alongside a silent but plainly pleased Pat on his quarterdeck, Barton at the wheel, as *Surprise* crept closer towards her intended anchorage, passing Killigrew's original Town Quay - the Custom House Quay - to larboard. The master ordered her course changed again, to north-westerly once more, the town now abeam and her bow pointing in the direction of Flushing village.

'It is a great while since I saw you so happy, brother,' Simon remarked conversationally. 'In such moments I could wish our voyage would go on for ever, all together in our contentment.'

'Fiddler's Green ain't in it,' whispered Pat, a little overwhelmed himself by the emotions engendered within him during the day.

There was barely a breath of wind, and the sound of her hull through the water - only the smallest ripple at her bow - was plainly audible even on the quarterdeck. The whole of the ship's company was on deck and the air of excitement was tangible as, inch by inch, *Surprise* approached the master's intended anchorage, the King's Road, the ship near silent, sliding along, tops'ls all backed, until the Fish Strand Quay lay two cables off her beam, the master declaring further beyond which he would not wish her to lie at low water. *Surprise* slowed as her way began to fall off, the current acting upon her, making a little leeway, slowing until stopped, no longer any forward movement at all upon her.

'Let go!' shouted the master, and the best bower was dropped with the distinctive sound of its splash heard all about the ship and the harbour. Pat looked all about him, then gazed over towards the town, where he saw, to his astonishment, lining the Market and Fish Strands, hundreds and hundreds of Falmouth people, recognisable and familiar faces prominent amongst them in his glass even in the distance, many of them former *Tenedos* crew, Jack Tars from prior voyages and new *Surprise* crew members too. For the most part they were standing together with their wives, sweethearts and numerous excited children. Suddenly the throng were roused as one and broke into wild shouts of greeting, then cheering, all waving exuberantly, clapping and shouting to greet *Surprise, their* ship as they now considered her to be, their menfolk now her crew, come home.

Pat was standing near the wheel, very moved by the spectacle, a deep sense of gratitude for such a welcome swiftly arising within him and a heartwarming feeling of well-being quite overcoming him. 'Welcome home, Mr Prosser,' Pat turned to the nearest man to him, the master, and grasped and shook his hand with enthusiastic vigour, 'Welcome home!'

*Wednesday 21ˢᵗ May 1823*                    *Falmouth, Cornwall*

After breakfast Pat and Simon remained in the great cabin with a fresh pot of coffee, reviewing the expedition preparations and awaiting the arrival of the mail coach from Truro, both keenly anxious to discover whether at least any letter of reply might be received from Pat's former officers. Duncan was away to the harbourmaster's office, attending to the port formalities. It being high water *Surprise* had been towed by her boats a little nearer to the Custom House Quay to facilitate the loading of her remaining stores and to allow boarding and disembarking for shore-leave of her all-volunteer complement, the Falmouth men making their farewells to excited families.

'Art happy, brother?' asked Simon, looking up from his papers. 'Tell me of your contemplations. I have the impression -

will I say - of a trifling lack of contentment about your person, a certain anxiety in your philosophy... if I may venture so?'

'I am a little put out, I confess,' Pat seemed to welcome the interruption of his thoughts. 'I have been considering our prospects, but there is one damn matter which plagues me and which I cannot shake.'

'How do we stand without our customary complement of officers if their arrival does not eventuate? Is it that which is oppressing you? Surely, they are still to be expected, if a trifle late?'

'I do not like to count all my eggs before they hatch.'

'I suppose not. Yet it would seem that we have only Macleod in the basket. If the others do not arrive, would you suppose this will present us with insuperable difficulties, being short-handed so?'

Pat exhaled deeply and nodded. 'Oh, without 'em we can sail the ship, of that there is no doubt, but to fight her... now that is a different barrel of fish... no officers on the gun deck and Lord knows how we will fare. A hundred and eighty men, let us say, to fight the guns, both sides together; forty and more to sail her and a dozen aloft with small arms and in the magazines; two hundred men and more but ne'er a one of officers, save for Duncan - *and me* - on the quarterdeck. And if one or t'other of us should be wounded... I will not say knocked on the head - I fancy I will never say anything as unlucky as that, I will not tempt fate - no, we could not fight her, that is plain.'

'I dare say. So, if not a one arrives this day on the mail coach, we are to pass a summer here in Falmouth... surely not?'

'You cannot have a ship sailing about without officers, it won't do.'

'What things you tell me!'

'Why, however would we find our bearing?'

Pat glared, momentarily lost for words, as Simon continued in great humour and enjoying himself; 'I am merely a surgeon, certainly no navigator...'

'Modesty fair suits you,' Pat growled.

'... and I have not the least familiarity nor indeed any acquaintance at all with the requisite instruments and charts... but

135

your observation is undeniable; indeed, it is the most commendable of such notions, none more so.'

Pat raised his eyebrows at Simon's tart comment. 'We will lack midshipmen too, and without officers I fear we will sit idling, knocked back on our heels, festering in some Ionian port... and that won't do... no, that certainly won't do. Why, I don't need no mumbo-jumbo seer, no astrological quack, nor any damn necrom... nec... necrophile to tell me what the Greeks will think.'

'Heavens! Let us hope not!' Simon could not suppress his laughter.

'Damned poltroons and cowards we will look... and what could we say to that? Precious little! Is there a tint of coffee in that pot?'

'There is none. Will I send Murphy for fresh? Perhaps we may enjoy a last glass of delectable stingo while we remain in port; that is to say if it is not too early. We might await the mail in some degree of comfort - *it offers the most inconstant service* - at the Marine Hotel; it a commendable tavern on the quay there. Perhaps your concerns will prove unfounded and this principled scheme of yours can still be delivered, the departure of this vessel as intended?'

'The mail is disgracefully late. We will wait a trifle longer, and if our officers ain't on it we will go ashore the moment it arrives.'

The crew, now that they were at full strength and numbering more than two hundred and forty men, busied themselves with the many and varied preparations for the imminent voyage, all to a man supremely pleased to be onboard ship once again and with a particular favour for *Surprise*. From all quarters there came the familiar noises of shipboard activity and bustle, so satisfying to Pat - not having been to sea since four years or more. From above him he heard the resounding thump of the 'Bible' holystones on the quarterdeck as they were shifted from place to place; through the door he could hear the hails aloft from the seniors of the crew on deck and the general to-ing and fro-ing of men occupied with a myriad routine tasks, and from below there came the rhythmical noise of the pumps. Even the shrill calls of the gulls were pleasurable and welcome to Pat's ears, the ambience of the whole - aside from his enduring concern for the lack of officers, save for Duncan - bringing about a quietude and relaxation within him which had been lacking for a considerable time.

Simon, never the most organised of souls, was similarly pleased to return to contemplation of the emerging and tidy inventory of his medical supplies, at that moment calculating his stocks of portable soup - a glutinous jelly requiring melting before it could be imbibed and a standfast of very doubtful welcome to all occupants of the sick berth.

From within the great cabin came the mutterings of Murphy, cleaning the windows at the stern - the lights as they were termed. And then came a pause, a suspension in the customary shipboard noises. It was replaced by a rising babble of voices, becoming louder and louder, coming from the quarterdeck. Pat, noticing after a moment and his contentment broken, shouted with some irritation, 'What is that infernal row? What is that din, Murphy? Murphy there! Tell 'em to clap a stopper over it. What's afoot?'

'Well, 'tis the mail coach arrived, sorr, and some visitors be here,' replied Murphy, looking through Pat's glass, staring intently through the lights and across to the Custom House Quay, his naturally excessive curiosity piqued.

Pat and Simon broke off to go up on deck. The mail coach had disgorged its passengers. Even at the distance of almost two cables, the figures on the quay were recognisable and confirmed with the glass. To Pat's great pleasure two of them were Tom Pickering and James Mower, both former midshipmen with Pat on *Starling*, Pat's first command, and Pickering a lieutenant on *Tenedos* after that. The crew had ceased work and were standing about, animatedly gabbling amongst themselves, pleased to see two more old shipmates, both held in the very highest esteem. Of William Codrington, Pat's third invitee, there was no sign. In high delight to see such welcome arrivals, Pat beamed with intense pleasure; he waved with enthusiasm across to the quay. 'Barton, you are to bring them aboard directly.' He turned to Simon, 'Why, ain't it a grand sight?'

'To be sure, a most pleasing event indeed. A more joyous development cannot be imagined,' a delighted Simon smiled beatifically.

The barge swiftly brought Pickering and Mower aboard, the two saluting the quarterdeck, as was the old custom, their faces shining with self-evident happiness.

Pat greeted his former lieutenants with vigorous handshakes, his enthusiasm unrestrained, 'Very happy, most exceedingly happy to see you both. Tom, James, come into the cabin. Murphy, bear a hand there, bring Mr Pickering's and Mr Mower's dunnage aboard... and ask Freeman to bring a brace of burgundy too, if you will. Shift along there. Please come in, gentlemen.'

'Well, I ain't got three hands,' muttered Murphy irritably under his breath. He left in search of his mate, Old Jim Lamb.

'Tom Pickering! By George it is grand to see you!' exclaimed Pat, shaking hands again vigorously as he came into the cabin. 'And James Mower himself! Upon my honour, how do you do? Please be seated. Allow me to press you both to join me for dinner. Freeman! Freeman! Where is that mumping villain? Ah, Freeman, there you are. Tell cook we will be dining a little earlier, and there be five of us eating now. Please to put dinner in hand directly. And look to my stores for three bottles of the best Portuguese red, the one with the red top and label; the Vasconcelos would it be? Will dinner be long, Murphy?'

'Well, it's just coming up, ain't it, sorr,' grumbled Murphy, though without the slightest of genuine discontent, as pleased as Pat to see Pickering and Mower come aboard once again. All sat at the cabin table, each gazing amiably at the others, their mutual joy in reunion so very evident, no one wishing to disturb the deeply satisfying moment of contemplation with the least intrusive of questions. Murphy returned and poured the wine.

'Mr Pickering... *Tom* - if I may be so forward - pray tell us of your experiences since *Tenedos* was laid up,' coaxed Simon eventually.

Tom Pickering was neither wealthy nor well-connected, and so his recent four years ashore as a half-pay lieutenant had not facilitated his financial obligations to his family life, being with

138

wife and four children. His lack of connections, as Pat had presumed, had precluded him from finding another ship. 'Why, Doctor, so very dull years they have been... no prospects for a ship at all, my letters to their Lordships bringing the very briefest of acknowledgements but sadly no promises. Half-pay at six pounds five shillings a month, just a little work in the Portsmouth dockyards to be had and in the most tedious of tasks; that is to say, negotiating on behalf of the port admiral with the repairers. The sole consolation being time with the family and seeing the children grow up. I oft wonder if prosperity is the surest protector of happiness,' replied Pickering in a downcast tone, the sparkling wit of many years ago seemingly absent. All felt their prior contentment just a very little diminished.

'Tom, let me offer you a glass of this delightful burgundy, if you will,' said Pat jovially, striving to restore the mood. 'James, what of you since *Illustrious*, when you last departed of us in the year 'ten? By God, so long ago... fully thirteen years since we was shipmates!'

'Aye sir, so it is, and in ne'er a one have I not thought of those days aboard *Starling*... and all her crew. Many a poem have I toyed with in my thoughts since, fondly remembering of her,' said Mower nostalgically and with the barest nod. He had left *Starling* when promoted to first lieutenant with *Illustrious* in the year 'ten, voyaging with her to the East Indies where she gained battle honours at Java. 'Well, sir, *Illustrious* returned from Java and the Indies in the year 'thirteen to Portsmouth, and since then she has been in ordinary, near all the crew laid off and all the officers on the beach. I came back very sick and stayed ashore for two years with the flux until I joined Captain Mould aboard the brig *Mutine* in the autumn of the year 'fifteen. I served aboard as First on the expedition to Algiers in 'sixteen, alongside *Impregnable* during the bombardment, and was discharged again sick when we came home.' The collective mood was diminished just a little further as all wondered what the implications of long-term ill health might be.

Simon, ever the physician first and concerned for all his shipmates in case of anything contagious being introduced so soon before departure, prompted quickly, 'My dear Mower, I am sure you will forgive me for asking: art thou still sick? Please to describe your sickness. Excuse us but for a moment, gentlemen. Mr Mower and I will shift to the gun-room for a more private consultation.' Simon, without hesitation, swept up the lieutenant with a broad grasp of his shoulder and moved swiftly through the cabin door, no murmur of objection being heard from Mower. Their departure left the prior cabin ambience of contentment entirely absent.

'Allow me to fill your glass,' said Pat, striving to recover the mood and smiling encouragingly to Pickering. 'We are sailing on Monday and I have but a single officer, Duncan Macleod as First. We will be accompanied on this voyage by *Eleanor* – you may recall her, my schooner – she will serve only as tender and messenger - and so I should look upon it as a most particular favour was you to join us on *Surprise* as Second. I explained in my letter only the bones of our purpose, which is to return to the Ionian islands, to render assistance to the forming Greek government resisting the Turk. Mind, 'tis not a mission for their Lordships, 'tis quite unofficial. Our status will be as a *letter of marque* for the Greeks... I dare say 'tis akin to how Cochrane operated for Chile and now the Brazil. We will be away for a year or two. We can offer full pay and but the slenderest prospect of prizes. What say ye?'

'I am most heartily glad of your offer, sir... and grateful to you for remembering of me. I would dearly wish to join you again, and on *Surprise* too - *Tenedos's* sister ship... I am doubly pleased, sir. If this crew is not the finest of company, where will I ever find it?'

'Capital, Tom! I am most heartily thankful to hear it, and welcome back, old friend; welcome back. Murphy will stow your dunnage in the gun-room, and after dinner we will take a tour of the barky. Murphy! Where the Devil are you? Murphy! Ah, there you are; light along to see cook and ask after our dinner, if you will.' Murphy was pleased to see Pat still in exceptional good humour, albeit for much of the interview his ear had scarcely shifted from the door.

In the privacy and silence of the gun-room Simon and Mower were conversing in near whispers, there being no place on a ship the size of *Surprise* for assured security of communication. 'You will forgive me, Mr Mower … *James,* for pressing you to explain your sickness. Whilst I naturally rejoice to see you again, I must be sure there can be nothing of any contagious nature introduced to this vessel. Particularly not just before we sail, and what I am minded to know is whether your long-lasting illness might persevere still and what may yet be done or be necessary... and – *if anything* – what help I may provide. Tell me of the very nature of your sickness.'

'You are very good, Doctor, and thank you for your kind interest for me. In the Indies I was struck down with the most severe flux, persisting for week after week until I was so ill I could hardly rise from my cot in the sick bay. I was in fear of my life, but the surgeon, good man though he was, could do nought to help me. I was bled four ounces every other day. For six weeks I was given no food save for onions, lemon juice, fresh fish and ship's biscuit aplenty. I recovered slightly afore we left Java and became a little stronger during the voyage home, but the dysentery was so bad that the captain took pity on me and allowed me to shift into the great cabin, where I spent more time in his quarter-gallery on the seat of ease than ever on deck. The Second was obliged to assume my duties, the Third his... and so forth. When we arrived back in Portsmouth, I was discharged sick. My wife, good lady that she is - *bless her* - nursed me back to health, but it was a full two years afore my strength returned such that I could beg a place on *Mutine.* But three months later, at sea again, my flux was back,' Mower recounted the sorry tale, his voice full of worry, and he was clearly ill at ease even speaking of his illness.

'Pray, how are you at present?' asked Simon tentatively.

'All a-tanto, Doctor; my wife has again nursed me back to good health.' Mower tried hard to smile, but his determination could not quite overcome his anxiety, plain in his voice, betraying a concern, a fear, that he might not be believed and so would be left ashore.

'Console yourself, dear James,' Simon's voice carried the conviction of kindness and friendship. 'You are to consider that the flux and dysentery are present on all His Majesty's vessels, more prevalent on some. Disease on His Majesty's ships has struck down many more men than Boney's sailors ever managed. You appear to have been singularly unfortunate, being stricken and incapacitated for so long and so very severely. You will subsist only on a light diet, the basis being that which my colleague specified for you in the Indies, onions being an excellent antiscorbutic; you will drink lemon juice, eat oranges when we can find them... *and plenty of fresh fish*, which is excellent for the fibres. We will allow you neither salt pork nor any salt beef. Vegetables you may eat aplenty but no butter or fats. No water unless it be of the very freshest... and only small beer for you *should there be any doubt of its provenance...* and that diet will answer wonderfully; indeed, I venture we will keep you in fine fettle. A glass of wine or brandy will do you no harm, and it will rectify the humours,' Simon concluded his reassuring prescription.

'You do me the greatest kindness, Doctor; thank you,' Mower replied, brightening with the realisation that he was not to be cast ashore, his acute anxiety dispelled with the greatest of relief and greatly heartened to find himself under the care of Doctor Ferguson, an infallible legend amongst his shipmates and well regarded in much wider circles: it being well known that he had been consulted by the First Lord.

When they returned to the great cabin, Pat was pleased to find that Simon had not discharged Mower, and he insisted he take another glass of burgundy, to which Simon nodded near imperceptibly to Pat. 'You would do me the most essential service, Mr Mower, were you minded to accept the duties of my Third, Mr Pickering here having joined us as Second,' said Pat, very considerably relieved by Simon's verdict on Mower and finding his satisfaction in securing another of his old officers now preserved.

'Gladly, sir; it would give me the utmost pleasure to serve again with you,' came the unhesitating reply from Mower, his relief evident for all to see. At that moment Freeman and Old Jim Lamb arrived, carrying the dinner, steaming on Pat's silver plate. They set it down to delighted looks all round and hastened away for more burgundy, the first two bottles being quite empty.

A little later, the main course having been eaten, a brace of bottles of fine port also consumed, all about the table were settled in the most amiable of moods, all present relaxing in a comfortable and convivially informal languor. Pat looked around his cabin, his mind absorbing the entirely restored comfortable ambience and the genial satisfaction of all present, himself included, before his gaze and thoughts settled on Simon. His mind continued its cogitations even as Freeman cleared the table, the steward eventually leaving the cabin, when Pat proffered his decision, 'Simon, I have given a deal of thought to your proposal to take aboard Mr Marston as your mate and as chaplain, and... and I realise I am quite brought by the lee there... and so I will be pleased were you to send our invitation to the gentleman, if you please.' Simon allowed himself a private smile, merely nodding by way of confirmation. 'Will you take a little of pot still with me, gentlemen?' asked Pat.

'Pot still?' queried Duncan, who had returned aboard.

'Whiskey, from the son of MacManus of Kilbeggan, in the fine County Westmeath. I have a bottle or two which Murphy ain't found. The glory of the world, so it is.'

'Och, certainly I will take a wee dram with ye,' Duncan replied with enthusiasm, heads nodding emphatically around the table.

'Mr Mower... *James*, will you grace us with a verse of your poetry?' prompted Pat in high good spirits.

'Why, yes sir. I have a new poem underway, the first stanza completed only yesterday... a return to sea and the parting with my wife prompting it.' Mower extracted a much-creased paper from within his jacket,

*'Amidst the rolling waves of oceans
comes the lovely thought of you,
Through the soughing of the breezes
and the sparkle of the dew,
In the shining light of morning
and the blackness of the night,
Come wondrous recollections
and dreams of past delight.'*

'Magnificent, to be sure,' complimented a delighted Pat as all clapped, '... though a trifle short.' He turned to his friend, 'Would you care to scrape a little, Simon?'

'Indeed, I would... with all my heart, brother.'

'What do you care to play?'

'That is for you to choose.'

'Allow me to suggest our old favourite, *St Patrick's Day; Bacon and Greens* as we mariners refer to it; and then we shall play *the Rakes of Kerry*. I have a hankering for a reminder of the Emerald Isle; 'tis plainly far too long since I have gazed over the rolling green hills of Galway and the fields of Connemara, so it is.'

'An inspiring choice, without a doubt.'

'Capital. Have you seen my rosin?'

*Friday 23rd May 1823*                    *Westminster, London*

On the day after the happy reunion with his officers, Pat and Duncan posted back to London, having arranged with the local carter in Truro to deliver all the remaining baggage packed by Sinéad to Falmouth on the morrow. The following morning the two friends presented themselves at the First Lord's private residence in Arlington Street. Mr Lowrey of the Foreign Office, George Canning's aide, was present to discuss all the political limitations associated with the arrangements for the expedition and to finalise the exact terms under which *Surprise* would be engaged and funded. The introductions were made without delay, the servant bidding them all to be seated around the large dining table.

Eventually, Melville, anxious to begin, rapped his spoon loudly and vigorously on his cup to gain the attention of the assembly, the concentration of several attendees not immediately perceptible, Pat and Duncan prominent amongst them. 'O'Connor,' said the First Lord, pausing for an instant to ascertain that Pat's focus was restored, 'until such time as you are engaged in Greek service with a proper *letter of marque* from the provisional Greek government – *not that such will count for much should you be taken by a Turk* – I am minded to suggest that *Surprise* will *ostensibly* be engaged in hydrographical surveying. We have a first-rate man in those parts: Smyth; *Mediterranean Smyth* as he is known at the Hydrographical Office; with *Adventure,* a sloop engaged in charting those waters.'

Pat merely nodded; Smyth was well known to him, but the sophistry of the scheme did not really interest him in the slightest. Duncan strived not to yawn.

After an hour of discussion had passed, the First Lord summarised, 'Well, gentlemen, we are in consensus now with *the arrangements*. It is incumbent upon me to remark again upon the strict political limitations of our association with the provisional Greek government... that is to say... that no connection with His Majesty's Government will be admitted *in any circumstances*. I trust that is plain?' Nods followed all around the table and Melville resumed, 'The *first* task... *of the utmost importance*... is to escort Lord Byron, who has joined the Greek Committee and wishes to go to Greece himself. I collect that Zante in the Ionians has been mentioned as his preferred *interim* destination... and thence from there you are to establish contact with the Greek military authorities – such that they may be – with the intention of offering the assistance of *Surprise;* which must - *note well, O'Connor - must* be formally arranged. However, there is one matter of necessary precedence in this situation: the latest despatches from Constantinople speak of a new High Admiral appointed to the Turk fleet. His name is Khosref, and he is seemingly held in high regard by the Sultan... who accompanied the departure of his fleet... *and that was quite unheard of ever before!* Well, at least as far as the Dardanelles. Our sources acquainted with the Porte are minded that the fleet may make an attempt upon a landing on Candia, the island being riven by feuding between internal Greek factions. You are therefore ordered *in the first instance* to attend Lord Byron in Genoa. You will offer to convey him to Greece. When you have effected that service - *and only then* - will you proceed *directly...* I speak now of all possible speed... to the island of Candia - *and without the least loss of time* - in order to assess Turk naval intentions in that theatre. Thence you will report your observations to the Greek authorities, most preferably to Alexandros Mavrocordato...

though where he may be is not clear to me.' Melville paused to see if his instructions were understood.

'What standing and influence does the man possess, sir?' asked Pat.

'He is favoured with an *Ottoman* title... of all things - *Prince of Wallachia* - on account of his Phanariot family; they hailed from Constantinople; indeed, he was born there. His family was long appointed as rulers of that province by the Sultan; yet whether he holds to that honorary title *which we might suppose no longer exists* since the rebellion in Wallachia against the Phanariots was crushed by the Porte two years ago... and Phanariot rule was ended... is unclear. However, Mavrocordato is known to be a prominent member of those influential Greeks who are promoting independence.'

Pat swallowed hard and gestured towards a nod. 'Politics, politics...' was all he could manage to utter, but his profound dismay was carried in his voice.

'Politics, O'Connor,' said Melville in a tone that would brook no rebuttal, 'is the polite term we use for human nature and its structures; and - like it or not - we are all bound by the dictates of whomever is King of the Hill; but in the present state of chaos in Greece, and in other Ottoman provinces for that matter, that is far from clear... but it is to Mavrocordato that you will pledge your service. Do I speak plain?'

On Pat's more emphatic nod he resumed, 'His Majesty's Government cannot become the recipient of any allegations of piracy from the Porte... and hence *Surprise* must become a Greek ship of war *only* after formal notarised request at the behest of the Greeks. Mr Lowrey will provide to you further instructions, as may be necessary in those parts from His Majesty's Government... in the strictest of secrecy and under cipher. He may deliver instructions personally or via a representative known to yourself and to Lieutenant Macleod. In the first instance Mr Lowrey will provide the appropriate code books in order that the lieutenant may decipher any instructions that you may receive.' Melville turned his gaze towards Duncan, 'You, Macleod, are to write and return encoded reports of all political and military developments to the Admiralty. In that respect it is anticipated that you may seek to associate yourself most closely with the highest of Greek political and naval authorities. A suitable translator will also be sent to assist you in that task.' Melville, keen to wrap up, directed his words towards Pat, 'A sum sufficient, as we have discussed, for the maintenance of *Surprise* and her crew during the expedition will be committed from the secret fund. This will be paid to your private account, O'Connor. It will be for Mr Lowrey to remit funds to you in specie or any other form of your choosing via His Majesty's Consul in Zante, as you will call for it. You will note that the value of any prizes taken by you in this venture will be deducted from the agreed subvention ...' Melville, perhaps noting the look of dismay on Duncan's face, swiftly added, '... *less forty per cent*. Such deduction will leave an adequate sum for the payment of prize shares to the officers and crew.' Melville paused before concluding, 'Finally, gentlemen, do note that should there be any capture by the Ottoman authorities of *Surprise*... know you well that their Lords and His Majesty's Government will disavow any knowledge of these arrangements and will plainly state that *Surprise* is *your private vessel*... and, I suggest, O'Connor, that you will be festering in a Turk prison with no prospect of release and will probably be hanged... *or worse*,' Melville concluded on a dark and sobering note.

'My Lord, if you will, please to authorise a draft on my account,' said Pat quickly. 'There are many pressing calls for considerable funds, very large calls indeed, and I must have this immediately if I am to complete all our preparations and make my tide. There is not a moment to be lost.'

Melville nodded to Lowrey in affirmation of his consent. 'It leaves me, gentlemen, only to wish you well and good fortune,' said Melville with finality. 'I must close our meeting; I have a deal of other matters to discuss later with the Foreign Secretary; and I bid you all farewell.'

After handshakes all round, Pat and Duncan left together, intending to overnight at The Feathers. Canning left accompanied by Lowrey, wishing them 'God speed.'

'A rum venture,' opined Pat, walking back along Pall Mall and deep in thought. 'I should scarcely have imagined it but a month ago. Am I not too old to be engaging in such... such... *disingenuous capers*?'

'Why, 'tis certainly unorthodox, brother; but ye are to consider that it has brought us - Simon, Pickering, Mower and all - back to sea, to our new home, our dear *Surprise*... a concentration of endeavours of which we have nae seen the like for many a year... and there is certainly something to be said for that.'

'I am very sensible of it,' replied Pat quietly, the weight of obligation settling heavy upon his mind.

# Chapter Five

*Must we but weep o'er days more blest?*
*Must we but blush? — Our fathers bled.*
*Earth! Render back from out thy breast*
*A remnant of our Spartan dead!*
*Of the three hundred grant but three,*
*To make a new Thermopylae!*

*Sunday 1ˢᵗ June 1823*                    *Falmouth, Cornwall*

The rising dawn sun cast its weak light over sleepy Falmouth town, the air dry but chilly as Pat stepped up from the great cabin, shivering a little as he paced about on his quarterdeck. A thin mist arose about the ship from the warmer harbour waters. He drew a deep draught of the cold salt air into his lungs and gazed up at the rigging, masts, yards and sails, his keen eye finding no fault with any of the arrangements. He looked through his glass towards the town. There were fishermen and merchants on the Fish Strand Quay but barely a soul to be seen on the Custom House Quay. He stepped all along the deck to the prow, nodding pleasantly to the three men on duty. Contentedly he paced back to his quarterdeck. Barton was one of the very few persons on deck, standing near the wheel and chewing his quid, only the three other crewmen forward being about so early. He was a constant reminder to all aboard of his late brother, always prompting Pat's recollections of his lost cox'n; and even now, ten years on, the bitter-sweet memories of those days still returned to his dreams with powerful and moving effect.

'Good morning, Barton. Tell me, did you know your brother well in his last years?' asked Pat conversationally, still reflecting on his sleeping thoughts.

Barton, pleased to be asked, smiled weakly and nodded. 'Like my right hand knows my left, sir; I cannot say it any closer. Every possible leave we stayed together at our mother's house, our other brother, Robert, having been killed on *Irresistible* in the year 'twelve. Mother passed but a few months after Brannon was gone... a broken heart, 'twas said.'

'He is, even now, mightily missed by his friends aboard too, Barton. A capital man he was, 'pon my word.' Pat, his spirits sinking, left the subject there. 'Be so kind as to rouse the bosun to pipe the hands to breakfast.'

'Aye aye, sir.'

Back in his cabin, Pat passed a few minutes in thoughtful solitude gazing through the lights, abstractedly watching a lugger coming in towards the Fish Strand. She was rolling in the smallest of swell, two score or more of frantic, swirling gulls behind her, their shrill squeals bringing his mind back to the day ahead. He sipped his strong black coffee whilst gathering his thoughts in preparation for *Surprise's* looming departure, a few minutes passing before he shouted for his steward, 'Freeman! Bring more coffee, if you please, and some soft tack and kidneys too... butter as well.'

'Coffee's a'coming d'reckly, massa, an' cook 'im relighting galley now,' came Freeman's cheery reply from the coach.

Murphy too peered fleetingly around the door of the great cabin, looking crisper than his customary self so early in the morning - or at any time for that matter - thought Pat absently. His thoughts were interrupted by a still sleepy Simon coming into the cabin.

'Ah, Simon! Good morning. Give you joy of our departure today. Will you take some breakfast with me? So much to do! Sinéad and the family are expected at four bells, the mail coach at five bells and we will then be away directly on the tide.'

'And what o'clock would that be?' croaked Simon, his grasp of nautical horology quite failing him so early.

'Why, ain't I explained that to you no more than two hundred times?' quipped Pat, only half in jest and mercilessly joshing his old companion.

'I believe you may have had occasion to mention it, soul. You navigators are sadly given to jargon and a devotion to clocks and bells so very incomprehensible to those of us whose genius is more akin to the land-oriented kind... but I confess I have never wholly held to a perfect recall of the principles.'

'Perhaps we might touch again on the... the menstruation of the maritime clock at dinner. Would that be of any help?'

'Non whatsoever, dear; but perhaps an explanation of the *mensuration* of the navigator's hours might serve... *vis a vis* that clock more familiar to the *less experienced* mariner. Pray, would there be a tint of glorious coffee forthcoming for a thirsty man?' Simon asked, yawning. At that moment Freeman returned with the pot, clutching too with obvious difficulty the soft tack and butter.

'Freeman, another plate for the Doctor... and ask the cook to double up the kidneys... and desire Murphy to attend,' said Pat in the mildest of voice, determined that nothing at all was to dampen his pleasure on this bright day of departure.

'Well, there ain't no bleeding peace already on this barky,' muttered Murphy almost inaudibly and only to himself - or so he thought - as he shuffled into the cabin.

'Murphy! Top your boom there, you scoundrel, and you are to lay out my best coat and breeches athwart my cot when Freeman has served breakfast... and nicely pressed, mind!' shouted Pat to a sour-looking Murphy who was departing in haste.

The early morning passed swiftly, the mist clearing, a brightening sun rising to warm the quays, the myriad gulls still calling, orbiting the later returning fishing boats still awaiting their turn to tie up at the Fish Strand Quay with their pilchard catches. With the high tide bringing plentiful depth of water, *Surprise* had been towed so as to be nearer the more spacious Custom House Quay where the families of the crew had gathered to witness her departure. Her best bower and a kedge anchor now held her position at two cables off the quay. The crew in their entirety were passing to and from the ship and the shore, all the ship's boats employed for this purpose, the men making their final farewells to family, friends and numerous other interested onlookers, a growing multitude of them gathering as the clock marched on. Indeed, Pat had noticed with infinite pleasure that the mood aboard was one of profound happiness generally; so much so that he had insisted the bosun lock and bar the spirit stores; he did not wish to see any instance of indulgence -

prompted by exceptional happiness - mar the day and the occasion. At the foretop the Blue Peter flapped vigorously, and at ten o'clock – four bells in the forenoon watch – the carriage arrived with Sinéad and the twins. Pat, in his best captain's attire, had previously stepped ashore to await and greet his family, who now came aboard *Surprise* in the boat. The ship's final preparations were left to Macleod, Pickering and Mower, the latter two sharing their time between their own families on the quay and their duties aboard, gently hustling along crew members dallying with their own kin whilst awaiting the mail and minding the tide. The crew had also made an extra effort for such an important event: their own best clothing, having no uniforms as such, had been washed, starched and pressed. Their pigtails were all replaited, as they sought as much as their captain did to look their very best on departure. The Wesleyans stood prominent amongst all, still garbed in red attire.

Pat had returned aboard to his quarterdeck where he contemplated the late arrival of the awaited mail coach. He was mindful with the very mildest of anxiety of the imminent ebbing of the tide. 'This is cutting it pretty fine, Mr Macleod. We will strike the Blue Peter.'

Sinéad and the twins were all standing on Pat's quarterdeck too and in a high state of excitement as the final preparations for departure proceeded all around them. Pat had no time to pass with them, his attention was all for his ship. 'Mr Macleod, the bosun is to send the topmen aloft,' he ordered, adding to himself, 'The mail coach is hellfire late.' He was hardly conscious now of his family's presence as his professional routine pressed in upon him, but he beamed in every direction, his own spirits never higher. Five bells came closer. The officers having called all the men aboard, only the arrival of the mail coach was still awaited. The quayside families continued to wave and shout excitedly to their husbands and sons, more than a few tears being shed by many of the wives and sweethearts. The crew busied themselves with the very final preparations, still shouting last farewells and waving to the excited, assembled throng when they could. Only the barge with eight rowers now still waited at the quay for the mail.

As the minutes ticked away, from the Custom House Quay came the distant clippety-clop sound of hooves and the distinct clatter of metal wheels on the cobbles. The mail coach approached the quay, brought to a halt amidst the excited throng. Two figures stepped out: the first a rather short man in His Majesty's most elegant uniform, the second plainly a civilian. 'By God, 'tis William Codrington!' shouted Pat with unrestrained delight.

'And my colleague, Michael Marston! To be sure, we have the blessing this day,' exclaimed Simon, great pleasure in his voice.

Pat shouted through his speaking tube to the quayside barge crew. 'Barton, bring those gentlemen aboard with their dunnage. Swiftly now, there is a mort of things to do, a tide to catch and not a moment to be lost!' He turned to the master and murmured 'Mr Prosser, stand by.'

Within ten minutes, Codrington and Marston had scrambled aboard, two of the barge crew passing up the arrivals' baggage and all following swiftly behind them. Pat waved his hat briefly to the two men before turning to his steward. 'Murphy, my compliments to Mr Codrington and Mr Marston, and will you kindly take their dunnage below.'

The high tide had passed near two hours earlier and the ebb was about to succeed slack water. Before *Surprise* could begin to swing on her best bower - as her bow still faced east towards the Carrick Roads, a kedge anchor keeping her station - Pat had decided that she would sail as soon as the ebb commenced. The gentle westerly breeze and lee-tide would greatly facilitate her leaving. All along the Custom House Quay the crowd, sensing the imminence of *Surprise's* departure, cheered loud and shouted vigorously, tears and joy all a-jumble. The crew, those that could spare a moment, furiously waved their scarves and shouted vigorously back, and exuberant loud whistling was heard from atop all the yards.

Pat was immensely pleased himself and minded not a jot this joyous breach of the customary, orderly routine of leaving port. 'All hands to unmoor ship!' he bellowed eventually. The crew, many more hands in comparison with her departure from Plymouth Dock, made light work of all their tasks: the kedge was brought in, tops'ls unfurled, yards braced, the best bower swiftly catted and slowly *Surprise* shifted away from her anchorage, a very happy Pat content to leave her control to Duncan and the master.

*Surprise* moved off, the distance between the quay and the ship swiftly increasing. Gradually she gathered momentum, the wind acting upon her tops'ls, the ship now being driven across the inner harbour in the strengthening ebb current. Gradually, *Surprise* picked up a little more speed, but still the families ashore could be heard shouting fading farewells from the quay.

After a further ten minutes *Surprise* cleared the inner harbour and shifted into the Carrick Roads. Pat turned to the master and his second lieutenant, 'Carry on, Mr Pickering.' This was said to Pickering as a convention and courtesy, but mostly for the ears of Mr Prosser, in the knowledge that no sailor knew the harbour and Roads better than the master, a native of Falmouth. 'Please excuse me, my dear,' Pat smiled as he spoke to his wife. 'Mr Macleod, Doctor Ferguson and I are going into the cabin to greet our late arrivals.' Sinéad nodded, content to remain on the quarterdeck with the twins, quite fascinated by the spectacle of *Surprise's* departure. Pat was quite out of his depth as to how to manage his son and daughter, hurtling with great excitement around his province, the quarterdeck. To Simon, Pat muttered, with some little exasperation, 'Anyone might think we were aboard the Margate hoy.'

Simon said nothing and simply smiled. Pat was more than a little relieved to go below, prompted by Simon's earlier and gentle suggestion that it was not a day to stand on the strictest of shipboard custom and etiquette. They came down together into the great cabin, the new arrivals already seated and sipping tea, Freeman hovering near the door.

'William Codrington, joy be with you; 'pon my word it is good to see you again. We had begun to wonder if the coach had overset. Mr Marston, how well you look, sir. Welcome aboard. Freeman! Rouse out two bottles of the best Madeira, if you please - *the 'seventy-five,'* said Pat pleasantly.

154

When Freeman had returned and was pouring the wine, all in the cabin had settled round Pat's table. Codrington explained that he had been away visiting relatives in the North Country, avoiding certain gentlemen of whom he declined to speak further, and had only very recently received Pat's letter. He had rushed immediately to Falmouth upon receipt of it, pausing only to don his uniform and pack the most meagre of baggage. Further necessities could be bought at their first port of call, Codrington declared, and *yes* he would be honoured to shift to *Eleanor* as Pat suggested, most honoured and pleased to do so. Codrington hurried on, explaining that his finances were in an assuredly temporary state of dysfunction, but he was in no doubt that a successful voyage would restore his treasury and his standing. Pat had not anticipated that all his officer invitees would become available in response to his invitations and so, the appointment of a fourth lieutenant for *Surprise* being somewhat superfluous, the surplus of officers would be satisfactorily resolved by Codrington shifting to *Eleanor* where Pat would be very pleased to have him in command.

Michael Marston had heard from the parishioners in his Cornish benefice of Pat O'Connor's planned return to sea two weeks previously. An educated, intelligent man, the past four years he had found increasingly tedious as parish parson to his tiny and generally unlearned congregation. His subsequent letter to Simon in Plymouth had enquired of the prospects for employment of any kind. It had reached Simon at precisely the moment that he had realised the necessity for a surgeon's mate, Pat more conventionally considering first of his need for sailors. In anticipation of the possibility that he could be called away from the ship, Simon had deemed it wholly prudent to engage a surgeon's mate. Hence Marston's letter was opportune. Upon Simon's affirmative reply, Marston had leapt at the opportunity to volunteer his services. He was a proficient surgeon's mate who had assisted Simon through a particularly bloody battle aftermath with serious casualties requiring immediate surgery during one of his voyages aboard *Tenedos*, because of which Simon was assured of his competency. The fact that Marston was also a knowledgeable naturalist further weighed significantly in

Simon's considerations, finding on occasions that the company of nautical men could verge some way towards the tedious; though Pat and Duncan were exceptions. Marston could also play the violin, albeit he had not been the most accomplished of musicians when last aboard *Tenedos*.

Pat looked out though his cabin lights and gazed at the white wake at the stern of the ship; *Surprise* was well out into Falmouth Bay, experiencing the customary chops of the Channel, sailing in a strong wind under all sail, white horses everywhere over a vigorous grey swell, spray spicules sweeping through the air and splashing on the glass. *Eleanor*, under the present command of Reeve, trailed a mile astern. A few minutes of reflection and Pat turned away to return to his table, to his officers. Duncan, Pickering and Mower had left the master in charge on the quarterdeck and had come into the great cabin at Pat's invitation to greet their former shipmate, Codrington.

It was a strict convention within the Royal Navy that no one spoke at the captain's table unless in reply to the captain. In this instance the tradition had seemingly gone by the board as Pat's four lieutenants and two surgeons happily engaged in an animated babble of mutual reminiscences and experiences since their last meeting. He did not mind in the slightest since he was as interested as they all were in hearing their stories and was particularly delighted that all three former lieutenants had accepted his invitation. Of Marston he was not so sure, but it was inconceivable that anything could shake his pleasure in this particular day. After half an hour and Freeman having coughed at least three times at the door, and having brought in after the captain's nod two large pots of coffee, Pat rapped the table with his knuckles to call them to attention. 'Gentlemen, I am very much obliged to you all for accepting my invitation to join me, to serve aboard *Surprise*. *Freeman, please pour the coffee*. Only a very few days ago I had a fine crew and but one officer, Mr Macleod; but here we are today... three more former comrades with me once more... together with and our old friend and surgeon Doctor Ferguson... *Simon here*.' He patted his friend's arm affectionately, '... and Mr Marston too.' Pat could not quite bring himself to think of Marston as *Michael*, to consider him in the same close informality as he thought of Simon, cordiality between the two in the past never having progressed that far.

Simon, in quite flagrant breach of convention but in the knowledge that the new officers knew precious little detail of the voyage, its purpose or the obscured drivers of it, interrupted Pat in his momentary pause and his informality, 'Be so kind as to outline your clearer view of our voyage, sir.'

'Thank you, Doctor,' Pat, taking his cue, reverted to a customary minimum of protocol. 'I must tell you, gentlemen, that I am no longer a serving Royal Navy captain; I have resigned the service.' There was an audible sharp intake of breath around the table. 'I have accepted the invitation of the provisional Greek government to advise and assist their formative navy on its methods to counter the Turk in the current struggle for Greek independence. Gentlemen, upon our arrival in the Ionians, *Surprise* will commence operating under a Greek *letter of marque. Eleanor*, however, will at all times retain her status as an English ship, sailing as a private vessel and thereby enjoying protection from Turk interference. She may be very useful to us with that safeguard and capacity should we need to separate our activities. As you know, I am accompanied by my family, who will become resident in Zante, and so on this first day aboard I must attend to them.' Pat looked around the table, 'Gentlemen, you will forgive me if I leave further explanations until the morrow when I hope you will all give me the pleasure of dining in the cabin... when we can speak further of these matters,' Pat concluded.

There was a murmur of further pleasantries before the officers shuffled out to settle in to their accommodation in the gun-room and to reacquaint themselves with the crew.

'Murphy, my wife will take my cot; please rig another in the cabin for myself; the twins will berth in the spare officers' cabins. Be so good as to shift their dunnage down there, afore dinner if you will... thankee.'

Murphy, only too pleased to be tasked with matters of a domestic nature and - in the most polite manner - even thanked by his captain, being mindful of Pat's imminent dinner busied away in some haste.

Pat returned to his quarterdeck where Sinéad and the twins were still evidently enjoying the novelty and vivid sense of adventure. The weather was particularly clement, the sun near its zenith, and the wind, a gentle westerly, propelled *Surprise,* close-hauled but with her clean hull, at a steady six to seven knots. She had passed the Manacles at noon, making good progress.

Many hours later, by supper time and Lizard Point far off to starboard, the chops of the Channel comfortably in the ship's wake, Pat sat down at his table to eat with Sinéad and the twins. The youngsters were plainly excited at the adventure they had embarked upon and had busied themselves all day speaking with many members of the crew, engineering encounters with them, asking many and varied questions about *Surprise*, their past voyages and the crew's past experiences with their father. To all enquiries they received only the most glowing of positive answers, all mention of blood-curdling events or setbacks being most diligently expunged in the telling. Sinéad, more soberly, investigated the domestic arrangements for the voyage and queried all on the prospects for the weather; not that anyone could vouch anything more than generalities and platitudes. After supper, before leaving the table, Sinéad pressed Pat for his views on the potential dangers of the expedition, but could glean near nothing about that, and so she ultimately contented herself with enquiries about the short term prospect of the voyage to Greece – via Mahon, via Genoa and via anywhere else that wind and weather might take *Surprise* – even as Pat laboured to explain the vagaries and vicarious nature of weather at sea.

As the twins, finally exhausted, went off to their berths below, Pat settled Sinéad within his cot. He decided on a little time for quiet reflection on his quarterdeck, the late spring evenings being pleasantly warm. It was these tranquil last hours of the day, the sun having set and dusk fading into the near total blackness of the approaching night that Pat, being a passionate astronomer, particularly enjoyed. At home, he had a telescope established in his own observatory. Aboard, he had a powerful glass which doubled for his military and astronomical purposes. He stepped slowly up to the quarterdeck with a great feeling of pleasurable anticipation, allowing his eyes to adjust to the darkness after the cabin's lamp light. The deck scarcely moved under his feet, the gentlest of motions barely discernible in a moderate wind, no strain at all on the rigging, merely a whispered creak from the blocks above his head and an occasional sigh from the canvas of the mizzen sails; and the atmosphere about the helm was calmness itself. The ship's activity was now subdued, supper having concluded long before, and on deck there remained very few of the crew. It had been a relaxing watch for them, the wind having being steady and westerly since sunrise, though veering north-westerly as the day progressed, and no tacking had been necessary during the day. Pat, Mower, the master, Barton and two helmsmen were the only ones present on the quarterdeck.

'All's well, sir,' declared Mower in quiet voice.

Pat simply nodded and gazed back over the ship's stern, her wake still visible for miles behind her with its trail of sparkling silver phosphorescence, her course so straight, unbending: two points west of south. He took a deep draught of the air, scented the salt, so deeply satisfying, and he looked up at her yards, all braced to catch the prevailing north-westerly; since late afternoon so constant in its strength and direction, presenting the helmsmen with little challenge to maintain her course with hardly any leeway. He paced very slowly up and down from the stern rail to the waist rail, enjoying the quietude of the moment, *Surprise* pitching almost indiscernibly in the exceptional wave tranquillity of the Channel sea state, the ship with only the slowest and smallest of roll, nearly unnoticeable to any seasoned mariner. He resolved to perpetuate the treasured moments of profound satisfaction with a walk all along the side, a few minutes passing before he stood on the forepeak, from where he swept the southern sky through his glass, the brightest of the stars already visible. The constants of *Vega*, *Cygnus* and *Altair* were shining brightly, the planet *Saturn* faintly emerging, and the last quarter of the moon was rising on the beam above a far distant France. He wondered what he would be doing if he had remained at home in Claddaghduff; concluding that he would be sitting beside a peat fire and considering or - more likely - *fretting* on the matter of his gold mine investment. He shrugged off the thought and reminded himself once more that he was at sea, his beloved place of all places; and, somehow, he suppressed all thoughts of the reason why, of Greece, of the essential rationale for the voyage. Ten more minutes passed, Pat gazing at the night sky in all its emerging splendour until, with a deep sigh of satisfaction, he slowly retraced his steps and regained the quarterdeck.

'A prime day, Mr Mower, Mr Prosser, Barton. I bid you good night, gentlemen, lads,' remarked a very contented Pat, holding tight to the precious moment as he paced past the wheel.

'Proper, sir, none better,' replied Prosser in his slow Cornish intonation.

'Good night, sir,' from Barton and the helmsmen.

Below in the gun-room, the officers were engaged in vigorous debate about aspects of the voyage that loomed large in their minds, principal amongst which was their captain's resignation. Simon, with possession of many if not all of the answers, could not freely comment and politely demurred from doing so when pressed, claiming scant knowledge. A strange look from Marston - who was peering out of his cot where he remained prone and in some little discomfort, the sea sickness having claimed him after such a long absence from sea - rather suggested that he believed Simon to know more than he was prepared to let on.

*Monday 2<sup>nd</sup> June 1823*        *The Bight of Biscay*

The Bay of Biscay weather was unusually but pleasantly clement, exhibiting none of the violent horrors that the crew had experienced on many a prior occasion. *Surprise* sailed on steadily at a comfortable five knots under a blue sky, close-hauled on a stiff north-westerly top-gallant breeze with scarcely the least heel on the decks, the air temperature rising incrementally as she made southing. From the gun deck came the sound of clicking hammers as the crew, a dozen men sitting about, chipped away at the round shot that had been brought up from the damp stowage of the hold where they had gathered a patina of rust. After smoothing with the chisel, the men greased them with slush begged from the galley, it being a valuable perquisite of the cook. On the forepeak three men were polishing one of Pat's two personal chasers, *Lucifer*, appropriated from *Tenedos* after she had finally paid off. They had long been neglected but all the old brown paint was now gone and the bronze had been restored to a lustrous shine.

Simon, appearing at Pat's side on the quarterdeck as he prepared to take the noon sighting, spoke in ebullient voice, 'Does it not warm the fibres so, to be at sea once more... the sky such a vast expanse for the philosopher to consider, and so very blue... truly the Heavenly colour... I stand with the Prophets on that perspective.'

'Sure, there is no doubt,' Pat was delighted to see his friend so happy, his face a picture of the most beatific of smiles.

'And a most temperate sea it is today... so particularly gratifying that there is nothing of the Bay's customary ill-temper to blight our passage... The swaying of the floor is as nothing when my mind is in contemplation of our prior voyages... indeed, the present tranquillity - *the absence of haste* - is quite sublime... and so very inspiriting for the more anxious mariner.'

'I dare say, and we are making steady southing... even if it is a trifle slow.'

'Will you believe, in my imagination I might almost be on Mull, atop Dùn Ara Castle and gazing across to the glorious Coll itself.'

What are you thinking about, tell?' asked Pat, Simon's conversation of an unusually thoughtful bent.

'I am in contemplation of our circumstances, in the present and the future; I do not greatly care to speculate on the latter... it is rarely fruitful to allow the mind to stray far ahead; and as for the present, the voyage is proving comfortable indeed... nothing of turbulence... and... *senso amplo*... that is both benevolent for the naturalist's interests and greatly providential for rectifying the depleted humours.'

'Eh? I never was much of a fist with the Latin, there was no great call for it in Connemara... in fact, none at all,' remarked Pat, adding, '*senso... senso...* what did you say?'

'*In the nature of things*; I refer particularly to the sea state; on such calm days one can truly appreciate its boundless enormity, it is feasible to perceive a sense of majesty and of infinity; that is ever more so when there is nothing of the contrary forceful billows and perfectly disconcerting storms which so much blight the prospects for observation. Indeed, to my memory, never before has it been feasible to enjoy such relaxing aprication... and... and I could stand here forever.' Simon smiled, a huge pleasure plain for Pat to see in his face in that moment. 'I am minded to say it is heartwarming.'

'The Bay is certainly at her best... and the glass promises uncommon fair weather to come; you may rejoice.'

'I am pleased to hear it.'

*Ding-ding! Ding-ding! Ding-ding!* The bell rang out its reassurance of comfortable routine and Pat stared up towards the sun, scarcely the thinnest wisp of cloud in a near unbroken sky of blue, his mind wandering to thoughts of the noon meridian and his sextant, still an hour away.

'The prolific wildlife of this watery realm has been such a joy to behold,' Simon resumed, 'Why, I have seen countless gulls - both the Lesser Black-backed and the Mediterranean... The Great Skua has also been with us... and gannets, petrels and fulmars aplenty... What splendour!'

'Give you joy of your pleasures, dear friend,' replied a fascinated Pat, for he could not recall Simon ever so effusive before.

'Why, when we were in the vicinity of that large island with the breakers all about it - *Ushant, did you say it was?* - I espied Warblers of all species... except for the Melodious; the Ictarine was above us for an hour or so... a veritable avian multitude... Marston remarked that they were to be expected in these latitudes. Glory! Why, Noah himself with all his collection could scarcely have enjoyed his epic voyage more. I have been in Heaven these two days.'

'Was you, though?' murmured Pat with interest. He looked closely at his friend, 'It pleases me - *for you* - that we could make safe passage in daylight, for the islands were ever a peril to the mariner at night time in Boney's day.'

'I do collect mention of them, sure; and rarely without an emphasis of respect and abomination.'

'We could be uncommon sure of south-west gales, and it was ever a care to stay out here in more than fifty-fathom water... far, far away from a lee shore.'

'I am sure of it. As for our aquatic friends,' Simon continued in enthusiastic voice, 'why, we have been accompanied by the Atlantic Spotted dolphin - aplenty at all times... pursuing a shoal of flying fish... Did you see them, the grand spectacle it was?'

'Perhaps I will ask the bosun to throw out a net before we go a deal further into the Bay, for the islands are capital waters for a fine catch... and I venture there is nothing tastier than a grilled fresh fish, straight from the briny.'

'... and the Common dolphin too... ever a pod of one or the other in our wake...'

'Doubtless they find cook's gash of an appeal,' said Pat; 'I did not, myself, much take to yesterday's pork. I venture it was too long in the cask... too salty... and not altogether quite agreeable...'

'I doubt it was the salt; it does fish no harm.'

'Eh? Fish? I was speaking of pork. I am minded that some crooked villain in the yard likely substituted our *fresh* salt pork with old, tainted and thoroughly execrable dross. Why, heart of oak ain't harder - *and I dare say it had been to the West Indies and back twice over.* I am quite put to the blush to say - *in your private ear* - that I have spent considerable time incommoded this morning... We need not dwell on the uncomfortable details... the infernal gripes it was... and for the most part I have been long sitting on the seat of ease.'

'I am concerned to hear it, my dear. You will allow me to administer ten drops of laudanum, which will serve to alleviate any enduring bowel pains; indeed, it answers most admirably for myriad ills, including the discomfiting, crapulous motions... *that is to say, when properly administered and without excess...* and you will persist on a low diet for twenty-four hours... an abatement from all rich victuals, nothing more than a piece of bread... it is still tolerably edible these two days past; but no cheese with it for you; no, a low diet is your only remedy; you are not to entertain wild notions of some quacksalver, *instant* treatment, for none exists; and you will drink only grog... *only grog - do you hear?* And, *exceptionally*, a modicum of spirits; gin will serve admirably.'

'Come, Simon, a man must avail himself of his dinner in timely fashion, eh? I must tell you that Wilkins has promised a Strasburg Pie fit for a king... with great quantities of fresh spinach and asparagus; a man cannot pass up such a meal as that; and Frumenty, too, has been in preparation this morning, so said Murphy. I much relish that pudding, I do; and I fancy it will all finish well with a half-pint of sherry.'

'You eat too well and you love your belly above everything else. God save you from gule! Greed will be the death of you, Patrick O'Connor. A Strasburg Pie, you say? Foie Gras and bacon? Pastry and a gross excess of fat? Such is rich food indeed. That is not for you today.' A pause, 'But, thankfully, all is not lost; no doubt I shall enjoy it... served with a bottle of burgundy. That delectable one with the red label would serve admirably.'

The Devil to bread; which, by the way, is now all uncommon hard crusts... and grog... which is scarcely more than the weakest water! That don't answer, no! How is a man to fortify the fibres?'

'Patrick O'Connor, your waist is in no want of fortification; indeed, I venture you could give even the Prince Regent an inch or two... I beg your pardon; I collect he is now become King.'

'Have a care, Ferguson; that is coming it a trifle high; I am no jollux. I may choose to clap you in irons!'

'I do not exaggerate, not at all; he is most certainly a grossly corpulent fellow. No, it is bread and grog for you; it will rectify the humours... and, speaking in my official capacity as the warranted physician of this esteemed vessel, such is not a voluntary matter; *no, it is not*. You will accept that I cannot possibly allow any other comestibles at this time.' Another pause, a momentary reflection, 'Did you mention Frumenty? Mmmm, a particular favourite of mine...'

'Sure, it is the great pudding of the world.'

'... but I could not, in all responsibity, possibly allow you to eat such an extravagance as that; why, you are to consider the rich composition: the eggs, the quite excessive cream... currants too... and as for the bountiful measure of sugar... no, it is quite out of the question for you. It will weigh heavily on the humours.'

'But I am amazingly sharp-set, I am so.'

'You are to consider: do you care to see out the remainder of our passage across the great Bay from your quarter-gallery?'

'God's blood, a man is deserving of a right proper dinner! Would even a beef sandwich be so very debilitating? Why, Mrs O'Donnell swears by a mutton chop for strengthening the blood, *eaten up hot*. In the name of all friendship, precious that it is, do you think you could countenance a solitary... *a small* mutton chop?'

'Certainly not; you are to eat nothing of that ilk. I will concede that you may be permitted to indulge in our favourite of all things... that is to say *coffee*.'

'Thank you!' declared Pat with feeling but otherwise crushed.

'Though tea - *without milk* - would be the better servant. For the moment I urge you to take a deep breath of this marvellous air, my dear... before you make further use of any of the more illiberal expressions of the King's English. Listen...' Simon's voice betrayed his excitement, '... will I tell you... I have recorded the Striped and Risso's Dolphins... but I have yet to remark the Bottlenose... What a joy it would be to see one of those perfect creatures!'

'Come, Simon,' Pat spoke with a modicum of disbelief and mild ire, 'Whoever heard of a dolphin with a bottle nose, eh? Do you seek to gull me with these fanciful notions?'

'On the contrary, dear; the processes of nature and evolution - slow that they may be - have gifted us a deal of marvels. Indeed, I am with child to see how the animal makes use of the nose to affect his wake and consequent turbulence.'

'I see; well, I imagine that such might be uncommon rare... and excite the naturalist's imagination,' murmured Pat, his testiness subsiding and adding, 'We were precious close to Ushant as we passed, but the isle is twenty leagues astern and we are bearing into deeper water, where the whale may be the next fellow you see... though I do dearly hope that they will not scrape our new copper.'

'God love us, I have already espied a solitary Cuvier's Beaked whale! What a sight! What a splendid creature! I venture she was a female, for she was all of a brown in colour... with much scarring; and - *would you believe it?* - a pod of Yellow Fin tuna, the broaching individuals of such a size as I have never seen before... So very large that I thought in the first instance they too were dolphins!'

'They eat well, if a trifle oily. Tomorrow I venture we will raise the Groyne...'

'Is that right? So soon...'

'... and some hours later Finisterre...'

'That perilous headland?'

'Sure it is; and we have certainly passed by with a fearful mind in the most perilous of seas during those dark days of the blockade... when there ever seemed to be a westerly gale... but, thankfully, *this time* - if the fine weather holds - you will see clear the mainland of Spain... and perhaps you may yet see your Bottled Nose... and certainly more birds aplenty; perhaps even the dodo!' Pat laughed out loud; 'Though whether they will be melodious I would not care to say,' Pat, forgetting for a moment his condemnation to a bread diet, was in good spirits, and he slapped the rail at his delightful words and laughed again; 'What a wit I am, eh?'

After his officers had enjoyed their dinner in the gun-room, fresh provisions being in plentiful supply so soon into the voyage, whilst Pat had tortured himself with bread alone in the great cabin, all his officers joined him for brandy and coffee: Duncan Macleod, Tom Pickering, James Mower and William Codrington all being present. William Reeve, being master's mate in rank but for so long in Pat's service and entrusted latterly with *Eleanor,* was also in attendance. Finally, there was Simon, seated alongside Pat and savouring the remnants of his coffee. All were in a high state of anticipation and curiosity. Michael Marston, still indisposed by sea sickness, remained in his cot in the gun-room. Mr Prosser skippered *Eleanor* in *Surprise's* wake.

'How does Marston fare, Simon? I gather he is laid up, indisposed with the sea-sickness. Will we put him ashore at The Groyne?' This was said with a smile and a wink, Simon well aware of Pat having no predilection for the clergy aboard his ships.

'Certainly not. He is merely slightly incommoded at present, a temporary state; the rhythmical motion of this vessel it is, after years ashore on firmer standing. He is dosed and sleeping. He did send his compliments before retiring to his cot. No doubt a low diet will answer the case...'

'The bread is getting uncommon hard. Let us hope his teeth will survive their watch.'

'... and he will likely return to his duty on the morrow... when his sea legs have developed a deal more fortitude.'

'I am gratified to hear it.'

'You are to consider that he is more of a landsman than you or I. Perhaps even Jonah had a similar disinclination for voyaging ever again after his release from the whale.'

'Simon, I beg you will not mention *that name* aboard this vessel; there are many - *and I do not exclude myself* - who consider it to be grossly unlucky to do so.'

'Yes, I see what you mean.'

Pat sighed, 'Oh, what I would give for a right luscious pork pie with thick, fat pastry. Oh dear, purgatory ain't in it.'

'Perhaps you will find one when we attain the sanctuary of Gibraltar.' replied Simon, enjoying his moment; 'I collect they serve their own particular dish in that place, *their equivalent* - if you will: the *rolito* is a delicious mixture of finely chopped olives, boiled eggs... with bacon or ham, and such vegetables as may be available depending upon the season; it is then coated with breadcrumbs... that is to say if they are not mixed together; with garlic added, herbs and spices all embedded, and the delectable entirety is enshrouded within a thin slice of beef.'

'Your soul to the Devil, Ferguson!' exclaimed Pat, striving to contain his curse to a whisper.

'I shall not take offence,' Simon could not restrain his laugh; 'I beg you will excuse my mirth; it is the rare day when I perceive I may make use of such an advantage.'

'Your good health, sir!' Duncan interjected, the mood in the cabin so jovial, 'A glass with you!' Pat scowled.

A pleasant hour was spent in the most delightful of reminiscences, Simon conceding the brandy bottle to Pat with a discrete nod, until Pat caught the air of restrained anticipation and rapped the table top before beginning his briefing. 'Gentlemen, we are bound for Genoa for provisioning, beforehand touching at the Rock for fresh water; and we will call briefly at Port Mahon. Thereafter we sail for the Ionians where we will... we will... *ostensibly* engage in surveying the Ionian waters...' Pat did not care to elaborate, still holding to an uncomfortable disquiet, '... until such time as we make contact with representatives of the provisional Greek government and so formally enter their service as a *letter of marque*. However, in the first instance we are tasked with a swift passage to the regions of Candia to ascertain the whereabouts of the Turk fleet, that we may report such to the Admiralty.' Blank faces all round, nothing said, and Pat resumed, 'Mrs O'Connor, my son and daughter, Mrs Macleod and Mr Macleod's daughter will remain in residence at Zante whilst we are engaged in that task. Only when we have our *official* Greek commission will we become a combatant ship, and then we will be lawfully entitled to any Turk prizes we may capture. Note, gentlemen, we do not serve in any *official* capacity on behalf of His Majesty's Government... and therefore none of us may legally continue with our service rank, and so all must resign...' Dismayed faces were the only response, and an uncomfortable silence persisted for what seemed an eternity before Pat resumed, 'However, the First Lord has pledged to restore all of us to our former rank and seniority when we have completed our service for Greece; but note also that this particular aspect is to remain confidential, known only to those at this table, and may not be communicated to anyone else. I trust you will remember this.'

There was a general murmur of affirmative response from everyone present, all mulling over questions that had come to mind; but in the more formal ambience prevailing now that they were at sea all observed the familiar protocol of the captain's table, withholding questions and comment until asked directly.

Pat continued his briefing, 'The Greeks have precious few vessels with which to fight against the Turk ships bringing reinforcements and stores to their troops in Greece. Two years ago, the island of Chios was sacked and thousands of Greeks taken from that place as slaves. The Greek islands of Psara, Hydra and Spetses provide the only Greek warships, and these are generally armed merchantmen only, no regular warships being available to them. Their crews insist on payment in advance and will not sail without it. Most of the shipowners will not hazard their vessels against Turk warships - they will only fight *merchantmen* - and who is to say they are wrong? A brig was never a match for a seventy-four. However, there are brave Greeks, Admirals Miaoulis and Canaris being principal amongst them, who *will* fight the Turk warships with what little they have to command. In this respect the Greeks have become adept at using fireship tactics to make up for their lack of numbers and ordnance.' Pat paused to look about him, 'New Greek warships *have* been ordered, notably two heavy frigates and six steamships; yet none are expected to arrive for some time, years even. Until then, gentlemen, *Surprise* will be the sole purpose-built warship fighting in the Greek cause. Our adversaries are many... and the Turk frigates may substantially exceed our size and ordnance. We will therefore choose our engagements with the utmost care... and - I make no doubt - we must *and will* flee before great odds... so as to fight another day. Mr Macleod has, in these past few weeks, studied the political and military situation. Mr Macleod, will you comment please?'

Duncan followed on, 'There is near civil war amongst the Greeks. Koloktronis is chief in the Morea, Odysseus in the East and Mavrocordato 'tween the twae. Missilonghi is under siege, Athens is in the hands of the Turk, and the provisional Greek government resides in Nauplia in the north-east of the Morea. Och, the situation, gentlemen, is bleak indeed for the Greeks. It is to be hoped that the Turk resupply by sea can be hindered... so weakening their forces in Greece... until the Greeks can act resolutely as one, their infighting ceases, and ultimately their wee state becomes more firmly established and with greater political support. If and when this occurs, gentlemen, it might be hoped that significant pressure might then be brought to bear on the Porte to accept or negotiate a settlement.'

'Thank you, Mr Macleod,' declared Pat; 'Let us for Heaven's sake return to our humble level of simple mariners and our own honest intentions... else we may forget ourselves and run foul of politics, the politics of foreigners even. As can be seen, the Greeks are in a proper lather. A greater dog's breakfast can hardly be imagined, and it is we who are to pull their chestnuts out of the frying pan.'

*Tuesday 3rd June 1823*                                    *Bay of Biscay*

It was the early morning of the third day out of Falmouth, the breaking chops of a turbulent south-west Channel left far astern, the sun just a finger's width above the horizon, and Marston was sitting with Simon in companionable reflection on adjacent gun carriages on the gun deck. The friends were taking the air, so refreshing for Marston after days of discomfort in the more foetid, wretched confinement of his cabin; indeed, he was feeling sufficiently recovered to consider taking some solid food for the first time. 'I am most thankful for your ministrations, dear colleague,' he said to Simon. 'Never did I think I would suffer so... and that after so many prior voyages at sea.'

'Oh, no doubt it was because of the lateral inclination of this vessel and its floor, which is more severe than customary when we are quartering and close-hauled... with the weather gauge. It obviates the necessity for repetitive changes of direction... which are so absolutely tedious; more so when the captain is fearing for a lee shore or... or *similar* natural eventualities - *so perfectly mortal to the navigator*; and, I regret to say, the process of successive turnabouts is inordinately customary for those more obdurate mariners with an affinity for perfidious haste... as I have come to learn over the years.' Simon was privately pleased to consider himself a mariner, although he never allowed himself to expound on this; at least not at length, perhaps conscious of the barely concealed mirth which he had observed in the past when uttering nautical terminology, the meaning of much of which he possessed only a somewhat imperfect grasp. However, there was not a man aboard who would ever seek to disabuse him of his trifling self-indulgence, such was the respect in which he was held. 'I venture a few days aboard in which to reacquaint your humours with the perpetual motion will answer tolerably well; and there can be no doubt that you will regain your sea legs in time; indeed, it would not be erroneous were we to consider you an old sea-dog, one making re-acquaintance with the watery realm.'

'That is most kind of you to say so, Ferguson,' replied an uncomfortable Marston.

'Allow me to offer you a trifle of this burgoo, Michael. Try for a few spoons whilst it remains hot... and here is a jug of the most excellent and medicinal negus to follow. Drink it down whilst 'tis still warm; you will feel the better for it. Then we will take a turn on the upper deck... that is to say *the quarterdeck.*'

The fresh sea breeze and warm morning sunlight both being so reviving, Marston had recovered some colour after a few hours and so was able to walk unaided, to go up the companionway steps and so to the hallowed quarterdeck. He stood at the rail on the lee side with Simon, grateful for the fresh air, leaning on the bulwark and gazing at the distant Spanish coast.

'Mr Marston! You have come by your sea legs at last!' shouted Pat, looking forward from the taffrail and seeking an opportunity to extend some hospitality and cordiality to his chaplain. 'How do you come along? I hope I see you well. What do you say to a pot of tea with the Doctor and me? I am told by Dr Ferguson that it is kinder on the digestive organs than coffee; and perhaps we will both enjoy the tiniest morsel of breakfast. That is to say, with the Doctor's permission.'

'With great pleasure, sir,' said Marston weakly.

'Carry on, Mr Mower.' After a few minutes they descended to the great cabin, Pat shouting for his steward, 'Freeman! D'ye hear me? Bear a hand there! Bring some vittles for my guests... some eggs and bacon, a fresh pot of tea too. Send word to the cook. Mr Marston,' Pat stared closely at Marston for the first time as they approached the table, 'Pray sit down, sir, you do not look well.'

It was a statement which struck fear, great fear, into Marston. For an instant the fleeting thought that he might be set ashore flashed through his mind. 'Oh no, sir! It was only a passing malady... a brief indisposition - *the briefest* - the perpetual motions... quite transient and perfectly abated now. Dr Ferguson assures me that the remedy is sea air, plentiful sea air... as much as possible; being aboard ship and far from land is the surest of cures. I am wholly contented, sir; it pleases me to say.'

Pat smiled, 'No doubt; well, I speak under correction; I am pleased to hear of your recovery. It pleases me that this wind is so much fallen away that the barky can sail herself. Well, Mr Mower would no doubt disagree!' Pat laughed, a little laugh and one which reflected his happiness. 'Why, I venture I am not needed at all.' Simon studied Pat carefully, his tone towards Marston almost verging on ingratiating, and he wondered what might be afoot. Pat resumed, 'Mr Marston, if you are in the way, I hope that you will give me the pleasure of joining the Doctor and myself for supper this evening, after which we will practise a little scraping. You *did* bring your instrument?'

'Why, sir, thank you... thank you. Indeed, it would give me great pleasure to accept your kind invitation... and yes, I have my violin, I am very pleased to say.' Marston smiled broadly, the invitation so significant, so welcome, and his face for the first time shifted from the mask of strain. 'I must caveat, sir, that I make no claims of great proficiency with the strings... and I possess no Stainer, merely the most modest of instruments which was given to me by one of my parishioners. It was a gesture of thanks for my small words of comfort at a particularly distressing time.'

'We will pay that no mind, it is of no matter,' declared Simon in emphatic voice, secretly delighted that both his friends would participate together in their cabin ensemble; indeed, it was a gigantic step towards a more cordial relationship between Pat and Marston, in which he delighted. 'With the best will of the world none of us may lay claim to the skills of such as Niccolò Paganini or Giuseppe Tartini. Oh, would that we might ever hear such perfection on the strings - one of the maestros present - with such as the likes of double stop trills and all from Tartini, eh?'

He sighed, 'We can but dream of a musical Heaven whilst we make recourse to our own imperfections; indeed, I have only the four fingers and one thumb upon my own left hand.'

'I beg your pardon, Simon,' remarked Pat, looking perfectly blank.

'Tartini: did you know there is a story - *a story indeed! I am sure it is no more than that* - that the great man had six fingers on his left hand, which greatly facilitated his playing?'

'Never in life!' exclaimed Pat, smiling. 'Well, I would settle for an extra inch on the length of my own when I make my attempt upon the 'cello!' adding, 'Perhaps they might stretch if I slide down from the masthead whilst hanging from the stay with only my left hand! What do you say, Simon?' Pat chuckled, plainly in good humour.

'Perhaps you might then also reach the lower parts of the harp and play with the skill of King David.' Both Marston and Simon laughed aloud, Simon delighted to see his friend's spirits reviving.

'I am so very hungry,' declared Pat; 'Why, another day on bread or biscuit with only grog and - *I heard this from Jack Aubrey on the old Surprise when we was both in Pompey and before he became Admiral* - I shall ground on my own beef bones!' Pat laughed, 'Lucky Jack Aubrey! What a grand man that fellow is... a true hero if ever there was one.'

'I believe his surgeon, Maturin, is of a similar, exemplary ilk ... and he is too a natural philosopher of extraordinary ability,' added Simon; 'Indeed, I once had the honour and great good fortune to meet him in Haslar. Long may that splendid hospital endure. Did you know that Lind himself served there?'

'Did he indeed?' Pat rarely admitted his unfamiliarity with Simon's reported personages, for to do so usually invited jest in the form of gentle sarcasm.

Freeman returned in that instant with a large, steaming silver dish, capturing all attentions, setting it down and removing the cover to reveal a visual delight to wide-open eyes, with bacon and sausages all aground upon layers of fried eggs and Black Pudding, and with none of the customary swilling fat; for Simon had remarked upon the necessity of care for Pat's stomach. The divine aroma of the fried bacon filled the cabin. 'Here,' said Pat, salivating, 'there is nothing like a right proper and full English breakfast to revive the body... *the humours.* Please to eat up, Mr Marston; do eat as much as you can; you look fair clemmed.' Marston smiled and nodded in emphatic reply.

'Soft tack 'im coming, Massa,' announced Freeman with a bow. Pat simply beamed, and Murphy appeared within minutes with a great plate of toasted bread.

Pat dispensed an initial serving upon the plates which he passed across the table to his guests, when all began eating, Marston most enthusiastically; indeed, to Simon's discrete eye he gorged with determination on the plentiful food; Pat, too, seemed intent on making up for lost time or, at least, for lost victuals; indeed, for the first few minutes he allowed his appetite free rein in making a most determined onslaught upon the bacon, his solitary remark, 'Mr Marston, may I trouble you for the pepper?' offered without a pause in the slicing of his thick rashers, and then he looked up momentarily to shout out, 'Murphy! Murphy there! Are you now about the coffee?'

As he said it, Pat's eyes cautiously scrutinised his table with a most careful glance ventured towards Simon in order to ascertain the least sign of condemnation of his express gluttony; finding none he looked to his other guest, a glaring vacancy already become visible on the chaplain's plate; indeed, Marston was staring towards the serving dishes but said nothing. 'Another slice of bacon or two, Mr Marston?' prompted Pat with feeling; his words were offered with some small sense of relief, perhaps reflecting his own; 'Can I help you to a fried egg?'

'If there is one that can possibly be spared, sir.'

Pat perservered, perhaps mindful of his own hunger, 'I beg you will allow me to cut you a larger piece of the Black Pudding.'

'Most certainly, thank you.' Marston paused and looked about him, as if conscious of and concerned about displaying his insatiable appetite, having eaten near nothing for two days. 'I confess that my own hunger brings a reminder of - and a new meaning to - my understanding of my parishioners' experiences of it and their constant fears of it perpetuating.'

'In the Isles, when I was last in Tobermory,' Simon interjected immediately and spoke with the utmost gravity, 'I took into my own home... *my tiny cottage...* two families evicted from Sutherland by the Countess.' Simon spoke with a voice of bitter contempt, 'They were two of hundreds, perhaps thousands, and they had eaten nothing for sixteen days - *sixteen days!* - when they arrived on Mull to seek assistance; and they possessed not a shilling between them - not a penny - *not even a farthing!* Indeed, the Countess's Commissioner, James Loch - *the damnable rogue!* - had promised them a bountiful life from the sea and its fringe: plentiful fish to eat and assured employment there for all... and this whilst their homes - their pitiful bothies - *scarcely fit for the sheep that replaced them* - were burned down before their eyes!' Pat had never seen Simon speak with such vehemence, such ferocity; indeed, it was akin to rage, and he said nothing as his friend resumed with evident difficulty, anguish visibly oppressing him, 'The mother of three bairns, *scarcely more than scarecrows - all of them*, told me that they had survived their trek by drinking water from streams, and they had eaten only such wild mushrooms, berries and dandelion leaves - *dandelion leaves of all things!* - that they could find in passing. They were skeletal, so weak they could no longer stand... I had to carry the bairns upstairs to the bedroom.' Simon thumped his fist upon the table, 'That is hunger!' He was plainly angered and much distressed by the telling of his tale, and an uncomfortable ambience descended upon the table as he relapsed into silence.

Marston eventually spoke up in a whisper, 'I beg your pardon, colleague; I am sorry to have spoken on the matter; it was ill-considered, and I ask your forgiveness.' Simon could find no further words in that moment of angst; he merely nodded and turned away to conceal his anger and distress.

Pat, most disconcerted to see his oldest, most dear friend in all the world so upset, turned to his steward and spoke in gentle voice, 'Would you have the great kindness to light along another pot of tea? Thank you.'

Murphy, who had been listening attentively to Simon, held his usual caustic tongue in check and whispered so quietly that his reply went unheard before he left the cabin.

Pat, sensing that the restoration of comfortable cordiality, that prized asset of all things in the cabin, might be slower than the return of the tide, tried again to break the silence, 'Mr Marston, it scarcely seems the thing to say... but... could you manage this last sausage? I regret to say that the bacon is quite finished... all eaten up.'

The chaplain, evidently discomfited by Simon's story, and seemingly embarassed by his own reference to hunger, declined. Pat seized the sausage with his fingers and relished it without hesitation, and the serving dish was bereft of the least morsel. He licked his fingers and beamed with pleasure, 'Ahh, what sublime joy to eat again after a spell of starvation, eh? Oh, sorry, old Simon.' He observed Simon's near-imperceptible shake of his head, a gesture towards resignation, and he changed tack; 'I have heard of the Clearances, of course,' he said eventually in cautious voice, '... even in far Connemara; indeed, on the rare occasion that I came up to London to attend the House there were stories of Scottish folk aplenty seeking a new life and home in Ulster... and even *further afield* in Ireland... not to mention the considerable emigration to Canada.' He sighed, 'It is my precious hope that dear Ireland will never find such tragedy.' Pat hesitated, 'But I find I am come on to dangerous ground and we are bearing towards politics, and that is the end of all comfortable talk. Mr Marston, I trust you are no longer hungry, and I thank you for gracing us with your company for breakfast.'

Marston accepted the hint gladly and left the cabin, suitably revived and considerably reinvigorated. Pat remained with Simon, and the surgeon was the first to speak, 'I too will beg your pardon, brother; I should not have spoken in such intemperate voice; I allowed anger to creep in. I hope that Marston was not greatly discountenanced...' A pause. 'His words on the matter of hunger touched my heart.'

'Never in life; it didn't signify; and I am sure he left in fine fettle... the finest.' A pause. 'It was a famous breakfast,' Pat added with a wide smile. His own mind was holding firm to pleasurable thoughts, all of which included desirable victuals; and he declared, 'What do you say to a fresh beefsteak... with beans... for dinner later?'

'With all my being, and conceivably might there be onions too? I venture the suggestion in the medical context. Whilst they lack the extreme efficacy of lemons, and oranges for that matter, they remain an excellent antiscorbutic; indeed, Lind himself remarked upon it.' Simon, sloughing off his despond, laughed at last as the recollection of such banter came back to him from their former voyages together.

'And perhaps we will enjoy another pot of tea. I confess I ain't enjoyed tea so much since... since God knows when.'

'It is become quite the fashionable thing in London town, so I am told,' murmured Simon; 'The Duchess of Bedford is the famous proponent in high circles.'

'Well, if ever I am called to wait upon her at such grand social occasions, I must remember not to call for the coffee!' Pat burst into laughter. 'Freeman! Show a leg, rouse out a right proper pot of coffee! COFFEE THAT IS!' he shouted, perfectly aware that Freeman's ear would be hovering close behind the door, likely alongside Murphy's.

'That was an exceedingly cordial gesture - your invitation to Marston - if my memory does not fail me,' remarked Simon; 'The more so as I collect you did not favour my colleague's playing when he was last aboard?'

'I am so happy, old friend, being at sea once again... with a prime crew, fine officers to a man... with Sinéad here, the swabs happy and the Bay behaving herself; Marston's playing, bad or worse, is of no consequence. A toast, if you will,' added Pat cheerfully, raising his cup, the tea dregs now cold, 'To our venture, and may no new thing arise!'

'Our venture, and may no new thing arise!' echoed Simon.

In the calming tranquillity of the early evening after supper Pat and Simon took their seats on an unusually stable deck in the great cabin, tuning their strings, sipping port wine and musing on the pleasant day; Duncan was patiently awaited whilst he went to his cabin to find his pennywhistle.

'Marston exhibits a modicum of nervousness... his first invitation to the cabin,' announced Simon as Pat paused with his bow.

'Poor fellow; I collect my first attendance upon my captain's table; the smallest of sloops it was, scarcely more than a captain's barge; it was back in the year 'ninety-five, if my memory serves. I was a young whipper-snapper of a reefer and fair quaking in my shoes,' Pat smiled, a small smile of pleasure in reflection.

'Brother, I beg you will forgive me for asking...' Simon spoke in low voice, '... and I speak as your friend here, as much as I might as your physician... Your intellects have seemed a trifle subdued at times during these recent days... or am I much astray?'

'Eh? No, no... not at all, not in the least.'

'That is an uncommon vehement denial, is it not? The painful memories which you have described as afflicting the ease of your spirit... are they oft recurring, tell? Is there some fundamental hesitation, a degree of uncertainty in your mind concerning our return to Greece, dear?' No reply forthcoming and Simon resumed, 'I fear you are low in your spirits... or am I, perhaps, in error?'

Pat reflected silently for several minutes as Simon studied his friend, eventually sighing before taking a sizeable swallow to finish his port wine; 'Will I tell you the truth?' Simon nodded cautiously and Pat continued even as he felt his throat constricting, his mouth drying in an instant; he swallowed to no effect, no moisture whatsoever remaining to him, and he spoke in an increasingly low voice, a near whisper, 'I am tolerably apprehensive about that place; indeed, I fear to see more of the vile and barbaric massacres of innocents that I witnessed when last there... when we return. Will we encounter such cruel barbarity as that again, eh? *Will we?* If so, I doubt I will long endure.'

'No man ever steps in the same river twice, for it's not the same river and he's not the same man,' murmured Simon in gentle voice.

'Eh?'

'Heraclitus.'

'Who is this hero, Clitus? I am not familiar with the man... A clever cove, no doubt?'

'Oh, the exceptional Greek philosopher of his age... in the times of Socrates and Aristotle; he majored on impermanence.'

'But his notions... *his writings* have endured?'

'To our great fortune; at least his *conceptual leanings*... will we say.' A pause. 'You were speaking of your angst, your hesitations, brother.'

Pat reflected for a few moments before resuming, 'I cannot shake ghastly recollections from my dreams - *my nightmares.* Even now, all these years later... I see the bloodied bodies of slain women and children in the ashes of that damnable village... I see the captive Turk seamen in chains on the Hydra beach, staring up at my face and affeared for what is to happen to them... and I hear their screams as they are being roasted alive... God rest their souls... and I am much affrighted by the prospect of more such horrors before my eyes when we return. It awakens me from my slumbers more often than I care to say. Indeed, when I awaken, I oft find myself in a muck sweat... and I am... I am...' Pat's voice tailed off; 'There, you have it; there are evenings when I do not care to retire... I dread my own dreams... I fear the foul memories...' He sighed again, a long, long sigh and with a deeply disturbed expression which seemed, in that instant, to fill the cabin itself with a mournful depression and left a silent Simon wide-eyed and aghast. 'Will they ever be athwart my hawse?'

'The mind and its memory have their reasons,' declared Simon eventually, trying hard to gather his own thoughts, for Pat had never before revealed his personal apprehensions, his fears, to him with such feeling.

'No doubt,' Pat murmured in offhand voice, without conviction and expressing not the least interest.

*'Our mind and memory,'* Simon spoke with emphasis; 'Let us consider that they are the most miraculous of our faculties.' He pressed on, finding his way to surer ground, 'Yet we are too often also burdened with their dark side: the burden - if you will - of *unwanted* recall, of a degree of derangement of the natural humours, perturbing as that is. In this matter there is something profoundly dismaying about those cruel past events - *for which no fault attaches to ourselves and of which we could do nothing -*

which so greatly blight our present life; indeed, for the physician it is deeply depressing to contemplate the more obscure fragilities of the mind... more so when we possess not the least medicine to address its injury... to quell or at least to suppress such frightful recollections when they arise.'

'I dare say that may be the case,' murmured Pat, wringing his hands; 'but *can* anything be done... the least thing... to... to treat this discomfit? What do you have at hand, tell?'

'There is, of course, the blue pill and... *and other remedies...* There are numerous such...' Simon's voice tailed off, for he realised that he had been speaking without the least projection of confidence, which Pat could hardly fail to notice, 'which will serve for the short term... *the very short term...* to foster sleep.'

'But, Simon, sleep is when it afflicts me so... the dreadful nightmares.'

'However, whilst there is no assured *physical* treatment known to the doctor - *and we must disregard with the utmost discipline that convenient refuge which is alcohol* (Simon baulked at mentioning laudanum) - we must also ignore the several quack remedies so often promoted by those of no credible standing... and we must fall back on the sole stalwart which is left to us.'

'That convenient refuge? Alcohol? I beg you will concede that a man must surely preserve the prodigious pleasures of such as a bottle of port wine... after supper most particularly.'

'Sure, but I speak of words. Words: I am of a mind that they are more powerful than the proverbial sword. Words: with words we may speak with compassion; with words we can express friendship... love even - *for those more fortunate souls*. Words: with words we may hold to the belief that we can convey the prospect - *perhaps even something approaching the likelihood* - of the burden diminishing with that other ethereal tool we possess...'

'Eh?' Pat was thoroughly confused, 'Ethereal tool? The other one?'

'Time. It is said since ancient times that time heals all ills. That may be a trifle reckless, a reflection of optimism... *perhaps no bad thing...*' Simon's mind momentarily drifted towards his own feelings in the matter of the loss of his wife, distressing to the present day, five years later; and he wondered if he was himself verging on the quacksalver; '... but those of us with more - will I say - *philosophical* leanings have not the least doubt of its veracity.'

'I see,' said Pat with a firm degree of scepticism, 'and how long does this take? That is to say, in the normal course of things.'

'Oh, as to that, the answer is far beyond the competence of even the most skilled of physicians, and I make no claim of being such a one; indeed, there is a notable paucity amongst those of us of a medical persuasion in the matter of the workings of the mind....' Simon continued in quiet voice, observing an emerging but still slight interest in Pat's eyes; '... for the complexities of it are endless, *quite endless*; and I regret are not explicable to the layman.'

'But I dare say that *you* understand the ins and outs of it, that you have a fair handle on it, eh? So, what is to be done to set me to rights, tell?' Pat spoke with exasperation, for in his recurring procession of sleepless nights and consequent fatigue he had reached the end of all patience.

'The only recourse for us mere mortals - for that is all that we are in this somewhat ethereal realm... *these uncharted waters, as the mariner might say* - is to reconcile ourselves to two things: *one*, we cannot know *when* such as a material improvement of any signification might eventuate, and *two*: the mind - as well as the body - is a great healer of itself *and will likely do so eventually*. Words will *aid* our progress; words *and time* will ultimately save us from our distress; with words we must look to our friends to speak with us on the painful matter, and we must not keep the subject to ourselves... difficult as that may seem to the layman. Do I speak clear?'

'You do; indeed, you speak well; and I am sure there is something in what you say,' declared Pat, calming and with a little less uncertainty. 'Thank you, old friend, and enough of our puling, eh?'

*'Ad meliora!'* declared Simon emphatically, adding - Pat looking blank - 'To better things!' Simon smiled, his foray into a

perfectly difficult subject completed, as much as he cared to perpetuate it or considered it decent to do so.

'Indeed,' murmured Pat grudgingly; 'Well, at the risk of falling back into that convenient refuge, will we call for a bottle or two of wine to... to lubricate our musical thinking, eh?'

'An excellent notion... Indeed, I rather think I will enjoy a drop... *ad vinum per aspera!'*

'There you go again, making game of me with the Latin,' Pat scowled, 'Topping it the nob... as if you are blathering about the *hoi polloi.*' Not caring to be outdone he added, 'That's Latin too, I believe.'

'I was not aware; perhaps it was a later, *humanist* addition.'

'Well, it ain't fashionable aboard ship... and a more fashionable fellow than I might consider it mere showing away.'

'Allow me to state that I have never conceived of you as fashionable, brother; never in life.' Simon ignored Pat's suspicious stare and laughed, '*Through adversity to the wine*; there, you have it. I believed it to be a sentiment with which you might accord.'

'A capital notion, it is; but you would oblige me if we might keep to our humble level of holding to the King's English! 'MURPHY! MURPHY THERE!' shouted Pat, disinterested in pursuing the subject.

Murphy appeared within moments, 'Well, Mr Marston's best compliments, sorr, and would you care to see him in the cabin... that is to say... if you are at leisure?'

'Ask his presence directly, Murphy; we await his company and we will be happy to see him,' replied Pat, not without a degree of hesitation; 'and please to light along a brace of port wine...' adding to Simon, '... that precious standby, eh?'

Both Pat and Simon recalled from prior voyages that Marston's abilities with the strings were competent but never of an exceptional quality, and so it was with a cautious degree of measured, indeed moderate, expectation that they took up their instruments as the chaplain entered and was seated.

'Good evening to you, Mr Marston,' said Pat with warm cordiality, though Simon could not be sure to what degree it was feigned.

'Thank you, sir; and a good evening to you all,' replied Marston with a mild anxiety in his voice.

'How are you feeling, may I ask?' added Pat, not ungenerously.

'Never better, sir; indeed, I am wholly recovered... and I am quite in the way for a testing piece or two upon my instrument; indeed, I have been polishing it these two hours gone...' Marston had the feeling that his hosts were not greatly impressed with his endeavours, all three exhibiting a certain fixity of expression, and he added in haste, 'and attending to the bow with a light rosin.' Pat merely nodded.

'Will you suggest a piece to your liking for our beginning?' said Simon to Pat when they had all taken up their bows. They started cautiously with Pat's old Royal Navy favourite: *Bacon and Greens,* before shifting to *Corelli,* Marston's violin and his bowing, to their surprise, magically bridging the customary, audible gaps between their usual thin ensemble of only two instruments, and bringing a minimal vibrato with pleasing high end sharpness to the pair of Pat's 'cello and Simon's viola, Marston with violin greatly contributing to their enjoyment of the melodic sounds of the Christmas Concerto, being Simon's particular pleasure.

'Your attentions upon your violin were certainly worthwhile, Mr Marston,' declared Pat when they paused, Simon marvelling in Pat's hospitality. 'Indeed, I am uncommon happy to play second fiddle to your bow.'

Marston beamed with obvious relief and plain delight, 'It is most benevolent of you to say so, sir.'

Simon's eyes opened wide; 'Did Pat have some nefarious purpose, hitherto unrevealed?' he wondered; 'Was this a welcome diversion for Pat from his depression?' He could not decide. In any event he was pleased to see that his friend appeared to be in better spirits than earlier.

The unexpectedly delightful opening greatly pleased them all, and so they played on for hour after pleasurable hour, wholly engrossed within their endeavours and revelling in the discovery of a quality within Marston which they had not anticipated in the least, the collective playing adding an utterly absorbing fascination to the sociable ensemble until late into the evening, even as they ignored an increasingly exasperated Murphy's tentative and periodic enquiries at the door about supper, whilst refreshed only by the steward's unsolicited deposits of coffee and red wine, later brandy, until wrists, hands and eyes were dog-tired, fingertip extremities were sore, right arms ached, and one of the two lamps began guttering as its oil ran low. The burnt smell had long permeated the air throughout the cabin before all paused with a deal of reluctance to take stock. Pat's eyes at last found the long-in-abeyance toasted cheese on his table, cold long since, but still palatable to a hungry man; certainly so, to Duncan's way of thinking, for he munched every remnant remaining after ten minutes.

The evening's musical quartet, even allowing for Duncan's sometimes quite indifferent improvisations with the whistle, had excelled everything previously heard in the great cabin; so much so that they were all greatly delighted, and they expressed volubly the most flowing of compliments to their guest, having been astonished by Marston's playing, exhibiting a depth, a warmth and a sensitivity upon the strings that Simon and Pat had oft dreamed of achieving.

'Very finely played, sir,' Pat said it again; indeed, he surprised himself with the degree of feeling, of warmth and emphasis, in his compliment to Marston.

'I venture that music is indeed the food of love,' exclaimed a tired but overjoyed Simon, adding quickly as Pat stared in enquiry, 'The Bard. Will we play on for a little longer?'

'Not another note, I do implore you!' declared a tired Pat; 'Why, in ten more minutes I doubt my bow will find the strings. Mr Marston, may I praise you most heartily on your violin,' he remarked with considerable geniality, much to his own surprise in instant reflection.

'I am much obliged, Captain O'Connor, deeply obliged. Thank you, sir,' replied Marston, a little overwhelmed by the warmth of his inauguration to the cabin social scene.

'I give you joy of your new... *your nautical* parish. May I trouble you to tell, sir: how did you impr ... *achieve* such an excellent talent since last aboard our barky?' asked Pat, still incredulous at the very substantial improvement. 'That is to say, I was not intending to infer any previous paucity of competence; no, not at all; and you are not to think so... upon my word and honour, I speak under correction; what I mean is... well... I... *please to continue if you will.*'

'The melancholia it was, sir,' Marston sighed; 'Long winters with dark evenings, then too the dwindling congregations in my benefice: my parishioners struggling to make ends meet, their long hard days working to simply survive, to keep the hunger at bay - the cost of bread now so very high - and Sundays tending their vegetable plot... those that had one after the enclosures that is. Great poverty abounded in my parish...'

'I am entirely of your opinion,' declared Pat in soft voice, empathising with audible and untrammelled conviction, 'Life for many a soul these recent years ain't been Bartholomew's Fair; no, not by a long chalk.' Being a landowner himself, albeit in a small way, and an Irish Member of the House, he understood full well the implications of the accelerating agricultural changes, post-war, particularly the enclosures. Worst of all was the very high taxation regime imposed on corn imports, and the peasants' staple food - bread - was consequently so very costly. He commiserated wholeheartedly with Marston, 'Yes, the abominable enclosures... and the damnable - *excuse me - the vile* Corn Laws... while the interest on bonds is now reduced to a trifling three and a half percent when tax has risen to thirty-four shillings a quarter on corn! Boney is long gone yet income tax is still at two shillings in the pound... *two shillings!* How is an honest man to feed his family? Aye, 'tis a pretty kettle of fish when bread is so dear. But I beg pardon for interrupting your tale.'

Marston sighed again, his face a picture of deep conviction, of sad recollection, 'It started at harvest festivals; for a while I took to drinking the local cider... from flagons left as my gift... until I decided one day to stop before things got out of hand. To cheer myself, I took to my violin, practising every day, and sometimes I would have a visitor, accomplished in the strings, who would encourage me until I mastered all the sheets I had. Then I gave solo concerts in the church and my parishioners trickled back, but their numbers were still so few, many so poor and gone to the workhouse, husbands even selling their wives for lack of even a shilling. That, sir, is why the news of your voyage was so welcome to me, and I am here with the blessing of my good wife, Mary, to seek a new purpose... a re-invigoration of my somewhat jaded spirits if you will.'

The latter comment struck a most sympathetic chord with Pat, his heart warming to Marston, and he spoke with great conviction in his voice, 'Mr Marston, I have so much enjoyed myself this evening; I thank you again for your company. Might I enquire if you would favour us again with your playing after supper on another evening... for an hour or so perhaps... as we cross the Bay?'

'Why, sir, I thank you most kindly,' Marston replied, as much taken aback as was Simon by Pat's gracious compliments and his invitation, his face positively shining with pleasure. 'And may I say how much - *how infinitely* - I am obliged to you for your benevolent invitation this evening? I will look forward to that with particular enthusiasm.'

'As will I, Mr Marston, as will I. You have my best thanks for joining our little ensemble in our musical endeavours.' Pat offered his hand, 'I bid you good night.'

Pat's transformation from his depression at the supper table and his somewhat half-hearted perception of Marston was quite incredible to Simon who in past times had come to accept that his friend could not bring himself to favour the chaplain, even in his capacity as assistant surgeon. Marston having departed, Simon looked to his friend, 'Pat, dear, may I say how extraordinary well the evening went off?'

'Indeed it did, capital; more of the silk purse than the wooden spoon we might have expected,' declared Pat, muddling, as was his wont, his metaphors; 'I had expected that we would dash off an attempt upon one or two pieces... to do the decent thing... before the toasted cheese; perhaps enjoy a night cap, and then call it a day - *a night* - and I had no inkling, none at all, that Marston possessed such a grand talent... Why, he quite lifted our game... there it is, I have said it! Truly he was a... a pearl... amongst a... a bed of roses.'

'I was thinking along similar lines, brother,' Simon replied with a huge sense of satisfaction, 'though I would not have presumed to say it myself... *unprompted*. Would it be premature, at all, to invite his presence again on the morrow?'

'I believe we may look forward to it,' declared Pat with obvious enthusiasm.

Murphy was less overwhelmed, as he complained to his sometime assistant, Old Jim Lamb, whilst helping Freeman and clearing the plates, glasses and cups back to the galley. 'Well, there be another of 'em now, all caterwauling; four of 'em, dinning away... 'tis enough to drive a man to the captain's liquor store.'

'Would you be meaning *more often*, Murphy?' asked Barton, who was also Old Jim Lamb's cousin and consequently privy to certain shipboard practices, overhearing Murphy as he was helping himself to cocoa off the galley stove.

By Corunna the quartet had become well established; before Cape St. Vincent Sinéad had returned from keeping the twins company in the sick bay after supper to attend the playing; by Cadiz the ship's officers were invited to join them for toad-in-a-hole and to enjoy the increasing ambience of informal bonhomie in the cabin after supper as the quartet played.

'God help us,' said Murphy, taking advantage of the absence of all officers from the quarterdeck, all being in the cabin, and chatting to Anderton, one of the helmsmen. 'What a screeching awful yowling they do make, to be sure; 'tis a din worse than the bar of the King's Head in Galway Town of a Saturday night.'

*Tuesday 17th June 1823*                              *Gibraltar*

*Surprise* had come into Rosia Bay at Gibraltar in the late afternoon of the previous day. In the brightness of the following morning, after breakfast and while the decks were being washed, Pat and his officers and most of the crew had gone ashore, Pat intending to show Sinéad and the twins his old haunts. Simon and Marston had left to climb the Rock and to observe the wildlife. Reeve and Barton remained aboard with a few hands to supervise the loading of fresh water.

Marston, by now fully recovered from his seasickness and his morale restored substantially by his welcome and playing popularity in the cabin, exuded goodwill for all things including O'Connor, the officers and the crew. Duncan, Pickering and Mower he had become accustomed to many years previously, and all had extended a friendly welcome to him upon his return. Codrington and Reeve were also very amiable with him, and unsurprisingly he contrasted the lonely times in his small rural parish with the companionship aboard ship, in which he delighted. Ships fare, whilst plain for the most part, was plentiful and invariably accompanied by wine which, although varying from indifferent to excellent, was not the norm at his Cornish home, and a full plate with a glass of wine always served contrasted so very favourably with his recent hard times.

Upon gasping their way up the final yards to the summit of the Rock, Simon and Marston collapsed for respite, sweating profusely and gulping the last of the water from their flasks. As their breathing recovered, they sat enjoying the magnificent views, content to recount fond recollections of their last time at Gibraltar when they had also climbed the Rock to observe the vultures, storks and eagles, all of which were still present and plainly visible. They sat basking in the hot sun, not a single cloud in sight, and when fully relaxed from their exertions they supped from a brace of red wine bottles which Simon had brought along, reclining and eating plentiful cheese sandwiches, munching on crunchy red onions purchased that morning and cracking Gibraltar walnuts - a great favourite of Simon's. An inquisitive group of monkeys was watching closely from ten yards away. 'Marston, art happy? I am considering a particular matter.'

'Pray tell, Ferguson; we have known one another long enough to speak our thoughts without giving offence.'

'Listen, will I tell you something? You know that O'Connor has resigned the service?' said Simon, 'This venture not being one in which His Majesty's officers can lawfully serve.'

'I am not unaware of this... this somewhat strange development,' said Marston cautiously. 'The officers speak of it in the gun-room... and there is a singular want of privacy for such discussions in that place... as you know full well. I am minded that the captain must be mortally cast down by such a change, the service being his life, even his very being.'

'To be sure, he did not choose this course lightly. It came about only after several years ashore and his dissatisfaction with their Lordships keeping him cooling his heels on the beach whilst all around him the fleet was shrinking. It has been a tolerably good decision on his part, I find. I do not collect seeing him happier than these past weeks. May I say, as you have now so providentially engaged with him in a social capacity, joining our scraping at supper, O'Connor could not be described as a philosopher, being something of a plain speaker in his honest tarpaulin way. You should mind where any dialogue might lead us; in particular you would be well advised never to let the term *privateer...* or even worse - *pirate! - God forbid...* cross your lips, for such terminology will attract strong reprobation, *the strongest*; and though one must never become the prisoner of words we must content ourselves with the term *letter of marque* should the subject of our capacity in Greek service ever arise; I understand it is a tolerably acceptable term in naval circles. I collect we may have spoken of such afore, though these matters of mere procedure... of protocol... I find oft slip the more – will I say – *philosophical* mind.'

'Is the nature of the privateer somewhat discreditable? I would be sure of my understanding in such a delicate matter.'

'Of course, the privateer fights for what O'Connor and his colleague officers would consider as the basest of motives: solely for gain, for profit; purely mercenary are the privateer's base interests.'

'And prizes hold no interest for O'Connor? I collect great joy abounding when prizes were taken in the past, the captain being particularly pleased. Surely so?'

'That is plainly undeniable, Michael. Yet the captain would consider the two to be wholly different. The taking of prizes in His Majesty's service bestows a legitimacy which is morally absent from the perspective - *from the thinking* - of the privateer.'

'Why, there's a distinction of course. No one would deny it.'

'Conceivably, your role will become of the utmost significance for our venture, and it would be a particularly unwelcome development were anything to arise so as to bring even the slightest of rift between you and O'Connor.'

'Never be so concerned, dear colleague. After years of shivering in Cornish winters, no fuel to be had save the odd windfall along the lanes, nothing of note ever occurring in my daily routine, no person of any education with whom to enjoy any meaningful discourse, this is most certainly the life I aspire to: interesting companionship and good commons. Be assured I will never cross him - no, such is inconceivable; you may be certain of that.' Marston nodded as he spoke, in emphasis of his understanding, whilst both stared intently at the whirling vultures overhead, entirely distracting Simon. His point made, Marston looked about him, his interest returning to the fauna, before loudly exclaiming, 'Over there, apes! Why, the rascals have seized our sandwiches!'

*Wednesday 25ᵗʰ June 1823*          *Western Mediterranean*

The wind was blowing a very favourable, gentle southerly as *Surprise* neared Port Mahon in the early afternoon, greatly facilitating her entrance to the harbour, a long and winding passage, no great width available in the approach, and safe access being so dependent upon the wind direction. Slowly she slipped past Fort Marlborough to larboard and Cape Mola to starboard, shearwaters flying vigorously in a swirling multitude all about them as they passed by with her courses furled; coming up next past the Lazaretto Fortress to starboard, now sailing on reefed topsails alone, keeping to the north side of the channel, passing Cuckold's Reach; until she was gliding through the narrow passage to the north side of the hospital island of Sant Felip Fort and approaching the Town Quay. At Pat's side all his officers had gathered with him, everyone staring all about them, drinking in the vista and savouring fond recollections of past visits. The northern side of the great reach of water was devoid of buildings for the most part and presented a dry and brown landscape covered with the scrub oak native to the island, contrasting so starkly with the cultivation amidst the scattered buildings set back from the harbour. Orange groves covered with white blossom stepped back up the hillsides overlooking the town, the wind gusts bringing occasional scintillas of their scent, alternating with wild jasmine, wafting towards all on deck. *Surprise,* her topmen working hard and her topsails now double-reefed, slowed to a near stop as she turned hard to larboard with the last of her momentum just as she came abeam the Town Quay, no other ships being tied up. The southerly wind now pressed upon her at the bow; her topsails were backed and she came quickly to a stop, letting go her small bower. The cable veered, *Surprise* drifted back slightly to leeward to set her anchor fifty yards off the Pigalle Steps, a notable landmark. Long known in the Service as the Pigtail Steps, they led directly up to the top of the town. It had been a homely place during the war, always welcoming to the Royal Navy; one which the Surprises had visited many times before and was well known to them all. The whole crew were now on deck, many of them gazing at a port in which they had, for the most part, lived for four years until the year 'two, when Minorca had been handed back to Spain after the Treaty of Amiens. Even since then the harbour had continued to be used as the occasional Royal Navy base in the western Mediterranean. Pat and Simon looked hard for familiarities and changes, not many of the latter being evident.

'Why, 'tis been a long time since we first tied up here; it seems a lifetime ago,' sighed Pat with just the barest hint of regret in his voice, a regret for something which had been so valuable and was now lost. 'It ain't changed at all, save that I see no brigs or frigates, not a one here.'

'It is as if we were never away. A glorious place it is, no doubt,' Simon smiled even as his voice with its tinge of melancholy betrayed him.

'Happy times here they were... happy times,' murmured Pat.

'To be sure, that thought is never far from my mind these days, brother,' said Simon very quietly, adding, 'I oft so dearly wish that Agnes could be here to share these peaceful days with us.' But Pat did not hear him, did not become aware of the more rapid beating of his friend's heart or the bleak flush of black despair that crushed his spirit in an instant.

'Mr Pickering, be so good as to roster leave ashore for the crew; we will be here two nights. The Doctor, Mr Macleod and I will be ashore for both of them. Pray take command of the barky, if you will. Gentlemen, I am in contemplation of a walk up the steps and a pint of sherry in Jeraldo's Coffee House - for old time's sake... on our way to the Royal, I fancy. Are you with me?'

'Aye, for sure,' said Duncan emphatically.

'I will be very happy, dear soul,' Simon replied wistfully, thinking of his prior, penurious days during numerous visits to Mahon for many a year after he had first met Pat.

Walking up the steps was something akin to a homecoming for all of them. Pat's mind wandered fondly to a discrete dalliance with a lady in Mahon before he had married, with the wife of one of the based squadron's officers, a liaison perhaps suspected but never coming into the open, the said officer losing his ship and his life in battle at sea a year later. He also fondly remembered a near romantic encounter with the wife of the landlord of the Royal, the lovely Marisol - near only because of the impromptu and timely arrival of Duncan who took an extremely disapproving view, with harsh words exchanged, and almost bringing them to an occasion of honour with seconds in attendance. The inevitably bloody conclusion was fortunately averted by an engagement at sea in which Pat was wounded; the passage of time during his healing, Simon's care and intervention, and Duncan's solicitude for him having smoothed the unwanted rift between them.

'Ain't it grand to be back here?' asked Pat of the warm air, neither of his companions hearing him, both in similarly delighted mood and utterly absorbed in studying their surroundings, casting their gaze about them as they progressed so very slowly to the top of the steps. 'Why, I might even retire here,' he added, the attention of his companions caught at last, 'For there is never anything pressing and nothing in the line of wayward, careless change... and an honest man cannot ask for much more in his world.'

Though it was some years since Pat had been in Mahon he felt immediately at his ease; indeed, he was acknowledged still by brief but friendly greetings from several near-forgotten, nodding acquaintances as he walked along, few officers ever having brought so many prizes into the harbour. He might even now be a welcome guest in many respectable houses of the town.

The appeal of the sherry at Jeraldo's was a nostalgic pull, but the Royal beckoned more strongly; certainly for Duncan, as that was where his wife Kathleen and daughter Brodie were accommodated, and so they resolved to pass by Jeraldo's and bear directly for the Royal, aware that Kathleen and Brodie, not knowing precisely when *Surprise* would arrive in Mahon, might not actually be there. Kathleen had written to Duncan before they left Falmouth, advising of her love of the island, never previously having left the British Isles, and she was usually engaged in roving far over the interior by horseback, always accompanied by Brodie.

They strolled into the Royal by the familiar back way, through the little courtyard of orange trees, greeting a pair of English mastiffs with scant interest in the arrivals.

'How agreeably familiar everything is!' exclaimed Simon with great pleasure.

Duncan threw two old walnut halves, found in the depths of his pocket, before the dogs would rise to greet them, slavering and panting in the heat of the early afternoon. Of Brodie and Kathleen there was no sign, but Marisol was still there: a little greyer, a little plumper, but still the same excitable and enthusiastic person that Pat was never likely to forget. 'Capitano Pat!' she shrieked, rushing to throw her arms around Pat's neck, to his evident joy as he swept her clean off her feet in the friendliest of embraces, Marisol squealing with undisguised pleasure.

It was becoming a little late in comparison with their customary dinner time aboard *Surprise* and so, with a raging appetite and after profuse greetings, several fondly remembered Royal dishes were ordered including a hearty beefsteak pudding, a solomongundy, and almond cakes to finish. A refreshing cold beer was served at the table immediately by Marisol, and then there was a healthy silence as they gorged with determination on the largest conceivable portions of those most memorable of all victuals, every man delighted that they remained firm staples of the house. 'Did I mention that things don't change in this place?'

declared Pat with evident satisfaction as he came up momentarily from his plate for air. The whole feast was liberally washed down with jugs of a very palatable local beer – English beer sadly no longer to be had – with a brace of bottles of red wine, and was followed by generous brandies accompanied by several large pots of strong coffee, Marisol remembering well their affinity for it.

Later in the afternoon the tiring effects of the food, the several beers, wine and brandies, together with the deep heat of the Mediterranean sun, combined to dictate a siesta, as was the local custom. The three friends slumbered comfortably in complete satisfaction in deep chairs within the draught and shade of the inside of the Royal. They were awakened several hours later as the afternoon began to cool by an excited babble from the kitchen, Marisol in audible exchanges with loud female voices. Within minutes an excited and delighted Brodie burst through the drape separating the kitchen from the public room, and ran across to greet her father as he slowly rose from his chair with a broad smile of delight which seemed to spread the width of his face.

'Och, my wee bairn, 'tis so wonderful to see ye, indeed it is,' cried a delighted Duncan, seizing her up from the floor as they hugged. He bestowed a gentler kiss on both cheeks for Kathleen, as is the Mediterranean custom, husband and wife settling into animated conversation, the reunion so pleasurable.

Another old Tenedos, Patrick Coghlan, now the ladies' escort, stood mute but smiling behind them. Pat's greeting, 'I see Murphy has dragged you from the Boora bog, Coghlan! I hope I see you well.' was met with a wider smile and his gruff reply, 'Aye sorr, thankee.'

*Friday 27th June 1823*                                   *Mahon, Balearics*

*Surprise* slipped out of Mahon harbour with the aid of a benevolent north-westerly, greatly aiding her passage along the several miles of channel from her mooring near the quay, past the Lazaretto and out into the open waters. Her courses, topsails and topgallants together gave her a steady seven knots as she set up for Genoa.

The previous day had been spent in shifting the little baggage of Kathleen, Brodie and Coghlan aboard *Surprise,* followed by their long-delayed visit to Jeraldo's. It had changed not one jot since their very first drink there together, of cocoa, more than twenty years previously, many pints of sherry having been shared there since. The day had ended with a celebratory farewell supper at the Royal, Marisol in tearful embrace with Pat at the end, a little to his embarrassment, Sinéad being present but not caring to ask about Pat's old times in that dimension, recollecting a suspected brief dalliance by Pat with a young lady in Halifax, Nova Scotia during the war.

Despite the emotive farewells of the previous evening, everyone aboard being loathe to depart the place which they so much loved, the mood aboard *Surprise* was buoyant. It was sustained all day through to a voluble and amiable supper in the great cabin, Marston and all the officers being introduced to Mrs Macleod and Brodie, and the crew welcoming back their old shipmate, Coghlan.

Accommodation aboard *Surprise* was now becoming full, and so the officers had kindly shifted around their tiny cabin berths off the gun-room so as to make space for all the guests. Murphy's loud voice was much in evidence as he carried things about whilst complaining at near every step in his customary whining voice, 'Well, no bleeding rest for another day...'

'Would you be meaning *for the wicked?*' cried Mower in passing, laughing out loud. The twins and Brodie adopted the larboard berths, Duncan switched to the coach; Pickering, Mower, Prosser and Marston took the starboard cubicle berths. Codrington and Reeve were serving aboard *Eleanor*. A little more space was afforded to the ladies because the captain had not engaged a clerk, and neither were there any midshipmen.

'Well, how is a man expected to carry on with so much washing?' Murphy loudly retorted - to himself, Mower had gone; 'Two weeks more and there ain't likely to be a deal of soap left.'

As the days of the voyage passed, the quartet of Pat, Duncan, Simon and Marston, playing with great pleasure after supper time, had already become something of a routine and an event that all four greatly looked forward to. Sinéad, now joined by Kathleen, was nearly always in the great cabin during their playing, and the lieutenants too were usually in attendance. Marston, in contrast to his diffident playing during earlier voyages, was now almost approaching virtuoso. His playing had, over recent weeks, inspired both Pat and Simon to strive harder to follow him. At other times the playing was so relaxed that they ventured enthusiastically and unprompted into surprising variations. Even Murphy by now was lingering close outside the cabin door, always helping Freeman serve the toad-in-a-hole or the toasted cheese, and had ceased grumbling at the much increased cleaning afterwards – except when with his mate, Old Jim Lamb; for even Murphy had his position and reputation to consider.

*Sunday 29<sup>th</sup> June 1823*　　　　　　　　*Western Mediterranean*

The evening being pleasantly warm and the four musicians having been playing with great exuberance, Pat had left the great cabin door open through to the gun deck so as to capture a draught of air to cool the cabin. Sinéad and Kathleen being with the twins and Brodie in the gun-room, the quartet had been playing with great enjoyment for more than an hour, interrupted only when Marston paused with a broken string. Whilst he endeavoured to change it, Simon suggested a brief recuperation, 'Might I suggest we take a turn on deck to enjoy a draught of the cool evening air?'

'With all my heart,' replied Pat, readily agreeable. They stood up, left the cabin and stepped up the companionway to the quarterdeck, the lingering weak and diffuse light of the gloaming still sufficient to make their way.

*Surprise* was heeled over slightly to starboard and making, Pat judged, a steady six knots or thereabouts in a stiff top-gallant breeze. With no tacking having been required for some hours, there had been a pleasing lack of interruption of noise and activity to disturb a certain engrossment in their playing. On deck there was only the reassuring noise of the bow wave slapping along the hull and the faintest sound of wind soughing through the creaking rigging. The sun having set just half an hour previously, the evening being fine and there being no cloud visible at all in the twilight sky, the navigator in Pat gazed up high over the starboard bulwark at the readily recognisable orange glow of the emerging two brightest of the stars, hundreds more twinkling about them.

'Look there, old Simon, over the starboard side – *the starboard side*. Ain't that a prime sight? Are we ever blessed with any finer? Have you ever beheld such wonders?'

Simon stared out, quite unable to fathom precisely what Pat referred to, nothing unusual being visible in the darkness. 'Quite splendid,' he ventured cautiously.

'Look up - up! *There* - so much to see. It is the clearest night sky for astral observations. Look! Do we have any greater splendours? Look there, a grand sight for you... 'tis our friends *Arcturus* and *Vega*,' Pat pointed high into the southern sky.

'Yes, brother, so I had understood. And also, one may say, so very significant for you mariners, I believe. Indeed, you explained the navigational processes to me once... at least to *your* satisfaction... but I regret I have not fully retained the principles.'

As Pat's eyes, after the bright illumination in the great cabin, became further accustomed to the gloaming and shifted from the stars, he turned and looked for'ard beyond the mainmast. He could now make out and was astonished that it seemed as if the entire crew – rough and ready jack tars for the most part that they were – were sitting silently along the waist gangways, backs against the bulwarks, all evidently having been listening to the music of the quartet and patiently awaiting more. As Pat paused to take this in, he turned as if to speak to Simon, when a ragged ripple of applause broke out, growing steadily until all on deck had risen to their feet and were clapping, stamping and whistling loudly, the scene a most joyous celebration of reunion.

# Chapter Six

*What, silent still? and silent all?*
*Ah! No; — the voices of the dead*
*Sound like a distant torrent's fall,*
*And answer, 'Let one living head,*
*But one arise, — we come, we come!'*
*'tis but the living who are dumb.*

*Monday 30<sup>th</sup> June 1823*                    *Gulf of Genoa*

The westerly *Ponente* blew *Surprise* steadily across the remaining leagues from Mahon towards Genoa. In the gun-room and on the lower deck, as proximity to Greece increased, discussion became rife over the mission. The old hands were wholly unconcerned about the nature of the enemy and the odds against *Surprise*, knowing little of the military balance between the parties. The officers were a little more knowledgeable of the Turk naval resources and those of their Egyptian vassal, specifically the French training of that particular fleet, although they were less familiar with the politics of the Greek revolution. Despite the uncertainties, all on board remained confident in the judgement and capabilities of their captain. Murphy in particular found himself very much more in demand with the crew, most of whom were aware that he had his ear to the captain's door and might therefore have gleaned a good grasp of the mission and its objectives. Yet, for all his persistent efforts, Murphy had not been able to eavesdrop with any degree of success as Pat had been circumspect with his briefings.

All knew that *Surprise* was no longer officially a Royal Navy warship, albeit she was still, in secrecy, *His Majesty's Hired Vessel Surprise*. All also knew that she was not yet actually engaged with the anticipated Greek *letter of marque* but floating on a sea of rather less certain arrangements, at least until she had arrived in Greek waters and was able to engage formally with the provisional government there. Because of this multiplicity of uncertainties, discussion of the mission within the great cabin was limited in the extreme, nothing of verbal substance crossing the table in Murphy's presence; indeed, there was little that Pat knew himself pending further orders which he understood would be delivered by messenger at some later date.

Notwithstanding the unofficial or indeterminate status of the voyage from Falmouth to Greece, Pat was in high good spirits. It was more than simply a return to sea, more even than the satisfaction of being once again aboard a frigate and with his long-cherished aspiration for a crack crew achieved – for assuredly that was what he now had, bar the absence of any marines. No; for the first time in his long and successful sea-going career he felt not the immediacy of seeking out an engagement with the enemy and had no longer to keep one eye ready for an approaching vessel bearing Admiralty instructions; and so he had discovered a deeper inner satisfaction, a calming self-confidence, almost a renewal of purpose. All of which made him feel quite at ease with himself and the world, to the extent that he even began to feel at ease with Michael Marston who was now a not infrequent evening visitor to the great cabin, accompanying Pat, Duncan and Simon in their musical relaxations, an addition to the trio that Pat, to his own surprise and satisfaction, increasingly welcomed.

'What do you say to another pot of coffee, Simon?' Pat prompted as they finished eating breakfast.

'With great pleasure, my dear,' Simon replied, adding presciently, 'I give you joy of your present satisfaction. Long may it endure.'

'Freeman! Light along another pot of coffee, if you will; and please to fetch a bottle of the best Madeira... Oh, and do see if there is anything left of the Sunday cake... the smallest morsel will serve!' Pat paused for a few moments and looked closely at his friend of many years before responding to Simon's comment. 'I cannot recollect in all our voyages this exceptional feeling of self-quietude.'

'I am entirely of your opinion, brother,' murmured Simon.

The gentle sea state for most of the voyage, the clement weather and the contentment that this had brought about, growing with the increasing distance from Falmouth, had created

199

an atmosphere almost of tranquillity for all aboard *Surprise*. No longer, as far as the crew were aware, was she a Royal Navy ship, and hence the customary Articles of War were no longer read on Sundays; there were also the families of both Pat and Duncan aboard. All these changes from regular routine had, quite unexpectedly, brought about great efficiency and sharpness in the crew in a way that Pat had never previously experienced, with an attention to every detail in the daily routine of *their* ship, for that is how *Surprise* was perceived. The officers never found occasion to pick up on any defects of the crew, for remarkably there were none. The regular evening playing of the string quartet had considerably enhanced this pleasant ambience, and the musicians had since several days shifted to playing on the gun deck on warm and dry evenings as appreciation of their music had become near universal amongst the crew. Morale was therefore exceptional and not a soul had reported sick since the start of the voyage.

'Freeman! Freeman! Break out a case of the Haut Brion, the one with the long cork, the 'eighty-nine, in readiness for dinner and see how it is coming along with my cook,' shouted Pat, sitting on the chest against the stern windows, finishing his coffee whilst discussing the powder and shot stores with Pickering and considering his position generally, noon fast approaching. 'Why, Simon, ain't you shifting your old clothes and shaving for dinner?' remarked Pat as an afterthought to his considerations for the forthcoming repast, one of particular significance for his wife.

'Must I? I shaved only yesterday... or perhaps it was the day before.'

'I could never introduce you in polite company in those grimy slops. Murphy remarked this very morning that in Falmouth we have cast away old sails - veterans of the Horn and battle - in finer fettle.'

'I am aghast, brother. You oft say that it matters not one jot at sea... that we may wear anything at hand which serves our comfort, and neither is it necessary for our vestments to be pressed nor washed particularly often... more than once a month, will we say.'

'It is Sinéad's day. The ladies will be present and - *I'm sure* - *they* will be dressed in all *their* splendid finery. You would not care to disappoint them, would you? Why, there is a lack of a deal of buttons on your coat, and its collar is torn away on the starboard side... while your old... *old* shirt exhibits plentiful witness to your surgery - *in blood* - and I venture your breeches - *it is plain to see* - have surely been used by Wilkins to clean his pans! What on God's earth has Murphy been doing these past weeks, eh? Simon, I am of a mind that clean clothes of all things *on this particular occasion* might better suit.'

'Why, there is only a trifle of fat lingering on the breeks from that memorable sauce with the crubeens and trubs of last week - *I forget the day* - with such excellent tatties too... the fat is scarcely bothersome, for all love; I will be there presently.'

'Well, not in them old rags ye won't, sorr,' hissed an extremely disgruntled Murphy, who could no longer refrain from comment. He had long been perfectly aghast at Simon's grubby attire and had been itching to speak; so much so that he was beside himself with frustration, seething with discontent, and holding his silence only because of Pat's well-directed glares.

Pat blinked as he heard the uninvited, unexpected interjection. He seized his moment to press his friend, 'Simon, I am of a wonder whether *you* will wish to present yourself before the ladies in fresh garb... but you will favour *me* most deeply by changing your clothes. Your sleeves resemble those of our young *Tenedos* snotties. This is surely a day on which our every effort will be remarked upon, our vestments particularly, and you would not wish to be laughed at when we are at the table; and must I remind you that the ladies' interests, being what they are, do lie along those lines, and any visible *aberration* is likely to attract severe *rebrobation* - the severest!'

'I am a modest sort. Clothes do not greatly signify in my mind,' protested Simon; 'Murphy, will you tell the captain that you washed these clothes a short while ago - *in May was it?* - and they are in *perfectly clean fine fettle.*' Simon's emphasis undermined his case to the objective listener.

'Not as who should say right *filthy,*' declared Murphy with vehemence.

'For the love of God, cast away those scabrous slops if you will! The ladies may believe that you have stepped out of your store without so much as a candle and fallen into the stove's coal. Indeed, will you care to embrace Sinéad whilst wearing such feculent rags! There, I have said it.'

'I see you will not be swayed,' exclaimed Simon in reluctant voice of resignation; 'Oh, very well; your soul to the devil, Patrick O'Conor.' Murphy managed an ill-concealed smirk.

'Clothes cover a multitude of sins, Doctor, particularly so as we get older; as you of all will know; and naked we have but little influence,' volunteered Pickering, bringing a bemused stare from his captain and a scowl from Simon.

It was Sinéad's birthday and Pat had invited all his officers to a celebratory dinner to join his and Duncan's family. Afterwards he intended to give them what small extent of briefing that he was able. It was therefore an expectant gathering that took its place at the table in the great cabin. All officers were in formal uniform, although without Royal Navy insignia. There being no marines on board, each was attended behind their chair by stewards in smart blue jackets with brightened brass buttons and white gloves. Nearly all of the men exhibited gold earrings. All were as keen as the officers to glean what might fall from their captain's lips for eagerly receptive crewmates. Before that the meal was to be eaten, to be enjoyed, the birthday celebrated. The captain's cook had been tasked with the provision of something a little above the norm. Pat's private stocks had been severely diminished for the occasion, and his cook, Wilkins, had quite excelled himself. After the customary glass or two of Madeira, very popular with the ladies, Freeman and Murphy, Old Jim Lamb helping, brought out the food on the captain's best silver plate. They began serving dishes of freshly caught tuna, prepared as floured thick steaks and served with pureed peas and white sauce. In that expectant instant before anyone began to eat and as all looked over towards Pat, he raised his glass, rapped the table with his knife and, turning slightly to take in his wife to his right, Simon at her other side, he announced, 'Ladies and Gentlemen, a toast, if you will. To my dear wife, to Sinéad: a most happy and joyous birthday!'

'To Sinéad!' was shouted by all with heartfelt feeling and followed by the loud chorus of 'Happy birthday!', echoed with gusto by everyone present in the cabin including the stewards.

To Pat's left sat Kathleen; to her left Duncan was flanked by his daughter, Brodie. Michael Marston was at Sinéad's other side beyond Simon. On the opposite side of the table the twins were seated amongst Pat's officers: Tom Pickering, James Mower, William Codrington and William Reeve. Only the master, Mr Prosser, was absent, in command of *Eleanor* and sailing independently for the approach to Genoa. Barton alone remained on the quarterdeck with the helmsmen.

'Mr Reeve, the bottle stands by you,' cried Pat, perceiving his most junior officer to be a little daunted by the very full gathering. With the family members present and the occasion being one of celebration, the customary formality of dinner at the captain's table, of speaking only in response to the captain, was quickly abandoned and a vigorous hubbub, the most amicable of conversation, ebbed and flowed around the cabin. Freeman and the stewards replenished the plate with more tuna steaks, eagerly consumed by the officers. Then followed fresh roast pork - one of Jemmy Ducks' number having been killed that same morning - served with crisp crackling and sage and onion stuffing with a brown onion sauce, carrots, shallots and mushrooms, all taken up in Port Mahon. The shipboard millers had not yet got to the supplies, the myriad cats at Plymouth Dock having decimated their numbers, and the solitary ship's cat, a most amiable cream tabby, was successfully keeping their numbers in check since.

'Brodie, my dear, allow me to cut you a little more pork,' Pat smiled to her, perceiving that she remained nervous throughout the gathering. At least until her covertly consumed wine, from a glass frequently refreshed from the bottle standing in Duncan's place, brought about a relaxation and she began to converse with a little more animation with William Reeve. The twins were delighted to be attended by Pat's lieutenants, to be regaled with tales of *Tenedos's* experiences in the deepest and farthest oceans, all events of severe personal setback and bloodthirsty battle being most diligently expunged.

Sinéad in particular passed a most enjoyable time and commented, her pleasure so very evident, on how much she had been enjoying the voyage, 'The crew seem to be in the finest of form, Pat, and such a pleasant band of men too.'

'To be sure,' said Murphy, letting slip a plate which crashed to the table to cover his comment, but raising smiles from the two nearby stewards who heard it and Codrington who pretended he had not.

'Mr Mower... *James*, would you care to read us a poem? Perhaps your most recent one,' asked Pat.

'Why yes, I have it here, sir; 'tis written for my wife, but will serve for all our wives... and today, with your permission, most particularly for Mrs O'Connor.' Mower clutched a wafer of paper taken from his inside pocket. The table quieted as he began, his softly spoken voice bringing complete silence to the great cabin.

*'Amidst the rolling waves of oceans comes the lovely thought of you,*
*Through the soughing of the breezes and the sparkle of the dew,*
*In the shining light of morning and the blackness of the night,*
*Come wondrous recollections and dreams of past delight,*
*In the horror of bitter struggle when my heart is gripped with fear,*
*When my soul seems lost in darkness, blind and frantic, you are near,*
*Giving faith and courage to carry me o'er the steepe roaring sea,*
*In those bleakest of moments, you shine bright in my memory,*
*Bringing rays of sunshine, my tired hopes restored anew,*
*I cast aside the darkness and cherish the lovely thought of you.'*

The contemplative silence around the table remained, all present looking to Sinéad. She smiled as she spoke, 'Why, Mr Mower, that is the most beautiful poem I think I have ever heard. I thank you most kindly and from the bottom of my heart, I do indeed.'

Loud applause erupted from all. 'Thank you kindly, James. A most prodigious talent; genius! Nothing less. I congratulate you,' said Pat amiably as the applause ended.

'Artistic creativity prospers well in the nautical mind! Congratulations, Mr Mower. Capital wine, sir, if I may say,' said Tom Pickering, turning to Pat.

'Thank you; 'tis a particular favourite of mine, a Romanée-Conti, a burgundy of the year 'seventeen. Another glass with you,' replied Pat, swiftly sweeping off the table a bargeman which had crawled out of a biscuit before Sinéad might see it, and stamping it flat on the deck.

'If you insist, sir. Nothing serves dinner like good wine,' Pickering replied, smiling broadly at his host.

With the ladies and girls being present, Wilkins had suggested and Pat had readily agreed to conclude the meal at pudding-time with a huge jam Roly-Poly, now brought out and presented to the table by Freeman, a generous portion of it having been put by in the galley for the later enjoyment of the stewards. This sweet pudding was immensely enjoyed by the two girls, in fact by all, and none escaped the plate's return to the galley. When the meal had concluded, with little marchpane cakes – Murphy having pressed the cook to make them, ostensibly at Pat's personal request but in reality the desire originating solely in himself, marchpane being his particular favourite – the ladies and youngsters retired from the great cabin so that Pat could present what scant briefing he felt able to provide to his officers.

'What are millers, Mr Murphy?' asked Pat's daughter in a whisper as they were escorted out.

'Well, they be the very smallest of the ship's complement, Miss Caitlin,' replied Murphy, stretching his tiny reserves of tact to hitherto unsuspected levels.

'Gentlemen,' the families had departed and Pat commenced his briefing; 'It may be some small puzzle to you that we are sailing to Greece *but will arrive in Genoa* tomorrow. Many reports of the war have come back to governments and unofficial bodies throughout Europe, from diplomatic missions and non-accredited persons. A Greek committee has been established in London - as in so many other capitals - and emissaries despatched to discover the nature of the situation in Greece. One such emissary has recently returned - so we are informed - to

Genoa, and we are to consult with this individual so as to ascertain as much as possible *afore we depart Genoa in escort of Lord Byron...* and arrive in some weeks time in the Ionian Isles...... to commence our service for Greece.

Pat paused to refer to his notes. 'Freeman! Freeman!' he shouted. As the happy black visage of Freeman peered round the door near immediately, Pat declared, 'After such a fine dinner - my compliments to my cook - I find I am in need of a brandy. Light along with a brace of bottles... and bring coffee for all, if you will.' Pat returned to his briefing. 'Gentlemen, we are but one fifth rate to face the combined Turk and Egyptian fleets, of which there be several first rates which we cannot expect to profitably encounter. Yet for the most part their fleet will be split into smaller flotillas throughout the islands. These will be engaged upon transporting stores to their forces widely distributed in the Morea as well as in western Greece. Our mission is to disrupt their commerce, their resupply; to encourage the Greek fleet as much as we can, to discourage the Turk; to bring hope to the Greek peoples throughout the mainland and the islands until better organisation and greater resources can be assembled... and a new and modern Greek fleet is raised and trained. There are plentiful stories in high places of loans to be raised for Greece... of new frigates and steamships yet to be built and purchased, but these will not be here this year... nor indeed *next* year. Yet the war must be sustained with but what little is available until they arrive. We have *Surprise...* and she has beaten many a Frenchman and others. We have a crack crew... and the Turks do not; they are served in large part by slaves, including Greeks. We can go where we please... and appear out of the night to strike hard and disappear, to re-appear where we will, to instil fear into the heart of the Turk. That is our mission, gentlemen, and I will cease prating away about it. I will entertain your questions, if you will.'

At that timely moment, Freeman sidled in with brandy and coffee, having dashed the ready boiling water on to the freshly ground beans the instant after Pat's request, 'Coffee here, massa.'

'Sir, may I ask whether we will be serving alongside the Greek admirals or sailing independently?' asked Tom Pickering.

'A very good point, Mr Pickering. I incline to the independent approach, not least as I expect *Surprise* alone will present a considerable confusion to any Turk she approaches to challenge; and that advantage would not be the case were she in the company of Greek vessels; but perhaps on some occasions we will be acting in concert with them.'

'Where will *Surprise* be based, sir?' came from Mower.

'Afore we begin our active service we will leave Sinéad, Kathleen and the children on Zante, it being a British Possession where they will be quite safe from the Turk. We will be guided by what we find when we arrive there.'

'Speaking without the least authority and with unsurpassed ignorance of all matters naval, may I enquire how long we anticipate voyaging against the Turk... and are we ourselves assured of resupply, Captain O'Connor?' piped up Michael Marston rather unexpectedly and with a deal more confidence than ever hitherto demonstrated in the captain's presence, perhaps since becoming a more frequent visitor to the great cabin.

'We will be roving far and wide throughout the Aegean, Mr Marston... and roundabout the Morea, resupplying in part from our captures - at least in powder and shot - and consuming our shipboard stores until such time as there arises the need for a more plentiful re-provisioning and a refitting, when we will return to England.' Pat explained his intentions, in truth with rather more thinking aloud than he cared to admit.

'Who will pay us for our prizes, sir?' The most prescient question of all came from William Reeve and it sparked an attentiveness amongst all present; indeed, eyes focused and ears pricked up for any reply that might come, for prizes were a most particular element of conversation and aspiration aboard the barky for officers and the people.

'Well, Mr Reeve, I expect that they will be condemned by some Greek prize court and sold, the monies to be held for our account. The specific arrangements we will have to see when we arrive in Greece,' replied Pat with greater confidence than he felt, for he doubted that the smallest part of any proceeds would ever be reimbursed by any Greek body. More questions of lesser significance were posed, but as it became clear that he had no precise answers at this very preliminary stage in the venture it was with some relief to him that the questions did not persist much longer. Eventually, Pat brought his officers attention to his final point with a knuckle rap on the table. He raised his voice slightly, 'Gentlemen, there is one point of the utmost importance which I will explain: Sailing alone we are very likely to encounter more than one Turk vessel; in such circumstances we will be hard pressed to fight them all, and so flight must be our sensible course. However, it will be of the very first importance for our survival - and will serve us well - were we able to fight both sides of the ship at the same time, keeping our distance so that we cannot be boarded. By that I mean fighting with complete crews for *both* sides and none of the running to and fro of the gunners in the customary way. Fighting *both* sides of the ship...' Pat paused to let this sink in as the mood of the cabin changed perceptibly and all eyes widened. 'Fighting both sides of the ship and firing all guns - were we to find ourselves between two Turks - will give us the best prospect of surviving *and of winning*. By all accounts the Turk is no more than an average gunner... not greatly competent. That objective, gentlemen, is where we will direct our training. We will exercise the great guns each day as we approach Greek waters... and damn the cost of the powder. I have some concept of appropriate tactics to fight the Turk, as I will explain when we are ready to exercise our guns. One last thing: as we have no jollies aboard, and so no sharpshooters to send aloft in any engagement, we must find our best dozen marksmen from the crew. There will certainly be poachers and the like familiar with a shotgun and even a musket. Mr Mower, you are to talk with the older hands and see whom you may find.' The conclusion of the meeting came with a degree of relief for a fatigued Pat, not wishing to let his own apprehension show through, and he held up his hand to stay any questions on his gunnery strategy before adding by way of emphatic confirmation, '*That will be all*. Thank you, gentlemen.'

After the officers and Marston had left, the families being still on deck, only Simon remained as Pat asked, 'What do you say to a glass of sillery?'

'Well, if you insist... I do not like to sound inquisitive, dear... but you seemed a whit uncertain... if I might venture the most trifling of observations.'

Pat thought for a moment before he answered, his own doubts permitting only a rhetorical answer, 'I suppose it is no use asking your opinion about the standing of the Greek government and any Admiralty Court that they may possess, and the likelihood of an equitable distribution from any prizes we may take?' A pause. 'Young Reeve was, as all saw, quick off the mark there on this prime question; he hit the hammer square on the head... and likely by now it will be a talking point all about the ship.'

'None whatsoever, my dear. I am no friend of speculation, and my opinion of that would be as valuable as yours on the prospects for a cure for the yellow jack.' Simon had replied to his friend's pessimistic question, rhetorically asked in absence of expectation of any helpful answer, as helpfully as he could. Perceiving a worry on Pat's brow, he continued, 'In so far as the officers and crew will be wondering about the prospects for prizes, for that is sure to be the case... as sure as Hestia's oath, you may care to collect that they consider Captain O'Connor exhibits the wisdom of Solomon in all matters nautical, and any indication from yourself on this matter or any other will surely remain unchallenged on this vessel. There is not the least doubt of that.'

Pat seemed to find this helpful, 'Well, there is something in what you say, and Solomon was - *by all accounts* - a sensible cove. Thank you... and now I believe I will take a turn on deck... take the air.'

Deep in thought he left the cabin and had stepped only a few paces along the gun deck when an indistinct noise caught his attention. From for'ard, from beyond the scores of Monday's shirts hung to dry on lines strung across the deck came the sound of singing. He slowly paced down the deck to hear more, his ear and curiosity intrigued. Beyond the foremast the singing became quite clear, the sound coming from an unfamiliar stringed instrument.

*'So fare ye well, sweet Ascoilemore, our lasses and families all;*
*I'm leaving that fair land, for the great plains us do call;*
*It breaks my heart for us to part, where I spent many happy*
*years;*
*Far away from friends and relations dear, I'm bound for*
  *Amerikay.*

*And above all the skies of the glen was the blue sky,*
*and I heard the birds singing for the dawning of the day,*
*but there was no work in Sutherland forthcoming,*
*just sympathy numbing the going away.'*

Pat espied Maclean singing and his Third, Mower, sitting for'ard near the galley with two others of the crew: Beer and Knightley. The singing ceased as he approached and the instruments were set down. Pat wondered briefly whether there was any convention which might permit or preclude an officer playing whilst accompanied by his crew, but dismissed the thought as he reached the quartet. 'A most pleasing song, Maclean. Indeed, I remarked you were singing with quite the passion. Is Sutherland where you belong?'

'Aye sir; I was there all my life *afore I was evicted from our family home.* The song was written for my brother; he left our home in Ascoilemore and has gone to faraway Canada... to the Red River. Our family was evicted by the Countess - *'tis said she owns near all of Sutherland* - but the bailiffs said she needed our croft; three acres it was... and we lived on its potatoes. I was there when Donald Bannerman - *the Sheriff* - ordered his drunkards to set our bothy afire. My mother was mortally set back; she died within the month, the winter so bitter cold... and I doubt I will ever see my brother again.'

It was an unpalatable tale, and Pat shook his head; he replied in emphatic voice, 'I am most heartily sorry to hear of such damnable actions; indeed, I can scarcely conceive that anyone *save for the most vile blackguard* can countenance them... and serve as a dun.' He turned away to hide his dismay; 'Mr Mower, pray tell me: what is that curious instrument? Is that six strings I see? Is that not a trifle ambitious? 'pon my word we mere mortals struggle to scrape with but four strings.'

'There is no bow, sir; 'tis customary to pick at the strings with fingers.'

'Well, I never! A rum device it is, though for sure it is certainly melodic.'

'It is Spanish in origin, sir. I took it up to set my poems to music, growing tired of the plain words. I bought it in London a few years ago after listening to a Catalan player, Fernando Sor.'

'A Catalan, you say? Our players will be keen to hear the story, no doubt.'

'Near my last half-pay guinea it cost, but when I heard its tone, so warm, I was lost.'

'Mellow it is, indeed. Your guinea was well spent, there is no doubt. We will look forward to hearing your fine playing and your singing in the cabin, Mr Mower. Beer, Knightley, Maclean... good night to you all.'

'Good night, sir,' echoed the reply from all. As Pat strode away, the melodic singing resumed to the gentle background sound of the Spanish strings.

*'And I wish I was by Loch Brora and seated on the grass,*
*And by my side a bottle of whisky, and on my knee a lass;*
*I'd call for her hand and her heart, and offer a kiss afore I go,*
*Then I'd hold my dear brother in my arms, with a lingering*
*grasp so slow.'*

The remainder of Pat's evening was spent very pleasantly with Sinéad who joined him on the quarterdeck until the evening air cooled when they removed to the great cabin, sitting near the stern windows and enjoying private reminiscences of their years together. Duncan and Simon had considerately shifted to join the exchanges in the gun-room. The twins, with Brodie, were being entertained by Kathleen, though they had last been seen pursuing Pat's cook for more marchpane and roly-poly; fruitlessly, Murphy long having removed the first and his mates, true hangers-on, having consumed the second.

'You lead a very happy crew, husband; that is sure, even to my inexpert eye in these matters. And, if I am not wide of the mark, you are yourself most splendidly pleased to be here... to return once more to voyaging in this ship... in the company of

Doctor Ferguson and Duncan.' A long pause. 'Will *we* be happy again upon our return to Claddaghduff, would you think?' asked Sinéad, her distraught voice wavering, perfectly in key with her spirits.

Pat gazed into his wife's moistening eyes with deep benevolence. 'Be not concerned for that in the slightest, Sinéad, my love. I have been at sea since I was much younger even than the twins; I have lived my life always in the company of sailors; fortunately, with the very best of companions in Duncan and Simon. Indeed, Simon has saved my life you know, when I was shot in a cutting out party...' Sinéad gasped. 'Did I never mention that to you? *Perhaps not.* We have seen many a successful cruise in *Tenedos*; success that has been the founding of our home and farm; 'tis ever the place which I very much look forward to coming home to, to be with you there... and I dare say I will not be at sea for many more years, my love, afore I am laid up... *in ordinary...* as we sailors say. Until then, in those few more years I have at sea, it is my dearest wish to see them out in command of a proper fighting ship such as *Surprise;* and since we have long since seen off Boney then there will be but few ventures in which we can profitably engage. All of us aboard do hope that this is one such voyage. Nor do I say *profitably* wholly in the mercenary sense; no, far from it; there are few men in this crew who *need* to serve again at sea, many of them having taken very substantial prize monies to their homes in Falmouth in the years of the French wars. No, I find a sense of contentment in this crew, a satisfaction founded on returning to our home at sea; for that is how we all feel about *Surprise*. Though usually we have no wives here nor any of our children, we share the companionship of those that have served with us for many years; we are together, officers and the people.' Pat hesitated as his wife became visibly distressed.

'Are you chasing after money?' she murmured in quiet voice, 'We have no great need of more if we hold to a modest life.'

'The most modest, perhaps,' replied Pat doubtfully. 'No, no, my dear; all are here not for the prizes... *though none would ever admit that*; no, we are here because this is where we have all spent the greater part of our lives, and we are comfortable in the traditions of the ship and the service, each man secure in the steady routines of the day – unchanging routines – as sure as the sun will rise in the morning; and that is pleasing to us all. So you see, my love, we are fortunate, all of us: we have *two* homes, but we all begin to see that we will serve in our shipboard home only for a very few more years... and that is really why we are here, all of us to a man enjoying the time we have left aboard, in our dear *Surprise*. We are content also in that we know – *we know* – that we will be coming to our other home... *our home ashore*, to our beloved wives, to our children... and in a near time which will be with us almost afore we know it. Is that a satisfactory answer to your question, my love?' Pat concluded, observing Sinéad's tear-filled eyes with great concern and seizing his wife, now overcome, into his arms in a crushing embrace.

'Oh, my darling, I love you so much,' was all that Sinéad could whisper in reply, blinking rapidly as the tears now flowed in great streams down her cheeks.

During the next day, the final day of *Surprise's* voyage to Genoa, the weather and sea state remained as tranquil as all those that had preceded it. As the warmth of the day faded with the sun sinking into the horizon of the western sky, leaving behind a splendid residual sunset, *Surprise* passed the western mole and La Lanterna to larboard and entered the harbour of Genoa under reefed topsails, slowing as they were backed, and coming gently to a stop, letting slip her anchor three cables off the quay.

*Wednesday 2nd July 1823*                    *Port of Genoa*

After the hammocks had been piped up and stowed, after the hands had eaten breakfast and the decks had been washed, the men lowered all of *Surprise's* boats into the water alongside. Her proximity to the Old Pier would greatly facilitate the taking on board of water and other provisions. With an unknown departure date, Lord Byron's specific plans not being known to either Pat or Duncan, the near quayside anchorage was considerably more convenient for going ashore, Pat anticipating much use of his barge.

'Duncan, pray tell, is there anything yet unremarked from Melville on the matter of our task to escort Lord Byron?' asked Pat as they, with Simon and Marston, were enjoying tea and a slow second breakfast in the great cabin. 'We must acquaint ourselves with his Lordship's intentions in detail. Do you know anything more of his plans, his travel plans particularly?'

Duncan looked up from his bacon and eggs, 'Lord Byron travelled previously in the eastern Mediterranean in the company of his longstanding friend, Hobhouse, now a luminary of the Greek Committee. I have here a letter of introduction from Hobhouse, given to me by Lowrey afore we left London, and I will send this to Byron's residence today. In a day or twae I imagine we will call upon his Lordship.'

'Until then, might I suggest that we take a day to see this magnificent city?' Simon interjected, sensing a rare moment of leisure at hand, wiping the grease from his chin onto his sleeve. 'It is a tolerably significant city for you mariners. By all reports one Christopher Columbus originated here, a mariner you may be familiar with. Those of us of the faith, of a more devout persuasion, will I say, are visiting the Basilica of San Lorenzo - Saint Lawrence in the English parlance. Duncan, Brodie and Kathleen are with me, Sinéad and the twins too.'

'I am not greatly familiar with Saint Lawrence,' murmured Pat with a bare modicum of attentiveness; 'Was he of considerable or even particular significance to those of a generally clerical leaning?'

'He was the primary of those seven deacons of Rome who were appointed by Pope Sixtus,' declared Marston, not detecting any real enthusiasm from Pat. He decided a degree of interest might carry his story, 'But his head was ordered to be cut off by Emperor Valerian. Indeed, the reliquary which contains his head is retained within the Basilica.'

Silence at the table; blank, speechless stares prevailed, until Pat spoke up at last, his voice expressing plain his disbelief, 'His head is in the church... *his head?*'

'Indeed, it is,' Marston continued, 'and Dr Ferguson, Mr Macleod and his family and I intend to visit to pay our respects today.'

'God between us and all evil,' declared Pat with vehemence. 'I was always of the opinion that saints - *of all people* - enjoyed a degree of protection from such brutal oppression... that they might reasonably expect to retain their head,' he remarked with an audible degree of despond.

'I do not believe he was generally recognised as a saint at that time,' said Simon.

'Oh, indeed? Murphy! Pass the word for Barton!' Pat shouted. 'Why, perhaps I will join you; I would not wish to appear singular.' He smiled, bowing to his friends' arrangements in pleasant accord.

Pat's cox'n entered within moments and touched his forehead. 'Barton, be so good as to deliver a letter ashore for Lord Byron from Mr Macleod. He will give you the letter directly. You may require a local guide.' Pat had by now established that Barton was of a similar, reliable ilk to his much lamented, deceased brother and had begun to pass small tasks of some significance to him.

At that moment Sinéad and Kathleen entered the great cabin, both in a state of excitement with the prospect of going ashore and the appeal of an escape from the close accommodation of *Surprise*. The near total absence of personal privacy was beginning to grate after the month's voyage. The youngsters too, the novelty of shipboard life fading, were beginning to evidence some youthful truculence and impatience with the shipboard routine. 'Will you be long, Duncan?' asked Kathleen.

'Not at all, my dear; just a wee few minutes and I will be with ye. We will all be with ye. Simon is minded to accompany us, and Pat too.' Duncan diligently wiped his plate of all egg remnants with the last piece of his bread.

'We will await you all on deck,' shouted Sinéad in high good spirits as the ladies left the great cabin.

'I will find the introductory letter for Barton. It is in my seachest. I will briefly scribe an accompanying note, and I will be with ye directly,' said Duncan.

'I will also be ready presently,' declared Simon.

'I suppose you could shave and change later,' suggested Pat sarcastically, a comment wholly disregarded by his friend.

The visit to the cathedral was a resounding success, the ladies and the youngsters being overwhelmed by the grandeur and scale of the edifice and its environs. Never before had they seen a city of such historic substance. Their walking tour continued for some hours, taking in the splendour of the palaces of the Strada Nuova before the long walk the length of the harbour to visit La Lanterna, the ancient lighthouse. In the late afternoon the long day of walking had quite tired them out, and so the youngsters were considerably more subdued walking back to *Surprise*, which was a relief to Pat.

After supper Murphy entered the cabin clutching a letter which he presented to Duncan who declared, 'Pat, 'tis a reply from Lord Byron. His Lordship has invited us to attend him on Friday.'

*Friday 4$^{th}$ July 1823*                                      *Albaro, Genoa*

After dinner, Pat, Duncan, Simon, Sinéad and Kathleen set off to stroll the near three miles to Byron's home, guided by Barton, walking up, down and through narrow streets that only gradually widened as they walked further from the port and higher up the hill of Albaro until, pausing for a brief measure of relief from their exertions, they enjoyed a commanding view over the harbour and the city. They gazed at the splendid panorama of the bay before resuming their climb, eventually coming with some relief to the Villa Saluzzo as they began to tire in the enduring heat of the late afternoon, all perspiring freely.

The maid ushered them in and served welcome jugs of punch. After a few minutes, which were most gratefully appreciated for recovery from their exertions, Lord Byron entered the drawing room and nodded towards his visitors. He walked with a limp on account of his club foot. He was a tall man in his mid thirties but looked older, youth having faded from his face, some spark having been lost; his curly auburn hair was now streaked with grey, his thin moustache near white. Yet he nevertheless retained an impression of energy, of quick interest; his large, luminous blue eyes exuded a sense of restlessness. 'Byron,' he said simply, offering his hand to Pat.

'Your most humble... devoted, sir,' mumbled Pat, unsure of protocol in the company of the most celebrated of contemporary writers. 'I am Captain Patrick O'Connor. Thank you for your invitation, my Lord. May I present my wife, Sinéad; my first lieutenant, Duncan Macleod; his wife, Kathleen; and my surgeon, Dr Simon Ferguson, who is also a natural philosopher.'

Lord Byron appeared to be in fine good humour and seemed genuinely pleased to receive his visitors. 'A pleasure to meet you all,' he declared with smiles all round. He was accompanied by a man with long black hair, bushy sideboards and an aquiline nose, dressed in - so the ladies thought - rather untidy clothing that seemed to have seen better days, an observation which never occurred to Simon. He continued, 'We are favoured today and it pleasures me exceedingly to present my earlier visitor, Signor Niccolò Paganini, the celebrated composer and violinist, a son of Genoa. He is residing here at his mother's home to recuperate from recent illness. He has called upon me to discuss my poem, *Childe Harold's Pilgrimage*. He has but a modest grasp of English and converses generally in Italian or French.'

Paganini bowed to the ladies and shook hands with the gentlemen. Simon scrutinised him professionally: he did not look well, an undefined air of malaise about him, but then again he had treated sailors that looked far, far worse. 'Un grand plaisir, monsieur, enchanté,' said Simon with some passion and a reverential nod of his head, being acquainted with Paganini's music, if not his playing.

Lord Byron continued, 'Before Signor Paganini leaves very shortly, he has most graciously offered to play his most recent solo piece. Please to follow me if you will.' Byron led the party to the music room where Paganini took up his violin and, without any preamble at all, began to play. In the five minutes that followed, the audience were bewitched by the most animated playing by a standing Paganini; his wonderfully dextrous fingering and bowing simply surpassed anything they had ever seen and heard before; his violin came to vibrant, resonant life in his skilful hands; and his music was utterly, blissfully exceptional to the ears of Pat - a talented cellist himself - and to Simon too, a considerably accomplished musician with the viola.

The flowing skill of Paganini was of an overwhelming virtuosity, unparalleled in anything that any of them had ever encountered before; the most vibrant long notes were held in the air for an age, others intensely resonated beyond that which Pat and Simon thought possible. The flowing continuity of the bow, Paganini's wrists flexing and shifting at astonishing speed, would have been simply beyond belief had they not been watching, whilst the sublime music and his playing of it was infinitely gratifying in its utter perfection. At the end they were in a state of near disbelief, almost of shock, at what they had seen and heard, before clapping from Sinéad and Kathleen jolted them from stunned silence to vigorous applause.

'Caprice vingt-quatre,' Paganini said simply before bowing to his tiny audience.

'My dear sir,' said Simon (in French), 'that was uncommon magnificent. We have never heard the like. We are both of us keen scrapers; indeed, we are; yet we could never aspire to such wonders, never in life... overwhelmed... We thank you most kindly, sir.'

'Merci, merci,' was all that an astounded Pat could utter before turning to Simon to suggest that he should invite Signor Paganini to dine aboard *Surprise*. 'Perhaps he could bring his violin,' he added as an afterthought, 'Signor Paganini's schedule in Genoa permitting.' To Pat's deep satisfaction Simon's reiteration of his invitation was accepted with evident pleasure, Paganini adding something along the lines of 'seeking Doctor Ferguson's opinion', although it was somewhat beyond Pat's pidgin French to fully understand, but Simon bowed to the great man and offered his hand.

After Paganini's departure the ladies remained in the music room, enjoying punch whilst the gentlemen shifted to the drawing room. 'My Lord,' Pat began, 'I have but recently become acquainted with the nascent developments in the Ottoman Greek provinces, coincident with my resignation from His Majesty's service. Lieutenant Macleod and I attended the London Greek Committee some few weeks ago, and having heard of your intended participation as an emissary of the Committee, perhaps we may be of some small service.' Pat ended his rather brief and vague explanation, not wishing to dwell on the background to his particular circumstances, and he awaited Byron's response.

'My dear O'Connor... that is most kind,' Byron smiled. 'However, my banker has located and I have already engaged a ship, *Hercules*, Captain Scott commanding, to convey my party from Genoa to Zante in some few days time. It is generally held that the Turks are preparing a large expedition for the suppression of the rising. I am fully disposed to assist the Greek cause and with every means at my disposal, hence my departure to offer my personal assistance. I now await only correspondence from Blaquiere, an emissary of the Committee who is already in the Morea, before we depart.'

Pat hesitated in thought very briefly before concluding the meeting, 'Well, sir, I am delighted that our aspirations are therefore similar. We are sailing to seek the Turk fleet, which - *doubtless* - is a constituent of the expedition you refer to. Allow me to congratulate you on your admirable intentions, and we wish you success in your noble endeavours.' With that they took their leave.

The next few days were passed in taking onboard those few stores which had been omitted in the hectic provisioning of *Surprise* in Plymouth and Falmouth. In respect of the sick bay, the crew shifted everything about to the satisfaction of Simon's assistant, Michael Marston. He being of an exceedingly tidy disposition, he was striving with an evident desire to please his master, to ensure every medication was readily at hand. The atmosphere onboard *Surprise* generally was relaxed, the crew having cleaned every conceivable part of the ship, all revelling still in their homecoming as they saw it, even to the extent that they had stripped the aged and peeling black paint from all the cannon during the voyage and then rubbed them down to the iron before repainting layer upon layer afresh until the guns looked as if they had left the manufactory that day, their new black paint gleaming pristine in the bright sun. They had also repainted the chequerboard sides of the ship with a precision that impressed every inspection, Pat insisting on the crew painting the Nelson yellow bands along the hull. All aboard concurred that it was a magnificent idea, the few Trafalgar veterans in particular being highly gratified. The officers had barely any need to direct the ship's activities, the crew being volunteers to a man, confident in their assured prospects under Pat's command for substantial prizes.

The ladies, Brodie and the twins were for the most part ashore in Genoa each day and even most evenings, enjoying the temperate early summer of the northern Mediterranean latitude, there being little for them to do aboard. They had hardly any domestic duties, Murphy being very jealous of and robustly resisting any attempted incursion into his personal province of care for Pat and Simon's accommodation and laundry – albeit it could have been argued that a little further help might have been justifiable in Simon's case.

*Wednesday 9th July 1823*                                    *Port of Genoa*

During the morning that Pat was to dine in the gun-room with his officers, word was received that Paganini was to come aboard to join them. To the astonishment and pleasure of the hands, the man delivering the message was a familiar face, a former comrade who had served with many of them long years ago in the Mediterranean. Giobatta Repetto was a native of Genoa, retired from sea service and now - still active in his late sixties - he delivered letters around the town for important personages including Byron and Paganini.

Pat was sure he had met the man and invited him into the cabin. 'We have met before, I collect, yet I cannot fathom your name.'

'Repetto sir, if you please,' the greying, old man touched his forehead.

'Ah... Repetto, yes, it comes back to me... It must be seven years or more since we were shipmates. I collect you was with us when we sank *Iskander* and captured *Half Moon*... larboard watch, *Hurricane* gunner - am I right? It was back in the year 'sixteen... so it was. It is greatly pleasing to see you again, so it is! You look in fine fettle, if I may say so,' said Pat, smiling, 'Are you keeping well?'

'Splendidamente, Comandante,' Repetto bowed, smiling broadly and deeply pleased that he had been remembered. He stood in silence, in awe and with transparent delight, being once again in his esteemed former captain's presence. He was pressed by Pat, with whom he soon commenced bantering about past voyages, to enjoy a glass or two in the cabin whilst Simon read the letter which Repetto had brought, mindful of the possibility of a reply being necessary. The subject of the letter revealed, Repetto declared that he was also a keen and proficient chef, and willing to help in the preparation of local Ligurian and Genoese specialities. Without further ado he was speedily introduced to Pat's cook.

Later Paganini was welcomed aboard with the utmost cordiality, and the much awaited dinner meandered through Repetto's simply stunning three courses; he had served them well: *zemin de ceci,* a chick-pea soup, followed by an exquisite *pansoti* pasta with spinach and walnut sauce; and finally a delectable cod stockfish cooked with potatoes, raisins and pine nuts in a tomato sauce. Nothing like it had ever graced Pat's table and the sublime food was a great success; the Genoese cuisine, unfamiliar as it was to the Surprises and the ladies - who marvelled at it - was relished by all in the most convivial of ambience. Several hours passed by in cordial dialogue and banter, Simon translating from Paganini's French to English for Pat's officers who were being very welcoming to their most distinguished visitor ever. Paganini himself ate sparingly and seemingly with a little difficulty, but he complimented effusively the food and the wine, though drinking little.

'Wilkins, there you are!' Pat cried out as the summoned chefs bowed to acknowledge the collective thanks at the end of the meal, 'Will I look to Repetto coming aboard or can you raise your game?' A great burst of laughter all around the table reflected the joyful mood.

Late afternoon slipped pleasantly into early evening with a pleasing acceptance by a relaxed Paganini of Pat's invitation to play for a short while. 'Perhaps your *Caprice vingt-quatre,*' said Pat tentatively, adding, '*Your* presence - *your playing* - on deck will be a delight for our people.'

With surprising alacrity, considerable bottles having been consumed during the feast, Mower and Codrington fetched the chairs from Pat's cabin out on to the gun deck, the two stewards bringing more from the gun-room. The officers and the ladies settled to listen to the maestro; the crew too, alerted, were all gathered about the gun deck in anticipation, alerted by the stewards, quite a press of them attending, an ambience of joviality abounding. The men had already enjoyed their supper and grog, and with little to do as the day slipped away the impromptu prospect of music was very welcome to them indeed. They settled, sitting about the fore part of the deck, the hubbub of conversation dying in anticipation. Paganini did not disappoint, launching into Pat's particular request and playing with consummate passion and skill, his bow flowing with an elasticity which Pat, Simon and Marston could only marvel at, his fingers shifting to positions that they simply could not comprehend how he had attained them. His music consumed all those listening to it, touching hearts and minds, its unrivalled and exquisite excellence registering even with the least musically-inclined old tars, the sounds reaching deep beyond their ears and, to their astonishment, striking chords within their souls such that all other thoughts were wholly eclipsed, and every man present gazed in wonder and utter silence as Paganini played the piece until, with a final flourish of his bow, it reached its unwanted end. The conclusion of this, the most magical playing that all had ever heard in their lives, was followed by raucous, uninhibited appreciation from all the ship's company, a riot of cheering, whistling and stamping of feet upon the deck.

'That,' said Paganini to his hosts after a bow to his audience, his face radiating with satisfaction, 'is how it plays in paradise.'

Pat, recovering from his absolute concentration in the music, complimented Paganini profusely, 'Very finely played, sir; the beauty of the world, so it was.' The sun was beginning to sink towards the horizon but the evening remained comfortably warm. Pat inclined towards and whispered to Simon, 'How I wish I could play like that, eh? Will I ask him... that is to say, would you think he might favour us by playing with us? We will never have the chance again.'

Simon simply smiled, his lingering contentment clutched firm as if to ensure its memory and precluding any contemplation of Pat's question. A deeply pleased and now somewhat emboldened Pat ventured to ask Paganini, 'Perhaps Signor Paganini would consent to playing just a very little more... and accompanied by the ship's musicians.' He was delighted, near overcome with pleasure, when his request was accepted. 'Murphy! Barton! Rouse out our instruments from the cabin; quickly now, there is no time to be lost.'

'Well, they be here already, awaiting your say so, sorr,' Murphy pronounced with a wide smile of perfect self-satisfaction, Pat's 'cello under his arm and carrying the violin; Old Jim Lamb held the viola and bows. With their instruments, the trio of Pat, Simon and Marston took their places alongside Paganini. They began, slowly at first as all adapted to their fellows, with Corelli's *Christmas Concerto grosso*, followed by a magnificent rendition of one of Pat's particular favourites, Boccherini's cheerful *La musica notturna delle strade di Madrid* - to Pat's mind a piece ideally suited to the collective shipboard temperament. It was a near twenty minutes of the most sublime playing by Paganini on first violin and waves of sheer musical bliss soaked up by the accompanying trio. It was with the utmost satisfaction and shared congratulations, akin to disbelief, that the piece came to its end. Vigorous applause followed once more from all the enrapt crew, young and old, *Surprise's* grizzled veterans realising that they were in the presence of genius. Simon and Marston rose as one, embraced, slapping their mutual backs while the delighted ladies smiled and clapped until their hands were sore.

'Och, that was the most glorious piece of music I think I have ever heard,' said Duncan, his voice trembling with conviction.

'Prodigious!' declared Pat in loud voice, for he could find no other word in his amazement, his pleasure, all so completely overpowering.

As the applause died down and the quartet took their bow, Barton and Evans - a popular Welshman living in Falmouth and a tolerably fine tenor - quickly stepped up in front of the players and turned to the crew. Barton furiously waved the applause and chatter to silence.

'What's afoot?' a puzzled Pat muttered.

From Evan's deep booming voice came the stirring first verse of *Heart of Oak*,

*'Come, cheer up, my lads, 'tis to glory we steer,*
*To add something more to this wonderful year;*
*To honour we call you, as freemen not slaves,*
*For who are so free as the sons of the waves?'*

With only the slightest of pause the happy and delighted crew, more than two hundred of them now on deck, by way of their own thanks and appreciation scrambled swiftly to their feet and without hesitation joined the chorus of the song, the Royal Navy's traditional anthem, singing with great gusto and enthusiasm.

*'Heart of oak are our ships; jolly tars are our men;*
*We always are ready; steady, boys, steady!*
*We'll fight and we'll conquer again and again.'*

At the end of the song an animated and impressed Paganini clapped his hands and turned to Simon. 'Bravo! Bravo! Cher amis, nous avons trouvé un petit coin de paradis ce soir!'

Pat, who had expected nothing like this, such a deeply pleasing and spontaneous gesture from the crew, beamed with evident delight, still speechless. The crew continued to cheer Paganini with great shouts of 'Hurrah! Hurrah!' At the conclusion of this revelry, Paganini and Simon with Marston retired to the great cabin in close discussion. Pat thanked the crew profusely for their impromptu singing, 'Barton, Evans... thank you kindly. Well done! Well done indeed! Barton, please thank the lads for a most generous gesture, most kind indeed, thankee. Mr Mower, an extra issue of grog to the crew, if you will.' He returned in high good humour to the gun-room with his officers, the ladies retiring to settle the girls and Fergal in their cots below.

In the cabin, Simon and Marston conversed with Paganini. He had sought a consultation with Simon when they had met at

Byron's house. They conversed in French which fortunately neither Freeman nor Murphy, both listening behind the cabin door, were able to understand. To put Paganini more at his ease Marston assured him that Simon had an Edinburgh medical degree, had studied Paré and had been consulted by no less a dignitary than the First Lord, Melville; and it was widely understood that he had also been considered as a candidate for Physician of the Fleet, though Simon had discreetly demurred. A clearly less anxious Paganini described his symptoms and treatment, 'I have been ill since January. I consulted Dr Borda of Pavia during June following weight loss and severe coughing up of sputum. Dr Borda has prescribed opium for my severe laryngeal cough and mercury for hidden syphilitic infection. I take the blue pill.'

Simon responded cautiously, 'Sir, your account does not suggest any fatal issue, and we are unable to differ with your own physician and his diagnosis, he being presumably more acquainted with your medical history than we. Yet, in candour, I must caution you against excessive and prolonged treatment with mercury, for such will most surely lead to undoubted deterioration of the physical state of the larynx and the gums, and to loss of teeth and general ill health. The consequences of the mercury will be far, far worse than the mere possibility of the emergence of hidden syphilitic infection. Mercury is generally recognised as effective principally in the early, *the very early* stage of syphilitic infection... as we see so often aboard ship. As the finest musician it has ever been my pleasure and great good fortune to hear, I must also caution you that the accumulation of mercury over some considerable time will lead to tremors in the hands. Surely you, the master of the most exquisite violin I have ever heard, would wish at all costs to avoid that?' Simon's voice and mind filled with infinite sadness, regretting bitterly that he could offer no more optimistic a prognosis to this unequalled musical genius.

Paganini sighed, his disappointment so evident in his face. He spoke in halting French, Marston translating, 'Dr Ferguson, Mr Marston, I am obliged to you both for your ministrations and professional advice, for which I thank you most sincerely.'

All shook hands, the two surgeons lingering in the last moments with their visitor, as if to save the moment, to preserve the memory of their encounter. Shortly afterwards Paganini departed, leaving behind an exquisite musical memory to be treasured by scores of men for the rest of their days.

'Was your consultation of any service to our guest, Simon?' asked Pat.

'Oh, I could not possibly say. Certainly, Marston and I passed some time contemplating on the efficacies of familiar processes.' Simon paused, unwilling to add anything of a confidence. Seeing Pat's frown, a self-evident concern for the esteemed patient, he continued after a moment, 'We may consider further of our interest in mercury, which in some instances will prove disappointing.'

'Yes, he is of little use for navigation, though assuredly of astronomical interest.'

'So I have always understood, but what I meant was the metallic element of mercury, brother; it is used in the blue pill.'

'Oh, I beg pardon. As to our guest's playing, we will never hear finer, never in life. Of that I am sure.'

# Chapter Seven

*In vain - in vain: strike other chords;*
*Fill high the cup with Samian wine!*
*Leave battles to the Turkish hordes,*
*And shed the blood of Scio's vine!*
*Hark! rising to the ignoble call -*
*How answers each bold Bacchanal*

*Tuesday 15ᵗʰ July 1823      Thyrrhenian Sea, bound for Leghorn*

Becalmed in Genoa for several days and no contact having been established with the anticipated emissary from the Ionians or the Morea, nor having received any further instructions from Lowrey or Melville, Pat was anxious not to lose more time idling in port. Such inactivity was wont to lead the crew into predictably regrettable diversions. *Surprise* and *Eleanor* therefore now left harbour, preceding *Hercules*. The wind, having risen little above a breeze since dawn, had further dropped to a near calm as two bells were rung. Pat had not left his quarterdeck since rising, the south-westerly *Libeccio* making for a very slow departure from the harbour and something of a laborious task, frequent tacking a necessity to make any progress at all until they were well past the entrance and La Lanterna left far astern.

'Precious little wind, sir,' said Pickering.

'Indeed. Though look to those high clouds, shifting along sprightly. I think we may see a blow tonight; 'til then let us put the fire hoses on the sails and we may see another half knot.'

'Aye aye, sir; engines to wet the sails. Mr Prosser, if you please.'

By mid-morning the frigate hardly raised a wake with every stitch of canvas set including royals, and her studdingsails were boomed out both aloft and alow. Pat retired to the cabin for a late breakfast. 'Freeman! Look alive there! Light along and rouse out my cook, and see what can be found in the line of bacon, eggs and plenty of soft tack.'

227

This came as no surprise to Murphy, waiting alongside Freeman and accustomed as he was to his captain's preferences after so many years. 'Well, 'tis all been a'waiting these two hours past. To be sure, 'tis all ruined,' he muttered as Freeman scuttled away to the galley.

By the time Pat had eaten his solitary breakfast, the ruination of which he had scarcely noticed, and returned to his quarterdeck there was more than a fierce drizzle sweeping the deck, for the wind had freshened considerably and was rather stronger than a comfortable topsail breeze. He wiped his eyes for the umpteenth time and made a swift assessment, shouting in full voice, 'Mr Macleod, let us get the stuns'ls in and the top-gallants off her as quick as quick can be!'

*Surprise* was now making respectable progress on a broad reach, well heeled to larboard, the necessity for tacking now long gone; indeed, she was demonstrating what she was capable of, her clean copper-bottomed hull cutting through the water and thrusting out great waves of flying spray and cleaving her passage through the violent turbulence of large waves as if impeded only by air in a spectacular display of speed akin to a carriage with a score of racing horses; huge showers of foam were flying everywhere as she ploughed down and up through the troughs, and the wind had long begun whistling loudly in the rigging, the stuns'ls and royals long since taken off her.

Within a half-hour, her royal and topgallant yards had been struck down, the topgallant masts housed on deck, and the lookouts had been called down from the mastheads which were rapidly becoming a precarious place for a man. Duncan Macleod, Tom Pickering and James Mower all stood by on the quarterdeck, heavy rain washing the face of every man. 'My duty and compliments, sir,' announced Pickering with a degree of trepidation in hs voice; 'The glass is dropping fast, and I think you are proven right. What a change! Not long afore we see a greater storm.'

Pat gazed about him, delighting in the progress but assessing the weather and contemplating the strain on the new sails. 'Mr Pickering, signal *Eleanor* to proceed independently to Leghorn. Yes, indeed; I do smell very bad weather coming... and she may not keep station with us. Mr Mower, she is behaving a trifle skittish; heave the line.'

The line indicated a not unexpected acceleration to a swift eleven knots, according with Pat's growing uneasiness as he surveyed the sky to the west, voluminous dark grey clouds having now near blotted out the sun. The temperature had also fallen noticeably and the storm winds were upon them, cross seas exerting an irregularity upon previously regimented crests. The high-pitched whine of the wind in the rigging had risen to an alarming degree and a greater profusion of furious spray was abounding all over the decks, a great profusion of foam flung up and over the lee rail. The ladies had long since retired from the quarterdeck to the relative comfort of the gun-room. 'Mr Macleod, we will double-reef her courses, we will brace in the upper yards just a very little - I do not care to see any spars knocked away - and we will have the fore-staysail set with double sheets.'

'Aye aye, sir,' Duncan reiterated the orders to the men in loud voice.

Another hour passed and the storm winds had strengthened further; rain sheets swept the decks in voluminous torrents akin to an onrushing wave and greatly more prolific spray flew in such dense profusion that simply keeping eyes open presented a challenge, every man on deck blinking rapidly every few seconds. All communication was difficult and shouting was a necessity beyond a few yards. 'Mr Macleod, we will take down the jib and flying jib!' bawled Pat. 'Mr Pickering, we will lash the gripes *diagonally* across the boats - *and double them while you are at it!*'

'She is steering ardent, sir!' shouted the master from adjacent to the helm, two men at the wheel and plainly working hard. 'She is carrying weather helm!'

'Is she griping?' shouted Pat in reply.

'No, sir,' Prosser cried out.

'Bring her to the wind! Luff!' exclaimed Pat, taking a step towards him to explain his assessment. 'I venture 'tis the new weather wheel rope stretching. She looks to be in good trim... the yards are all a-tanto.'

'Aye aye, sir. Luff and lie!' the master shouted to the helmsmen, adding after a few minutes when he regained the wheel, 'Steady so!'

'A considerable change since the early morning, for sure,' said a hesitant Simon, who had with difficulty joined the officers on the quarterdeck and who clung with the desperate grip of both hands to a backstay. He shouted in disgruntled voice to Pat, 'We are shifting with considerable celerity... and with a resumption of the customary frenetic haste which is such a lamentable attribute of this nautical dominion... *I dare say on some form of bowline*... and doubtless with a plethora of back-braces and preventer-tackles... and numerous other such mariner's mechanisms engaged.'

Pat smiled, 'You are seeing her at her best; she is certainly being put to her shifts!'

'No doubt,' Simon cried out with a look of incomprehension, his concept of best being far, far different to Pat's; 'But there is an exceptionally discomfiting lean.'

'*List*; it is the perfectly natural tilt to her lee side. But what brings you to take the deck in this weather?' asked Pat, surprised to see his friend.

'It is scarcely less comfortable in the cabin, where Murphy is kicking up a loud commotion... all our cots and vestments getting wet; I swear he also mentioned Bob's-a-dying... although I do not believe there is anyone so unfortunate... so severely indisposed... but, may I say - *with emphasis* - there is a veritable tumult of water coming in... incessantly dripping from the ceiling.'

'I dare say the Dock caulkers have skimped their duty and her working has exposed it; the wicked dogs! Mr Sampays and Mr Tizard will doubtless have their hands full when we raise Leghorn.'

An exasperated Simon laboured his disquietude, 'Will I also say... there is a deal of urgent activity throughout the entirety of this vessel; I saw it as I endeavoured to manage the stairs... and a most erratic exercise that was.'

''Indeed, there is a heavy swell with us and, I venture, dirty weather ahead.'

'Ahead? *Ahead, did you say?* Did I ever mention your leanings towards understatement?'

Pat affected not to notice the remark, wanting nothing to disturb his obvious exhilaration, the least thing. 'We are under close-reefed tops'ls and courses, and making fully thirteen knots! Why, I dare say that with this press of canvas and at this speed we could raise Alexandria by dawn, eh?' Pat laughed out loud in a hearty bellow but Simon stared, speechless and disgruntled.

'Lord, how do you preserve such calm, *such equanimity* - indeed, it is nothing less than a disconcerting ataraxy - in the face of these most intemperate... *these exceedingly vigorous* billows; tell?'

'I do so love a blow,' exclaimed Pat with evident pleasure, 'and this may be a right stronger one than I expected... but there is nothing like it for setting a man up... to see who is a right proper salty dog and who is a half-pint lubber...'

'Just how salty does one have to be in order to shed the derogatory diminutive?' Simon was increasingly discomfited and shouted loud in testy voice.

Pat blinked to clear water from his eyes and hesitated, recognising his friend's apprehension. 'But with the ladies and children aboard we will treat her tenderly,' he bellowed.

'I had supposed that our departure from Genoa might have been predicated on indications of propitious weather... such that we might have avoided this extreme aqueous adversity!' screamed Simon, wiping the spray from his face.

Pat's appreciation of a blow was not something with which Simon personally accorded, despite his now long years as his seafaring companion. The rising violence of the waves had for the past hour sent spray flying across the waist of the ship, and the few crew of the duty watch that still remained on deck had long donned oilskins and awaited the next order to further reduce sail. Pat was now certain of his suspicions and turned to Simon, 'It is coming on to blow hard indeed. Look to the leeward clouds - *to leeward* - where you can see the wind-galls - *the brighter halo* - all about the cloud edges; to the mariner that portends storm. If the wind much strengthens and if this dirty weather becomes uncomfortable... then we may have to lay to.'

231

'What? What did you say - *if* it becomes uncomfortable?' Simon bawled into the wind, clutching his tightly buttoned but inadequate coat, heavy rain soaking him and the deck rearing up beneath him before sinking as fast into the trough of the steep swell, the rapid and contrary motions most unsettling. 'Pray tell, just how uncomfortable would it have to be? It is very disagreeable up here! 'tis a dreich day! I am fair drookit. I do not wish to sound discontented, but will this infernal hurricane last long, would you think?'

'Why, of that there is no sure thing... no telling: one day, perhaps two or three if we are unlucky. I would not care to say... I do not wish to tempt fate.' At that moment, as *Surprise's* bow rose from the depths of the trough, she was struck full by the wind and rolled violently until her lee gunwhale was nearly subsumed within the furious bow wake streaming along her side, the unexpected ferocity of the lurch throwing Simon violently to the deck where he lay on his back but sliding towards the scuppers, borne by the torrential wash of water. The men at the helm started, two of the four on duty hastening to the scene, pausing only for Pat's nod to take up the surgeon. They rapidly hauled a bedraggled Simon to his feet with ignominious abandon.

'I do not much care for the navigator's horrible burden... another of these vile tempests... such inclement weather... such forceful squalls,' shouted a humiliated Simon in ill-temper, scowling whilst gathering his senses; 'and now my shirt and coat are beyond cold... and the damnable wet has entirely soaked in.'

'Your grego is the only sure attire in this weather; why ain't you wearing it?' asked Pat, his alternating concentration wholly shifting to his dishevelled friend and his clothing, more nearly resembling a sodden and shapeless cloth rag.

'My mind was turned elsewhere... doubtless afflicted by the reminder that we are living in a small wooden compartment - *cabin* - which is damp and lacking in the least comfort... *and the violent motions*... the cumulative tally, no doubt, weighing heavy upon my contemplations.'

'I see. Well, you had best go below and away from the falling damps,' said Pat, with difficulty saving himself from a mischievous smirk, 'for they are falling uncommon aplenty.'

'The blessed notion has been affixed in my mind these few minutes,' exclaimed Simon with despondence plain on his face.

'Get along now; Murphy will assist you, no doubt; and I beg you will look to the ladies... and ask cook for a hot meal without delay; we may extinguish the galley presently. Mind now, clap on!' Pat shouted, his words almost drowned out by the wind, wild and constantly shrieking through the rigging, 'One hand for yourself and one for the ship! Dalby!' Pat shouted to Clumsy Dalby, standing near the helm, 'Dalby! Be so good as to aid the Doctor to go below.' The sky had darkened considerably and the light was more akin to an evening dusk than late afternoon.

Pat had no fears, for *Surprise* was in perfect fettle after her long refit at Dock; furthermore, all her crew were the cream of his veterans of past voyages; and, to Pat's sweeping gaze, more often that not filled with spray, he could see very well that the crew had taken every precaution with the rigging: preventer-braces a'plenty, topgallant masts long struck down, stuns'ls and booms similarly - and lashed to the deck, a surfeit of blocks and pendant-tackles hooked on, relieving-tackles ready at hand for hooking. He had noticed with approval that the guns most particularly were well lashed to the bulwarks, and the ship's boats were tight-strapped per his earlier directions against the slightest swinging movement. He found everything just so and all to his satisfaction. The sea state had deteriorated in the past few hours and vast torrents of spray bodily scoured every man upon the quarterdeck, whilst the gun deck was awash more often than not with tons of cold, green water, flooding forward as the bow pitched down and clearing momentarily only as the bow violently reared up, precious little seemingly escaping the lee scuppers, before crashing down into the next trough, the cycle repeating itself interminably since several hours.

'An uncomfortable night ahead, sir,' shouted Pickering, clinging desperately to the life-line as *Surprise* tilted further.

At six bells of the afternoon watch, and movement on deck only possible by clinging hard to the life-lines rigged from bow to stern, Pat made his next declaration. 'Mr Macleod, this sea will have our hide if we keep our sails... 'tis time to take them in. I think we will pipe all hands on deck.'

'Aye aye, sir,' Duncan nodded. Prosser, listening in, seemed very relieved to hear the order and bustled away to rouse his men, almost all of whom had been below for some hours, few remaining on the exposed deck as the sea flooded it frequently as *Surprise* rolled and pitched violently. The order was passed along and the men came tumbling up from below in great haste, assembling on the foc'sle and all along the waist, all staring about them, assessing the sea state and considering what might serve as the most appropriate set of sails, every man looking back to the quarterdeck for instruction.

'Mr Macleod, send the men aloft; double-reef all tops'ls and take in her courses!' ordered Pat in animated voice, Duncan standing alongside him. The crew hastily scrambled to do so as the first lieutenant bellowed out the order. 'Mr Prosser, luff up!' shouted Pat. 'Bring her to the wind! Let her lie! Nothing off! Handsomely now!'

'Aye aye, sir, luff and lie, nothing to leeward. Barton, steady so.'

The rain, heavy for several hours, became heavier, fiercer and so thick that for all on the quarterdeck it seemed to merge with the fury of the sea. Huge black rollers swept all about them as far as the eye could see and the most violent of wave tops were perpetually breaking all over the deck, the water never clearing from the lee scuppers before the next wave crashed over them. The fury of the wind about them and the crashing all around of the tremendous seas made hearing difficult and orders nearly impossible to communicate, yet the wind was noticeably still increasing, as was the height of the rollers, white water breaking off their crests, torrents of spray whipping away within the wind's wild fury. *Surprise* was both pitching and rolling, lateral stability now solely afforded by her double-reefed tops'ls and fore-staysail, her officers beginning to wonder whether she would roll further, perhaps even to lie on her beam ends. The afternoon had slipped away into an uncomfortable evening and the light was nearly gone under the press of black cloud and sheeting heavy rain, the wind screaming aloft in the halyards. *Surprise* could do no more than lie-to. Yet for all this press of extreme seas and weather, four men now being necessary to hold the wheel, Pat kept his deck and remained unperturbed; indeed, his officers still alongside of him on the quarterdeck believed that he was actually enjoying himself, for he was too. Precious few others shared the feeling; all on deck were soaked to the skin, all below thoroughly uncomfortable. No hot food had been served since the crew ate dinner at midday and no hot drinks were available, the galley fire having been extinguished as a safety measure; but Pat munched with satisfaction on damp, disintegrating biscuits from his grego pocket. Little light now permeated the gloom below deck and the severe rolling and pitching made even those with the strongest of stomachs nauseous. The ladies and children were badly sick, retching so violently that Simon was called to attend, and he administered a particularly strong dose of laudanum. Marston too had succumbed once again to sea sickness and was of no use. At four bells the men of the first dog watch disappeared gratefully below for respite and to eat hard tack with grog.

'The carpenter reports a deal of seams working, sir; and eighteen inches in the well,' reported Mower.

Pat received the report with unconcern. 'Oh, the barky is stretching her legs... and flexing her new timbers; no doubt teasing the yard's oakum. Doubtless there will be a paucity of tar for us to discover in some small number of the seams.' Pat mused despite the torrential rain, 'I collect her sisters were always reputed to be wet ships. Chain pumps, Mr Mower, if you please. Mr Pickering, pass the word for the carpenter and the bosun.' Hours later, by five bells of the first watch and the sky being inky black, Pat retired below to check on the ladies, leaving Mower in command on deck. Duncan had already retired to rest, the sea state and wind having been gradually diminishing for some hours: the reefed tops'ls and fore-staysail had sustained her throughout the violence. The severe rolling of earlier hours had subsumed to something less uncomfortable and the ladies and twins were all lying in their gun-room cots in a semi-sleeping state, their discomfort having been eased by Simon's laudanum. Brodie alone was sitting up, quite unconcerned, talking in Gaelic to a somewhat discomfited Patrick Coghlan. 'How are you, little one?' asked Pat, smiling encouragingly.

'Quite well, sir; thank you kindly,' said Brodie in obvious good cheer, most pleased to be able to assist Simon tending the sick and distressed.

'The worst is past, my dear,' soothed Pat.

All through the long night the wind continued to decline, and at six bells of the middle watch the men were able to take the reefs out of her tops'ls, which greatly further aided her stability and progress. It was close on dawn, with a perceptible lightening in the eastern sky, before the storm finally blew itself out, the sea state declined and the gale dropped to a tolerable blow as the orange orb peeked over the rim of the horizon as if in curious inquisition of the night's varied damages, when the hatches' battened tarpaulins were removed. The galley fire was relit, to the deep satisfaction of the crew, and hot food was once again served. *Surprise* shook out her courses to give a respectable spread of canvas once more and she resumed her voyage.

To Pat's great satisfaction, Freeman appeared in the cabin with coffee and a hot breakfast, and with too the welcome news, 'Ladies be feeling very better, taking tea, massa.'

A very tired Pat, for he had not retired all night, was much relieved to hear it, 'Pass the word for Mr Pickering.'

As Pickering entered the cabin, Pat asked, 'Tom, is there any sight of *Eleanor* or *Hercules*?'

'None, sir.'

'Well, keep us set firm for Leghorn, we will most likely meet them there. Mr Macleod is resting and I will sleep now for a few hours. You have command.'

*Eleanor*, a most weatherly sailor, had preceded their arrival at Leghorn, but of *Hercules* there was no sign. It was a full three days before she arrived. Captain Scott had returned in the storm to Genoa, the horses having become unsettled, kicking out their stalls in the hold.

*Tuesday 22nd July 1823*                                        *Leghorn*

Little time was needed by *Surprise* in Leghorn other than that necessary to take on water, to revictual the supply of a few fresh comestibles and to repair the slight storm damage. *Eleanor* had suffered no discernible damage at all and *Surprise* required only the most minor attention. Captain Scott, having rectified in Genoa the damage wrought by the panicking horses, had no need to dwell in Leghorn at all. Nevertheless, it was Lord Byron's intention that *Hercules* would stay for a likely two more days before departing, during which time he would seek news from the Morea and Greece generally. Hence *Surprise* and *Eleanor* left without *Hercules*, Pat mindful of Melville's urgent reconnaissance task about the island of Candia. Whilst in Leghorn, Byron had kindly communicated to Pat that it was now his intention to land in Cephalonia rather than in Zante, upon the advice of his passenger, Hamilton-Browne, a knowledgeable Hellenic sympathiser and a friend of the Zante governor.

'Cephalonia, Zante... 'tis all one for us, Duncan,' Pat remarked with some small degree of acerbity whilst playing chess with his First after supper.

'Whining will serve no purpose,' muttered Simon, his head not shifting from his book.

Duncan did not look up from contemplation of his long-planned knight's move, merely riposting, 'I think ye are in a wee difficulty. Does the game begin to tire ye, at all? There, my friend - checkmate!'

As greater southing was gained Simon and Marston were keenly anticipating passing by Etna and more particularly Stromboli, both men in great hopes of witnessing a spectacular eruption. 'With the blessing, it is to be hoped that we will witness fire atop one or the other of them,' said Simon in the dispensary one morning after breakfast.

'Has Captain O'Connor some worry with which he is pre-occupied, colleague? I have received no invitation to the cabin these past two days. Am I in his disfavour, in breach of some nautical protocol or convention with which I am not familiar?' ventured Marston anxiously when they had finished up the dressings.

'Not at all, dear colleague; be not concerned: The captain's mind is a military one. Such souls have a predisposition towards order, regularity and... *and convention* in all their affairs. I fear that he finds this venture a trifle unorthodox, and with no channel of communication being apparent to him - an expected envoy never appearing in Genoa - the further distance we are from home the greater his discomfort... No doubt matters will take their irregular course.'

Pat had completed his breakfast in Sinéad's company, and after she had left to join Kathleen, Brodie and the twins, he hailed his servant. 'Murphy! Pass the word for all my officers... compliments of course.'

His lieutenants, Simon and Marston accompanying, appeared and they all sat at Pat's table. 'Gentlemen, we are but one frigate... *one*... yet we are expected to engage the Turk whenever we can. Most likely we may encounter more than one of their warships. They have several seventy-fours - *which I certainly do not intend to engage* - and many frigates, a deal of them more modern than our *Surprise*. I have been considering this and my plan to fight with best prospects for success... for flight too. Indeed, as my plan assumes that we will likely be outnumbered, it will be necessary to maintain all possible celerity at all times... and such will best be preserved by strictly avoiding course changes and any manoeuvring... which would usually slow us...' Pat paused to assess the attentiveness of his officers, all of whom were wholly fascinated. 'In action we will fire the foc'sle long nines...'

'The long nines... sir?' whispered Marston.

Pat turned towards his surgeons in explanation, 'That is our *bow chasers*... during our approach from astern of our enemy... in the hope of damaging masts or rigging so as to degrade his speed and steering. As we close, the carronades will open with shot only, no grape or canister. For three rounds their fire will be directed low, near the waterline of our enemy. At the range I intend *Surprise* to open fire from... that is to say... *no further than four hundred yards*, the smashers will assuredly penetrate the enemy hull and may - *with the blessing* - start their sinking. After three rounds - as we get closer - the carronades will switch to shot with grape too, the better to cut their rigging. The long guns will open double-loaded with shot and with grape, seeking to tear their rigging. For their second round they will switch to canister replacing grape so as to smash their guns and kill their men. I have no intentions of slugging it out... and so if it don't look like they will strike their colours then we will be away at all possible speed.' Pat observed the affirmatory nods from his officers. 'To repeat myself for clarity, gentlemen... depending on our enemy - brig or frigate - we will make a direct approach to close to two cables; we will *ne'er mind manoeuvres and go straight at 'em...* as Nelson advocated.'

The lieutenants all looked doubtful. Pat could plainly see their glum faces. It may have been advocated by Nelson in the great heyday of fleet battles but it was a high risk tactic that could be very costly: the approaching attacker could be battered by its prey, possibly even raked, bow to stern, particularly in the final one thousand yards of closing which was the maximum truly effective range of ship's guns. The attacker could not reply except with bow chasers until she crossed the bow or stern of her adversary, and so the tactic had been abandoned long before the end of the French war.

It was Marston who interrupted again, 'I am no sailor, sir, but what will your enemy do with his great guns while *Surprise* strives so to reach him?' Pat disbelieved his ears and stared in astonishment; it was such a gross breach of protocol, so rude. He was still speechless as Marston, realising full his error, spoke again, 'I beg your pardon, sir; I imagine you have considered of this.'

Pat looked about the cabin - the lieutenants were aghast, more so with Marston's comment than Pat's surprising tactics - before he continued, 'Yes, gentlemen, I see your concern; but we may expect that the Turk is not yet as expert as the French and the Americans became. Thus, it will be necessary to retain the weather gauge throughout our approach, to preserve all possible speed... and to change our own course swiftly if the Turk comes round. One final point, gentlemen: we will not extinguish the galley fire in action.'

This comment drew sharp intakes of breath from the lieutenants - the tactics were certainly testing convention - but Pat pressed on, 'I intend to fire red-hot shot... and with reduced charges so that the ball will lodge within the target and will not

239

penetrate through both sides of her hull. The consequent fire will give the Turk something more to struggle with. Of course, we may only be able to heat a very few shots in our galley. Mr Mower, you will discuss this with cook and the gunner. We shall practise heating and firing red-hot shot in our great guns.' With this Pat concluded his briefing, his lieutenants' initial doubts being only partially dispelled, but to some extent replaced with a keen interest to find out if the aggressive, innovative tactics and the increased gun crew capabilities afforded by hot shot could be developed successfully.

*Wednesday 23rd July 1823*　　　　　　　　　　　*Tyrrhenian Sea*

After hammocks were piped up, after breakfast and divisions, Pat announced an exercise would be carried out, explaining to his experienced gun captains his intentions of fighting the ship from both sides, all the crew listening with manifest interest. '… that is fighting with gun crews serving the great guns on *both* sides *concurrently – at the same time, Dalby!*' He glared at Clumsy Dalby, who plainly was seeking some clarity as to his role and muttering to his gun captain, Old Pennington. 'Mr Pickering will command the larboard battery and Mr Mower the starboard. Mr Boswell... Master Gunner... you will favour me by commanding the carronades on the quarterdeck. You are not to raise their elevation such that it presents any danger of the muzzle flash or flaming wad igniting the barky's mizzen shrouds. Aim low or level as she rolls.'

'Yes, your honour, sir,' grinned Boswell, delighted by his captain's instruction.

'Lads, we may find ourselves in situations where the odds are very much against us. We are but one small frigate... though all of us would vouch the very best of frigates, WOULD YE SAY?'

There was a barrage of affirmation from all present, as if anyone could doubt it, before Pat resumed, 'We must fight fast... and fire from both sides. Fast! That is three broadsides within five minutes. If we can do that there is not a frigate that can stand against us. CAN YE DO IT?'

240

Huge roars of confirmation erupted, subsiding as Pat raised his hat. 'Lads, we have not been at sea aboard the likes of our dear *Surprise* for four years or more... and it will take time to recover our past form. We start today. Look lively lads... and God speed!'

The crew became instantly alert; the spectacle and occasion of firing the guns was always exhilarating, but firing both sides together was a rarely experienced tactic: the crews by convention and training switched from one side to the other. As their larboard gun was reloaded, they trained and fired their starboard one and vice versa. Would there be enough men to fire both sides together and still achieve three broadsides per side, all within five minutes, Pat's minimum competency standard, as they all knew well? Would depleting the sailing crew to furnish more gunners diminish the ship's speed of manoeuvrability, a critical function in battle, as they all fully understood? The loss of such manoeuvrability could well bring the potential for catastrophe, which some, including Pat, had experienced personally when *Java*, critically unable to steer, had struck to *Constitution* in the year 'twelve. For this first exercise, no shot would be loaded and wasted, no targets set afloat; it would be simply running out the guns and firing the powder, with extra wads rammed as shot. They would see what timing could be achieved firing three rounds. Pat had no intention of keeping the new and old gunners wholly separate, a division which would slow the firing rate from many of the guns, and so every experienced crew had been diluted with new men, most with at least some experience of firing the guns. Most men in a man-of-war had had occasion to do so at some time in their career; even the cooks were retired gunners in many cases, but the new men had been drafted from their customary stations, standing by to make sail and course changes as required, to bring the frigate closer to its enemy or away as the battle dictated. Thus, the experienced gun crews all found themselves with a new crew member or two whom the captains invariably instructed to 'Keep out of the way! Jump when I says so! Mind the recoil! And be ready to heave that gun in and out as fast as fast can be! As if your very life depended on it – as it surely will! D'ye hear me?'

'We will ripple the firing, bow to stern, to spare her timbers,' declared Pat. 'Stand by on my command.'

There was not a living soul below decks as the exercise was prepared, save for the powder crews in the fore and aft magazines. The ladies and girls – although it had been firmly suggested by both Pat and Duncan that they retire below to the gun-room – could not hold their curiosity in check and they stood on the quarterdeck in keen anticipation, never having seen the guns firing. The bulwarks forward of the great cabin were also taken down. Pat gazed down from his quarterdeck, reflecting that it had been over five years or more since *Tenedos* had fired her great guns in anger, even longer for *Surprise*. It was five years of almost total inactivity and four or even more years in many cases since any of the crew had even run out a gun, let alone fired one: what would happen? The gun captains - every one of them as keen as mustard to actually open fire - shouted encouragement to their men 'Attend! Look alive! Stand ready!'

The carronade captains and crews were less happy. It was only with severe cajoling that the lieutenants had switched gun captains and experienced gunners from long guns. Not one had volunteered for the short carronades, considered ugly by most gunners. And who would expect them to transfer willingly, for they were attached to their own guns, all of which were fondly named – aptly as far as their crews were concerned – with such striking names as *The Nailer, Axeman, Dutch Sam, Hell's Mouth* and *Hurricane*. Long years before, Pat had found the nearest thing to a mutiny aboard *Tenedos* when some gunners had been switched to the carronades, and only personal intervention alongside his lieutenants had smoothed things over. He reflected that it was no longer like the Royal Navy of Old Jarvie's day, but perhaps that was for the best. The morale on board *Surprise* was better than ever he had remarked before in all the ships he had previously served on. Perhaps it was just a reflection of the fact that every gun crew dearly wanted to show their best and they doubted that they could do so if relegated to a carronade, for that is how they saw things and who was to say that they were wrong. The carronades were close in smashers, short of range but absolutely deadly when they were close enough to be fired, firing a ball nearly twice as heavy as the guns. They could also fire canister, two hundred and fifty balls each of two ounces which could sweep an enemy deck clean if used at the opportune moment; they could fire grape, nine balls each of almost four pounds which would tear sheets and rip away rigging and thence substantially degrade the enemy's speed and manoeuvrability with a single broadside. They were usually fought by a crew of four, now reduced to two so that Pat could implement his plan, spreading his experienced gun crews a little more thinly and fighting both sides of his ship concurrently.

If *Surprise* encountered two ships and found herself between them, and if both sides could be fought and deliver three broadsides in five minutes and red-hot shot then *Surprise* would be the deadliest of adversaries. Of course, there was *Surprise's* transitioning to the firing position to be carefully managed. A slow approach could expose her to repeated broadsides from two enemy ships, and depending on her relative speed she could be under sustained fire for up to fifteen or so very unpleasant minutes. Pat had considered this before deciding on his tactics, for they gave *Surprise* – if she did find herself in a position to fire her broadside from close in – a potentially decisive advantage: the near certainty of holing the enemy hull and the red-hot shot starting fires. Were they also to clear the enemy decks with canister and grape then it would be so much the better to deter enemy boarding parties, very important with *Surprise* in her unofficial standing not carrying any Royal Marines.

Before commencing firing, the decks had been wetted and sanded, and the magazines were flash-protected with thick 'fearnought' screens over the hatches to prevent any danger from sparks. The more experienced crew had stripped to bare chests, had stuffed cotton waste in their ears and wound scarves about their heads to afford a little protection from the anticipated loud thunder when the guns fired. All stood by their guns clutching rammer, sponge and powder horn, the slow-matches having been replaced some years before in favour of the modern flintlocks. Pat had adopted this change with reluctance and still kept slow-matches lit alongside the guns by way of precaution against the flintlocks misfiring.

The great guns had all been aligned with one of several marks Pat had ordered to be painted on the deck whilst in Plymouth so that every gun's fire would converge on the target at differing ranges. It was an aid devised by Captain Broke of *Shannon* where Pat had first noted it. His tactical preparations for their mission lacked not the slightest detail: the magazine had been filled with best red, large grain powder; all guns had been fitted with spare breeching ropes in case of damage to the tackles – a gun recoiling with cut breeching rope or damaged tackles represented a substantial danger; the deck had been wetted and sanded to prevent slipping of barefooted men - straining with every sinew to haul the heavyweight guns through their ports; and near each port stood a water bucket for the sponge - wetted each time before it was run into the barrel prior to loading the charge. At each gun another bucket was filled with water for the crew to quench their thirst and to slake the bitter taste of smoke; every gun captain retained a lit slow-match within a third barrel, to keep it dry in case of spray. Behind the gun captains stood the second and third lieutenants, both pacing the deck, each one overseeing one side, there being no midshipmen aboard to share the task. Pat sorely lamented the lack of them in that moment.

Pat and Duncan looked down from the quarterdeck. 'Mr Prosser, you will oblige me by hauling our wind three points... keep her steady at six knots, no more,' declared Pat.

At last, after a final survey of his deck, he spoke to Simon, 'Be so good as to mark the time on your fine repeater, Doctor.' He turned to his wife, 'Sinéad, Kathleen, girls; be ready! We are about to commence firing.' He turned forward and shouted to his men, 'Cast loose your guns! Out tompions! Run out your guns!' Within moments there came a drumming, roaring noise as twenty-eight guns were pushed forward over the deck, the six quarterdeck carronades shifting more easily on their wheels within their constraining slides. 'Prime your guns!' Pat bellowed, and finally, 'From forward, a rolling fire … FIRE!'

To the passengers on the quarterdeck the loud great crack of the guns – for they had never heard it before – and the spectacular jets of shooting red-orange flame were simply beyond anything they had ever experienced, and they shrank away in awe. The effect of the rippling barrage progressing down both sides of the ship and the firing coming closer overpowered them as they looked down from the quarterdeck. The noise was louder than the loudest thunderclap they had ever heard. The girls shrieked in excitement but the ladies cowered. After a few moments the carronades fired from behind them, a higher cracking sound in comparison with the deep boom of the long guns. Noxious black smoke enveloped all on the quarterdeck and Simon shouted to the ladies through the din, 'Come! Come below! Swiftly now! There is nothing here for you, as you can plainly see.' He shepherded them down to the gun deck and on down to the gun-room, the rolling thunder of the continuing barrage following them.

On the gun deck the forward crews, now glistening with sweat, were worming and sponging their guns, ramming in fresh cartridges and wads - though no shot - and re-priming the flashpans as fast as they could go. Newcomers were being cursed by their captains, communicating with gestures, nods and a rare shout. Two had fallen on the deck, squealing like stuck pigs, not shifting quickly enough as their guns had recoiled - leaping from the deck before crashing down on their wheels. The unfortunates had forgotten their captain's instructions to stand clear, and their legs had been struck by the gun trucks. Another new gunner was being berated for dropping the wormer as he leapt back in panic. Two captains were screaming at their powder monkeys for the cartridge. None of this escaped the immediate attention of the lieutenants. As the aftmost guns fired, the lieutenants waved their hats, ordering the forward ones to fire again. The noise was deafening, even below in the gun-room where the passengers trembled as the second broadside rippled aft, the shaking of the deck being only very slightly less violent than it had been on the quarterdeck. Smoke drifted down the companionway, and they coughed in the noxious air.

Amidst the frenetic activity, the thunderclaps and the bilious smoke from the guns firing, smouldering fragments of burnt wad drifting with flickering red edges in the air, two men could be seen coming from the galley stove attired in heavy gloves and carrying a glowing red-hot shot between them in steel pincers, moving towards larboard number seven gun, *Hurricane*, the nearest gun to the galley. *Hurricane* had already fired its first shot and was back inboard from its recoil, the barrel being swabbed before a fresh powder charge was loaded. The gun captain, Old Pennington, was coaxing his crew, 'Faster! Faster, you lazy buggers! D'ye think the Turks will wait whilst you fumble about at the breech?' Their evident reluctance to load the red-hot shot and their severe grumbling was only overcome by the confidence they had long placed in him. The marked reduced-charge bag was rammed down, followed by the wad and then the ball was gingerly introduced by a nervous crew, men in great trepidation and plainly aghast: loading red-hot shot with just a wad separating it from its powder was, to their minds, surely asking for disaster. Another wad followed and all was rammed tight, the man with the rammer fearing for his hands. The gun crew edged away from their captain, away from their gun, surreptitiously, a pace or two back from their customary stations, as far as they could decently shift. To their astonishment and very great relief no spontaneous detonation occurred. Old Pennington shouted to them, the gun was hauled forward by the crew, the lanyard pulled and the flintlock pan powder flashed through the vent to fire the charge and send the glowing ball out across the waves. No gun crew ever felt more relieved.

Some little time later, as the aftmost gun fired its third shot, Pat shouted, 'Avast firing!' and the guns fell silent. Simon had long since returned to the quarterdeck; he peered at his Breguet repeater in anticipation of Pat's only question, 'How long?'

Simon replied with an answer that he knew would dissatisfy Pat, 'Seven minutes forty seconds. Would that do tolerably well for our first time after all these years?' One glance at Pat's glum face confirmed his expectation that it would not, not by a long chalk.

'Draw and house the guns, if you please,' Pat, standing above the waist, shouted the command, which was echoed all down the gun deck by his lieutenants.

In the evening a visibly downcast Pat settled to his supper of toad-in-a-hole with Duncan and Simon. The dish appeared to be more blackened than the norm, though a distracted Pat seemed not to notice. 'Pray tell, brother, what ails thee?' prompted a concerned Simon, for the atmosphere about the table was discernibly dismal.

'Eh?' Pat looked up, frowning. 'We must fire faster. We will likely be outnumbered... and only the very fastest of firing will preserve us... and 'tis clear that the crews are rusty, like a half-baked old hinge.' His dissatisfaction was pronounced in a very strident, gloomy voice.

To Pat's muddled metaphor Simon could only offer a sympathetic, 'Surely, dear, there is time enough to improve on today's tolerably promising start?'

'Sweat, Simon, saves blood. Very poor, it was. We will be sunk afore we fire our second at that rate.'

'I am concerned to hear it. But would you expect the finest horse, though in want of training, to win the King's Plate at the Curragh? Not even Patrick O'Connor... the optimist of all the world... could hold such a glorious hope, and 'tis little different.' Simon laughed out loud, amused by his quote.

'Optimist of all the world? That is coming it a trifle high.' The timbre of irritation was now plain in Pat's voice.

'I can scarcely imagine that you have forgotten your considerable expenditure in canal stock and East India stock? And I also recall *bank* stock being mentioned at the table.'

'I venture you may be thinking that you are more familiar than I with corporate investments and the market?' said Pat in indignant voice, his ire rising. 'Will I tell you I have my doubts about that?'

'Oh, and latterly was there not also mention of South American bonds?' Simon laughed again.

'My money is firmly anchored in solid ground - *safe investments, the safest!*' exclaimed Pat.

'Indeed, I collect there was even talk of gold mining... *gold mining, for all love!*' Simon laughed out loud in unceasing, uproarious fashion and slapped his palm on his knee. He resumed in moderate voice, 'You are assuredly not frittering your capital away in such a venture, eh?'

Pat glared, 'Gold, I assure you, was found in Wicklow in the year 'ninety-five... or was it 'ninety-six? The promoters, Mrs Webster, Mr Mills and Mr King, were introduced to me; they explained that the gold was in the granite, in the bedrock through which flowed the Ballinvalley River...'

'Is that so? I was not aware,' said Simon in extremely dubious tone.

'... and from which it was a mere simple task to pan for it in the water... where bountiful quantities awaited simple harvesting. You will be amazed... their colleague, Mr Sharp, showed me the nuggets found there...'

'And *sharp* described the nature of it, no doubt,' murmured Simon, though Pat was not listening attentively, his ire rising, and so did not detect Simon's glib pun.

'... said that some early prospectors had cleared thousands, declared that my farm sat on the very same granite... and for sure it was only the want of financing of explorations that had precluded the discovery of gold in Claddaghduff itself. Sure, I have a little capital now in the Gannoughs, in the very smallest of mine on the low hill there. Investments... *investments* they are, and 'tis a bull market at present, though there is never a certainty in them. There is no sure investment, as all men of commerce will know. There is but little return in leaving precious funds in Consols and Navy five per cents when prices are rising again.'

'I dare say there is not. I do not set myself up as an authority on investments... I rub along,' declared Simon, 'My father's bequest was so very small that I have ever persisted in financial mediocrity, and hence my penurious nature would never permit of such follies. Nor could I tell a bull from a bear, save they were standing alongside of me,' Simon laughed again; 'Sure, I have been too long immersed in the medical world and that of the naturalist to contemplate on the absurd pursuit of wealth!' Simon laughed aloud once more.

Pat scowled, 'You would surely never say I was rich? I have but scarcely a dozen acres; three quarters are bog and the remainder provide but the smallest of potato crop, and that only in a good year – it has failed these two years gone – and my cow was stolen when I was in London; 'tis only the accumulation of prize monies that has kept us from the workhouse. My half-pay could never feed even the wife and wains.'

'For God's love, it seems to me that if the boggies will believe our beloved Jesus did raise Lazarus from the dead then 'tis not remarkable that unscrupulous sharps will always find plenty of blunties to gull. Gold, Pat? Gold? In Ireland? I am amazed! Have these proficient thaumaturgists also mentioned their discovery of the methodology for the transmutation of metals?... the changing of lead into gold?... the philosophers' stone perhaps?... or even the very elixir of life itself? Pat, do you leave your precious sense in the cabin when you step ashore?'

'John D'Arcy did assure me there is gold in Galway and in Mayo too; on Inishturk island it has been found. Many a day have I fished near that place... and the prospects for this promising enterprise have been scrutinised by the most sagacious of advisers.'

'I fancy salacious might answer better than sagacious.'

'Salacious, of course. I knew there was something not quite Bristol-fashion there. Salacious: a prime word; I dare say that is with an L?'

'An impecunious man should never indulge in speculation, brother, nor a wise one, even when he can afford it... and such is plain even to the meanest intelligence.'

'Simon, this is quite different, an uncommon opportunity... *'tis investment*... not speculation. Can ye not see that?' Pat spoke now in a raised voice.

'Far be it for me to affirm anything about investment, although I have heard the promotion of it forever in those circles where persons profess with airs and graces - invariably self-bestowed; and generally I am of a mind that they are projectors - *scoundrels* - who seek to cod honest folk of their last shilling; but I confess I know nothing about it and speak only with the most general of perceptions; but in the matter of money, folk have the strangest notions of what is sound and what is more akin to the throw of the dice.' A momentary pause. 'I collect that you said that the discovery of gold in your mine did not eventuate at all.'

'No, not yet; however, plainly it is early days for the venture... and I merely seek a sound home for my precious small capital, as you know full well,' Pat replied, his tone growing increasingly more irritable.

'There is no call to grow chuff,' retorted Simon after a silence and somewhat acerbically, his own ire rising.

'You would have me laid by the lee again,' Pat's vexation and voice deflated; he knew he could not better Simon, save in matters nautical, where his friend had scarcely the sense of the greenest midshipman. He relented, 'I'm sorry I flew off the handle; I know you mean it very kindly... and there was no call for me to be hipped so.'

Simon heard the resignation, most amiably accepted, 'Let us have a pot of coffee... and what do you say to us scraping a little? A cheering ceilidh tune or two... and perhaps a bottle of your admirable port to follow. Is that trifling portion of toad-in-a-hole in the dish spare?'

A suggestion of a little playing customarily brought Pat round to his sociable side. 'Yes, yes, of course we will... 'tis just that my mind had shifted from the pleasure of being back on board after these past four years to thinking how best we would be fighting the ship once more. Murphy! Murphy there! Light along with a pot of coffee and a bottle of my best port, if you will... the seventy-five... and no breakages; d'ye hear me?'

'There's no need to boil your cabbages twice,' said Simon.

'Eh? Cabbages?' Pat stared at his friend; 'I collect we were speaking originally of the slow rate of firing of the guns.'

'An Irish pearl of wisdom you once offered me... which I have never forgotten: there is no purpose in fretting because it solves nothing.'

'Yes, yes...' Pat sighed, 'Of course we have time to improve, and so we will, and without sparing the powder. Here you are.' He passed the little silver dish, two shrivelled slices of toasted cheese, unusually, remaining; 'I have quite lost my appetite.'

*Friday 25th July 1823*                                    *off Sicily*

Stromboli, to starboard as *Surprise* approached the Messina Strait at the top of the day, presented none of the keenly hoped-for signs of eruption, and Etna, once through the Strait, displayed only a very little smoke, the somnolence of both being a great disappointment to all on board. The sky, an infinite blue and wholly cloudless, together with a relatively mild wind, presented the perfect day for Simon's ornithology interests, a passion he shared with Marston. Weather permitting, Simon customarily passed much time of every day on the quarterdeck with Marston, the two of them watching keenly for birdlife. Despite spring being a far more favourable time to see large scale northbound migration, late July still presented opportunities to see some birds returning early to their African wintering grounds.

'Look there, quickly! Over there! Surely that is another Montague harrier... *Circus pygargus,* the third one today?' shouted Marston, waving his arm.

'No, colleague; I think not. I believe it is a fine example of Eleonora's falcon, the bearded vulture*, Falco eleonorae,*' said Simon with audible complacency, wholly immersed in his fascination, 'Such majesty... what a delight to see him!' He peered intently through Pat's best Dollond five-lens achromatic telescope; it had been loaned solely to Marston with the strictest of instructions as to its care, Pat not wishing to see it in Simon's hands where it had been nearly lost on several occasions; but Simon had seized on it exclusively upon their first sighting, to Marston's unspoken irritation.

'But look to the leading edge of his wings... the underside is plain to see, so very black,' Marston persisted.

'Indeed, but you are to consider that the black of the Montague's wings is customarily *at the tips*, my dear,' replied Simon in smug, self-satisfied tone, intently following the bird's flight with the telescope.

'I do beg your pardon,' Marston, somewhat piqued, spoke with a shade of indignation, 'Perhaps were I to avail myself of the glass then all would be clear.'

The birdwatching was necessarily abandoned after dinner as the great guns exercise was resumed every day as *Surprise* sailed east, holding her course for the Ionians, the times for firing three shots from both sides steadily reducing until Pat pronounced himself satisfied only when this was achieved once again in his

251

self-imposed maximum five minutes. By then, they anticipated arriving in Ionian waters the next day.

In the evening a great concern came upon all aboard as Duncan's wife, Kathleen, became unwell. For several days and nights, she had suffered a return of the mild symptoms of her former illness, suffering night sweats and struggling to cough up a glutinous white phlegm. It was exceedingly painful for Simon to see, even more so to diagnose it as likely to be consumption, and it brought back the most heartbreaking memories of his deceased wife who had long been afflicted by it before she died. A believer in the recuperative qualities of fresh air, he ordered a cot made up for her on the quarterdeck, and he sat with her all night to the exclusion of all other activities, Sinéad attending, whilst Duncan was relieved of all duties by Pat and sat with them, both men striving to maintain a cheerful, encouraging demeanour in front of the ladies whilst privately harbouring the most desperate of fears and anxieties.

*Saturday 26th July 1823*                                    *Ionian Sea*

The first faint glow of morning twilight, and Pat called Simon and Duncan across to the stern rail. 'How is she?' he asked with a feeling of immense trepidation. Duncan, in his distress could find no words; he merely nodded.

Simon spoke up, 'She has not been best served in her accommodations. The small cabins are incommodious even for those of us who are well... *and a trifle short*... but the dear soul has been suffering for some days, and she has feigned good health when asked; but I regret to say it is not.' Grave anxiety visible on the faces of both his close friends, Simon resumed, 'However, I am minded that given blessed recuperation from the tiring motions of this vessel... and a lengthy spell of taking the airs... with the most benevolent of diets...' He paused as if to check himself before making his pledge, '... then she will make a recovery. I am minded the dis... *her illness*... is not advanced. She exhibits the mildest of symptoms, and we may - with the blessing - *confidently* anticipate a goodly degree of recovery. Of course, I cannot vouch that it will be a complete one, for such knowledge as we physicians have of this drea... *this matter* is far from complete.' He stared closely at fearful faces. 'Duncan... my dear friend... you will allow me to attend her until she recovers; indeed, I insist upon it.'

Duncan, gratitude mixing with fear, still could not speak; his breathing was coming fast and unconcealed tears were constantly wiped away on his shirt sleeve as he strived for an equilibrium.

Pat, his arm upon Duncan's shoulder, reached his decision, 'Gentlemen, we will touch at Cephalonia this day but only to put Kathleen ashore... with Sinéad and the children... before we go directly to our mission... to Candia in search of the Turk fleet.'

Shortly after dawn the heights of Cephalonia came into view from the tops. *Surprise* continued her steady, easterly course all morning until she eventually turned north to enter the great bay of Argostoli in the early afternoon, making frequent short boards against an adverse but weak summer north-easterly *Gregale* before heaving to and letting go her anchor in seventy-five feet of water in the Roads, a little outside the harbour proper. Pat had not the slightest wish to encounter officialdom in the short spell of *Surprise's* visit, possessing no official papers.

'Simon, you will stay with Kathleen... that is my order,' declared Pat emphatically. 'I have no intentions of any engagement; it is a reconnaisance only that we are engaged upon. I anticipate no action.' Simon simply nodded, preoccupied with his patient.

Without the slightest delay, a breathless Kathleen was lowered with the utmost care into the barge. Simon and Duncan accompanied her for the short pull to the quay, Duncan fretting, Pat's bargemen taking no more than ten minutes, whence Kathleen was carried gently up the steps. Sinéad and the youngsters followed.

It was after dinner, in the late afternoon when *Eleanor* appeared, anchoring a cable away from *Surprise*. Codrington crossed to *Surprise* by barge on Pat's signal.

In the great cabin, as the hot and breezy day shifted to the relative stillness of early evening, warmth still plentiful, the gun port lids were hauled up to capture what cooling breeze might still be had. An anxious and plainly fretting Duncan had returned aboard from the shore, and he listened without his customary and complete attentiveness as Pat briefed his officers, 'Gentlemen, we are arrived in Greek waters. Politically however, we are in Ionian waters. That is to say the United Islands of... principally Corfu, Cephalonia and Zante... with four lesser ones: Lefkas, Kythira, Ithaka and Paxos. Together they are a British protectorate, quite independent of Greece and free of any Turk suzerainty. No Turk ship will venture here. The Governor, Maitland, has placed the islands in a state of quarantine from mainland Greece. No one can cross to them without incarceration on account of the plague so prevalent on the mainland. At present we are flying English colours and perfectly welcome. When *Surprise* hoists Greek colours we may expect that to change. For that reason, we shall take every possible sounding afore we change our flag. Mr Codrington, *Eleanor* will at all times maintain her English status, and so may come and go as she pleases... save for any contact with mainland Greece. I anticipate that we will be formally in Greek service afore many more days have passed. Make your personal preparations, such that they may be. We are departing without the slightest delay for Candia, to find the Turk fleet.'

With no more than another half-hour elapsing as her anchors were hauled up, catted and fished, the wind no more than a gentle influence upon her topsails and the sea surface scarcely more than a flat calm, *Surprise* departed the anchorage with an ethereal slowness to disappear into the grey tranquillity of the gloaming.

# Chapter Eight

*Trust not for freedom to the Franks —*
*They have a king who buys and sells;*
*In native swords, and native ranks,*
*The only hope of courage dwells;*
*But Turkish force, and Latin fraud,*
*Would break your shield, however broad*

*Monday 28th July 1823*                    *aboard Surprise, off Candia*

The sound of creaking rigging was the solitary noise breaking the rare silence, with only the exception of an occasional bird call. Even so early in the day the windsails, rigged to provide a little relief to those below, could do nothing against the heat. Upon leaving Argostoli, *Surprise* had benefited from a benevolent north-westerly *Maestro* but since the dusk of yesterday she had been struggling to make only the slowest of progress, tacking frequently to make headway against a summer southerly coming from the far North African shore. Overnight, *Surprise* had glided with infinite slowness and across the calmest of flat seas towards Candia, royals hoisted up and stuns'ls all boomed out; but these made no difference, she barely moved in the feeblest of zephyrs. The frigate had eventually arrived within distant sight of the island's peaks shortly after the dawn, scarcely closing a league since then.

The dawn itself had been quite exceptional, a spectacularly glowing red orb rising infinitely slowly, for so it seemed in the general fixation of the barky; it's majestic presence was plain, throwing a brightening hue through and above the low haze of the sea's surface, and projecting a pink blanket over a sea quite devoid of any ripple, slowly turning orange and finally yellow whilst burning through the few wispy cloud remnants lingering over the clearing mountain extremities of Candia off the larboard bow, Mount Ida's summit prominent. With barely the slightest wind to disturb the flaccid sails, the air temperature already hot and the deep blue sky promising much greater warmth to come later, there was no prospect of any cooling effect from the weak breeze, and all aboard anticipated another smouldering day, an enforced inactivity which was so unwelcome.

The ship's bell, rung by Clumsy Dalby – who had seized the role with alacrity and who struck the bell with unequalled vigour – tolled loud its declaration of eight bells. *Surprise's* officers stood on the quarterdeck, Duncan determined to stand his duties with them without favour; all anxiously swept the horizon in every direction with their glasses, the crew on watch washing the decks in the background: wholly unnecessarily, for so they thought, having done it every day for as long as anyone could remember, and with scarcely a speck of anything necessitating cleaning to be found on them. The crew laboured half-heartedly, with a sense of expectancy, an awareness of unknown events about to happen, for they felt an omnipresent foreboding, a keenly sensed anticipation. Of what they knew not, but every one of them had picked up the discreet signals, the frequent conferences of Pat's officers and their alertness with their glasses, and heard their urgings to the topmen to stay vigilant.

'How far off Candia are we would you think, Mr Prosser?' asked Pat.

'To pass Cape Vouxa, perhaps another four leagues, sir.'

'What does the line signify, Mr Mower?'

'Barely half of one knot, sir. We may as well be anchored.'

'Very well. Mr Pickering, let us pipe the hands to breakfast while we are becalmed.' Pat descended the steps to the gun deck. 'Ah, Mr Marston, there you are; will you take a bite with me? I think there is still some bacon - *if it ain't gone off* - and maybe some sausage.' They entered the cabin together, Pat calling to his steward, 'Freeman, a fresh pot of tea, bacon if we have it, and sausages, eggs, and soft tack; and enough for Mr Marston too.'

Murphy was also present, keenly aware of the sense of anticipation pervading the ship, and he hastened as quickly as he could to the galley with Freeman to fetch Pat's breakfast so as to ensure no time was lost and his ear was returned as close to Pat's door as he dared without precipitating admonishment from his captain, who was, fortunately for both of them, long inured to Murphy's foibles and irritating shortcomings.

Pat stared as unobtrusively as he could at Marston, wondering whether he had decided well in leaving Simon behind. 'Should we sight any Turks, Mr Marston, you may yet find some wet work below. I pray we do not... with Dr Ferguson remaining on Cephalonia to care for Kathleen,' said Pat, adding, 'Please take a seat, I doubt that Freeman will be long.'

'How was Mr Macleod's wife, sir, when we departed Argostoli?'

'Oh, tolerably comfortable and no more in danger. He did assure me of that... though the prior days were as anxious as any we both ever found at sea. Her illness was thankfully not severe, so said Doctor Ferguson. Indeed, Kathleen remonstrated with me from her cot to depart when I declared that I would wait another day afore sailing. She quieted herself after accepting my promise to depart directly only if she would accept that Dr Ferguson remained to care for her.' Pat paused to reflect, another matter pressing on his mind. 'Oddly, we have seen ne'er a one of the Greek fleet... which Mavrocordato's agent in Argostoli assured me was bound for Candia too. There is no relying on your foreigner, Mr Marston... and this Greek enterprise is a damned fine pickle of fish.'

Marston did not dare to correct his captain's metaphorical muddle, and just at that moment Freeman returned with their breakfast: a huge pan of sausages, highly spiced and peppered so as to disguise their advancing term and doubtful flavour; served with eggs, coffee and plentiful toasted soft tack, baked fresh by Wilkins - a rare treat and offered as if in compensation for the ageing sausages. He brought too one of the few remaining pots of Falmouth marmalade, though the butter, beyond rancid at the end, was long gone. Freeman set it all on the cabin table, bowed his head and withdrew to return to his station outside Pat's door. Pat nodded his appreciation of Freeman's endeavours but then peered at the sausage, sniffing, as if seeking to verify or assuage his doubts over the desirability of Wilkin's efforts. 'Allow me to help you to a little of this sausage,' he murmured in a rather cautious, subdued voice. He continued quickly as if to preclude any objection, 'I fancy Dr Ferguson will be following us in *Eleanor* by now. Reeve is a prodigious fine master of her, and with Codrington to spell him there will be no speedier vessel on God's ocean. I'm sorry, please forgive my reference to our Lord,' Pat added hastily.

'No matter, sir; I imagine our Lord would wholly concur with your opinion,' Marston replied, smiling. 'Is the Greek cause now precarious in Candia, sir?'

Pat looked up from scooping eggs on to his guest's plate. 'Sadly, it seems so. The Porte has sent its Egyptian vassal's army to subdue the Greek rebellion... and it is feared that Candia is their first port of call. The Hydriot commander, Tombazes, has struggled unsuccessfully against internal fighting amongst the Greeks for some time. It seems that the Greek fleet has other matters to deal with, for we are here alone; but with this absence of wind neither *Surprise* nor any other ship, Greek or Turk, is likely to fetch Candia. Tombazes's men - we hear they are fighting in Lautro - may soon find themselves sorely pressed, if they are not already,' Pat opined gloomily, adding, 'We may yet have to employ sweeps.'

'Where is Loutro, sir? My knowledge of the geography of these parts is weak.'

'Oh, it is near Sfakia, on the south-west coast of the island, the province of some or other Greek band of brigands.'

'What could have happened to the Greek fleet, sir?'

'Without doubt they have a difficult task. The Turk is unfettered to arrive at any part of their coast and all their islands, to sack and plunder any of the Greek port towns. Perhaps they are already engaged in evacuation elsewhere. Perhaps their admirals have received reports of the Turk fleet movements and sent their ships away to find them. Perhaps the crews have again refused to sail for want of pay. Certainly, they have fine admirals in Miaoulis, Canaris and others, and they do not lack for bravery. In the year 'twenty-two at Chios they defeated a Turk fleet much larger than their own with the deployment of fireships, the Turks being terrified of them. Even the Turk admiral was killed in the engagement... after running his ship aground to seek an escape from the *bourlotas* - as the Greeks term them. No, 'tis far from sure who will win this war, but the advantage must still lie with the Greeks, for it is they who are defending their homes and their families. If only they would agree a consensus of government and military command, for the want of such is the Turk's greatest weapon, and we will be here for many a year yet until the Greeks can speak with one voice; of that I have no doubt. That is unless our lads develop the Greek approach, for want of pay.' Pat laughed out loud with great mirth at this thought. Marston smiled, pleased to see his captain in good spirits. The prior years of naval inactivity with its inherent uncertainties and then the sudden thrusting upon him of a command in the service of a rebellion had placed a degree of strain upon him, he thought. Now, as a first mission of some importance was developing, the becalmed state of *Surprise* was plainly unhelpful. Would Patrick O'Connor be up to the emerging danger and the challenge before him? Marston put the question aside, recollections of past times quashing his concerns. A sociable time passed in the hour until breakfast was finished when Pat looked to his companion with a smile, 'Come, let us go up and see what we are about.'

The studdingsails and royals had made little difference: *Surprise* was sailing, near drifting, with every stitch of canvas she possessed aloft but hanging lifeless, and she made barely half a knot, rolling gently in unwelcome immobility. Three more dreary hours passed, the sun blazing down with unprecedented heat from high in the sky, and Pat found his boots sticking to streaks of pitch oozing out from between the deck planks. Spots of tar had also fallen from the rigging aloft as it melted, spattering everywhere and quite ruining the crew's earlier efforts to wash the deck. Even below deck the air temperature was as hot as anyone could recall, the windsails utterly ineffective, and the unpalatable stench of mould - and worse - rose from the bilges throughout every vestige of the ship. A despondent Pat had long retreated to the shade and hoped-for relative cool of his cabin where he sat writing up his log when, from the tops, an excited shout was heard, indistinct but clearly audible, as the cabin doors through to the gun deck were latched open in futile attempt to catch the tiniest scrap of breeze. The words remained recognisable and alarming nevertheless. Pat ceased writing and set down his pen, and he hastened up the steps to gain the quarterdeck.

'Mr Pickering, what's afoot?' he asked. 'Ships? Where away?'

Pickering indicated to larboard, towards the east, into the still lingering, low haze, 'Over there, sir. The topman thinks he sighted a vessel, perhaps two... hull-down on the horizon... but I can see nothing.'

Pat stared hard into his glass. The sun had climbed away in the past half-hour but, oddly, the haze had thickened, and it no longer hurt his eyes to stare carefully for long, tense minutes before he finally exclaimed, 'There! Four points off the bow. Look hard, Mr Pickering, they come and go. Damn that haze! Mr Mower, we will beat to quarters!'

'Clear for action, Mr Prosser!' cried Mower.

Prosser shouted down to the deck, 'Beat to quarters.' *Surprise* having no marines aboard, the task was carried out by Clumsy Dalby who had a particular enthusiasm for the drum and strived on every occasion to tear the skin with his vigorous beat.

Pat remained all the time peering into his glass, declaring at last, 'I see no sails.... no sails. Why, they must be Turks; xebecs, their sails still furled and men rowing. That is why we could not see them! Xebecs for all love! I would never have thought it. Why, I ain't seen one bigger than a fishing smack for twenty years, and that in Venice. Have you ever seen such a vessel, Mr Mower? Well done that look out! Half an hour more and I doubt they would ever have been sighted with the Candia headlands behind them. Who saw them?'

'Young Pennington, sir,' declared Duncan.

'By God, that fellow has the very best of eyes,' said Pat. 'There's a shilling in my purse for him... a capital hand! Well done Pennington!' He lowered the telescope, cleaned it with the briefest of wipes with his handkerchief before peering again through the indistinct, early morning haze, a thin wispy mist rising from the warmer waters into the colder air. 'Doubtless they have seen us before we saw them, and their captains are crafty fellows, creeping up on us with no visible sailcloth to gain the advantage. I see her masts plain on the nearer vessel; she is a poleacre-xebec - *a large one* - with square-rigged yards on the main... and... and I espy ten guns per side. Why, they are capital vessels for manoeuvring, they can row into any position to their advantage with their oars... where we cannot strike them... and with no wind we will be uncommon sore pressed.' Several more minutes passed; all the time Pat continued to gaze through his glass at the approaching xebecs. Finally he spoke, very quietly as if he did not wish his words to carry, 'Mr Macleod, we may shortly find ourselves in some difficulty. No wind to shift or turn, no means of training our guns to bear if they come for'ard or astern of *Surprise* - save for our chasers. As xebecs they will have powerful bow and stern guns as well as a significant broadside weight of metal. Quite likely they have twenty-four-pound or even thirty-two-pound bow and stern guns, which will far outrange our own. They can stand off all day and beat us to a pulp.' A minute of silent thought and Pat spoke again, 'However, need teaches a plan. We must confuse them as best we may. We will hoist the Turk pennant which the sailmaker has run up, and below it fly a yellow jack.'

'Would that be entirely regular, sir?' came the unexpected interjection from a concerned Marston, looking on aghast, his question spoken with the most anxious of voice. Eyebrows were raised by all on deck within earshot.

The interruption - such impertinence - was such a gross breach of protocol that Pat was entirely taken aback himself; however, his mind solely focused on the imminent threat from the xebecs, he simply stared at Marston without expression for a bare few moments, his look becoming very cold, before turning back to his First. 'Mr Macleod, I want the Turks to see no one on deck. Every gunner is to crouch behind the ports and not to show even the top of their head around them. Send a man to the heads, to lie there as if dead. Set everything aloft all ahoo, our royals and tops'ls all a'fluttering - and her courses too - everything all loose and flapping. We will look like Bedlam. Mr Mower, leave the gun port lids down but unshackled; prime the flashpans; send half a dozen shot to be heated in the galley stove... and run it hot so we - *and the Turks* - see no smoke. We will let them come close; our deception will reel 'em in. Remember, Mr Mower, be sure to tell the captains of both those two guns a'side firing red-hot shot to load only reduced charges. It will serve us well if their

261

balls do not break out of the Turk hulls... so much the better to
start fires burning inside. Mr Pickering, remind all other captains
- *of the eighteens that is* - to fire low; they will break scores more
of splinters as they strike - and so better to kill their men. We
will load both shot and canister: hundreds of iron balls - *a right
proper slaughter-house* - served out from fourteen guns will
quickly disable the rowers. For the carronades, Mr Boswell, load
shot only and aim low, so that they may smash holes in their
hull... perhaps below their waterline. We shall clear our
quarterdeck from Turk sight.' Pat now turned to his cox'n,
'Barton, put the strongest twelve lads we have in my barge and
eight more into the cutter. You are to command them both from
the barge. Make fast the boats to *Surprise* at her bow with short
lines, thirty yards only, no more. Stay behind *Surprise,* close by
her hull at the starboard beam so the barge and cutter will not be
seen by the Turks... and Barton,' Pat spoke gravely to his cox'n,
'it will be for you and your lads to haul her round by the bow
when we signal so that we may fire our guns; 'tis our only
chance.'

'Aye aye, sir, twenty men into the boats, hide and haul her
round on your signal,' Barton repeated his instructions and
hastened away to gather his men.

As the boats, all filled with the chosen men, were being tied
to *Surprise's* bow, Pat looked back at the xebecs, still far distant
but clearly approaching. 'Mr Marston,' he said quietly to his
immediate companion, 'You may care to make your preparations
below.'

Marston appeared quite unprepared for Pat's prompt at that
moment, the responsibility of ship's surgeon now thrust upon
him and the prospect of an engagement looming large. 'Those
xebecs, sir, will it be necessary to engage them? Perhaps flight
would better serve our cause if we are to reach Candia and
without hindrance to our purpose in that place.' The helmsmen
and the master, also near the wheel, exchanged shocked glances.

Pat's reply was infused with only the mildest of indignation.
'Do not think me a warmonger, Mr Marston, a death-or-glory
merchant. I assure you, I had rather see a brace of fine ships
burnt and sunk than lose a single man of my crew killed or

wounded. You are to consider that we have no wind... no means of flight. Those xebecs will soon be upon us before we know it, and to fight presents our only prospect for salvation.'

'Sir, pray forgive my - *doubtless* - ill-considered notion, but can we not fly His Majesty's colours as *His Majesty's Hired Vessel Surprise...*' Marston pressed, a little nervously, '... and would they not then pass us by?'

Pat looked again at his assistant surgeon and chaplain with mild astonishment and not least a modicum of irritation, and he replied with as much impassivity and formality as he could find, 'Why certainly we could, Mr Marston... until they asked for such Admiralty papers as His Majesty's ships all possess - but of which we have none! Since we have also not received our Greek *letter of marque* we would be treated as pirates, and to be taken without any flag flying would likely condemn us to be hanged. No, we must run or fight. As we have no wind we cannot run, and so we must fight. We can fight only as a Greek or strike our colours as a Greek. We may hope that the Turks may not yet know of any frigate in Greek service, and that small thing may yet set things in our favour.' The latter point was said more confidently than Pat felt.

Marston, now realising from Pat's tone of gentle rebuke and his eye catching the condemnatory faces of men all about the helm that he had overstepped the mark, anxiously sought to make amends, 'I have expressed myself badly, sir; plainly I am not to teach you your trade; I ask that you forgive my maundering impertinence, and please accept my most sincere apologies; I beg you will.'

'Oh, I think we may overlook it this once, Mr Marston,' Pat relented, smiling, bearing no ill will towards his chaplain, his respect for Marston undiminished. 'Mr Macleod, all sails loose to a bowline. We will likely need to shift away quickly and at best speed. There will be no time to make sail. All canvas flapping will aid our deception.'

'Aye aye, sir.'

'Mr Mower,' said Pat, 'Prepare our marksmen. They are to stay out of sight, and on my mark to climb into the tops to fire down on the Turk officers only, *officers only!* Make that plain to them. And were they to clear the Turk quarterdeck, then gun captains next, but only *after* they have swept the xebec quarterdecks clear. Each man is to carry two muskets, both primed and ready to fire, and to carry powder and shot for six reloads. I doubt this business will last longer.'

'Very good, sir. We have ten men to send aloft with some competency with the musket.'

'Keep them all close below the bulwark 'til I shout,' Pat reiterated. 'Mr Pickering, all hands to keep silent as the Turks near. Pass the word.'

An anxious hour slipped by with infinite slowness until the nearing xebecs became clearly visible without a glass, their three lateen sails all furled and a score of oars pulling along each side. On *Surprise* not a soul could be seen, neither about the gun ports nor on the quarterdeck where Pat and his companions crouched low out of sight. He turned to Marston, alongside him, and whispered 'God between us and all harm.' The chaplain only stared in silence, aghast and wide-eyed.

All of Jemmy Ducks' brood had been taken below and at the heads a very convincingly dead seaman lay over the prow. Barton and his men were waiting patiently, tied alongside in the boats. Pat, lying on his chest on the deck, peered through his glass through a gun port wedged just ajar, scrutinising the approaching Turks.

'Mr Marston...' whispered Duncan, Marston lingering still on the quarterdeck and looking very dismayed, '... will ye go below, sir? Ye may be needed in the cockpit presently. Afore ye know the shot and splinters will be a'flying about.'

'The wind is freshening, sir,' said Pickering quietly as the loosened topsails began to flap vigorously, the southerly wind picking up.

'Aye, Mr Pickering, and that may yet be our saviour,' Pat replied. 'The xebecs are diverging now, the first heading to come at our bow and the second to hold back, nearly on the line of our stern... as would I, were I their captain. I imagine they intend to position so as to rake us, one after the other. They are half a mile away now, no more. Our guns are all double-shotted?'

'Yes sir.'

'We will hold our fire for short range when our shot will smash straight through both sides, even double-shotted and with canister too.' More tense minutes passed. The only noises that could be heard were the loosened sails rattling their lines and the creak of timbers, *Surprise* rocking with the gentlest of motion. The crouching crew held their silence, anxiously awaiting their orders.

From the nearest Turk xebec, closing from ahead of *Surprise*, came a hail. Her oars were raised, and the Turk, a mere hundred yards or so away, began to slow perceptibly. From the Turk the shouts came louder and more frequently. The second xebec was some hundred yards or so behind her companion, but coasting to position herself at *Surprise's* stern, losing way as she too slowed, her oars raised. The moment was eerily quiet, merely the slap of wave against hull breaking the near total silence as the vessels converged. Time, to Pat's mind, seemed to be standing still. 'God between us and all evil,' he murmured the familiar prayer to himself. He looked again at his watch, mentally noting the time. Never before had the closing seconds to an engagement ever passed so slowly.

A very few tense minutes more and Pat judged the critical moment had arrived; he leaped to his feet to shout his orders, 'Note down the time, Mr Pickering, and give the order to our boats - to row as if all our lives depend on it, for they surely do!'

Pickering leaned over the side and bellowed to the men below in the boats, 'ROW, LADS! PULL FOR ALL YE ARE WORTH!'

'Mr Prosser, strike the Turk flag and the yellow jack; hoist Greek colours. Swiftly, gentlemen, to your guns, if you will!' As Pickering and Mower hastened to the companionway, Pat rushed forward to look down over the waist rail to his gunners on the gun deck below. 'NOW LADS!' he shouted through his speaking trumpet, 'HAUL THOSE GUNS OUT! SWIFTLY NOW!'

The change aboard *Surprise* was instant: up sprang sixty men on the quarterdeck and gun port lids were hauled up. On the gun deck a hundred and more hastened to run out their guns. The eighteens on each side began to be hauled out; at each gun six men were heaving and sweating to haul the two tons weight until the barrel protruded far through its port. At those two guns held back their crews waited. From the galley came four men carrying two red-hot shot in tongs which they hurriedly loaded into the two remaining guns, numbers seven and nine, *Hurricane* and *Delilah*, on the larboard side. The unfamiliar Greek flag, blue stripes bold on white, fluttered lively at the mizzen gaff in the strengthening wind, as if with its own vitality. No one aboard *Surprise* had time to notice or consider the strange flag. The startled Turk xebec had also sprung into life and her men had resumed rowing. Urgent shouting of orders and whips cracking could plainly be heard by all on *Surprise* before the xebec's bow guns spoke with a fearsome thunder, blasting roundshot and flames from their barrels. Great clouds of bilious smoke thrust out, enveloping the gap between *Surprise* and the xebec on her bow, the two vessels just a mere fifty yards apart. Fortunately, the shot flew high, making a sound like tearing silk in passing twelve feet or more over *Surprise's* quarterdeck. A falling block missed the splinter-netting, clattering to the deck amidst curses all round, the bosun being a particular recipient of abuse.

'Greek slave gunners amongst the xebec crew perhaps sighting their country's flag at *Surprise's* mast and firing high,' was the thought that struck Pat. The swell too was noticeably increased in the past hour, and the xebec's bow alternatively rose and fell as she approached. He pondered on this as he looked about the sails and rigging. Little damage was evident on *Surprise* save for some holes and tears in her main course and foresail – which had not been furled as they would normally be in an engagement, they being left loosely hung as part of Pat's deception, and a section of rigging had been torn away. *Surprise's* marksmen were sent hurrying up the shrouds, their burden of two muskets being no weight at all in their haste. He leaned far over the side and shouted loud encouragement, 'HAUL HARD, LADS!' to the men in the barge and the cutter, the twelve and the eight, who were now pulling frantically, as they had never pulled before; and gradually, in agonisingly slow progress, *Surprise* began to come round by her bow.

'HOLD FIRE! HOLD FIRE! NOT YET! NOT YET!' shouted Pat over the rail and down to his officers and gunners.

Lieutenants Pickering and Mower, standing just below the boat stations forward of the quarterdeck, repeated his orders. A further tense minute passed, Pat nearly biting through his tongue, looking about and behind him, studying the approaching second xebec with some anxiety for a long, long ten seconds, a lifetime in such desperate moments. From aloft on *Surprise* a ragged musket fire was opened upon the Turk quarterdeck and several figures on it fell down, stricken.

'The Turks will be reloading, sir,' remarked Prosser unnecessarily, he being more than a little nervous, adding, 'The second xebec nears our stern quarter.' *Surprise* had now been hauled further round, and although no more than a little way past half way to parallel with the forward xebec all her guns could just be brought to bear, their shouting captains having driven their sweating crews to haul the gun carriages round to their very limit.

'FIRE AS THEY BEAR! FIRE AS THEY BEAR!' shouted Pat with all his voice, waving his hat; 'FIRE!' he screamed again, and the ear-shattering crescendo of noise was near instantly reached as all of *Surprise's* larboard battery opened fire in a devastating ripple of violence all along her side, great flashes of red-orange fire and dirty, grey smoke belching out from the guns and the smashers, two red-hot shot amongst the missiles, the deck shaking violently and the masts quivering. A ferocious bellowing erupted from two hundred men and more as the great guns violently recoiled and the carronades were flung back on their slides with a crash. *Surprise's* crew had not missed, could not possibly miss, the distance now no more than forty yards. Along the xebec's side, from *Surprise's* shot strikes great gaping holes could be seen by Pat and all his larboard crew; many of the xebec's oars were smashed into broken stumps and many more were wholly missing, wrenched away by iron shot. Much of her bulwark was battered into jagged shards and her bow guns had been thrown aside by shot strikes. From the thousands of canister shot projectiles, the effects at such short range were horrifying: dozens of dead and dying men lay strewn across her deck, as were severed body parts: legs and arms, even a head. Such carnage could plainly be picked out, but not a single officer could be identified and no shouting of any further orders could be heard amidst the carnage aboard her.

On *Surprise* the gun crews had no time to stare; amidst the shouts of 'Hurrah! Hurrah!' the most frantic reloading was taking place and the frenetic activity on the decks was spurred by the orders and curses of the gun captains, the powder monkeys rushing as fast as they could shift to bring fresh charges. All along the larboard side the guns were being wormed, sponged, charges and wads rammed home, shot and now grape reloaded, and guns run out as fast as any crew had ever managed to do so before. *Surprise* was turning as the desperate rowers hauled her round. The second xebec was directly astern of *Surprise*, one hundred yards away, and none of *Surprise's* ready starboard guns could yet bear on her. The barge and cutter crews were still rowing frantically, not yet tiring, Barton's shouts of encouragement hardly audible. Few could still hear with any clarity, the noise of the guns drowning out all else. *Surprise* was coming round further each minute by the head yet it did not look to Pat as if *Surprise* could fire before the second Turk fired, and so all attention remained on the first xebec, clearly stricken very badly and aflame too, black smoke rising from amidships. She was plainly shearing off, some semblance of command restored, and a very desultory rowing could be seen at her beam. *Surprise,* larboard guns swiftly reloaded, fired again, delivering another fiery series of hammer blows on the first xebec, and this time firing grape too. The missiles inflicted the severest carnage on the xebec crew, still reeling from the roundshot and canister of the first broadside. It looked as if the deck had been swept clean. Barely a man was left standing or sitting. Scores lay dead athwart her deck and on her benches; dozens of corpses had already been thrown into the water. The first xebec was clearly in great distress, presented little or no danger and so could be relegated from Pat's attention. He turned away to consider the second, less than sixty yards or so astern, and her guns, he thought, bar a miracle could not possibly miss *Surprise*.

'LIE DOWN, LADS! LIE DOWN!' screamed Pat, 'FLAT AS YOU CAN! LIE DOWN!' and, convention abandoned, he threw himself on to his chest on the quarterdeck. Instantly,

BOOM! BOOM! thundered as the second xebec fired. The near shots, so close, did not miss their target. The sound of the explosions was heard just fractionally before the balls smashed through the stern of the ship, the lights of the great cabin not the least impedance, the shots flying through the coach and rising, tearing across *Surprise's* deck midships, cutting rigging and rising to rip through foremast sails. Pat's command to his men to throw themselves down to the deck had probably saved at least several of their lives. He turned his head and looked about him whilst still prone, seeing anxious faces staring back towards him from the quarterdeck gunners. Within minutes the xebec's guns roared once more. Again, the shot entered *Surprise* below them, striking and smashing through planking, breaking the companionway and its steps from the quarterdeck to the gun deck into kindling, having entered again through the great cabin, shattering much of the remaining glass panes in its windows. One shot smashed into the capstan and the second struck one of the guns amidships before ricocheting off into the heavens.

'UP LADS! UP NOW!' screamed Pat, leaping to his feet. 'Mr Pickering!' He leaned over the rail and shouted down to the gun deck, 'Mr Pickering, send the larbowlins to haul tight the tops'ls, the courses and to brace every yard all a-tanto, topgallants and all. We will need to catch every breath of wind in every stitch of canvas if we are to survive this day.'

'Aye aye, sir. Larbowlins to make all sail.'

On *Surprise*'s gun deck, as the men of the larboard gun crews swarmed to their task, the starboard gun crews waited anxiously for the command to fire. Double red-hot shot had been loaded in those two guns nearest the ship's galley: *Pure Poison* and *Old Nick*. On the barge and the cutter, the crews were tiring, drenched in their own sweat, breathing heavily, and all their strength was nearly gone. Yet still they valiantly but feebly pulled at their oars. Fortunately, their efforts were no longer necessary as the second xebec was now abeam *Surprise*, to starboard, but backing her oars frantically. The first, to larboard, had plainly had enough, had broken off any intent of further action; command had been restored to her and the few remaining unwounded oarsmen were plainly striving to shift her away from

*Surprise* as best they could. *Surprise*'s starboard gun crews now had the second xebec in their sights, barely forty yards off her quarter. A few shots still rang out from the tops as the last of the marksmen's powder and shot was fired, seeking officer victims aboard the second xebec, although the still-billowing smoke much obscured any targets.

Pat looked about him, seeing many a gun captain's enquiring face staring towards him, and in that same moment he observed with an almost overwhelming surge of grateful relief – which welled up from deep within him, suppressing momentarily his anxiety – that there seemed fortunately few casualties. He raised his arm and, sensing the roll of the ship being at the precise position to unleash the cannonade, in an instant brought it sweeping down, his cap in hand, with a simultaneous shout of 'FIRE!' to his starboard crews, his shout echoed by Pickering and Mower, 'FIRE!' All *Surprise*'s guns, it seemed, exploded together instantaneously, with a cacophony of deafening, roaring, thunderous sound, the deck pulsating and the masts shivering violently under the great strain; vast long fiery flames belched out, the guns sending their deadly missiles on their way, for *Surprise* too at this short range could not possibly miss.

Frantically the crews rushed to reload their guns, the anxious captains urging their sweating men to haste amidst more shouts of 'Hurrah!' The powder boys were running amidst the frenetic activity of guns recoiling and men heaving them out again to bring their fresh charges from below, shot together with grape being rammed into the barrels. As each gun was run out, it was fired again without delay or any order being given, and a second ragged barrage erupted again from *Surprise's* starboard side, hurling more death and destruction at the xebec.

Thick, sulphurous smoke enveloped all on deck in its bitter, choking maw. In moments, as it began to clear, blown off to larboard by the still freshening wind, all aboard *Surprise* could see that the xebec was utterly destroyed. Its larboard side was near totally crushed along its length by the heavy blows from the great guns, the carronades in particular firing a very heavy ball and doing frightful damage. Barely a solitary intact oar remained and a huge list was now remarked upon. Of the xebec's boats, wheel, capstan and binnacle there was no trace left, not even fragments. Her mainmast had also been shot away, its sail half in and half out of the water. Alongside it floated great swathes of timber jetsam with many wounded and dying men visible all about it. Smoke rose from the xebec midships as the embedded, red-hot shot did its work.

On the xebec, all was in chaos: dead men were strewn about her deck; oarsmen struggled to rise from their positions; a very few men at her ends were striving still to ready their guns; shouts of command could still be heard from determined officers, urging shocked and stricken men to action. At that moment *Surprise* fired again, the third volley not nearly concurrent as each gun crew reloaded and fired as soon as the grapeshot could be rammed into the muzzle and the gun run out again through its port. At a bare thirty yards distance the carnage on the xebec was immense: the shocked survivors of the first and second discharges were swept away as if by a hurricane. The devastation wreaked by the shrieking hail of grape left not a single man standing or sitting. Bodies upon mangled bodies lay prostrate all over her deck; blood ran in small streams across the deck and out from the scuppers. Shrill, screaming wails of agony could plainly be heard from men who would never be whole again.

Pat averted his gaze from the xebec, the ghastly, gory business being done. The horror unleashed from his guns had removed all danger to *Surprise* with just five broadsides. He shouted, 'CEASE FIRE! CEASE FIRE! ALL HANDS TO THE BRACES!' He called down to his second, 'Mr Pickering, recover our lads from the boats. Swiftly now, afore the xebecs turn about; we are still vulnerable to an enterprising captain, and one against two... though I doubt they have still any spirit for a fight. Mr Prosser, luff up and touch her; south as best you can.'

'Aye aye, sir. Are they finished... would you think?'

'Were I their captain, I would be hastening towards land at best speed so as to beach and save what may. Let us capitalise on this freshening wind and be away as quick as we can,' ordered Pat, huge physical tremors of relief shaking his body. His thoughts were mixed: anxious feelings of caution tempering the momentary jubilation he felt at a miraculous victory, for assuredly that it was. He strived consciously but with a degree of difficulty to hold fast to a composure which radiated assurance, fortitude and conviction, but in his heart of hearts he felt sick, a physical nausea rising at the thought of the men whose lives he had destroyed, a tightening of his throat coming upon him, a blood-soaked vision of human detritus on the xebecs' decks filling his mind; and a black depression swiftly enveloped his spirits even though it had been a relatively painless victory for his own shipmates, one to which he attached not the least jubilation. 'I find I am getting old,' he said to himself, out of earshot of all on the quarterdeck, minutes passing but hearing nothing of the customary shipboard noises all around him.

The Turks would not fight again and might not even make any beach let alone reach home, the damage they had suffered being so extreme. The attention of all aboard *Surprise* now turned to gaining as much speed as she could achieve in the stiffening but weak breeze, for it was still no more than that. Course and topsail yards were braced at their extremes to harvest what they could and studdingsails were rigged again on their booms. The Greek flag still streamed vigorously at the mizzen. The barge and cutter crews had been recovered, utterly exhausted and dripping, so little strength left that they were barely able to clamber up the ship's side, the boats left in tow, bobbing far astern on lengthened ropes. All the rowers collapsed on the deck, the ship's boys bringing them water which all gulped gratefully, pint after welcome pint, speech quite beyond them. The near activity broke Pat's rigid introspection at last and he stared all about him in a drifting return to focus upon his own careful evaluation.

'WELL DONE, LADS! WELL DONE!' Pat found a moment for a grateful shout of praise and a wave of his hat from his quarterdeck before returning to gaze at the xebecs, for they were now three hundred yards or more astern of *Surprise*, not moving in the water and more smoke, dense and black, visibly rising from both of them as, presumably, deck oakum steeped in highly-flammable pitch was burning. Pickering and Mower had now joined him on the quarterdeck. Of Duncan, who had shifted below to the gun deck at the beginning of the battle at Pat's bequest to help his other lieutenants - *Surprise* having no midshipmen - there was no sign. 'How are we doing, Mr Pickering?'

'Mighty fine, sir,' Pat's momentary uncertainty did not escape Pickering's eye.

'Might fine... mighty fine, eh?' murmured Pat, becoming conscious of a raging thirst even as he strived to clarify a confusion of multiple concerns.

'And I venture the wind is stirring at last,' added Pickering, the tone of relief plain in his voice.

'Not before time, I venture. Mr Mower, go below and ask Mr Marston of our casualties, if you will,' said Pat softly through dry lips, great fatigue now clearly evident in his face and sweat having streaked the black powder smoke particles engrained in every pore of his skin; a bloody gash was evident above his eye and blood was running copiously down the side of his face. His physical strength seemed to have greatly diminished throughout all his body in the unconscious registration of release from danger, and he wrestled to control his thoughts, to steer away from reflection and to face the present with all its immediacies, for indeed there was no luxury of time for reflection; not a single minute of leisure was available to him, not in the least; and in such moments the responsibilities morphed into burdens and all weighed heavily upon him.

'Aye aye, sir,' Mower replied wearily, tension fading as the adrenalin rush subsided and exhaustion set in.

'Water, massa?' asked Freeman, emerging, proffering a cloth and the ladle from a bucket he was carrying.

'Thankee Freeman, thankee... obliged,' was all a grateful Pat could say, gulping greedily, the water gushing from the ladle into and out of his parched mouth as he swallowed the warm pints, pausing to spit to wash away the foul and acrid flavour of the gunsmoke whilst an anxious Murphy strived to mop the blood from his face even as Pat waved him away with few words, 'Wait... wait until I gather my wits... WAIT... Thank you, Murphy.'

The shattered xebecs were still watched closely until they had been left some five hundred yards in *Surprise's* wake, a very weary crew settling to recover from their exertions, the ship's boys bringing water buckets along the deck to quench the thirst of every man, for the sun had yet to reach its zenith and the air temperature was measured already at eighty-seven degrees on the Fahrenheit scale.

'I think they will have their hands full for some hours or more, Tom,' Pat eventually said to Pickering, relief now awash in his voice and formality slipping away. 'That was damned uncomfortable... we are well out of that.'

'Aye sir,' Pickering spat to clear his throat before speaking through an exceptionally dry mouth. Pat passed him the ladle from which he drank great gulps of water until it flowed down his chin.

'How many men have we lost, James?' asked Pat in apprehensive voice; Mower had returned to the quarterdeck. 'God, how I wish the Doctor was here with us.'

Mower wiped smoke from his eyes and sweat from his brow, and with the barest smile of relief reported, 'I am relieved to tell you, sir, that we have suffered no deaths... at least not yet...'

'No deaths... no deaths; not yet, did you say? Thanks be to God, Mary and Saint Patrick!' declared Pat with heartfelt feeling; 'We have come off easy.'

'... though Mr Macleod has been struck down...'

'What! Macleod? Knocked down, did you say? How is he?'

'He is below, unconscious. Mr Marston is tending him. Ten more men are being treated; eight with splinters, two of them severe. One of the new gunners has a crushed foot as he did not move swiftly enough when his gun recoiled. The last has a severe burn on his leg from the red-hot shot. I know not yet how it came about,' Mower concluded.

'A cheap victory,' said Pickering in subdued voice. 'Here, sir, take my scarf, for you are bleeding well from above your eye.'

'Yes, indeed it was, Tom. Thankee, 'tis but a scratch. I thought we surely would be dished that time. I find I care little for the taste of this victory. Perhaps I find I am becoming old,' muttered Pat, wiping a renewed small stream of blood away from the side of his face, his collar already blood-soaked.

'And only twenty minutes since the first xebec opened upon us,' Mower added.

Pat looked his Third squarely in the face for a few moments, as if collecting his thoughts from far away, before replying very quietly, 'Would anyone wish such horror to last longer, James? I collect that *Chesapeake* struck to *Shannon* after just fifteen minutes... and for only eleven of them was we firing. Yes... I was there... and that was a bloody affair... Captain Broke severely wounded and poor Lawrence of *Chesapeake* losing his life. No, twenty minutes is plenty enough for me... such bloody butchery. I venture the Turks have lost scores of men this day... and most likely many Greeks amongst them... galley slaves at the oars, poor souls. Now they know there is a frigate in Greek service... and our next engagement will afford us no surprise.'

An agitated Murphy reappeared, his gaze fastening on the red runnel over Pat's eye, cheek and chin, 'Well, sorr, 'tis time to look to a dressing over that bloody eye... this d'reckly minute.'

'Eh? No, it don't signify... No, later will answer. My handkerchief will serve for the present; Mr Marston will have his hands full, no doubt. I must look to see how the lads are doing... I must go round the ship.'

One of the aft companionways being smashed to pieces by a ball strike and the other obstructed by the debris, Pat walked forward to the foc's'le and descended the steps to the gun deck. He paced aft very slowly amongst his weary gunners and crew, looking at each of them as he passed by, staring about him and assessing the damage, exchanging a word here and there, passing many a compliment and asking of many an old shipmate until he returned to the point amidships where his men could congregate about him and hear his words. He halted and the animated discussions amongst the crew faded away as all became aware he waited to speak to them. The furore and hubbub had now ceased, and the slap of the bow wave along the hull was again audible, *Surprise's* speed increasing with the strengthening wind. The sound of cut shrouds slapping against halliards, against yards and masts, passed unnoticed, and nothing interrupted his words to his men, spoken with great pride as he stood amongst them. 'Well done, lads; you may rest easy now. Well done, every one of you.

A bloody business, but never better gun handling did I ever see on *Tenedos* in all our actions, and you have my compliments and best thanks.' There was a growl of appreciation from scores of voices before Pat continued, 'Lads, we cannot tarry here to take prizes, nor to sink those xebecs, for we have no official standing with any flag, neither Royal Navy nor Greek. Let us eat now, rest awhile afore we clean guns and ship, but remain vigilant, for the Turk has many more ships in these waters and we are but one. Mr Tizard, it seems that you have much work to do,' said Pat wearily, waving to the smashed planking and the steps.

'Right away, sir,' replied the carpenter, striving for a cheerful countenance.

Pat continued his tour, accompanied by Pickering, stepping down and walking forward to the gloomy cockpit, in near darkness to Pat's eyes after the bright daylight of the deck. A very busy Marston laboured under an Argand oil lamp. To Pat's nose the foul stench was almost overpowering after the fresh air of the quarterdeck, so vile that it seemed akin to a putrid cesspit, and interspersed with the smell of human detritus came the coppery smell of blood, the brutal meld hanging in the torpid, hot air, an insufferably high temperature. 'Mr Pickering, will you look to the rigging of a windsail and without the loss of a moment, and I am minded we will be best served by opening the sweetening-cock.'

'Aye aye, sir; without the loss of a moment.'

The surgeon was helped by three assistants in attendance, including Mrs Boswell, the gunner's wife, one of the few women permitted to sail with them by long convention. As Pat's eyes slowly adjusted, and as the sweat began to form all over his body, he could see that the deck near the surgeon's table was strewn with bloody dressings and - Pat could not quite make out enough to be sure - what looked like small fragments of flesh. As he stared, his mind reeling in revulsion, the quick movement of a brace of rats darting out momentarily from the shadows for a shred of their intended bounty caught his eye. Pat hesitated, he timed his single step forward to perfection, and he kicked one rat hard against the side, its fellow squealing in pursuit into the darkness. He looked around him as from all corners the moans of pain registered as unceasing and the occasional louder, shrill scream of acute distress was a torture to his ears.

Fortunately, the generous dispensing of laudanum had quieted the agonies of the four most badly wounded seamen: one with a foot quite crushed by the recoiling gun carriage of *Hell's Mouth*, amputation being at the forefront of Marston's deliberations but inexperience and doubt staying his hand; and a second who had taken a deep splinter right through his thigh, fortunately missing all the major blood vessels. It was a large splinter which, Mrs Boswell explained, Marston had struggled to remove, only succeeding with the patient strapped to the table with two assistants to hold his struggles and one to quieten his screams, the injured man biting down on a block held in his mouth to safeguard his tongue as the splinter was drawn back and out as fast as fast could be but, in all care, still taking two agonising minutes.

Mrs Boswell continued her dismaying briefing in low voice to Pat; the third casualty, Symes, had taken a significant splinter into his chest, penetrating his lung, and his life expectancy was short, draining away like the red froth bubbling from his mouth and nose, whilst his brother sat by him, silently weeping whilst holding firm his brother's hand. Marston himself was in visible despair, finding the wound far beyond his limited competency to treat. The fourth casualty, a man burned by the red-hot shot, William Currie, had also been given plentiful laudanum, and now slept a deep sleep, his pain temporarily suppressed for some hours. Six others were awake and talking amongst themselves, their smaller and less critical splinter wounds all cleaned and dressed by Marston. All would, bar any infection, recover completely.

Pat's halting steps had carried him to the surgeon's table; 'How... how is it, Mr Marston?' asked Pat, deep concern very evident in his voice, low and wavering.

Marston looked up, wiping the sweat from his brow with the back of his bloody hand before replying to his captain, striving to project a quiet confidence and conviction in his voice despite his inner agitations, 'Sir, I believe I may answer for all but one of these men. I am very fearful for Symes here, who I am not competent to treat; I doubt that even the finest surgeon could preserve him. I have sewn him up; that is to say as best as I am able given the... the... extent... *the severity* of his wound, and I shall keep him as comfortable as can be until he is gone. That is to say if he will accept the draught of laudanum, for he is struggling to breathe let alone drink. He will be with God this day.' Marston sighed, a deep, enduring sigh of depair. 'He has an hour, perhaps two; I doubt it will be more.'

'May God, Mary and Saint Patrick preserve his soul,' whispered Pat, his mind confused and bewildered in the shared moment of distress, the sense of responsibility bearing heavy upon his every thought. He stooped down to the cot and looked at his stricken shipmate, wretched anxiety searing his thinking and writ plain in his face; he stared for some moments at the unconscious Symes whose breathing was short and greatly laboured. He bent down and leaned over Symes; gently he laid his hand on his forehead and he whispered close to his ear, 'Ye are not alone, Symes; your shipmates are here with you, your brother too. All your friends are hereabouts.' There was no reaction from Symes, and Pat remained, unmoving, the distress greater than ever he could recall in similar circumstances in the past, and he stared intently at his shipmate as if willing something, *anything* ... but quite what Pat did not know. He nodded to Symes' brother, his eyes blinking rapidly, turned his face away and sighed, a long, long inhalation and even longer exhalation, and his spirits sank as low as they had ever been; and as the tears began to well from his sore eyes he strived to conceal them by ineffectually wiping away the runnels of blood smeared across his cheeks.

Marston, determined to return his own attentions to his patients, interrupted Pat's gaze and silent thoughts after a long minute, 'Mason should recover, given time. It will be some weeks at least, perhaps months, afore he will be fit and about on the leg that took the splinter. Edwards here may lose his foot, but I do not despair for him; I will defer to Doctor Ferguson on that and keep him tolerably comfortable until then. The six men over there will be fit within a few weeks,' he concluded, waving his hand towards the more fortunate half a dozen of the wounded.

'How... how is Mr Macleod? Where is he?' Pat's careworn face was a picture of absolute distress as his thoughts focused on his friend.

'Freeman and Old Jim Lamb have taken him to his cot. His head was struck hard, a splinter most likely. Fortunately, its force was surely spent when it struck him for there is no wound, save a deep scratch or two and a heavy bruise. He is unconscious, a great swelling on his head. Freeman remains with him, attending, should he awake.'

'When do you think he will recover?' a badly shaken Pat asked nervously, unsure that he wished to hear the answer in case it was bad.

'Sir, I can saw, cut, stitch and dress wounds, but his injury is far beyond my paltry skills. Our Lord may preserve him, but I can do nothing more. Rest is the only remedy. We must leave him be, sir. Silence will be beneficial... and we... we will pray for him.'

'Thank you, Mr Marston... I am much indebted to you... and... *and God bless you*,' murmured Pat, looking back at Symes; his relief at so small a butcher's bill was tempered by the impending loss of one of his crew. Symes was a long-serving Tenedos and a Wesleyan elder too, back home in Falmouth, if Pat's memory served him; and in that moment, when death in all its cerebral brutality was once more before him, Duncan's critical status pressed harder than ever upon his worries and his downcast feelings.

'I must see that wound above your eye,' added Marston.

'Oh, 'tis nothing, merely a scratch; thank you.'

'That's as may be, but an inch lower and you would have required Nelson's patch. I will attend you later. Here, take this cloth for the moment... and I beg you will endeavour to ask Murphy to wash the gash clean when you are afforded the least time.'

'Thank you, Mr Marston... Thank you... *Michael*,' Pat offered his heartfelt thanks very quietly and left Marston to his ministrations. He walked slowly aft to the gun-room, deep in thought, and so to Macleod's cot, where he stared in silence at his unmoving, unconscious friend for some minutes, nodded to

Freeman, and paced disconsolately back the length of the lower deck, to and up the for'ard steps, looking again in assessment and nodding to the treated casualties with the best effort at a smile that he could manage. He reversed his path and moved aft in further inspection as he passed once more along the gun deck, a slow wave of his hand to more of his men in passing. The after-battle exhaustion, the onrushing severe debilitation of his energy which came every time with the release of tension, and the great shock too of finding his friend so dangerously wounded all left him unable to speak further with any of them. He nodded with what he hoped was a supportive expression to several enquiring faces staring at him as he passed by, his thinking frozen, save that he felt a salt stream of tears streaming down the side of his face, mingling with the blood oozing from his head wound, which obscured his tears from his men's sight, for so he hoped and for which he was in that moment very grateful.

Back in the great cabin an exceptionally tired Pat sat alone at his table, deeply unhappy, oblivious to the ship's familiar movements, a gentle rise and fall at the bow and the smallest sensation of roll, his head in his cupped hands, his chair amidst hundreds of glass shards scattered all over the deck from his shattered cabin lights, half of them smashed away and half remaining intact. The adrenalin rush of the battle was gone at last and exhaustion was draining his every fibre as its customary successor. He wiped his bloody forehead and his smeared cheeks with his handkerchief and, gratefully, he sipped a large tot of fiery Greek brandy accompanied by strong black coffee, freshly brewed and delivered since the battle had ended, several men having remarked on Pat's visible distress to Wilkins. He had been reflecting on the engagement and the casualties for an age, for so it seemed, when Murphy entered, together with his chum, Old Jim Lamb, another long-serving veteran of *Tenedos*'s many voyages and these days still serving as cook's assistant and Murphy's dogsbody.

'Well, Jim here will clean up the cabin, sorr, and I'll fetch your dinner d'reckly. Will I take a look now at that scratch on your head, sorr?' asked Murphy, very concerned; 'Sure, 'tis still all a'bleeding o'er your collar?'

Pat gingerly raised his head, his reply quiet, despond plain in his voice, 'Oh! Thankee, Murphy, a wet cloth will serve; 'tis nothing... and dinner will be fair welcome, I am mighty clemmed. Would you ask Mr Pickering and Mr Mower if they would care to join me? Pass the word for the carpenter. Perhaps Mr Tizard could board over some of these broken panes.'

Murphy, with a gravely discontented air, the plain and urgent necessity for attending his captain - as he saw things - refused, was gone when Pat looked up again, but within, it seemed, bare moments his officers had joined him, and Wilkins had appeared with a large pot of lobscouse, bowls and all. Old Jim Lamb clutched two bottles of claret and glasses. Murphy still fussed about his captain, wiping the flowing blood from his forehead and the side of his face, and would have pressed on to clean the shirt with Pat in it had he not waved him off with a softly murmured, 'Thankee Murphy, thankee Jim,' as Lamb was affectionately addressed by all aboard, the captain included. 'Gentlemen, we shall not stand on ceremony this day. Please, allow me to help you to this food whilst 'tis still hot,' said a very muted Pat, as he ladled out generous bowls and pushed them to his officers, realising in that moment just how acutely hungry he was, having eaten nothing since leaving his breakfast uneaten. Mower poured the wine, and for a few minutes all three said nothing but ate hungrily, the lobscouse soon devoured.

When they had finished eating none spoke; indeed, there was nothing of initiative or the least zest in all their faces, and every man looked to his fellows as if seeking to avoid any inappropriate comment as Murphy busied about them collecting the bowls. Pat looked up to his steward as Murphy's hand hovered about the bottle; he could not shake from his mind the sight of Duncan lying unconscious in his cot. 'Murphy, will you kindly take the cold ham and a jug of ale, and set it alongside Mr Macleod? Mr Marston will be busy for many an hour, and I would not care for Mr Macleod to come round in the night with thirst and no drink nor any bite at hand.'

'Well, sorr, I will be taking turn and turn about with Freeman, sitting with Mr Macleod until he does,' Murphy replied, no trace of the curmudgeon in his voice.

'You have my best thanks, Murphy... thank you kindly,' whispered Pat, nodding gratefully to his steward, a profound appreciation in his voice.

It was Mower who spoke first, seeking to lift the gloomy ambience in the cabin and in breach of the custom that the officers did not speak except to reply to their captain. 'A bloody business, sir; there must have been scores and scores of dead and wounded on the second xebec from the close firing, and after our grape I could not see a soul sitting or standing on her deck.'

Pickering too had sensed the mood, and seeking to lift his captain's spirits added his own observation, 'The first xebec took a pounding too; I doubt either will see the Golden Horn again.'

Pat looked up at his officers for a few moments and settled his glass on the table. He licked away the blood from his lips, trickling still from the gash above his eye, and his quietly spoken words seemed to struggle from afar, a long way back, pulled from deep down in his memory, 'At Trafalgar, I collect when *Colossus* took *Swiftsure*... the Frenchie that is... *I was serving on her as Third in those days*... we had inflicted five hundred casualties in her crew of seven hundred... and her sides ran red from the scuppers. It was said that *Victory's* first broadside, fired at Villeneuve's flagship, *Bucentaure*, inflicted four hundred casualties and smashed or shifted twenty guns on her decks. It is assuredly a bloody business we are engaged in, gentlemen. We may take small comfort from the thought that the Greek cause is just... *and our few casualties*.' He took a draught from his glass and, no one else caring to speak further, he resumed, his voice revealing his sorrow, his fatigue, 'I am much set back because we will lose another old shipmate this day... poor John Symes. For many a year he made his way, with me... with us... I think since the year 'six. I collect he was with us, alongside of me, when we captured *Half Moon*, seven or more long years ago.' Pat sighed, 'To be sure, our lease on this life is short.'

'What now for our mission, sir?' asked Pickering in apprehensive voice.

'We're done with that,' replied Pat. 'If the Turk fleet was here, I doubt they would patrol with merely two xebecs. No, it's back to Cephalonia for us, to Doctor Ferguson at all speed.'

Later, a few minutes before sunset, as the light began to diffuse after the longest day a greatly unsettled Pat could remember for a long time, he wrapped his grego around him and stepped up to his quarterdeck to pace silently fore and aft, fore and aft, taking in the mood of his men at the helm, looking to the slowly shifting, thin, wispy clouds high in the reddening sky, their varied colours a spectacular display of all the shades at the red end of the spectrum, the sun fast descending towards the western horizon, fine on the bow. He looked to the log-board, showing six knots; he gazed at the sails, the merest hint of an occasional shiver on the weather edges, *Surprise* close-hauled, six points off the wind - she would not hold closer - and making long tacks, Pat having decided in principle that the new ropes throughout the ship would afford him the luxury of dispensing with the slower but more gentle wearing of the barky. He continued to pace, unceasing fore and aft, fore and aft, as the sun bid final farewell and slipped gracefully into the horizon just as Dalby rang out two bells of the last dog watch; and as he did so he wondered, *perhaps*, whether the barky might have fought the xebecs in any better fashion; for, as ever, the losses sat heavy in his thoughts, disturbed his conscience and vexed his spirits; and he wondered, *perhaps*, if Symes might not have been so very severely wounded had he changed tactics; and *perhaps* Duncan and his other shipmates too might not have been injured; but as for what alternatives might have been open to him he could not fathom. On he paced, fore and aft, fore and aft throughout the prevailing silence of the twilight, still deliberating in silence, chaotic doubts persisting in his tired mind; he ignored the concerned looks from the retiring helmsmen at the change of watch, ignored Murphy's repeated suggestions of supper, 'Vittles is up!' and ten minutes later, 'Well, the toasted cheese be a'ruining!' His anxious steward was dismissed with a wave away of his hand. In the final dim vestiges of the gloaming he ignored both Mower and Pickering suggesting he retire and that they would spell him, the ship safe in their hands; and, all the time, his mind in turmoil, he considered the battle in retrospect, his thoughts a deeply analytical review of his decisions. The air temperature was still warm even in the moderate breeze, and the only sounds disturbing a total tranquillity on the quarterdeck were the gentle creak of the rigging and the near imperceptible splash of the bow wave washing along the waterline, and to Pat's ears an occasional and quiet prompt from the master to the helmen to 'Let her go off' and 'Steady so'. He was still there at the taffrail two hours later as the full moon rose in the sky directly astern, presenting itself in all its spectacular glory, its brilliance illuminating *Surprise's* wake as an unbroken silver streak of glowing phosphoresence in the moonlight on the most moderate of seas, trailing away into distant darkness, when Pat's mind, at last and with difficulty, reined in his painful deliberations, and he reconciled himself to what would be on the morrow, to an assuredly agonising day when Symes would go to his watery grave. With the slowest of movements he navigated the carpenter's hasty repairs to the steps and made his way back to the great cabin where he removed his boots and his coat only with difficulty; and, too weary to discard more of his clothing, he lay back on his cot, intending to undress after a few minutes of physical respite, his mind a'whirl within a maelstrom of tumultuous doubts and raging confusion. However, another hour passed in anguish, in sleepless mental discomfort as his mind refused to relinquish its grip on his body until he eventually fell into a deep sleep of absolute physical and mental exhaustion. Five minutes later Murphy crept in quietly to examine Pat's bloody gash on his head - thankfully dried to a crusted scab - and to extinguish the solitary Argand lamp, the beatific moon shining bright through the remaining panes of the shattered stern gallery as if in tiny consolation for a dreadful day.

*Tuesday 29th July 1823      aboard Surprise, off NW Candia*

After breakfast, after pumping the bilges dry, the crew mustered on the deck. The day was a quite beautiful one, another brilliantly blue and infinite expanse of cloudless sky and with scarcely the least whisper of a breeze. The hands gathered on the gun deck, so many that some stood as far forward as the galley, the majority standing just forward of the mainmast. The seaman with the lung splinter, Symes, had fought hard for his life and lingered, but he had died shortly after midnight, Marston despairing at his inability to save him. It was a glum mood as Pat and his officers stepped forward on the gun deck as the crew, standing in their divisions, the customary drum dispensed with on this solemn occasion, talked quietly amongst themselves. Just two topmen remained aloft, ever alert; and the only other men not present were the two men at the helm and the injured, who remained below. The Wesleyans, six score or more of them, had turned out in their best red and white attire, washed and starched. Every man was adorned with a purple scarf, their customary colour for funerals, in due deference and respect to their deceased comrade, Symes having been one of their number. At six bells of the forenoon watch the temperature had risen steadily to a baking hot eighty-five degrees, but the weak south-westerly wind, no more than a light topgallant breeze, did little to cool the assembly. Marston waited in introspective silence to begin the service. Behind him stood all the officers, hats removed and looking silently forward to the people, the Wesleyans prominent at the front. With a sharp tap of a fid on the repaired capstan, Mr Prosser captured the hands' attention and the assembly came to order.

Pat stared at his men for some moments in silent contemplation, his gaze roving across them, picking out those nearer faces he long remembered from his earliest commands. Nearly all he could see were old *Tenedos* hands. The crew's few whispers finally quietened as all became aware that he was waiting to speak. He was, of course, oft acquainted with death and funerals at sea, but the first such in many years struck hard at his mind's equilibrium, and it was some minutes, all the people holding their silence and not a single whisper uttered, before he was able to begin as the bleak significance of the moment weighed heavy in his thoughts. He bit hard on his lip as he felt his eyes beginning to water, and he removed his hat, tucked it under his arm and began, 'Lads, it is the long road we have travelled together... all these years... and we are gathered here this day to respect our old shipmate, John Symes... who has sadly lost the number of his mess. Long-serving he was... with us aboard our dear *Tenedos* and now *Surprise;* 'tis assuredly a loss to us all.' There was a general murmur of accord in the briefest of pauses before Pat continued, finding increasing difficulty with his words, as was visible to all; 'Our dear friend, John Symes... *our dear friend...* has crossed the bar for the final time... but let us remember him today and long in our future.' He looked about him again for a few moments, as if seeking guidance in this, the most painful of his duties, and he wondered whether his crew were finding the least comfort in his words because he was not himself. He resumed, speaking very softly and striving to keep his composure and at least the semblance of steadfastness in his voice, 'I have asked Mr Marston to speak a few words... afore we bury our shipmate... but first we will hold our station... and... and we will stand in silence for a minute of reflection... and give our respects to John Symes.'

Silence, save for the gulls drifting and calling aloft; silence, save for the rising topgallant breeze rustling through the strands of the rigging and the sail edges vigorously flapping on unbraced yards; silence, not a murmur from any man, the people with heads down, the thoughts of all kept to themselves; silence, save for the wash of successive waves which slapped the sides of the barky. No one was counting the seconds and it was two minutes more or longer before a distraught Pat raised his head and cried out, 'THANK YOU, SHIPMATES!' His emotions on fire, his feelings running riot, his mind in a total disarray of dismay, he could say nothing more.

Every man, every old tarpaulin that they were, held the utmost respect for their captain; and his discomfort was perfectly evident, for he looked careworn as never before in his whole demeanour; and - it was plain to see - no further words could he find. Another minute passed in silence, with no man uttering the least murmur.

Eventually, Marston - seeing plain his duty and obligation - stepped to Pat's side and put a gentle hand on his arm; 'Will I speak to our people now, sir?' he whispered with an emphasis that left no doubt that this was the timely moment.

Pat said nothing in his distress and simply looked down again, but he waved Marston forward before stepping back for a few paces, finding his way around the detritus of the smashed companionway and halting behind the mainmast, a flimsy sanctuary where he felt he might decently allow his tears to flow and where they might not be remarked; for in his overwhelming despair in that moment it was completely beyond his sensibilities to halt them.

Marston stepped forward to the makeshift lectern. The chaplain began to speak, a little slowly at first yet with the assurance of deep conviction, his words firm, steady, unwavering, 'I am mindful of a prior eulogy, a very famous one by Pericles at the end of a previous Greek war, long past. I could never do better than to borrow just a few words of that most magnificent speech, so famous in Greek history.' Marston paused for a few moments to gaze upon his audience, all silent, all reflecting on their past acquaintanceship with their lost shipmate, no one showing the least cognisance of Pericles. From all about them, from the air and from *Surprise* herself, the customary sounds of their sea-going routine, of gulls calling, of the bow wave slapping on the hull, of the creaking rigging, all pressed on them with particular clarity as Marston took a deep breath and resumed, 'Pericles said this... *In doing good we are unlike others; we make our friends by conferring not by receiving favours. Such a man may benefit his country or his cause whatever the obscurity of his condition. On the battlefield their feet stand fast in the confidence of freedom, and in a frank and fearless spirit, and in an instant, at the height of their fortune, they passed away from the scene, not of their fear, but of their glory.'* Marston paused again to look up, sweeping his gaze slowly across the gathering, looking closely at every face in the front row: all remained mute and quite still. In the reverential silence he continued, *'The value of such a spirit is not to be expressed in words, but in foreign lands there dwells also an unwritten memorial of them, graven not on stone, but in the hearts of men. Make them your examples and - esteeming courage to be freedom and freedom to be happiness - do not weigh too nicely the perils of war...* We bid our farewell to our comrade, our friend, our brother... John Symes... May he rest in peace.'

Marston's short reading found favour with all his listeners, grave nods and murmurs of "Hear him" signalling their accord with the deep sentiments expressed in Pericles' eulogy. Marston took another deep breath, looked about him again and resumed speaking, 'We will conclude this sad day with but a fragment of Psalm one hundred and seven... *They that go down to the sea in ships... and occupy their business in great waters; these men see the works of the Lord... and his wonders in the deep.*'

As Marston finally concluded and raised his head to gaze at his audience, Pat - who had returned, a concerned Pickering standing close at his side - cried out 'AMEN' and looked to the four sombre Wesleyans including a greatly distressed John Symes' tiemate holding the bier on which he lay, bound in his hammock, two eighteen-pound shot at his feet, and at Pat's sad and silent nod they tilted the bier through the open gun port and John Symes slid overboard to his watery grave.

'THANK YOU, SHIPMATES!' Pat cried out in relief at having come to the end of such an upsetting event, adding, 'And now to dinner before work; see to your duties.'

Pickering shouted to the bosun, 'Pipe to dinner!'

The crew dispersed, only a few whispered words exchanged between a minority of them as they returned to their station or ambled slowly forward towards the galley to speak with the cook about their forthcoming dinner; for Tuesday was a meat day, either pork or beef, both long in salt, and whichever it might be it was long in the steeping tubs. Pickering turned towards Pat and, speaking in gentle voice, remarked, 'My duty and best respects, sir, and I beg you will forgive me for... for remarking that you looked to be... to be - *will I say* - tolerably distressed... stepping behind the mast there for some few minutes.'

Pat sighed, 'Yes... yes... my thinking was all ahoo... and I did not care for our people to think me some puling milksop... a right Jack Pudding. Perhaps I am in want of fortitude... my intellects gone astray.'

'Listen, will you, sir? I was myself shaken... to the bottom of my heart, I was so; and I was scrutinising the faces of every man at the front of our assembly... and the spirits of every man - *every one* - were demonstrably out of kilter... That was as plain as a pikestaff.'

'God and Mary bless you,' whispered Pat, his spirits as low as ever they had been.

In the last flickering moments of the fading light in the dusk, little wind also remaining, *Surprise* slowly came about in the approach channel into Argostoli, no Greek flag in evidence on this occasion, Pat being mindful of the necessity for diplomatic conventions not to be breached, as would be the case were the Ionian government to be made officially aware of her real duties in Greek service. Whether the islands' government was now actually aware at all of her duties, officially or otherwise, he knew not, but the hastily repaired battle damage along her sides could not be concealed from even the most inexpert eye, particularly the smashed windows of the great cabin. Although the carpenter had done his best to patch the worst of the splintered planking along the gun deck (fortunately no shot had penetrated *Surprise's* hull below the waterline) and had replaced, after a fashion, the disintegrated companionway steps to the quarterdeck, lacking suitable materials and with so little time available much of the repairs could only be described as jury-rigged at best.

'We will lay a little farther off from the harbour this time, Mr Pickering... and perhaps a kedge might keep her damaged stern lying away from prying eyes in the town,' Pat suggested to his second lieutenant as the crew prepared to drop anchor, *Surprise* moored a little over three-quarters of a mile off from the quay.

'Aye aye, sir.' Within a few minutes Pickering reported, 'The lads are lowering the cutter now to get you quickly ashore.' As *Surprise* steadied on her anchor, Pat clambered down into the cutter, helped aboard by Barton who had stowed Pat's small bag under the prow. Marston remained aboard ship to tend the wounded and Codrington joined Pat as companion for the short ride to their accommodation outside the town, a tiny house which had been offered and rented for the shortest of term in the village of Metaxata. The row for the most discreet landing place at the far end of the harbour quay was swiftly accomplished. *Eleanor* was tied up alongside the quay, but of her crew only a watchman could be seen. It being past 11 p.m. the port office was closed, and so there was no Customs agent at hand to delay them. The horses were rapidly procured from Pat's agent at the fringe of the town, and in the cool of the very late evening they made light of the familiar road at a steady pace, slowed only by Codrington, he being unaccustomed to horses and so most uncomfortably served by his poor riding proficiency.

At midnight they reached the house, candles visible through the windows. The horses were tethered at the trough and, without any ado, Pat - anxious to see his wife and to enquire of Kathleen's health - swept through the door into the small living room. To his very great relief Sinéad sat talking to Kathleen and Simon, all of whom leapt to their feet with great pleasure to greet the arrivals. Without ceremony he swept his wife into his arms and stood hugging Sinéad tightly for several minutes, their private exchanges whispered between them after initial exclamations of mutual joy. It fell to Codrington to greet Simon, Kathleen hastening to the kitchen to procure refreshment for the arrivals.

'Is that coffee I smell? By God that is welcome!' said Pat. Sinéad was now free of his embrace, the two of them seated opposite Simon and Codrington, Sinéad tightly clutching Pat's hand but fretting about the bandage wrapped around his head.

'Here it is and there is brandy, warmed bread, olives and local cheese,' said Kathleen, placing all on the small adjacent table.

'Thankee kindly, my dear; that will answer the case,' said Pat, consumed with happiness. 'I am greatly thankful to see you much recovered.'

'No small thanks to Doctor Ferguson here... and my beloved sister's attentions.'

With Kathleen visibly near completely recovered from her illness, the most unsettled man present was Simon, plainly greatly fretting about his absence from *Surprise*, away without him, his fears rising on his close scrutiny of Pat's healing head wound, small as it was. 'Pat, what is that head wound I see above your eye?' Simon spoke with acute concern in his voice, his anxiety rising in the closer study of Pat's injury.

'Oh, it is of no matter, scarcely a scratch.'

'What has happened?' Suspicions of conflict flickered immediately into his mind. 'Pray be good enough to tell me of your voyage, brother.' In his acute and pressing anxiety Simon was wholly forgetting the presence of the ladies, pausing only until after Pat had gulped a great draught of his coffee; 'I have languished anxiously in this place since your departure, my proper place being aboard our dear *Surprise.*' He spoke with a discomforting feeling of premonition, 'Did you engage in any conflict, pray tell; and were any of our crew stricken? Be so good as to clarify the situation; am I needed now aboard?'

'Perhaps the ladies might wish to retire?' Pat volunteered cautiously, though his suggestion was completely ignored by both. Accepting that, he recounted his story, 'Even afore we reached Candia we were assailed by two Turk xebecs... though we saw 'em off with little but a few of our spars knocked away and some broken windows in the cabin.' A long pause, Pat was concerned for the ladies; and, indeed, the acute and corrosive feelings of grief, only a little diminished with the briefest passage of time, lingered still within his heart; he took a deep breath, swallowed hard and spoke in low voice, 'Symes was killed by a splinter into his lung...' There was a sharp intake of breath from all listening, and Pat himself was grateful for a pause. 'Sadly, there was nothing that Marston could do for him. Mason too, took a tolerably sizeable splinter in his upper leg... which Marston pulled out with some difficulty... It will be some months afore he can reach the tops again. Then there is Edwards, one of the new gunners; his foot was crushed by *Hell's Mouth*... He was careless and did not mind the recoil.' Squeals from the ladies. 'He is in some pain, though Marston did not care to amputate the foot and awaits your lights. Another of our gunners, Old Tom Currie's younger brother, William, is mightily burned on his leg from hot shot... Marston can keep him comfortable only with plentiful laudanum. Half a dozen others have lesser splinter wounds... but doubtless they will recover within a week or two.'

'Dear Lord,' Simon gasped, 'I was not there in their hour of need.'

Pat, unsure of how to put it, Kathleen being present, had kept mention of Macleod to the last. With great trepidation he returned to his story, 'Duncan was struck down by a splinter...' - Kathleen screamed - '... a blow to the head... and he... he ain't *fully* woken up since... but I assure you that Marston is caring for him.' With that dreadful finale Pat concluded his grim list.

Kathleen screamed again and rose from her chair, dropping her cup. She stood stock still. Sinéad gasped and rushed to embrace her sister. After a few moments the two ladies turned to stare at Pat. They looked horrified but said nothing, the shock so great, even as Simon sprang to his feet. 'Hell and death! If only I had accompanied you. I will be away directly... at all speed for the ship... I must attend to help Marston.'

'I am sure the morrow will serve,' Pat suggested, 'Marston is a competent doctor and is with him.'

'I need not tell you, brother,' declared Simon, 'that there are occasions when one may fairly state that there is not a moment to be lost; indeed, I would not linger another moment were Saint Patrick himself imminently awaited; no, I am away directly.'

'I will ride with you,' Kathleen declared, and - strong-willed woman that she was - she would brook no protest, asserting that her recovery was complete. No one - including Simon - cared to contradict her.

'Take our horses. They are outside, and though not fresh will not mind another hour. William Reeve on *Eleanor* will take you across in the cutter. I will return in the morning,' said Pat, realising any further effort to dissuade Kathleen and his friend from leaving until the morrow would be fruitless, realising too that Sinéad would never release him until many more hours had passed.

*Friday 1st August 1823*                    *aboard Surprise, Argostoli*

Late morning brought Pat, somewhat restored in spirit, back aboard *Surprise* to check on his wounded crew members. A bruised Codrington could not agreeably contemplate the immediate return ride to Argostoli and so remained at the house in Metaxata, intending to walk back in the cool of the evening. Brodie and the twins had left the house together, earlier in the morning to walk to the port. Looking about him, Pat noted agreeably that repairs were underway to the planking, several of his crew busy painting over previously damaged and repaired timbers. Before lingering further to inspect his ship he went below to visit his severely wounded shipmates. All had now been accommodated in the tiny cabins off the gun-room, previously occupied by Sinéad, Kathleen and Marston on the voyage out from Falmouth, the lesser-wounded having been discharged to rest in their hammocks. There was no sign of his surgeons, and so he looked in first to Duncan's cabin. Brodie was sitting at the side of his cot on a small stool, gripping his hand, the evidence of plentiful tears streaked down her face. She looked up as Pat entered, her face so very pale. In answer to Pat's unasked question she shook her head, all the while her wide, liquid green eyes seeming to bore into his face, questioning, imploring, her physical stillness at odds with the frantic racing of her thoughts, the deep, deep pain pressing, tearing through her mind.

'Courage, child,' said Pat softly, 'He is in the best of care. Dr Ferguson will surely set him to rights. Where is your mother, lamb? Where are Doctor Ferguson and Mr Marston?'

'Mother has stepped out for a moment. The doctors have been here, watching over father all night, one ever present... whilst the other was looking to their other patients. They retired but an hour ago.'

'I will return in a minute or two, my dear. Will I send Murphy with some tea... with a sandwich perhaps?'

Brodie shook her head, could say no more and turned back to her father. Pat moved along to look in at the next cabin.

'How goes it with your brother?' he asked of Tom Currie.

'Mending slowly, sir; thankee. He has taken some burgoo today, and the Doctor has given him laudanum against the pain, so he is a'sleeping still.'

'I venture 'tis the ramrod for him next time; no more hot shot for him,' Pat joked weakly.

'Aye sir, that's sure,' smiled Currie, pleased with his captain's interest for his brother.

'Mason, how goes it?' asked Pat of the patient in the next cabin.

'Topping, sir; stitched up better'n the wife's sewing, thankee,' came the cheerful response from Mason.

'Good man. Ye'll soon be back to my barge crew,' Pat replied encouragingly. The last patient was Edwards with his crushed left foot. Happily, no infection had set in although the foot was swollen to the monstrous size of twice normal and was deep blue, black and yellow in colour. 'Ye won't be at the Maypole next year, Edwards,' smiled Pat to the obviously pained sailor.

To his credit, Edwards returned a sickly grin, and in a laudanum-slurred voice answered his captain anxiously, 'Will I keep the foot, sir? To be sure, I won't be any use in the rigging if 'tis gone.' To which Pat could only reply, 'If anyone will heal it, Edwards, it is Doctor Ferguson; of that you can be assured.'

After Edwards pained 'Thankee, sir,' Pat headed to the great cabin, intending to speak with Simon and Marston. 'Murphy! Murphy there! My compliments to the Doctor and Mr Marston, if they are at leisure; and please to ask their attendance in the cabin at their *earliest* convenience.'

Within a few minutes the surgeons entered, both looking extremely tired. Murphy, needing no bidding, brought in a great pot of steaming coffee and withdrew from the cabin. In Pat's absence overnight, Murphy with Old Jim Lamb had removed the last of the shattered glass and timber shards whilst the carpenter had boarded over many of the gaping holes of the window remnants. The cabin, though much darker, was no longer so exposed to the elements.

'Gentlemen,' said Pat, 'I beg pardon for calling for you if you were intending to sleep; you look so greatly tired, *quite destroyed.*' No reply other than weary nods and Pat resumed, 'How are the wounded, Simon?'

'All are tolerably comfortable; no small thanks to my colleague here who has served them as well as ever I could.'

Pat managed a nod towards Marston. 'How is Duncan?' he asked Simon anxiously, the surgeon's face grave.

'He is still unconscious... you will be aware, no doubt. His pulse is steady, which is a comfort; but the blow to his head must have been very great; I am minded that the swelling is receding...

but it will be slow. It would not be erroneous to believe that he may not come round for some time. I have known such cases to last many days, weeks even. You are to consider that generally such injuries do heal in time, though we must pray that his intellectuals are not impaired. If I may say so, his daughter exhibits the greatest fortitude.'

'The precious angel. Will Edwards keep his foot?' asked Pat when all were seated.

'With the blessing, we have some small hope of that. Thank the Lord there is no infection - no smell of the gangrene - and no cut vessels, it seems. When the swelling recedes, the prospect will be plainer to see, though in any event I cannot see him ever running again, for the damage to bone must be so very severe. He may retain a club foot, with luck... and 'tis Marston to thank for that, the foot cleaned and set as neat as ever it could be... as are the splinter cases. No better a job could I have done.'

Pat turned to Marston and spoke gently whilst nodding as if in confirmation, 'Mr Marston ... *Michael*, you have my particular thanks for your most excellent service helping those men. I have spoken with them and, for sure, they are in good heart because of your attentions.'

Marston's heart swelled and his eyes watered: never before had Pat referred to him in company as Michael. This was recognition as a friend and comrade of the very first order, and his pleasure ran deep. It was all he could do to reply with the briefest of words, 'Thank you sir. It was no more than any other man of medicine would do.'

Pat would have none of this and spoke further, deep conviction in his voice, 'No, that is not true. I am informed that you have barely slept these five days past; never leaving your patients and tending to them as they have recovered, ministering too with words of support and comfort all these days and nights. They... *and I*... are surely in your debt. There is no doubt of that, no doubt at all... and I thank you with all my heart.'

'Thank you, sir,' was all that Marston, quite overcome by his captain's thanks, could manage to mumble.

'Most excellent work, Michael. I could not do better. Neither could I have saved Symes, for I understand that his wound was so severe... beyond the abilities of even the finest of surgeons,' added Simon, which was some small comfort to his friend.

Murphy entered the cabin to announce, 'Well, the dinner is in half an hour,' adding, 'There is plenty enough sea pie for three, sorr... fresh tunny it is... 'twas a monstrous big fish.'

Pat, when such thoughts occurred to him – which was very infrequently – marvelled at Murphy's efforts to manage the minor details of his life. The implied invitation to the two medical men, who were generally held in the very highest esteem by the crew - Mr Marston now having joined those Olympian heights of crew respect after his treatment of their wounded shipmates – could never have been respectfully delivered by anyone else aboard other than Murphy. 'Thankee, Murphy. Sea pie for three it is, in half an hour... and a bottle or two of the best wine in my stores, *if you will*. Look to my favourite: the Portuguese, the red label! Rouse out a brace...' Pat bellowed after his exiting steward who, despite the boldness of his suggestion, was departing in haste before any unwelcome rejoinder could come from his captain, '... and without the loss of a moment! And I will not countenance any excuses that the rats have got at it; d'ye hear?' He turned back to the table; 'I trust you will tarry for dinner, gentlemen?' he asked, to observe the proprieties, the answer assured.

Within mere moments, Murphy hastened back into the cabin, excited and quite breathless. Without ceremony or invitation, he gabbled out his message. 'Mr Macleod, sorr... Mr Macleod... he's a... a...'

All shot up from the table, fearing the worst, Pat shouting at his steward, 'Calm yourself, Murphy. Mr Macleod, what of him? Spit it out. man!'

'Well, he's a stirring, maybe a'coming round, sorr.' Murphy was physically shoved aside as Pat and his surgeons pushed round him and out the cabin door, hastening to the companionway and below to the gun-room, to Duncan's tiny cabin berth, the illumination so poor after the light of the great cabin that they could barely see the pale face, the lips quavering, nor hear the murmurings which were so indistinct, his eyes still closed. A very nervous Freeman stood outside the door, his customary cheer quite absent. Kathleen was now seated alongside Duncan's cot, holding a cloth with which she had been wiping Duncan's brow. Brodie sat in the corner, clinging tight to her father's hand, silent, openly weeping, tears in profusion visibly soaking the handkerchief she clutched.

'Please to stand aside, Pat,' ordered Simon, stooping to listen closely to the barely audible words and to feel the pulse: steady, constant, unwavering, a little stronger; his breathing was nearly normal once again. 'Duncan, you are awakening, tell?' the words were laden with relief.

'Aye, these past few minutes,' came back the very faintest of whisper; 'A glass of water would be the grandest thing.'

Pat's own long, long exhalation of relief was audible to all. He stooped and seized Duncan's hand, but did not speak as Simon resumed. 'Listen, brother, do not speak further or call out; rest, do not agitate yourself. Freeman is here with the water and will attend you until you can sit up. You have had a very severe knock on the head and must keep your bed for some days more.'

But Duncan had already slipped back into sleep. Pat stared at him for a few moments before turning his gaze to Simon, his questions unsaid, his face saying all, a flood of extreme relief combined with unrelenting concern.

'He will do well, with the blessing. Only time and rest can serve him now,' Simon opined, nodding in emphasis, his quiet words bringing a tidal wave of release to all pressed into the tiny space, the palpable fear and tension visibly diminishing in anxious faces. With great relief they exited to return to the great cabin, leaving Kathleen and Freeman hovering near Duncan; she gently wiped his brow and face and the steward very quietly resumed his low singing of an African song as they left.

Seated once again around the table Pat and Simon sipped sweet Greek white wine, *Santorin Vino Santo*, Pat's original cellar so very substantially diminished, and nibbled on stale *Captains' Thins* brought by Murphy until he served the sea pie within a quarter hour. 'What of you, in our absence, Simon?' asked Pat, 'I am pleased to see Kathleen now so well.' His relief at Duncan's recovery was still very evident in his voice, low and wavering.

Simon set down his cup and replied in the gravest of voices, his tone strong in emphasis of his disapproval. 'My ministrations to Kathleen were comforting only and not strictly necessary. As I thought it would be, Kathleen was mending not long after you departed - the beneficial effects of land, plentiful fresh air and good comestibles. I beg of you... I must never be left behind again. My place is on this ship, alongside of all our shipmates who sail in her.'

'On that, my dear friend, you have my solemn word,' pledged Pat with heartfelt conviction.

In the lingering warmth of the evening Pat arrived home and sat with Sinéad on their terrace, high on the south-western flank of the island's premier peak. Their small supper was slowly consumed with few words said. Later, Pat sipped his brandy and held hands with Sinéad as they contemplated the southward vista of the gently descending terrain of small farmsteads, irregularly-shaped fields and green copses leading down to the coast, the heady scent of rampant honeysuckle so prevalent in the air, and the constant chirrup of cicadas the only sound in the tranquillity of the moment. He gazed across the calm, still waters of the channel between Cephalonia and the low, gentle hills of Zante to the south in the distance. The light was beginning to fail but it was also just possible to look upon a hazy view of the far hills of the Morea, still just visible in the soft, near dusk light to the far left before Mount Aenos blocked out any nearer view of the mainland. 'Will I tell you about poor Duncan?' Pat asked, gently breaking the contemplative quietude of the past hour.

'How is he?'

'He is mending. He has awakened for a minute or two before settling again to sleep. Simon and Kathleen are tending him. He will be well, with the blessing. I hope I may speak with him in the morning.'

'Thank God, Mary and Saint Patrick,' gasped Sinéad and then fell back into silence.

Another half-hour passed before Pat spoke again, 'I am much set back by Kathleen's illness... and I noted Simon's shock in recognising her condition, her particular sickness. You will recall that he lost his wife to it... to the consumption. It was when we were at sea aboard *Tenedos* in the year 'eighteen.' A pause. 'I venture that he has served Kathleen very well.' Another minute elapsed before Pat resumed once more, 'I am mortally cast down to see Duncan wounded so. The poor man insisted that he would serve... *with his wife in Simon's attentions*... and then... to be struck down so. He is the unluckiest soul... And what will I make of it? We have all - Simon, Duncan and myself - served our turn... yet here we are again... amidst blood and damnable death - *excuse me my dear.*'

Sinéad turned to gaze at her husband, the tears in her eyes beginning to stream down her cheeks, 'My love, these thoughts are natural to all of us. Patrick O'Connor is getting older and perhaps becoming more like us *ordinary* mortals. Would you wish us all to return to Claddaghduff? Perhaps it is time to enjoy retirement there. No one would deny you have earned it.' Sinéad was now sobbing profusely and struggled to add, 'We have no longer any great want of money... you have no need to fight any more battles.'

Pat embraced his wife gently. 'Here, take my cloth,' he offered, wiping the tears from his wife's face. 'Let us go inside, the air is cooling.' An hour went by, Pat sitting with Sinéad at the fireside. Darkness had descended outside and the flickering light of the fire's flames and the candles reflected off the windows. Pat continued to sit close to his wife, holding her hand.

'Give me hope, Pat... Hold me... please. I cannot endure much longer. Promise me we will leave these struggles... I beg you will. Poor Duncan... poor Kathleen.' Sinéad was crying softly and shaking uncontrollably. Pat pulled her gently into his embrace.

A long and pensive pause followed as Pat considered his wife's pleas. Finally, some few minutes later whilst still holding her tightly about him, he answered her, 'Sinéad, my love... I do not want to come it the philosopher... no, not at all; but I am sensible of your sound thoughts... and that is where we will set our course. Yet... for now... I am here... with many all about me, old shipmates and new; and we are - *all of us* - engaged in Greek service.'

'But will we ever return home... *to our proper home*, to Connemara? I begin to wonder... I do so. Tell me we will, I beg you; tell me... for the love of God... please.'

Pat sighed and for a brief moment gathered his thoughts before replying in gentle voice, 'Let me tell you, my love, that in my dreams I imagine our fireside at home... the low flames of the smoking turf and the divine smell of the burning peat... and I cling to the blessed thought with a passion, I do so. It is the only comfort when I am in contemplation of this return to Greece, to this land of brutal murder and savage revenge.' Pat hesitated, 'I confess that I have ever been in two minds about coming back - *to Greece* - I have... but I beg you to understand that this is my life... aboard ship; it is the only life I have ever known... I am no farmer...' Pat managed a weak smile and squeezed his wife's hands. 'Rest assured that before too much longer... we *will* return to Connemara together... I beg you not to doubt it... though afore that I - with Simon and Duncan... and all our people... together *we* must finish this undertaking... see this task through to its bitter end; I have given my pledge... but after that it is my hearth and horse for me... at home in peaceful Claddaghduff; no more voyages, neither for King nor foreigner; no more battles; no more deaths. I have seen plenty enough of that.' Pat seized a crying Sinéad once more into his arms, 'Thank you, my love, for your thoughts... and... *and be sure of this*: we will enjoy our retirement together... *we will*... afore all of our time has slipped by.'

# Chapter Nine

*Fill high the bowl with Samian wine!*
*Our virgins dance beneath the shade —*
*I see their glorious black eyes shine;*
*But gazing on each glowing maid,*
*My own the burning tear-drop laves,*
*To think such breasts must suckle slaves*

*Saturday 2<sup>nd</sup> August 1823*                    *Argostoli, Cephalonia*

In their finest dress attire of starched and pressed white dungarees, blue smocks, black hats, neckerchiefs and with the most carefully plaited of pigtails, Pat's barge crew, Barton in command, rowed him dry across to the quay of Argostoli accompanied by Simon, Pickering, Mower and Codrington. The captain of the port was standing on the quay as they tied up, a frigate being a most rare arrival in Argostoli. He was a native Cephalonian and an affable man, welcoming Pat's party and introducing himself with neither airs nor formality, 'Teodosio Cazzaitti, at your service, gentlemen.'

After introductions had been completed, Cazzaiti readily opined his belief in the imminent arrival of the Greek fleet and his anticipation of its destruction of the Turk.

Pat did not think fit to disabuse him of his optimism, 'Captain Cazzaitti, please to introduce us to the Resident.'

The port captain explained in heavily accented and imperfect English, 'Colonel Napier away... he with General Adam, with Admiral Moore, gone see Turk Pasha. You see secretary, he is here.'

'Very well, Captain Cazzaitti, the secretary will serve. Please, if you will, lead on,' said a resigned Pat.

Cazzaiti was pleased to escort Pat's party to the Resident's house, a short walk away albeit tiring in the blistering heat – though it was only a little after nine in the morning. A servant met them at the door, bidding them wait whilst summoning the

301

maid. After a short while, Pat growing irritable in the intense humidity, the maid brought them to the office of the Resident's secretary.

Captain Kennedy, a most amiable man, seemed genuinely pleased to greet them; his voice resonated with natural warmth and with the gentlest of Ulster inflections, 'Good morning to you, Gentlemen. John Kennedy, captain of Royal Engineers and secretary to Colonel Napier. The Colonel is away presently, likely for a few more days.'

Pat's impatience drained away in a moment, presented with this hospitable aide. After Pat had introduced himself and his officers, Kennedy replied, 'Your servant, Captain. Gentlemen, may I offer you tea? Punch perhaps?'

The temperature had been rising steadily since breakfast and it was now hotter than Pat could recollect it ever being, even hotter than his days in the West Indies. 'Thank you, Captain Kennedy; punch would be most welcome.' Pat was now sweating heavily in his best dress uniform of a particularly heavy cloth, pressed to perfection that morning by Murphy. It was now bereft of any Royal Navy insignia save for the Nile medal in his buttonhole, a paucity of official status which Kennedy could scarcely miss.

Kennedy smiled, 'The maid makes a particularly fine punch with green tea... and we may even have a little Trieste ice left in store which we receive with tolerable frequency from Corfu.' As Pat and his officers were seated in the secretary's office, the maid promptly returned and served the iced punch. Kennedy continued, 'The Resident will return within a very few days, Captain O'Connor, and will no doubt be pleased to receive you. Until then may I enquire as to the purpose of your visit? We have received no prior notification of your arrival in the Islands, official or otherwise.'

With no change of expression, Pat looked carefully at Simon on the opposite side of the table who, almost imperceptibly, shook his head, just once. It was enough of a signal for Pat who replied cautiously, recalling a now distant briefing from the First Lord. 'Captain Kennedy, *Surprise* is not a Royal Navy vessel as such. Rather she is chartered to engage in hydrographical surveying in the waters of His Majesty's Protectorate. We are here to provide our assistance to Captain Smyth, *HMS Adventure*, whose fine surveys are much appreciated by their Lordships at the Admiralty. Their Lordships are minded that in the present - will I say - *delicate* political circumstances a survey vessel of some military standing might well be more respected by any belligerents she may encounter in the course of her task.'

Simon was most impressed with Pat's credible polish added to Melville's stratagem. Pat, though no academic, was remarkably quick of thought when pressed in such circumstances, a particularly valuable talent when engaged in and considering his immediate military options. Pat's lieutenants had all assumed blank faces.

Whether or not *Surprise's* self-evident damage had been reported to him and whether Kennedy believed or doubted Pat's story, his face did not register either way and his reply was noncommital, albeit in a tone that suggested he was a little sceptical, 'I *see*, Captain O'Connor. No doubt Colonel Napier will be pleased to discuss that with you on his return. In the meantime, if I may be of any assistance to you and your assignation please do not hesitate to ask of me.'

After the customary pleasantries of leave-taking Pat and his officers returned to *Surprise,* Pat and Simon to take their supper together and to discuss matters further. Later, Duncan being somewhat recovered, Pat visited his cabin and chatted with him in his sickbed, recounting the visit to Kennedy and the declared intentions of surveying. 'What else was I to say, Duncan?' Pat asked of his friend.

'An admirable answer it was, sure, and one which will endure tolerably well until we are in possession of our *letter of marque*. If ye collect our briefing from Lowrey in London, in a wee few days I am to meet with his promised contact here in Argostoli, who will make himself known to me... and who will have the most recent information on the political and military situation in the Morea and in Greece generally. Until then we might seek some larger and longer-term accommodation for the ladies... and assume the task of surveying... whatever that may involve. I have nae doubt that ye will make a credible fist of it for the benefit of any onlookers, for there will surely be Turk agents in this place.' With that, the exertion proving greatly taxing for Duncan, Pat determined to let him be, much to Kathleen's relief, and he fell asleep within moments.

*Sunday 3ʳᵈ August 1823*                    *Argostoli, Cephalonia*

It was during Pat's second breakfast with Simon that Mower reported *Hercules* entering the bay and proceeding slowly towards them, her courses reefed as she approached the outer anchorage of Argostoli's port.

'Pat; listen, will ye now?' said Duncan who had insisted upon joining them for an hour in the cabin. 'I say this advisedly... Might I suggest that we maintain just a wee dialogue with Lord Byron for the moment, only that which is necessary; and perhaps it should be conducted solely through myself until at least such time as we have secured our Greek *letter of marque*. I widnae care to see any association between ye and such a well-known Hellenist to be remarked upon, particularly when ye are here officially for hydrographical purposes.' Duncan's glance wandered towards the table, 'Oh, would there be any more of those tolerably flavoursome kidneys left in that pan?'

'You are truly more suited to these... these engagements under false colours than ever I will be, Duncan,' Pat mused, 'being just the simple jack tar I am. Do we, I wonder, ever profit by them?'

'Och, to be sure it would all be much simpler were such trickery and deceit never necessary, my friend.'

'You may consider this...' Simon interjected, 'Would the Greeks ever have taken Troy without the deception of the wooden horse?'

'Such sharp practice... that is scarcely my line of country, Simon,' said Pat.

'Forgive me if I am in error, brother, but I do collect our dear *Tenedos* hoisting certain colours on occasion, colours which were never strictly in His Majesty's gift?' Simon failed to conceal his mirth, laughing out loud at his jibe, which did raise a smile from his captain and a little weak laughter from Duncan, the first in many days, both Pat and Simon being very pleased to hear it.

*Tuesday 5<sup>th</sup> August 1823*                    *Argostoli, Cephalonia*

Colonel Napier came aboard *Surprise* at eight bells of the morning watch, being sighted beforehand by Barton as the Resident was being rowed out from the quay. He was accompanied by Kennedy. Barton alerted Tom Pickering who entered the cabin as Pat was finishing his first breakfast, Duncan recovering well enough to be sitting longer with him.

'Sir, we have a visitor approaching the ship. Possibly the Resident as he is accompanied by Kennedy.'

'Very well; I shall come on deck directly. Murphy, light along and ask the Doctor to join me in the cabin in ten minutes. And Murphy, ensure that he is shaved and clothed respectably for our visitors,' said Pat pleasantly. 'Duncan, I must visit my closet, and then I will speak with Simon. Tom, please to welcome our guests on deck, if you will.' Pat stepped in to the quarter-gallery.

'Of course, sir.'

'Napier,' said the visitor simply, introducing himself as he climbed aboard up the accommodation ladder and on to the deck, hand outstretched towards Pickering, Kennedy following.

'Lieutenant Pickering, sir, at your service. Please to step into the cabin. I will tell you that our First Lieutenant is there, recuperating after... *after a fall*, sir; he remains weak and is unable to rise.'

Napier nodded and strode behind Pickering into the cabin, proffering his hand to the invalid without ceremony, 'Napier; how do you do, Lieutenant?'

'Lieutenant Duncan Macleod; my pleasure, sir. I am a wee tait indisposed, as ye can see,' Duncan replied, shaking his hand. 'Captain O'Connor invites ye to please sit at the table, he will be here in a moment.'

Freeman, familiar with Pat's expectations, appeared unbidden after a peremptory knock, setting glasses and cups on the table. He whispered to Duncan, 'Doctor coming, massa; he no find wig.'

'Are you associated with the other vessel recently arrived, *Hercules*, Lieutenant Macleod... with Lord Byron aboard?' Napier came straight to the point.

Just at that moment, Duncan's reply hanging in the air, Pat entered the cabin with Simon, having just caught the question. Simon stood quite resplendent, Duncan thought, in clean pressed clothes and freshly shaven, his wig newly-powdered atop his head - a rare sight indeed. 'Colonel, will I present Captain Patrick O'Connor and our surgeon, my particular friend, Doctor Simon Ferguson.'

'Your servant, sir,' said Simon with a theatrical bow.

'Good morning to you both and a grand morning it is, to be sure,' said Pat, shaking hands with Napier and Kennedy whilst looking keenly at both guests. 'How perfectly considerate of you to visit us.' He was speaking with his usually indistinguishable Irish lilt very much to the fore, Duncan noticed, a little puzzled. Pat continued quickly, leaving no opportunity for anyone to interject. 'To be sure, 'tis a pleasure and a very great honour to meet one of Ireland's most illustrious sons...'

'Most kind, Captain, but I am hardly that...'

'Sure you are, sir... a veteran of the Peninsula and the 1812, and a staff officer to His Lordship, Wellington, to boot. Did you know that, Lieutenant Macleod?' Pat nimbly diverted all thoughts from Napier's unanswered question but left unsaid the other thought on his mind: 'and cousin to Lord Edward Fitzgerald, leader of the United Irishmen and the Rising.' It was a subject Pat was particularly keen to avoid, being a sympathiser of the brotherhood in his enthusiastic, younger days. Pat continued, brooking no interruption, smiling as he turned to Kennedy, adding, 'Captain Kennedy, you are of the Donegal Kennedys, I venture?'

'Why, yes indeed, a Donegal man I am, Captain O'Connor. Are you familiar with the county?' replied Kennedy.

'Most certainly I am, sir. The glory of the world, so it is. I once hooked a prodigious fine salmon at the leap in Ballyshannon and I have played 'cello in the Donegal style with Hugh Doherty in Glencolmcille. I visited in the year Boney was sent to Elba. My colleagues and I are particularly fond of our music and often tend towards the traditional rather than the classical. Perhaps you would like to attend our playing... We have a fine quartet aboard; that is myself with my officers and our assistant surgeon, Michael Marston - who exhibits a particular talent with the violin. Excuse me Colonel, Captain, I blather on inexcusably. Would you care for tea... a glass of Madeira?'

Pat paused only for long enough to draw breath, but Napier interrupted. 'Thank you, Captain O'Connor,' he said, a little taken aback by Pat's verbosity. 'Doctor Ferguson, are you, perchance, acquainted with the Emerald Isle?'

'I am familiar with the sweet County Clare, having once visited the Burren... a wondrous place for fritillaries you know, the water beetle too, very rare... Yes, 'twas a splendid few weeks that I was there... before I reluctantly bade farewell to return to my position in Plymouth Dock.'

Fortunately, just at that moment Freeman entered bearing a tray of Madeira and tea. Duncan could bear his captain's rambling diversion no longer and, seizing his moment, interjected, 'Thankee Freeman; well done. Colonel, Lord Melville has requested us to assist Captain Smyth, *HMS Adventure*, in his hydrographical surveying of the Ionian waters and thereabouts... with particular interest in the Corfu Channel. His Majesty's Government is keen to help the economies of the United Islands prosper, given the Turk blockade of the Morea and the merchants of Corfu wishing to stimulate their olive oil sales, greatly depleted since the end of the war with Boney... and likewise the local currant producers, their trade also being much down.'

If Napier and Kennedy were astonished by Pat's blathering and Duncan's subsequent efforts at a plausible explanation for *Surprise* – a warship of some significance - appearing in this emerging place of congregation for foreign supporters of Greek independence, ostensibly to facilitate further the growing principal commerce of the Islands, of which they were perfectly aware, by additional hydrographical surveying they gave no sign: both their faces remained blank, as if weighing the truth of Duncan's remarkable statement.

307

'Colonel, there is one matter in which I might beg your assistance,' said Pat, 'My family and Lieutenant Macleod's seek accommodation ashore, their present lodgings being suited only for a very few weeks and *Surprise* being oft away. Can you suggest some suitable place of abode for them within - *shall we say?* - no more than an hour of the port... and suited to a horse and carriage?'

'Of course, I will assist. If I may, I offer the assistance of my brother, Charles. He is here on the island and perfectly acquainted with suitable locations,' Napier volunteered.

After finishing the Madeira and tea, Napier stood to leave, bidding farewell and adding pleasantly, 'If we may render any service, however small... Captain O'Connor... Perhaps you and your officers might join us for dinner in the Residence at your convenience. Captain Kennedy and I would be delighted to accept your offer to hear your ship's musicians. We must away now to *Hercules* to attend His Lordship. I bid you all good day, gentlemen,' Napier concluded and departed with Kennedy.

'That went well,' declared Pat with audible relief; 'I was much affrighted that Napier would come aboard topping it the nob, but no, he was a good egg! Duncan, you are indeed a dissimulator of the very first order. That was a tolerably entertaining story: olive oil and currants! How did you conceive of that?' asked Pat, puzzled and intrigued.

'Och, I know nothing of such things, but Codrington joined us yesterday for dinner in the gun-room, and we discussed *Eleanor*. She is in need of a deal of new canvas now; ye collect she was nae refitted when *Surprise* was in Plymouth Dock and 'tis four years since she was last out of the water. Codrington was explaining over the very finest of plum duffs for pudding – with fresh raisins which came aboard only yesterday morning – that his family had some interests with a Venice merchant, one customarily buying the olive oil of Corfu and the currants of Cephalonia and Zante, all unobtainable for him 'til the Turk blockade of the Morea removed the mainland competition from the market. So ye see,' Duncan concluded with just the slightest note of triumph, 'I venture 'twas nae the fanciful story ye thought it to be.'

'My compliments, brother,' said Simon, smiling.

'Eh? For what?' asked Duncan.

'That hocus pocus; what a capital tale! Olive oil indeed! Would there be any of that plum pudding left? Tea leaves the strongest of craving for just a very little morsel of something sweet.'

Pat smiled, 'I venture *Surprise* has a greater prospect of sinking a seventy-four than our duff had of surviving Murphy's return to the galley.'

*Thursday 21ˢᵗ August 1823*                    *Argostoli, Cephalonia*

Near three weeks had elapsed since *Surprise's* arrival, and no contact had been received from the provisional Greek government, although Duncan did at least expect to hear news from Lowrey in due course. A larger house in the village of Metaxata had been found for the O'Connor and Macleod families for a longer term, the short distance of only some five miles from the port presenting no great inconvenience for travel to and fro by horse. The house belonged to a relative of Captain Cazzaitti who had immediately offered to assist their search for accommodation. It offered a fine view of Zante to the south with a distant glimpse of the Morea far beyond. The ladies were very pleased with the location and threw themselves enthusiastically into arranging their accommodation as they wished it to be. Patrick Coghlan with some half a dozen of *Surprise's* crew – principally those hands who had served in Pat's Claddaghduff household – was tasked with cleaning the house and the fresh painting of its walls, all without the slightest delay being brooked by the ladies.

Simon had accompanied Pat and a much-recovered Duncan to inspect the new house. 'Here we be, Simon; 'tis a plain, honest abode... if a trifle small,' pronounced a delighted Pat.

'Little is what I behold, Pat, for so many of us. Would there be a room for me? There is a veritable cornucopia of intriguing plants and diverse avians about this place which are not familiar to me. There is always a want of time to study such fascinations when we are engaged in your briny world... plants and birds alike all being absent... save for the gull.'

309

'Why, of course there is. Eight bedrooms there be, though in some, as tiny as they are, I would not care to swing the cat out of the bag; but here is our new home... in the Ionians... and small as it may be - with wives and children - it will serve; for wide is the door of a little cottage.'

'Why, my own home...' Simon hesitated instantly with his use of the word, memories of his lost Agnes flashing into his mind, '... my *house* is likely the tiniest of all in Tobermory.' The instant surge of melancholy was profoundly disturbing. 'And a very cold place it is too,' Simon's unspoken addition overwhelmed his whole being; the recollection of his first return to Mull after Agnes had died there was profoundly distressing: no one to answer his unthinking knock on the door, an empty parlour when he had found his key, the kitchen as tidy as ever but every surface covered with dust and dead flies, moths flickering when disturbed, the swept hearth and a log stack long awaiting a fire, and the fingers of the clock stopped as if in echo of the end of all happiness. Simon recalled the all-consuming feeling of emptiness, the bitter realisation that some significant constituent of his heart had been lost to him with his wife. Indeed, the dismay and heartache never left him, being particularly intolerable in the dark hours of the night; and he whispered to himself, 'Thanks be to the solace of laudanum.' But none of his had he ever confided to anyone, even as after years the pain had dulled to a barely tolerable degree; and so he chided himself for allowing these feelings to escape, possibly noticeably, in the presence of his closest friend; and, cursing that his strength was not all that he wished it to be and digging deep to find resolve, he entered the house with the best that he could muster as a smile for the ladies within.

Pat felt obliged to stay and assist in the establishment of the family abode for several days, Duncan recuperating there. A handful of Surprises helped out with the moving of all the baggage from the ship. Such enforced domesticity increasingly grated with Pat as he considered the lack of progress with the mission proper until, to his delight, the morning arrival of Surprises from the port brought welcome news. He spoke to his wife immediately breakfast had been consumed, 'Sinéad, my dear, Duncan awaits a most important letter from London... and the packet from Corfu is expected today. Hence we will be away directly for the port.'

Shortly afterwards Pat and Duncan departed for Argostoli, carefully riding two locally purchased, fine Thessalians at a snail's pace. It was a gentle hour for the horses whilst Duncan was being carefully favoured in his recovery, and Pat was mindful of the extreme heat. To their great surprise a most familiar old acquaintance awaited them on the quay, sitting outside the port captain's office in the shade.

'Abel Jason, so it is! How it pleases me to see ye again!' exclaimed Duncan, delight in his face and voice. He vigorously shook the hand of his old shipmate and friend, *Tenedos's* former purser.

'I am very happy to see you, Mr Jason,' declared Pat, gripping his hand until Jason near winced.

'It is most pleasing to see you both again, Captain... Mr Macleod,' replied Jason, extricating his sore hand from Pat's excruciating, steely grip. After the customary cordialities, enjoyed by all, he apprised them of his own mission. 'I am arrived today from Corfu, having taken a packet there from Falmouth in great haste at the bidding of Mr Lowrey, and herewith is a letter from him.'

'Pat, perhaps we should repair aboard the ship; here is nae the place to discuss any letter, nor indeed to decipher it, for I am certain it will be encoded.'

'Let us go aboard, directly, out of this damn furnace; and perhaps we will find a cold bottle of Sillery,' said Pat, irritable since reflecting on his abrupt departure from his wife and his whole body seemingly bathed in sweat.

They returned to the great cabin and settled, sipping pleasantly cool champagne fetched from the lower hold by Freeman. 'Jason, I hope we see ye well,' declared Pat, 'and will ye tell us of your activities these past four years.'

'I am in perfectly good health, thank you.'

'Heartily pleased,' said Pat with evident pleasure.

Jason resumed, 'After our return from the eastern Mediterranean, my cousin pressed me to assist him in the further

311

development of the family estates, an occupation of which I had long begun to tire, and so the letter I received from Mr Lowrey enquiring as to my interest in rendering him some assistance was manna indeed. I hastened to London, and now I am here... bearing this letter.'

'Perhaps we should look to the letter.' said Pat. 'Likely it will be of significance; indeed, perhaps it is a matter of urgency.'

Duncan looked across to Pat, 'Will ye excuse us, sir; it may take some wee time to extract Lowrey's message from his letter, it no doubt being in his code?'

'Why of course. Stay here in the cabin, if you will. I shall be on my quarterdeck. Please to shout for Freeman should you require further refreshment.'

Jason brought Lowrey's letter from his inside breast pocket and pressed it on to the table whilst Duncan, Murphy assisting, shifted the table itself towards the stern windows where the sunlight could aid their deciphering. 'It is in the D3 code with one shift I see,' Jason pronounced after a few minutes.

'One moment, I shall find my key.' Duncan went down to his cabin to search his dunnage, re-emerging after a quarter hour.

Nearly another hour passed before Jason spoke again, 'It has been some considerable time since I last engaged with this task... and I have found some difficulty with all these combinations. However, the message has emerged in principle, and we will bring this to Captain O'Connor's interest without delay.' Duncan sent Freeman to find the captain.

Pat appeared after a very few minutes with something akin to worry across his latterly unperturbed face as he looked at Duncan's grave expression. 'Freeman, we will take coffee now, if you please, and look to see if cook can find any of those marchpane biscuits.'

Though Freeman was gone, Murphy lingered in the extremities of the cabin until Pat waved him out. Duncan, well acquainted with the steward's tendencies, whispered, 'Pat, 'tis clear from those parts of this letter which are satisfactorily decoded that the situation in Greece is far worse than we had thought. Internecine strife abounds throughout the provinces... and the government in Nauplia, since January, carries nae sway either in the Morea or elsewhere. So much so that the *letter of marque* for *Surprise,* promised by Secretary of State Mavrocordato, cannae safely be brought to us here with the Turk embargo on all marine traffic throughout these waters associated with the United Islands - save for His Majesty's ships. The letter will therefore be brought and entrusted to the Greek government's representative in the western provinces, in Missilonghi, where we are to collect it. However, the town has been besieged by the Turk fleet under Khosref since late in July.'

Freeman returned, looking downcast, 'Ain't no biscuits left, massa. Cook baking more. Here be coffee, fresh now. Anything else, massa?'

'No, Freeman. Biscuits when ready will be most welcome, thankee,' said Pat, preoccupied with his contemplation of the letter's contents and having no intention of enlightening Murphy's self-evident curiosity, even as he loitered near the door. 'I dare say there will be some significant Turk ships 'tween Cephalonia and the mainland. We know little of the lagoon and shallows afore Missilonghi, and with no pilot available to us it would be a passage with some hazard. No, we cannot take *Surprise* there. No doubt her arrival would be remarked in Constantinople within a week and Corfu in just a day or two when King Tom... *Maitland* would throw us out of this place directly.' Pat pronounced his assessment rather gloomily before continuing, 'A way must be found to collect the *letter of marque* when we know it has arrived in Missilonghi. We surely must not act again without it, for such would be plain piracy... and if taken we would all be hanged from the yard, and rightly so. We will send *Eleanor,* if necessary, to fetch the letter. She can slip over in some fog and, being so much shallower in draught, she will better cross the bar and navigate the lagoon approach to the town. Without a local navigator or the finest of charts we could not hazard *Surprise* on such a venture.' A plan began to form in his mind, 'As we are here supposedly assisting Captain Smyth in hydrographical surveying, it would not go remarked were we to ask of him his charts for that place... and, I dare say, they would be uncommon useful. Until we possess the letter, we will offer our assistance to Smyth and see what can be done.'

After breakfast, church and divisions had concluded, Pat, Simon and Duncan, together with Marston, Jason, Sinéad and Kathleen went ashore in the barge to join Napier and Kennedy for dinner, the musicians taking their instruments. Pickering and Mower accompanied them; Mower too, desperately keen to meet his poet idol, Byron.

Napier, with his colleague Kennedy, welcomed them all most warmly to the Residence. Lord Byron, having already arrived, greeted them in the friendliest of manner, Mower being rendered tongue-tied as he shook hands with the great man. 'I am, sir, a devoted admirer of your most excellent works,' whispered Mower, in complete awe.

'Thank you kindly, Mower. Are you a poet yourself?' Byron asked in an encouraging tone.

'Why, yes, sir; indeed, I am.'

'Then I hope that we may find occasion to read your own works together...' offered Byron smiling, '... here in this most pleasant and tranquil place; none finer for any bard could there be. Perhaps we will both enjoy the creation of further works. I will await you. Please call at your convenience.'

'Thank you,' replied a delighted and grateful Mower; 'It is my most precious hope that I may do so.'

Byron introduced his companion, Count Gamba, who had accompanied him from Genoa. It was a most affable gathering at the Colonel's table, several bottles of a superb Amontillado enjoyed by all as they sat waiting to dine. The chef had excelled himself, serving a superb selection of grilled fish, the food accompanied by a local retsina. The main course was followed by sofrito – albeit his Lordship demurred in favour of cheese – served with a magnificent burgundy, and then baklava puddled in honey. Finally, there was copious local brandy and the strongest of Greek coffee to conclude, a finale wholly to the taste of Pat, Simon and Duncan.

It was with tremendous satisfaction that Pat thanked the Resident. 'A capital dinner, Colonel Napier. We must see how *Surprise* can thank you. If only we were still a commissioned vessel, I think we would assuredly press your cook,' he joked in the cordial ambience of satiated contentment.

'Most assuredly, sir, I have not eaten as well since leaving London,' added Jason.

'And what are your activities and intentions here in Cephalonia, Mr Jason? We are already accompanied by probably the most well-known Hellenist of all, here beside me in his Lordship,' Napier said, smiling towards Byron whilst seizing his opportunity for a prescient question, which alerted them all to some caution. 'Would you be another, at all?'

'My dear Colonel, my sympathies lie wholly with the Greeks,' Jason protested; 'Of that I make no secret, but I am here merely as linguistic assistant to Captain O'Connor, for I have some proficiency in both the Greek and Turk languages - which may conceivably be called upon should *Surprise* encounter any of the ships of either side in the current strife. I am come from Corfu on account of attending to pressing family affairs here on the island... arriving before my Admiralty letter of appointment was delivered to me. It was too late for me to reach Falmouth ere *Surprise* left. Tell, Colonel, how do you anticipate matters developing in this conflict... and how are you affected here in the Islands?' With this question Jason smoothly switched the interest of the ensemble.

For Colonel Napier, a distinguished veteran of the Peninsula war and the Hundred Days, such questions held no fear as all looked to his answer. 'My dear Jason, as an officer of the Crown and being subordinate to Sir Thomas Maitland, my duty lies in maintaining the avowed neutrality of the United Islands. Sir Thomas, who may fairly be called a rough old despot, is very strict on that and will brook no infractions of our neutrality, as is rightly so; and my own personal opinions must be subordinate to that. I must tell you all that Sir Thomas insists on a policy of strict quarantine for anyone coming to these islands from the Greek mainland... where disease and pestilence is rife. We will brook no traffic at all with Greece.'

Lord Byron interjected, 'It is sure that Maitland's neutrality prevails, even here, for I can find no means to cash my bills of exchange. Both Cariddi and Corgialegno, the richest proprietors and merchants in the island, have refused me... which is a considerable inconvenience.'

'Virtue never has been as respectable as money,' remarked Pickering.

Pickering's comment did not distract Napier, who was assuredly aware that Byron's pro-Hellenic sympathies would not find favour with Maitland, and he continued, 'As a military man it is obvious that the Greeks lack a great deal: professional officers and a standing army are woefully absent. Their struggles are contingent on little more than militias, who are in reality brigades of bandits... fighting amongst themselves more often than against the Turk. They have no artillery, no cavalry, no training regime, no commissary... and they feed off their impoverished fellow countrymen. Our sources report that the German Legion survivors in Nauplia are starving and subsist only on tortoises!' There was a laugh from all present, several thinking that perhaps salt pork was not so bad after all. A smiling Napier resumed, 'Such is likely not wholly unpalatable to you mariners, accustomed as you are to eating the turtle, but plainly it evidences the woeful lack of money and any kind of proper administration. The Greeks have very few of warships, but no one would doubt their courage. If that alone can deliver them, then delivered they assuredly will be. They have two particular admirals: the Psariote, Canaris; and the Hydriote, Miaoulis. Both have fought the most successful actions against the Turks. Yet for all that, their fleet lies inactive, their crews in want of money, and so the Turk, Khosref, blockades Missilonghi in impunity with his squadron of fifteen of sail whilst twenty-thousand Ottoman troops besiege it by land. The Greeks have several generals: in the east, Odysseus; in the Morea, Kolokotrones. Everywhere there abound innumerable politicians, all squabbling amongst themselves, the prominent one being Secretary of State Mavrocordato, who I believe has now fled to Hydra under threat from Kolokotrones.'

At this long litany of news, most probably throwing their plans into disarray, Duncan glanced quickly at Pat who had similarly taken it in and who now seemed to be sunk deep in thought.

Napier continued, 'Should the Greeks succeed in uniting their forces by land and securing stronger warships, then they have a prospect of victory. Until then they will always be suppressed - if not controlled - by the Turk who, by virtue of his fleet, can place his brigades anywhere throughout the Greek communities in any of the Ottoman provinces. Any seasoned general would relish the task of bringing the disparate Greek forces to a concerted direction, but that seems unlikely to come about on account of their political chaos. They have plentiful foreign volunteers... adventurers and dreamers for the most part... and ill-equipped to meet the full force of even the most lamentable Turk brigade. Yet any capable admiral with but the smallest squadron of warships might well intercede with great success in choking off Turk resupply... as, gentlemen, there is certainly no Turk Nelson.'

At this, as if prompted, there was a polite but subdued laugh from around the table before Lord Byron interjected, 'Colonel Napier, surely that is too pessimistic? Greek heroes, as worthy as any of their predecessors of antiquity, are dying every day, most recently the brave Marco Botzari, and the honourable aspiration for freedom surely beats as firmly in Greek hearts as it did in Napoleon's subject peoples. Even that man... one of arguably military genius... *as is said by some,*' - a few frowns around the table - '... could not hold the tide of freedom at bay. And so are these adventurers, whom you state are so ineffective, not providing a beacon... to illuminate the path to follow for the peoples of Greece to throw off the Turk yoke?'

'Very admirably put, my Lord,' said Napier, 'but it cannot be denied that Bonaparte was beaten only by the most experienced and substantial forces of the Alliance, on land and by sea, and only after very many years of costly struggle... and even then it was a near run thing. No, it would not do to underestimate the Greek difficulties nor the time it may take them. Yet, were I pressed to conjecture I would have to favour the Greeks.'

Neither Pat nor Duncan wished to pursue the subject of the discussion and so they politely refrained from comment. A little further time passed before it became apparent to all that no confluence of opinions would be established between Napier the soldier and Byron the poet. It was therefore a moment of some relief when the maid announced the return of the ladies and Pat brought the military debate to a timely end. 'Colonel, might we conclude your most excellent dinner with a piece or two from Corelli ere it becomes time to depart?'

'A most admirable suggestion, Captain O'Connor,' Napier replied, beaming jovially at Pat. 'Captain Kennedy and I have been keenly awaiting your concert. We hear so little of the classics here in Cephalonia. Please to continue.'

'If your Lordship pleases,' Pat looked towards Lord Byron, 'My colleague, Michael Marston, will precede our Corelli with his version of a most magnificent piece we encountered first in his Lordship's home in Genoa, where it was played by the finest musician it has ever been my good fortune to hear. He will play Signor Paganini's *Caprice Vingt-quatre*, though with Dr Ferguson's viola rather than the violin. We find it adds a pleasing warmth to the piece.'

'Most happy, O'Connor,' Byron replied; 'Please to begin.'

Whilst Marston could not achieve the exquisite perfection of Paganini, his own playing was close to virtuoso, and at the conclusion the small gathering was deeply impressed, thanking him with robust clapping, Duncan, Simon and Pat included. The quartet then played on for another twenty minutes or so of Corelli, Duncan contributing his own gentle and subtle additions with his whistle, before the convivial occasion came to its end.

Napier and Kennedy were delighted, applauding with gusto as the musicians finished. The Colonel stood, as if in timely summation of the event, and spoke with boundless gratitude, 'Gentlemen, so very invigorating! I congratulate you all most profusely. Sadly, there is little opportunity here for us to enjoy such stirring musical talents. I beg you to accept my invitation to dine with us again, and allow us, if you will, another blessed moment in which to hear such prodigious fine musicians.'

'Most kind, Colonel, and thankee for your hospitality on behalf of all of us,' Pat replied, delighted to establish such good prospects for future dialogue. 'I regret we must now away to our abode, sir, my officers to the ship.'

As they prepared to depart, Byron, being kindly solicitous to the ladies, enquired of them their contentment with life aboard ship, he himself still being accommodated on *Hercules*.

'Thank you for your interest, my Lord', replied Sinéad. 'We have shifted from *Surprise* and now reside in a little house in Metaxata... on a warm south slope. It is a most pleasant village where we enjoy the vista towards Zante.'

'Perhaps that place would suit my own modest needs, for I must very soon quit the ship. Indeed, I collect that the Colonel's brother may have suggested it,' Byron remarked.

The Colonel thanked them again for their playing, smiling and shaking hands with them all as they left the house, and bidding farewell as Captain Kennedy escorted them out to the street. The afternoon was passing into early evening as Pat, Duncan and their families, Simon with them, set off in contented, jovial spirits to stroll back to their new home ashore, Mower and Pickering to return to the ship. An hour later they sat in comfortable relaxation upon their easy chairs on the terrace in the approaching dusk, the whirring sound of cicadas all around them, the air still warm and scented with pungent honeysuckle and wafts of the gentler, more subtle, wild rosemary.

'The prospects of securing our Greek commission are receding like the tide, Duncan. Will we leave for Hydra, would you think?' asked Pat, his mention of the very word *Hydra* sending a searing flush of anxiety through his mind and veins.

'In this uncertainty of political stability, I fear such a move might serve only to prematurely disclose our intentions, and would secure little were we to find Mavrocordato absent from Hydra. The close preservation of our intentions for the moment must best serve our interests. Better to send *Eleanor* to Hydra - with Jason perhaps - to find out what is afoot... and 'til then we will persevere with sailing up and down the coast.'

Simon interjected, 'Indeed, 'tis a pleasant enough prospect, though I marvel that such repetitive contemplation of your watery realm holds such evident interest for you mariners. Is there a shard of that toad-in-a-hole left at all?'

'Surveying, Simon, for us mariners is a most engaging pastime; the understanding of our realm is of prime importance.

You are to consider that his Majesty has lost many more ships to rocks and reefs in poorly charted waters than ever struck to Boney's fleet. But I see you jest. *Adventure* and Smyth will be here afore long and then you shall meet a surveyor of the very first order. Until then we are in accord, *Eleanor* with Jason will be sent to Hydra tomorrow to see the lie of the land. Freeman! Ah, there you are. The Doctor has set his fancy on another of your admirable toad-in-a-hole rations, if you will. Thankee kindly... and perhaps we will share another claret!' Pat shouted to Murphy, even ashore never far from earshot.

*Wednesday 17th September 1823*                    *Argostoli, Cephalonia*

It was more than two weeks before Captain Smyth and *Adventure* eventually arrived in Argostoli to revictual and to take on fresh water, having spent some weeks off the west coast of the Ionian Islands in assessing modifications to charts made some years previously. The west coast was reckoned to be generally free of Turk warships and to a lesser degree the Greek pirates who still abounded throughout those waters despite the risks from Ottoman patrols enforcing the blockade.

'William Smyth, sir, at your service, Captain O'Connor,' said Smyth, proffering his hand as he stepped upon *Surprise's* deck. *Adventure*, with her shallower draught, had tied up to the quay that afternoon, Captain Smyth replying to *Surprise's* almost immediate signal of invitation.

'As am I at yours, sir!' pronounced Pat with keen enthusiasm; 'Upon my word and honour, may I say how much of a great pleasure it is to make your acquaintance once more!' Pat turned to Duncan and Simon, 'Did you know, this man saved my life... rescued me from Hydra in 'twenty-one... *that Godforsaken place.*'

'Come, sir,' murmured Smyth in polite surprise; 'You embarked upon *Adventure*; that is scarcely my saving of your life.'

'You will believe me when I tell you that never before was I so relieved - *indeed, I was overwhelmed; I was so* - to gain the deck of your vessel,' replied Pat with feeling.

All being keen to engage in cordial dialogue with the undoubted expert of Mediterranean surveying, Pat and his officers shifted swiftly inside the cooler great cabin. Smyth too was delighted to be in the presence of one of the Royal Navy's officers well known to be particularly interested in hydrography. 'May we offer you a trifle of refreshment, Captain Smyth? Perhaps a glass of wine, sir,' Pat prompted hospitably as they settled around the table.

'I would not suppose, Captain O'Connor, that you might have a cold bottle of sack?' enquired Smyth.

'Freeman!' shouted Pat, who was through the door before he had uttered the second syllable. 'Check the stocks and see if we have any sack. I collect we may have a few bottles left of the Manzanilla.' It was on such occasions that Freeman excelled, having taken aboard a very few days beforehand a small supply of ice from the Corfu packet, well-wrapped in stout hessian within wooden boxes and now deposited low in the ship, melting slowly at the extremities. From such carefully-husbanded stores, Freeman was able to chip out just a very little ice on each occasion to chill the cooled bottles further after they came aboard from the net.

Around the table and in good humour, all enjoyed hearing Pat exchanging recollections with Smyth of their earlier times in Ionian waters, whilst Pat was also pondering how best to make his intended request for the charts he sought. Freeman returned with two bottles of the Manzanilla and six glasses. Pat was impressed by his steward's success and all were most happily pleased by the chilled sack. 'Well done, Freeman; a colder glass I ne'er had when we were off the Horn... and tolerably welcome in this heat. Thankee, Freeman. Captain Smyth, we are engaged by the First Lord to offer our assistance with your surveying of the Ionian and neighbouring waters... *should you have need of it.*'

Pat paused momentarily to assess Smyth's reception of his ruse. No response other than a cautious nod, he pressed on, 'Lord Melville is most anxious that the charts of the waters 'twixt the United Islands and the mainland be as accurate as can possibly be, so as to avoid in the current troubled times any conceivable charge of territorial infraction by the Turk authorities... however

321

unlikely that might be. Their Lordships have sent our ship, though she be only a fifth rate, on account of the very troubled situation with the Greek risings in the Morea and western Greece, anticipating that she may go to waters where any prudent captain would well baulk at any prospective challenge to his ship from the Turk authorities. *Surprise* – well, her predecessor that is – was, as you are aware, from former times a ship known well in these parts. I have been particularly charged by Lord Melville to survey again the waters at the approaches to the Gulf of Patras...'

'My own survey of those waters is particularly detailed, sir,' Smyth could hold his tongue no longer.

Pat nodded and resumed in apologetic tone, 'I have no doubt, sir, that any such further survey will find no distinction from your own most commendable charts from the year 'thirteen, excellent as they are. I have always used them myself - *indeed, I was using them when you found me on that accursed island, Hydra, in 'twenty-one...* and I ne'er found fault, but when their Lordships request... well, we find it is our unfortunate and thankless lot to obey. Captain Smyth, might I enquire, sir, if you could possibly provide to us - *on loan of course* - your most recent charts of that particular area - *the Gulf?* With any additions you may have personally annotated... including the region of the lagoon of Missilonghi. Should we find ourselves disoriented in, say, the most extreme instance of fog or of storm, no pilot being available to us, such charts would be of quite inestimable value.' Pat concluded with his principal objective - his important question - credibly asked as best as he could put it.

Smyth, graciously and having taken no offence at their Lordships ostensible request, replied without hesitation, 'Of course, Captain O'Connor. I have indeed my own charts with many a marking that never was printed by the Admiralty... and I will be most pleased to loan them to you. If I may have them returned at your conclusion I would be in your debt, sir.'

'And I in yours, Captain Smyth; thank you kindly,' Pat replied, finding Smyth something of a kindred spirit and having himself plotted a useful chart or two during his voyages. He added, 'As a most proficient hydrographer, it is to be presumed that you have an interest too in our celestial aids. Jupiter is prominent these past few nights, and I have an excellent Dollond glass. Would you care to join me aboard this evening for supper and celestial gazing? We are surely blessed here with these wondrous clear skies.'

Smyth was noticeably pleased by Pat's invitation, swiftly according with it, 'Most kind, Captain O'Connor. I shall return after six bells of the last dog watch. It is a particular interest of mine since visiting Piazzi and his observatory in Palermo, and I will greatly look forward to our evening.'

'And I too, sir,' replied Pat, smiling warmly as he shook hands with the departing Smyth.

*Saturday 15ᵗʰ November 1823*                    *Metaxata, Cephalonia*

Considerable time had passed aboard *Surprise* surveying the Ionian waters but, no news having being received from the provisional Greek government, *Eleanor* had returned from Hydra several weeks previously, and Codrington had been unable to provide any further information. Jason remained absent, having failed to meet with Mavrocordato, and so he had stayed on Hydra, lingering in the hope of doing so until eventually *Eleanor* had been sent once more to recover him.

*Surprise* having recently returned to Argostoli, Pat and Duncan were staying with their families in the Metaxata house, which the ladies had put into admirable order. After supper the two friends sat contentedly on the terrace contemplating the view towards Zante, two bottles of the finest quality Robola finished.

'Will I tell ye of the recent news, brother?' asked Duncan. 'Our neighbour Lord Byron has abandoned his plan to go to the seat of the provisional government at Tripolizza... his Philhellene colleagues, Hamilton Brown and Trelawny, having returned with news of further internecine strife. His Lordship had sent with them his personal letter urging an end to this fratricidal insanity... which is jeopardising the London Greek Committee's loan, and they returned bearing a letter from Mavrocordato seeking an interim loan from his Lordship himself in order that the wages of the Hydriot fleet could be paid, without which they will nae sail to relieve Missilonghi.'

Pat set down his glass and turned to his friend, replying only after a long sigh, 'Dear Lord above! Had we conducted our affairs like this in the year 'fifteen, Boney would now be presiding in Westminster, His Majesty would likely be left languishing in the Marshalsea to rot, and *Surprise* would be sailing under French colours!' He sighed, 'His Lordship is plainly of a more benevolent mettle than us mere mortals... and what is he to do about it?'

'Admirable man that he is - *were there more of his ilk* - he has sent his emissary to Tripolizza affirming his personal commitment to providing a loan of four thousands sterling or the equivalent in dollars upon the arrival of the fleet, and he is now disposed to go directly to Missilonghi to assist the Greek defence there.'

'It is to be hoped that the fleet will bear with them our long-awaited *letter of marque*,' said Pat with more hope than conviction, his dolorous face exhibiting the despairing pessimism he felt at that moment.

# Chapter Ten

*Place me on Sunium's marbled steep,*
*Where nothing, save the waves and I,*
*May hear our mutual murmurs sweep;*
*There, swan-like, let me sing and die:*
*A land of slaves shall ne'er be mine –*
*Dash down yon cup of Samian wine!*

*Saturday 22nd November 1823*         *Metaxata, Cephalonia*

After breakfast Pat and Duncan with Simon, who had joined them early that morning from the ship, strolled through the village to visit Lord Byron in the hope that his Lordship, who was most presciently receptive to the political winds blowing from the Morea and who received many letters from his several emissaries throughout much of Greece, might be able to apprise them of the current circumstances generally and Mavrocordato's specific situation, his location particularly.

On the first floor of his apartment the poet was gazing from his window as the maid showed them in. 'O'Connor, Macleod, Ferguson, how pleasing to see you all. Look here, I do so enjoy this vista,' declared Byron, looking tired but smiling. He turned again to the window, 'I was admiring it only last night, my daughter only latterly recovered from sickness, and I have myself been sleeping ill. The calm, though cool serenity of a beautiful and transparent moonlight showing the islands, the mountains, the sea... with a distant outline of the Morea traced between the double azure of the waves and skies. These sights, of such beauty, have quieted me enough to be able to write. Look, Zante is there to the south... and in the far distance one can glimpse the hills of the Morea. Here in my modest home, in this blessed landscape and amongst these simple people... I have found tranquillity such that has eluded me for too many of these past years. Do you not find it acts upon you in that way?' Byron turned again to his visitors, 'Excuse me, may I offer you tea?'

Simon, was plainly moved by the poet's eloquent words, and before Pat could answer he replied softly, 'I am the most modest philosopher, sir, but I find that too often our hearts are oppressed by our minds, and sadly our mind can be oppressed by our heart. When we are fortunate to find that neither is the case, we oft know not how to embrace the absence of anguish and but slowly do we come to rejoice. I give you joy, sir, if that is where you find yourself. Leave that place only with the utmost reluctance. Speaking as a medical man, these feelings are beyond our gift... but of their recuperative benevolence one may not praise them too highly.'

Byron had listened patiently to Simon and continued to look at him as if contemplating the sense and the merit of his words. He stepped towards Simon and grasped Simon's hand between both his own; and he murmured, 'Thank you kindly for your words, Ferguson; none finer could come from any poet's lips. Would that we had more time together to enjoy such discourse.'

'Sir, I am gratified by your kind words.'

After a few pensive moments, Byron still firmly gripping Simon's hand, each of them silently contemplating the other, Pat intervened, 'Beg pardon, my Lord; by that, do you mean... that is to say... is your Lordship leaving this place?'

'My dear O'Connor,' Byron replied, breaking as if reluctantly from his thoughts and his grasp of Simon's hand, 'I have recently received a letter from Secretary of State Mavrocordato, whom I pressed to state the intentions of the Greek government so as to assist the formulation of my own plans. He reports that President Conduriottis has himself paid the first month's pay for the fleet in Hydra, which is to sail shortly in anticipation that I shall loan their continuing costs. I am minded to do so... and I shall reply urging Mavrocordato to come to Missilonghi, to show himself there, the better to demonstrate some restoration of political unity. I am now resolved to go to that place and assist their efforts. I will go first to Zante to cash my bills; Messrs Barff and Hancock there have offered to do so... and on the most generous of terms. It will surely be a loss to leave this place, but sitting here I can do little for Greece.' Byron sighed, his weary voice reflecting his feelings of dismay with

Greek disunity. The maid returned with tea and announced a further visitor, Colonel Napier, had arrived. 'Pray, do come in, Colonel,' shouted Byron with a friendly inflexion.

Napier entered the small room and the maid busied about to serve all with tea. 'Good day, my Lord. I have called first upon Captain O'Connor... to be told he was here. Captain O'Connor, as I left Argostoli your schooner was approaching the quay. I am sent by the Governor - the packet recently arrived from Corfu - to determine and report the further interests of yourself and Lord Byron... Maitland lamenting that I tell him nothing at all.' The reference to Sir Thomas was spoken with a knowing smile on Napier's face.

It was Byron who replied, 'Napier, we have known each other for some months... and I will say a respect akin to a friendship has arisen between us in that time. So, I will tell you in honesty... I am quitting this tranquil place where I have been pleased to find a home - *which I shall sorely miss* - and I am going to Missilonghi in some few weeks time. I will presume upon our friendship and ask that you retain that confidence until I have left. I wish, Colonel, that you might accompany me. I am sure that no more admirable leader of military men could the Greeks aspire to secure. I will gladly write you a letter of introduction to the London Committee to that effect.'

'You are too kind, my Lord,' Napier replied. 'In the first matter, my report to the Governor must be sent by the December packet to Corfu, but I understand that Maitland is not well and has gone to Malta, and so it may be some time before he receives my letter... and by then you will have departed Cephalonia. In the second matter I cannot comment, but I thank you for your sentiment. Captain O'Connor, in frankness, sir, may I presume that surveying is not *the sole interest* you have in and about these islands?'

The question produced only a pregnant silence for a few moments before Pat replied after evident deliberation, 'Colonel, *Surprise* has completed her work on the *west* coasts of the islands of Cephalonia and Zante... but there remains interest to the *east*.'

It was the most circumspect reply, with everything left unsaid, which Napier could hardly fail to notice, though he did not press further before Pat resumed, 'We must away, gentlemen, *Eleanor* having returned.' Pat, Simon and Duncan left after cordial but swift farewells.

The news from Jason when they reached *Eleanor* at the quay in the early afternoon was deeply significant. 'Finally, I was received by Mavrocordato, he being for some weeks reluctant to confide in me, and he was also uncertain of the intentions of the combined fleet. It consists of nine Hydriot and five Spezziot brigs; quite small for the most part and hardly armed at all in comparison with the guns of *Surprise*. How they will fare against Turk vessels of some size is far outside my province, yet they are intending to sail at the end of the month. Mavrocordato himself will accompany them; not in any official capacity but as a volunteer, he being no longer in office. They will sail to Missilonghi, and their intention is to break the Turk blockade.'

After the shortest of pauses Pat replied, his officers all with him in *Eleanor's* small cabin, 'Thank you, Mr Jason; that is news of the very first importance. Gentlemen; Doctor Ferguson, Lieutenant Macleod and I will return to Metaxata this evening to make our arrangements. We will convene on the morrow at eight bells of the morning watch. Our plans will be revealed after we have mustered to divisions. Mr Mower, please to replenish *Surprise's* water. Mr Pickering, provisions for thirty days. Mr Codrington, the same for *Eleanor*. Mr Reeve, my barge is to be ready at the quay tomorrow at seven bells, if you please. I bid you all good day.'

The ride back to Metaxata was a little more urgent than usual, the heat of the day slightly cooler than in prior weeks, despite which it was a hot and perspiring Pat who dismounted outside the house. 'I shall be mightily pleased, Simon, to be astride my quarterdeck once again... in the fresh sea air, salt wind in my face. I tire of many more days astride this horse, willing that he is, on this damned inferno of an island. Praise be we are hauling up our anchor tomorrow... though when we might see our long-awaited *letter of marque* the Lord only knows.'

'In the plainest of speaking, I fear you have been eating rather better here these past months and tending again to obesity, brother. Salt horse and ship's biscuit will serve you well until you can shed at least thirty pounds,' replied Simon, disregarding his friend's personal feelings entirely. 'Will I prescribe a daily purgative to assist you? It will act in several ways and is sure to rectify the humours!' Simon laughed out loud, but the comment was wholly ignored by Pat, and they drifted into a contemplative silence for the remainder of the ride.

At supper, shared with their families, Pat announced to their considerable dismay that *Surprise* and *Eleanor* would depart next morning and be away for some weeks. *Eleanor* would return to apprise them of their circumstances were *Surprise* unable to do so; for such seemed possible once the Governor became aware of any participation by *Surprise* in the conflict, when the strict Ionian neutrality policy would preclude her returning to the Islands without fear of seizure or even forfeiture, the United Islands authorities most likely having no present knowledge of her covert appointment.

### *Wednesday 10$^{th}$ December*                    *near Ithaca*

The ship's bell had just rung six times in the morning watch. The weather, hazy but dry, promised a fine day, or so Pat thought as he contemplated yet another uneventful day; for nothing of note had happened in the two weeks since *Surprise* had left Argostoli. He picked at his first breakfast. *Surprise* was a few miles off the east coast of Ithaca with a light and following north-westerly wind. 'Another week of cruising up and down this channel, Ithaca to Zante, Zante to Ithaca, *ne'er any ship to be seen*, and I venture the crew may soon be minded to press us to join the enemy; the only vessel we have seen was that Greek mistico running the blockade yesterday. Much more of this wretched to'ing and fro'ing and we will be looking to our pension ere we ever see so much as a Turk... and no commission yet in hand neither. We are blighted by delay, infernal delay, and I am sorely hipped,' an irritable Pat grumbled.

'What news from the captain of the mistico, brother? Ye hailed and spoke with him, I collect,' asked Duncan, reaching for the bacon dish. Pat, unusually, had not consumed much.

'Very rum developments if he can be believed. The captain said that he hailed from Hydra. The Albanian besiegers of Missilonghi have marched away... fearing to starve in the winter, no doubt. The Turk fleet has retired to beyond Patras and sits under the guns of the Little Dardanelles; hence, the mistico was running in daylight. The Greek fleet has plainly sailed, but the mistico is faster by a knot or two and will sail at all speed at night, accustomed as they are to running the blockade. The captain said the fleet was but an hour or two behind him as he passed Modon. I think I shall go on deck.' With that he took his Dolland glass and stepped up to his quarterdeck.

A half-hour passed and the masthead lookout shouted, 'Sail ho! Two points off the larboard bow.'

Training his glass, Pat, his instincts sparked by the report, could see a brig followed closely by several more sail, too indistinct as yet to clearly make out, the morning mist persevering. 'Mr Pickering, maintain this course until we close and can see who is there. They are beating close-hauled into this north-westerly. It will surely be slow progress. Stand by to come about in good time, and then we will keep a parallel course,' added Pat, keen interest having replaced his prior lassitude.

The next half-hour passed inexorably slowly in growing anticipation as *Surprise* closed on the approaching ships, Pat studying them closely with his glass. Puffs of smoke erupted from the leading ship and cannon fire could be heard. 'A Turk brig, I fancy. She is pursued by four or five Greek brigs... smaller vessels. Her captain is handling his ship well.' Pat murmured his commentary aloud, watching frequent course changes as the quarry sought to use her longer-range guns to disable or rake her pursuers. 'Mr Macleod, we will wear ship,' Pat declared, reaching his decision. 'Bring her about and maintain our distance at two miles from them, not a cable less.'

The first lieutenant reiterated Pat's order and the crew with supreme efficacy brought *Surprise* gracefully on to her near reversed course. She, like the combatants, now required frequent tacking to make the slowest of progress into the wind. The Turk ship and her pursuers gradually approached as *Surprise* still sought to recover speed.

'Mr Macleod, we shall clear for action!' ordered Pat.

The sound of Clumsy Dalby's drum brought every member of the gun crews running to their stations, all gun ports opening. With the thunderous rumble of the carriages across the deck, their frenzied crews heaving with all their strength and sweating with their exertions, the long guns were swiftly run out on both sides of the ship and the men stood ready, a great sense of expectation prevailing.

'The Turk is being harried at every tack by two or three Greek brigs and her escape must be doubtful. Her captain is surely weighing his prospects at this very moment,' said Pat quietly to no one in particular but heard by all on his quarterdeck, Marston and Simon too, they having stepped up to see what was afoot.

The nearest Greek was on a converging course with *Surprise* and the distance closing quite rapidly, she having separated from the chasing pack. She was now no more than one mile off *Surprise's* starboard beam but presented no danger to the frigate, it being within *Surprise's* far more considerable fire power and range to maul or destroy the Greek brig before she could even engage.

'Steady, Mr Macleod, he wishes to see who we are; let us steer two points to leeward and do so without haste,' ordered Pat.

The Greek was now a mere half mile abeam of *Surprise*. Perhaps content with the identification of her as an English ship – her unauthorised colours flying prominently in the stiff wind – she turned away towards her compatriots, a mile or more ahead.

'Maintain course, Mr Prosser. Mr Macleod, I think we will see what is about over there,' said Pat, beginning to wonder where the end of this chase might lie. The Greeks lay between the Turk and the approach to Patras. The Turk was cut off with no prospect now of escape: she plainly could not outrun her Greek pursuers. The sound of cannon fire became louder, more frequent, more vigorous as *Surprise* gained slightly on the protracted skirmish.

'Set topgallants, Mr Macleod.' Pat stared with professional fascination through his glass. 'Look, the fox pursued by the hunt, I fancy, and no bolt hole available. The Turk is in a dreadful dilemma, quite damaged. Her trysail is shot away and her boom spar shattered. Look, she is steering for Ithaca now. I doubt that she will make the turn into the bay for the port afore the hounds close for the kill.' *Surprise* had closed a little and the action was no more than a mile ahead. 'The Turk is plainly finished now; she has turned away to leeward with no sea-room available to her. Her captain must be intent on beaching her to save sinking or capture.'

Another half-hour passed. 'The Turk captain is a most determined fellow. Look, the brig has struck the rocks. The Greeks are standing off now and lowering boats... 'tis a flagrant breach of Ionian neutrality and plainly there will be the devil to pay for someone. Mr Pickering, we will come about and approach no closer; stand down the gunners. Mr Prosser, set course for Missilonghi, if you will. I am set fair for my second breakfast. Will you join me, Mr Macleod?' asked Pat.

'Certainly, sir, I would like it of all things, and I have a sure craving for a pot of tea this past hour. Would it be wise to approach Missilonghi in *Surprise* rather than in *Eleanor*, d'ye suppose?'

Pat wasted no time in thought, 'Whether or no, we are going. We have wasted far too much time; we have seen precious few Turks, and I venture it will be as well to find Mavrocordato ere too many more weeks are gone.'

The tedium at the start of the day had now gone and the decisive Pat O'Connor of old was returning, Duncan thought. Some further hours elapsed with the crew remaining in a state of excitement, the officers scanning the horizon and Prosser bringing *Surprise* close to the approach to Missilonghi until he enquired of Pat, 'Shall we stand off, sir, and send our cutter to seek a pilot? I have not the least acquaintance with these shallows.'

'Never fear, Mr Prosser, I have Smyth's personal chart in the cabin. Barton shall fetch it, and we will be assured of safe passage. Smyth is a perfectionist you know,' declared Pat buoyantly.

Within the hour, *Surprise* had passed by the outer islands and cast her anchor a mile and a half south of Vasiladi island. Pat was swiftly aboard his barge, and his immaculately dressed bargemen rowed him through the gentle chop to the distant shore of Missilonghi. Some two hours later, the Greek fleet having followed them to the deepwater anchorage, *Surprise* was surrounded by a dozen or more small brigs. A tumultuous reception, which seemed to consist of the whole population of the town, had gathered to welcome their fleet. Firearms were discharging and even the odd cannon could be heard above the good-natured demonstration of the newly relieved residents. The besieging Ottoman army had departed some two weeks previously and now resupply by sea was once again at hand. The port captain, once he was eventually found, declared that there was no quarantine - unlike the Ionian Islands - and no papers would be required whatsoever; Pat's crew were at liberty to come ashore; indeed, they would be warmly welcomed, for assuredly there would be festivities and celebrations until the dawn.

'I think that we shall return and remain aboard the barky until the morrow,' Pat declared after short consideration. 'It would not do to be here, the crew ashore and drunk, all kicking up *Bob's-a-dying* were the Turks to return. No, we shall allow shore parties of no more than two score... but only from tomorrow and for a few hours only. Let us get back to the barky, back to *Surprise*.'

Supper was eaten on deck, the crew watching the distant lights and listening to the noisy festivities of Missilonghi, all wishing they were there, for the celebrations continued all night.

*Thursday 11ᵗʰ December 1823*          *Missilonghi Town*

It had been very late when Pat had finally turned in, and he was therefore most displeased to be roughly shaken awake shortly after first light by Duncan shouting directly into his ear; for that is how it seemed. 'Wake up! Quickly now! Hurry, ye must come on deck. Wake up! There is a great deal of commotion between the Greek ships. What it signifies we cannae tell.'

Throwing on his cape, Pat hastened up to the quarterdeck, Duncan trailing. 'Mr Pickering, what's afoot? Why am I shaken awake at this ungodly hour, pray tell?'

Pickering pointed towards the Greek ships. 'There seems to be some disturbance between the Greek brigs, sir. I think between the Hydriots and the Spezziots; even several have run out their guns and are hoisting anchors. Look there, sails unfurling now and the crew hauling on a kedge to swing her round. Will we beat to quarters?'

In an instant Pat decided, 'Yes, beat to quarters, but do not open our gun ports until we grasp what is happening here. We do not want any of the Greeks to see us as a threat. Murphy! Murphy, there!' Pat shouted down to Murphy, loitering below the steps to the quarterdeck and chattering to Old Pennington, all within Pat's earshot. 'Will we send down your hammock? Rouse up Freeman and ask him to bring fresh coffee on deck!'

'Well, Jesus bejabers, the water ain't hot yet and Freeman's been grinding the bleeding beans this past half-hour,' moaned Murphy, not loud enough for Pat to hear.

Pickering turned to Dalby, 'Dalby, beat to quarters.' The resonant beat swiftly brought bleary-eyed Surprises rushing up from below. Slow-matches were fetched lit from the galley, and powder boys stood by their guns with reloads. Hammocks were hastily tied into the rigging, with many loud curses heard from men who had until recently been watching the shore festivities before retiring late to their sleep.

'My glass, Murphy,' shouted Pat, grasping his coffee gratefully from his steward, Freeman not returned from the galley. He took a deep draught of a lukewarm, bitter liquid. 'Murphy!' he shouted to the fast receding steward, 'Did you find this vile stuff in the bilges? Toss it over the side and bring me fresh!'

'Take my glass, sir,' proffered Pickering, 'Here!'

'Well, coffee first, rush, rush, glass next! To be sure, I'll be a'labouring all bleeding night afore long,' muttered Murphy, bearing away the coffee pot on its tray.

'Never fret when busy, Murphy; save it for when idle,' Pickering remarked as Murphy passed by.

'Thankee, Mr Pickering; an admirable notion indeed.' Pat peered through the glass with anxious curiosity. 'What on earth are they doing over there... anchors hauled up and sails unfurled with yards all ahoo? What do they know? Is there any news or sightings of Turk ships?'

'None, sir.'

Within a half-hour there seemed a general awakening of all the Greek fleet; several had caught their wind, sails filling with a steady north-easterly off the land.

'Mr Codrington, you are to take *Eleanor* to the quay and see if you can determine what is happening. Mr Mower, take Mr Jason with you in my barge and approach one of those brigs still anchored. Hail and ask them for an explanation. Mr Macleod, let fall tops'ls and spanker, leave them slack; warp her bow round to the south and prepare to get underway.'

Murphy returned, holding out Pat's Magellan jacket. 'Well, put it on d'reckly, sorr,' he remonstrated, 'afore ye catch your death.'

'Are we departing, sir? And what of our purpose here?' asked Duncan anxiously.

Pat had by now scrambled into his clothes, brought up by Murphy, 'No, we ain't leaving; 'tis just a precaution. No ship has fired, though some have run out guns and are leaving so swiftly - sails and rigging all ahoo - that I wondered if they might even cut their cables, but no. It seemed for some minutes like hostilities were about to break out between the Hydriots and the Spezziots. Who is to know what is up? They are foreigners, you know. Where is Mr Mower?'

'Over there, sir. He is aboard the near brig... gone to find out what he can.'

Another half-hour passed and the barge returned alongside, Mower and Jason swiftly scrambling aboard. Pat hastened towards them, anxious to ask their news. Mower revealed the startling story which Jason had gleaned from the captain of the Spezziot brig. 'It seems, sir, that the Hydriots captured a huge booty from the Turk which ran aground on Ithaca yesterday - half a million of piastres. They have refused to share it with the Spezziots and are running away with the lot. The Spezziots are boiling with rage, as might be expected; hence guns being run out... though her captain said he doubted anyone would actually fire.'

'Such conduct cannot be considered amicable,' remarked an irritated Simon, who had appeared on the quarterdeck barely half dressed.

Pat looked up to the heavens and turned to his First, exasperation plain on his face, 'Tell me, lest I forget... these are the people we have come here to assist? Eh? Running away with the prizes, with no fair distribution... and readying to fire upon their brothers! What brings these people to such acts? Will we haul our cable and return to England directly with no more time wasted here? Stand down the crew, Mr Pickering. I shall take breakfast and then go ashore to see if there is anyone in charge of this house of Bedlam.'

With some exasperation and followed closely by Duncan, Pat stomped back into the cabin. Murphy was there before he arrived, and, perceiving his ire, announced in the meekest of tones, 'Well, Freeman has your breakfast ready, sorr.'

'Tell him to bring it in directly, Murphy; thankee,' replied Pat, a great tiredness coming over him and returning to his voice. He sat down with some relief to enjoy his breakfast.

Later in the town, the atmosphere remained highly charged; excitement at the fleet's arrival and their delivery from the Turk blockade was now mixed with consternation, the fleet having left in haste. Pat had gone ashore with a small landing party, and Codrington came striding briskly towards them along the quay, accompanied by Reeve and a Greek civilian, seemingly of some standing, he being surrounded by an entourage of a score or more civilians and militiamen, all cheerfully mingling with half a dozen Eleanors. A somewhat flustered Codrington brought the march to a halt in front of Pat. 'Captain O'Connor, sir. Will I introduce Mr - *that is to say* - *Prince* Mavrocordato?'

Pat could not have been more surprised had Nelson himself been introduced. The many months of waiting to meet this very man, weeks of surveying, more weeks of fruitless patrolling the Ionian waters off the Greek coast, two successive days of beating to quarters, and now the man was here himself, standing in front of Pat and Duncan. He was at first glance an unimpressive man in his early thirties with unkempt long black hair, a huge drooping moustache, slightly short, a little overweight and with thick-lensed spectacles, though his companions exhibited considerable reverence towards his person.

'Your Maj... *your Highness*... it is an honour to make your acquaintance at long last,' Pat extemporised, much taken aback by such an unexpected development and inwardly floundering.

Duncan interjected to save his captain's embarrassment, 'Prince Mavrocordato... sir... Lieutenant Duncan Macleod at your service. I believe we have some business of a confidential nature to discuss. Will ye join Captain O'Connor and me aboard our vessel, *Surprise*, so that we may engage with some confidence of privacy?'

'Captain O'Connor, Lieutenant Macleod, I would be honoured to visit your ship. Let us do so without delay,' replied Mavrocordato with a sigh. He gave instructions to his cohorts and turned back to face Pat, 'Captain O'Connor, would that I could have arrived in this place sooner. Alas, the wheels of Greek politics do not turn smoothly...' He sighed again, '... and the consequences are sometimes quite brutal... as you saw this morning. Let us away to our business before we are overtaken by other necessities... Please, lead on.'

'Barton, help his Highness into the barge... and row dry back to the ship,' said Pat. His barge crew had mingled with the Eleanors, seeking further explanation of this evidently important Greek about to come aboard. A half-hour later and back in the great cabin, coffee having been served and a brace of bottles of cooled Amontillado consumed - which his Highness seemed to favour - Freeman was sent away to seek something better than biscuit to offer their guest. Pat remained unsure of how to begin and, being no diplomat, he struggled to find a start, 'Your Highness, it is an honour to welcome you aboard His Maj... that is to say aboard our dear *Surprise*. We have passed the summer in these waters gaining but little understanding of the current political situation. You will readily understand therefore that we are most pleased that we now meet with you.'

'Captain O'Connor, the honour is all mine, sir. It is a very great pleasure to meet such a renowned naval officer. My aides have provided to me the most interesting of information, the quite exceptional account of your prior service in our waters and an account of your sinking of the Turk ship *Iskander*. It is an exemplary record... of no equal.' Pat nodded politely and simply stared.

A slow but most cordial hour of pleasantries elapsed until Duncan could discern that Pat's reserves of patience and diplomacy, limited as they were even at the best of times, were being sorely tested. He brought matters to a head, 'If ye will permit me... your Highness will collect that Captain O'Connor and his ship arrived here in the Islands since some months past... and we remain anxious to assist your struggle for liberation... yet lacking any commission we are unable to engage without the most serious consequences. Indeed, a charge of piracy might well be levelled against us... were we to do so. Does your Highness possess the *letter of marque* that we understand has been prepared for our arrival?'

Mavrocordato peered genially over a pair of half-spectacles. 'Of course, Lieutenant Macleod. The letter is here with me, signed since some months by President Mavromichalis and by myself as Secretary of State, though it is an office I no longer hold.' Reaching inside his jacket Mavrocordato removed and handed over the much-anticipated document to Pat, who grasped it eagerly: it was the long-awaited key to their endeavours, an entirely legal start now possible. Mavrocordato continued, 'Perhaps you could study that at your convenience, sir; and if it proves acceptable then the Hellenic Republic will be pleased to consider that you are in our service. Sadly, as I am no longer Secretary of State and am come here only in the capacity of a simple volunteer, no changes can be made to the terms. However, the President has consulted closely with one of your compatriot officers in our service, one Captain Hastings, in preparing the letter. He therefore trusts that you will find it acceptable. My aide, Monsieur Léli, will come to you in Cephalonia. He will tell you of our priorities and communications when you return there. Captain O'Connor, I must now go ashore else no doubt some other burden will accost us. Thank you for your interest in serving Greece, gentlemen; we are assuredly poor of funds but do not lack for appreciation of our friends.'

Pat gingerly placed the precious letter inside his table drawer, shook hands with his esteemed guest and replied cautiously, 'I am sure the letter will serve, your Highness. It is an honour to commence our service for your country.' Pat paused for a moment before resuming, 'My First here, Lieutenant Macleod, is particularly tasked by our Admiralty with facilitating communication between this ship and your naval colleagues. In the first instance, it is proposed by their Lordships that he shall pass some time with you to gain a familiarity with your procedures.'

'That will serve us well, Captain O'Connor. The Hellenic Republic is obliged to you.' They shook hands.

'My crew will set you both ashore. I will bid you good day, sir.'

Duncan hastened away for his sea chest as Pat escorted Mavrocordato to the ladder for the barge. Returning to his quarterdeck after they had disembarked – Duncan with time for only the briefest of farewells to his fellow officers before he departed – Pat stood there, sadness returning to his mind as he contemplated prior occasions when he had seen off one or the other of Duncan or Simon, but the acute feeling of anxiety never relented. His attention was restored by Tom Pickering standing in front of him, enquiring of his intentions as the men at the helm looked across, patient enquiry written all over their faces. Pat pondered their new status: should he now hoist a Greek flag? Should he make any announcement? Instead, he simply murmured to Pickering, 'Take us out of this place, Mr Pickering. We will return to Argostoli. Keep a sharp watch for any ships, Turk or Greek.'

*Monday 29th Dec. 1823      17:20      Surprise, Gulf of Patras*

Christmas had been a greatly subdued affair in Metaxata despite both Pat and Duncan's families being in attendance in the house. For Simon it had been a somewhat demoralising episode, still missing his dear wife so much after five years, and his spirits had appeared to his friends to be greatly downcast. Duncan, something of a bystander but so greatly concerned for his dear friend had remarked to Pat that perhaps Simon had found something of a small renaissance of spirit in his burgeoning friendship with Lord Byron, for the poet had attended the household on several festive occasions.

Ultimately Lord Byron had declared his wish and intention to be set upon Greek territory, specifically at Missilonghi, before the new year; indeed, he had emphasised that such would likely represent and deliver new hope for the town's defenders and for a wider Greece generally, his determination to assist their fight for independence being well known. Accordingly, Pat had ordered *Surprise* to sea to escort the small vessel within which Byron would make the passage, a chartered mistico with a master who was greatly familiar with the islands and waters all about Missilonghi town and its lagoons.

Pat had persuaded Byron to accept the company of Abel Jason as a proficient translator; indeed, he had also convinced Byron that his personal companion, Count Gamba, should make the passage quite separately aboard a second small vessel - a local bombard with a master equally familiar with the waters thereabouts had also been procured - in order to mitigate the possibility of both being captured by Turk patrols. In his own crossing from Cephalonia it had also been decided that Gamba would be joined by Simon Ferguson; the Doctor would attend to any medical needs of the two philhellenes for at least the first few weeks until the local availability of medical resources was understood.

Simon himself had declared that he was keen to accompany and support Lord Byron, but after the brutal and fatal encounter *Surprise* had experienced with the Turk xebecs off Candia, Simon being absent from the barky, it was an arrangement that Pat had been loathe to accept; indeed, he had been adamant that he would not accept it. For several days it had been the subject of vigorous debate and harsh exchanges which near veered into hostile statements before Pat had reluctantly accepted Byron's and Simon's wishes, reconciling himself to them only because the essential priority in his Admiralty orders remained the same: the safeguarding and delivery of Lord Byron himself.

Pat had spent the whole of a slow day's approach to Cephalonia in a seething cauldron of mental anxiety, holding back progress with frequent sail manipulations, despite a weak wind, with the intention of entering the Gulf of Patras and closing on the mainland only in the coming of darkness.

'Can you still see them, Mr Pickering?' asked Pat, rubbing his eyes as his gaze wandered away and towards the last of the sun, blinking its farewell over Cephalonia.

'Aye sir, the mistico appears to be going ahead of the bombard, but 'tis now very difficult to be sure in what little is left of the weak twilight, it fading so.'

'Let us pray this wind remains a favourable westerly,' Pat opined, straining his eye into his glass and searching for the two vessels, now near three miles distant and disappearing into the diminishing light, sure to vanish into the colder darkness of the eventual night. 'Let us pray too that the Turk fleet stays at Patras Roads, for that is where it is said to be... from our reports obtained in Zante. It is to be hoped that both vessels reach Missilonghi without interception and without any help from us. I would wish that the Turks did not yet know we had come to the aid of the Greeks, and so I prefer not to be sighted with them. That is why we shall keep our distance from the bombard and the mistico.'

'What are the Doctor and Mr Jason to do, sir, in Greek company?' enquired Pickering.

'Mr Jason is to translate... *he speaks both the Greek and the Turk...* should his Lordship be accosted by either side. The Doctor is to aid Count Gamba similarly. Though he speaks nothing of either the Greek or the Turk, he will support the Count with his story that they are bound for Calamos; *that is should they be waylaid.* Let us hope that will not be the case. We will shadow them, principally his Lordship, and interpose *Surprise* between them and any Turk that comes along seeking to stop them; *that is if we can stay in sight of them during the night.* They are showing no lights whilst running the blockade,' said Pat, explaining a strategy with which he himself remained most uncomfortable; 'Will you double the watchmen?'

'Aye aye, sir; that we will,' replied Pickering.

Just at that moment Freeman appeared. Since *Surprise* had left Falmouth he had assumed a right to tread Pat's quarterdeck, at least as long as he professed to be bearing any message or refreshment, a presumption that Pat had not thought fit to disabuse him of, the formalities of the whole voyage having become somewhat less than that which the strictest Royal Navy captain might have mandated. 'Stirabout he spoilt, massa, gone cold. You want fresh?'

It was a welcome reminder to Pat that he had quite forgotten his customary supper in the activity of the departure from Zante, plus the near sleepless crossing from Cephalonia having been made the night before, and Simon, his usual companion for supper, also having transferred to the bombard. In the close following of the two vessels for five or so hours since leaving Zante he had not shifted from his quarterdeck. 'Thankee Freeman, I will come to the cabin shortly. Supper will be most welcome... I am amazing short set. Mr Pickering, would you care to take some supper with me? Ask Mr Mower if he will join us too. Freeman, supper for three if you will... and look out a bottle of port from my stores; a bottle of the da Silva of the year 'fifteen would serve admirably,' said Pat pleasantly, continuing half in thought and half in speech to his lieutenant, 'Now there is an enterprising man. I met him in London one year, I collect it was in Black's... Bruno da Silva, would you know? He also had a *letter of marque* to arm his ship and more safely bring his wine to London. He kindly gave me a case of his port wine. I have always bought his wine since and ne'er opened a spoiled bottle. Come, let us go to the cabin. All this talk reminds me it is time to eat. Mr Prosser, you have the barky.'

*Tuesday 30ᵗʰ December 1823, 07:30*          *aboard the bombard*

Simon, and Gamba had remained on deck throughout the lingering light of the prior evening whilst the mistico had been in close accompaniment; however, as twilight had ceded to dusk, it had been lost from their sight. After a cold supper of black bread and cheese with thin red wine they had gone below to seek rest as midnight had approached and as the wind had freshened to a much colder northerly when progress had near stopped. For hours they had sought uncomfortable sleep huddled below deck, swathed in blankets of doubtful provenance, until after seven o'clock in the subdued twilight of the emerging dawn they had stirred; the sensation of the motion of the vessel increasing had awakened them. Now, in the visibly brightening air, as it gained speed, Simon gazed, shivering, at the grey and choppy waves, the wind having shifted round to the customary north-easterly *Gregale* of those island waters. Having returned to near the wheel, Simon spoke to the captain, his voice carrying his worrying uncertainty in his words, 'Would it be uncivil, sir, to ask you of your intentions... *indeed, your expectations...* of our landfall?'

'Can we ask the wind of its intentions, Doctor Ferguson? I know not. These are very difficult waters for the navigator... shoals and rocks all about us,' replied Captain Valsamarchi cautiously. He had declined to continue at best speed in the darkest hours despite the danger from Turk patrols, being concerned for the shallows, preferring to mark time and await first light.

'Pray tell, Captain: are we far now from Missilonghi?' Simon persisted.

'We are approaching the Scrofes, the small islands and rocks outlying the lagoon. In several hours we will be in the anchorage some way off the town. The water will become very shallow soon for all the remaining distance from here to the town. Great care of navigation is now our foremost priority,' replied Valsamarchi, his cautious reservations plain in his tone of voice as well as in his words.

*Tuesday 30th December 1823,      07:45      aboard the mistico*

'Will you take tea with me, Jason?' Lord Byron asked. The two men had enjoyed the most cordial of conversation since losing sight of the bombard in yesterday's sunset, the two crews having continued firing pistols and carbines for another half-hour or so in an ultimately fruitless effort to maintain contact. The captain had shortened sail so that the following bombard, slower and lagging a mile or more astern, might keep up with the faster mistico, but all was to no avail, the bombard had been lost to them. A largely sleepless night had followed.

'That would be most welcome, your Lordship... WAIT!' Jason exclaimed. 'Look there! Look! Over there! Do you see it? A ship, larger than the bombard, I venture... just there!'

'Keep silent and do nothing,' ordered the captain, appearing beside them, great anxiety plain in his voice. 'It is a Turk frigate and he will be near alongside in a few minutes. We cannot escape him. Our only hope is to pretend we have not seen him for as long as that is credible... and hope we reach the shallows where he cannot follow. Keep silent if you value your life... and pray to your God.'

With a sinking feeling Jason could not take his gaze from the approaching frigate. Indeed, the eyes of all were focused upon it, the mistico's crew urging every last half knot of speed from their vessel as they contemplated two very different destinies: which one would occur would be made plain in the next few minutes. The Turk frigate was plainly bent on their interception and fast approaching, sailing large, wind astern of her, a creaming bow-froth plainly visible as she swiftly closed.

*Tuesday 30<sup>th</sup> December 1823,*        *08:00  aboard Surprise*

The low light, not long after the dawn, was weak and diffused, nothing of bright radiance through the thin, streaky cloud above the Morea to the east, when the loud shout from the foretop reached the quarterdeck, 'Sails ahoy! D'reckly off the starboard bow!'

Pat, astride his quarterdeck since before the dawn twilight, peered long into his glass before eventually shouting, 'Mr Mower, beat to quarters!' Pat bellowed his commands to all around him, the crew hastening up to the yards with alacrity, the alarm and urgency clear to all in his voice. 'Mr Mower, open gun ports and run out the guns! All crews to stand by their guns. We will leave our English jack flying for now, but prepare to hoist the Greek flag on my command.'

'What do you see, sir?' asked Tom Pickering.

'It is a Turk frigate, I venture, and closing on the mistico, perhaps a league between them,' Pat announced, looking again for a few minutes through his glass. 'The mistico will surely be struggling against this northerly, as are we to close on her. We cannot reach the mistico afore the Turk hauls alongside of her and takes them, but - *God speed* - we may yet distract him... *if he has seen us*. He is on a beam reach, a league and a half from us if he is a yard... and barely one from the mistico, though he will be sailing with some southing too. It will take us three parts of an hour to close on him,' said Pat, the urgency diminishing in his voice as he had now calculated the likely time before any action could commence.

*Tuesday 30$^{th}$ December 1823,*      *8:15*   *aboard the mistico*

'Pray earnestly to your God, gentlemen, and keep still your silence,' reiterated the captain with a degree of despair. All aboard could no longer ignore the hailing from several crew on the quarterdeck of the Turk frigate, which had swiftly crossed their bow barely fifty yards ahead, firing a gun to reinforce her command. The frigate had now come about and was approaching the mistico's larboard side, slowing from only fifty yards away, the two vessels converging. Angry faces were visible on the Turk deck, as all aboard the mistico could not fail to notice. The Turk guns were also run out and - at such close range - were the frigate to fire, obliteration of the small mistico and all on board her could not fail to be the result.

'I do not understand why he is passing by close-hauled under full canvas with no notice of us,' said the captain to Jason. 'Perhaps he thinks us simply the stupid crew of a stinking fishing boat; we are not dissimilar in size and rig.' After another minute he added, 'We are too close now to the rocks for him to come about once again; I pray we may be saved; thank God, thank God.' The captain was breathing more easily, his relief so evident in his voice as the frigate cleared their stern, though she loomed large still with her bulk and presence so close to them.

'Captain, will you now put us close into those rocks so he cannot possibly reach us again?' asked Lord Byron with the utmost concern in his voice. 'Never fear for any damage to your vessel for I shall guarantee you any necessary repairs.'

From the deep sigh of relief from the captain, no bidding or any guarantee was necessary at all; no slackening of sail or speed was made, but the little mistico seemed now so close to its destruction from a different means as the shallows were upon them. The captain, knowing the waters intimately and with a sure touch, ordered a swift series of course corrections to bring the vessel through between two islets and to safety from both the frigate and the rocks. 'We can go no further, the wind being so much against us now,' he declared. 'If the Turk so wishes, he may yet launch boats to capture us, and we can do nothing. We have but a very few sidearms and to use them would be folly, ensuring our certain execution after capture. We must await a change in the wind to continue to Missilonghi... or we may beat for hours into this wind and sail for Dragomestre where we can at least take to the land and away from any Turk pursuit. What is your preference, sir?'

On this sobering note, Jason and Byron paused very briefly to consider their fate before Byron declared, 'To Dragomestre, Captain. We must not be apprehended. Let us proceed as best we may to that place.'

'Yes, my Lord,' nodded the captain, his own profound relief so evident in his voice.

*Tuesday 30th December 1823,        08:30        aboard Surprise*

'The Turk has seen us, Mr Pickering, and he has left the mistico alone. He is coming towards us with a full spread of canvas and at best speed. Another twenty minutes and we shall see his mettle,' said Pat, staring intently through his glass. Within the minute he added, 'No, he is slowing. I venture the light is good enough for him to see our colours, and I doubt that he would wish to challenge an English frigate, even as we are in their claimed territorial waters and off the through channel for the United Islands. I fancy the Turk will be no trouble. He is turning away... yes, he is going about and so does not fancy engaging with us.'

'Look, a sail over there, approaching off the starboard beam,' the captain announced, a little more buoyantly, to Gamba and Simon as they peered with straining eyes into the rising but low sun, just barely above the horizon. 'We are still some twelve miles out from Missilonghi... but the Turk fleet is said to be beyond Patras at Lepanto.... and I believe it will be a Greek warship sent out to ensure that the whereabouts of the Turks remain known. We are hoisting the United Ionian Islands flag. The topman reports he also saw another, a smaller vessel - perhaps our mistico - beyond the Scrofes islets some two leagues ahead.'

'May I borrow your glass, Captain?' asked Simon, being far less sure than the confident Greek captain. 'Thank you,' he added, taking the proffered glass, and after peering intently for a few moments he enquired mildly, 'Would I be correct, Captain, in thinking that a red pennant might signify a Turk?'

At which comment Captain Valsamarchi brusquely snatched back his glass and looked hard at the approaching ship, a frigate, as could plainly now be seen and flying a Turk red flag at her mizzen. 'Hell and damnation!' he shouted - or the Greek equivalent, for that is how it sounded to Simon, no translation being necessary. The captain and his crew were stunned, in some disbelief that this was happening to them. The Turk fleet was supposedly shut in at Patras or even beyond the forts of the narrows, the Little Dardanelles as they were called, and at that moment they began to despair. Within what seemed like moments the frigate approached, turning swiftly into the wind to lose way and within a very few minutes came near alongside.

'They are hailing us now,' said Gamba to Simon, gazing at him with the utmost concern, 'What should we do?'

'Might I suggest, sir,' Simon replied in a measured tone, 'that were you to have any papers of a confidential nature – *confidential that is in the matter of his Lordship's intentions in the Morea and for Greece generally* – aboard this vessel, that they would be better for his Lordship's and indeed our own interests and prospects were they consigned over the side... and with the benefit of a large leaden weight?'

347

'Of course, of course, I will do so immediately,' said a greatly agitated Gamba, and he rushed off in great anxiety to his berth to retrieve them.

'What can I say?' asked the captain of Simon. 'God help us! They will surely ask why we, flying an Ionian flag, are so far away from the Islands channel. What conceivable explanation have I to offer? We will be taken as blockade runners and likely put to death.'

Gamba now having returned and the revealing documents being clutched by his frightened servant on that side of the bombard which was opposite the Turk frigate, he whispered to Simon, 'My servant shall throw our papers - they are weighted - into the sea should any boat put off from the frigate.'

Just at that moment the Turk ship lowered a small boat. The servant panicked and threw everything into the water where all sank immediately from sight.

'My dear Gamba, do you have anything else of a conceivably incriminating nature?' asked Simon as the Turk boat drew alongside. The Greek captain was summoned into it without any of the pleasantries as are customary between navigators.

'Nothing,' replied Gamba with some relief.

'Then I will join the captain and go aboard the Turk vessel. We are merely en route for Calamo and have lost our way in the night,' said Simon with some measure of sang froid which he did not feel in that moment.

At that moment there was shouting from the Turk frigate and some pointing of hands to the south-west. All looked about, towards far and approaching sails in the direction of Zante. Simon could not be sure at this distance, no longer having the benefit of Captain Valsamarchi's glass, but he wondered if it could be *Surprise*, possibly with her consort, *Eleanor*, coming to their aid. The Turks were obviously nervous, the shouting from their quarterdeck was becoming evermore shrill and strident. Simon hastened with alacrity to scramble down the net to join Captain Valsamarchi in the barge, and its crew rowed hastily across to the frigate. The Turk captain was shouting to his first officer, now taking charge on the bombard, to bring her behind the frigate and follow its lead. Within a few minutes both vessels were underway, heading north-east towards the Straits, beating slowly into the wind.

*Tuesday 30ʰ December 1823,        09:00        aboard Surprise*

'It is the bombard... alongside the same Turk frigate,' said Pat, his spirits sinking; the realisation that the bombard was captured was hitting him particularly hard. He continued to peer through his glass, the morning light still weak through an overcast sky of cloud, visibility poor. 'They are getting underway, towards Patras; the bombard is captured... and Simon too. Mr Pickering, send to *Eleanor*, "follow *Surprise* closely, bombard and Turk together".'

Just then there was a shout from the foremast topman, 'Sails Ho! Two point off the starboard bow... six ships... seven.'

Pat swept his glass to the north-east, pausing to study the horizon for long moments before lowering his glass. 'By Jove, 'tis a whole fleet of ships,' he exclaimed, looking again through his glass as if to confirm what he knew he had seen, 'and plentiful frigates amongst them. It cannot be the Greeks. It is the Turks come out from their anchorage at Patras. I think we must leave the bombard to the Turk. Plainly we cannot prevail against such numbers. We must turn away.' This was declared in a sinking tone of deep dismay and resignation. 'Well, that surely signifies our departure, gentlemen,' he added. 'Signal again to *Eleanor* "follow closely". Mr Pickering, Helm up! Let her go off! We will go west and away, back to Cephalonia. Home, gentlemen; we can do no more here this day and must await another time afore we try again for Missilonghi.' Pat ordered their turn away with considerable disappointment in his voice, tiredness creeping in after a second night of very little sleep.

*Tuesday 30ʰ December 1823,     09:15   aboard the Turk frigate*

Simon, sat alongside Captain Valsamarchi on the planks of the Turk deck, surrounded by towering, deeply hostile Turk sailors, angry faces prevalent. A frightened Captain Valsamarchi whispered to Simon, 'The Turk captain feared the mistico was a fireship and so left her alone when they espied an approaching ship of war behind it, coming so as to take off its crew when it became ablaze; and then we appeared and they became concerned that we too were another fireship, set to grapple with and consume them.'

'Are we in extreme peril?' asked Simon nervously.

Valsamarchi nodded towards a most ferocious Turk, speaking loudly with his captain who was holding his drawn sword and staring closely at them. 'There, that big fellow, he may be the second officer; he is urging the captain to cut off our heads and throw us over the side, and then to sink our vessel.'

'Oh, dear God,' exclaimed Simon, fearing the worst as the Turk captain stridently shouted something to the crew.

A great babble of vehement exchanges now took place amongst the Turk captain and his officers, Simon growing ever more anxious by each passing minute. Though he could understand only the barest smattering of the Turk language, the exchanges were so fast and furious that nothing could he comprehend, and so he looked with great anxiety to Valsamarchi for translation. 'What is this intemperate fellow shouting about, tell?'

The Turk captain, thankfully, appeared to be gaining control of the argument, his officers subsiding yet staring menacingly at their captives. Valsamarchi strained to hear whilst gazing unblinkingly at the Turk captain.

'Put them in irons,' bellowed the captain.

Valsamarchi translated for a very frightened Simon's benefit, adding in a whisper and with great uncertainty, 'The captain seems familiar to me.'

The captain himself had shown no such sign of recognition and shouted his question at them, asking if they were bound for Missilonghi. By now Simon and Valsamarchi were closely surrounded by a deeply hostile, gabbling crew, two of them clutching chains and close enough for Simon to smell their foetid breath, even to see a plethora of rotting teeth and to observe the hostility in their unwashed faces.

'Be not afraid,' advised Valsamarchi.

A bewildered Simon thought it advice of very doubtful validity, for rarely had he been in such a perilous predicament, one which seemingly offered only the immediate prospect of chained confinement; perhaps even death was now close at hand. 'Your advice is kindly meant, sir, though you will understand why I find myself hesitant to accept it,' he whispered, fearful as another four Turk seamen approached closer with rattling chains, every one glaring viciously at them.

The next development was utterly astonishing to Simon: his companion stood up, the Turk seamen halting in their intentions, as taken aback as was Simon. Valsamarchi gulped, rose unsteadily to his full height, the Turks pausing, and then he addressed the Turk captain in a loud and confident voice, 'Will Captain Zachiriá kill the man who saved his life, the man who saved his brother's life, who saved his crew from shipwreck in the Black Sea?'

The Turk captain started with indignation: that one of his miserable captives should address him was impudent in the extreme! He swivelled swiftly towards them and stared at Valsamarchi, intense curiosity now in his eyes, peering closely at Valsamarchi's face for some moments but saying nothing. A long minute passed before uncertainty flickered across the face of the Turk, and then in an instant a change of demeanour came about, anger giving way to curiosity, concern even. He stepped closer, no more than inches away from Valsamarchi, and said in the most fluent Greek, 'What? That cannot be. Is it you, Spiro?' The Turk captain dropped his still unsheathed sword to the deck, raised both his arms in the air and, without further hesitation, seized and embraced Valsamarchi tightly, as if meeting a returning brother – one long deemed lost, holding him close as if to prevent any second separation, for clearly that is how he felt. His demeanour displayed huge happiness, astonishment and joy, all of which was showing on his face, quite unconcealed, and then he stepped back a pace, grasped and shook Valsamarchi's hand vigorously for several minutes more, seemingly lost for words. Both of them were now smiling widely at each other. The crew, all tension relieved, relaxed immediately; indeed, they too, once their captain's story was understood, embraced his evident happiness, and the chains were removed from sight, and all hostility ceased with this most unexpected turn of events. A very welcome turn, thought Simon, relief flooding through his every fibre. He marvelled at this swift reversal of fortune and stood staring at Valsamarchi and Zachiriá in a state of complete disbelief.

'Come Spiro, with your companion to my cabin. We shall have soup and coffee together, my friend,' declared Captain Zachiriá, his attitude so positively reversed from the frightening moments of their first minutes aboard the frigate. 'Captain Zachiriá, at your service sir,' he nodded to Simon when they were in the cabin.

'Please introduce me and thank the Captain for his attention, Captain Valsamarchi, if you will,' Simon replied, savouring every sip of the proffered Turkish coffee as if it were his last, but grateful relief now nearly superseded by a degree of restored normality in his voice.

For almost an hour Valsamarchi and Zachiriá exchanged reminiscences of the intervening fifteen years since they had last met in extreme circumstances - so Simon gathered - before their conversation turned to recent times and their present situation. Zachiriá explained his particular fear of fireships, having been captain of the Turk admiral's flagship that had been engulfed by a Greek fireship at Chios in the previous year, and swimming from the burning ship to save his life; but the Admiral, Kara Ali Pasha, had lost his when struck by a falling, burning spar. A further hour passed as Valsamarchi and Zachiriá continued to reminisce, Simon content to allow his anxieties to further subside as he enjoyed the Turkish coffee, and then it was time for Zachiriá to return to his duties.

'We are to be taken to see the Admiral later. Zachiriá will vouch for us,' Valsamarchi explained. After Zachiriá had left them and returned to his deck, Valsamarchi concluded his scarcely credible story of how, at some risk to himself and his crew, he had rescued Captain Zachiriá, his brother and his crew from their sinking vessel some fifteen years beforehand; so long ago that mutual recognition had dimmed but had not, fortunately, been totally extinguished.

Under the close scrutiny of its captors, the captured bombard had reached Patras, letting go her anchor alongside the Turk frigate amidst a Turk fleet of fourteen ships. The captain's barge came alongside the bombard, and Gamba crossed to the frigate, summoned by Captain Zachiriá. On boarding Gamba was greeted by a somewhat more relieved-looking Captain Valsamarchi, waiting with Simon. Valsamarchi repeated his explanation of the recent turn of events for Gamba's benefit. Gamba listened without interruption until the end of Valsamarchi's story and he offered only, "tis strange but true, for truth is always strange, stranger than fiction. That is verse fourteen of his Lordship's poem *Don Juan*, did you know?'

'Count Gamba,' Captain Zachiriá spoke sternly, 'your captain, Spiro Valsamarchi, has confessed that it is your intention to reach Missilonghi in contravention of the blockade. What say you?' This was translated by an Italian, Captain Francesco, in the service of the Turks as pilot at Patras.

'That is most certainly not the case, Captain. We are bound for Calamos and merely became lost in the dark of the night,' replied Gamba valiantly, glaring coldly at Francesco. 'What Valsamarchi has to say is of no worth whatsoever, for I have chartered his vessel for Calamos, as his papers will vouch, and therefore I must remonstrate against our detention and that of our vessel.'

Simon, then interposed, shrewdly observing more than an intermediary's interest on the part of Francesco - perhaps a pecuniary one; perhaps too he was anticipating a goodly share of the prize, as the eight thousand dollars aboard the bombard had likely been discovered. He spoke very seriously, surprising himself with his calmness, 'Captain, respectfully... as one seafaring man to another and as personal physician to Lord Melville, His Majesty's First Lord of the Royal Navy, I appeal to your undoubted goodwill as a fellow navigator and to your considered observance of the appropriate diplomatic formalities. Our continued detention will not sit well with his Majesty's ministers at the Court of St. James's. It will no doubt bring the severest remonstrations to the Sublime Porte from his Majesty's ambassador in Constantinople. Will you care to consider that?' Simon concluded, studying Zachiriá's reaction closely.

Captain Zachiriá was by no means an unintelligent man, and the potentially dangerous implications for himself of his arrest of the vessel he readily perceived. He peered closely at Simon as if in assessment of this unkempt, unimpressive man before him, until his face broke into a great slow smile, 'Captain Valsamarchi's story was no doubt motivated by fear, Doctor Ferguson. By the grace of God and his Prophet Mahomet I have no doubt that the Admiral will release you and your vessel without delay.' This Zachiriá declared after only the briefest of thought – roundly sinking his interpreter's aspirations for a share of the booty, acceptance of that being visible to all in his countenance.

'That is a comfort,' murmured Simon, his mind awash with a huge surge of relief.

Zachiriá continued, 'I am so sorry to detain you, but perhaps you would be so gracious as to complain to the Admiral of your capture at my hands, so far beyond the Gulf, so far from the forts and many, many leagues beyond the line of blockade; for that will surely be well received on my return to Constantinople, the Greek warships being known to be in those waters. With God's grace and that of his Prophet Mahomet this recommendation will be worth at least a half million of piastres to me.'

'I will assuredly do so, Captain. Thank you kindly, sir,' replied Simon with great relief, contented by the success of his reference to his somewhat exaggerated credentials, as was Gamba who continued to glare at Francesco with deep hostility for the remaining time of the interview.

Captain Zachiriá continued affably, 'We must all be grateful to God and his Prophet this day, for they have granted me the opportunity to thank again the man that saved my life, Spiro Valsamarchi. He is a good man, and it pleases me that I can repay but a small portion of the debt I owe him. God in his benevolence has smiled upon us all this day.'

Simon, permitted himself a wry smile and replied simply, 'I am of your way of thinking, Captain. All men have need of the

Gods, and that, sir, is the opinion of a wiser man than us. Homer it was.'

The mood of the interview now being more cordial, Gamba picked up the bag he had brought across from the bombard. 'Captain, may I present you with my very modest gifts?' he said to Zachiriá, handing over a small cloth-wrapped bundle. 'Here are bottles of rum and porter, and a telescope. The latter may be of some use to you in your professional capacity as a seafarer and navigator.'

Zachiriá seemed genuinely pleased, particularly with the telescope, and after thanking Gamba he announced, 'Doctor Ferguson, Count Gamba... until tomorrow, when we shall meet the Grand Admiral, his Excellency the Pasha.'

Zachiriá shook their hands with emphatic warmth, and with that the interview was concluded, Simon and Gamba being escorted to the deck and taken by barge back to the bombard. When they were returned aboard and alone in Valsamarchi's cabin, Gamba seized Simon's hand and shook it with both his own, saying, 'A companion's words of persuasion are effective. That too is Homer, Doctor Ferguson. A most fine intervention; you have my thanks, sir. I am greatly in your debt.' His overwhelming feeling of relief was plain in his voice.

'Not at all, Gamba, though the Dear knows it is not a day I would care to repeat. Would there be any prospect of good coffee to be had on this vessel... and perhaps a tot of brandy? For medicinal purposes only; it will relax the fibres.'

'I will press Valsamarchi. Assuredly there will be brandy, perhaps coffee too.'

'And a final quote from Homer will serve us well this day,' Simon added, the tension within him near gone, his energy near wholly exhausted.

'By all means,' replied Gamba, curious.

'There is a time for many words...' whispered a deeply fatigued Simon, '... and there is also a time for sleep.'

# Chapter Eleven

*A king sat on the rocky brow*
*Which looks on sea-born Salamis;*
*And ships, by thousands, lay below,*
*And men in nations; all were his!*
*He counted them at break of day---*
*And when the sun set, where were they?*

*Wednesday 31ˢᵗ December 1823*　　　　　　　　*Dragomestre port*

In the morning of the final day of the year, Lord Byron mused aloud about their predicament in a somewhat melancholy review, his words steeped in great sadness consequent to the loss of his friend. 'Jason, Gamba has been taken by the Turk frigate yesterday; that was plain to see. My horses are all lost and also some eight thousand dollars of mine all gone; but never mind, we have more left. We had a narrow escape last night, being so close under their stern... hailed even, and again this morning. Perhaps the Turks are searching further for us. But here we are, with the sun and clearing weather... run away once more and within a pretty little port. Whether the Turk may seek us again and send in their boats to seize us is another question, especially if we remain long here, since we are blocked out of Missilonghi by the direct entrance.'

Jason searched for some consolation. 'We are at least safe here from the Turks, my Lord. If necessary, we can take to the hills and walk to Missilonghi... should any of their vessels approach the port,' he offered, seeking to cheer Byron.

'No, such thoughts had occurred to me also. But the mountains are impassable... so the captain of the mistico has explained to me. So steep that land affords no road to reach Missilonghi; indeed, plentiful snow now abounds upon them and far below their summits... we see it here in the wind. There is too the matter of roaming brigands - Turk and Greek - 'twixt here and there. It is quite impossible, a desperate resort for us at best.

No, we must await Greek ships from Missilonghi to escort us ere we leave this place... and hope that they might arrive before any inquisitive Turks.' Lord Byron concluded a sobering assessment.

### The Fort of the Morea, Patras

After hours of unsettled and anxious waiting, Simon and Gamba were finally escorted to meet the Ottoman supreme commander and Governor of the Morea, Yusuf Pasha. The Pasha was lying on a sofa smoking a pipe and did not rise to greet them. With a wave of his hand he indicated an adjacent sofa on which they were expected to be seated. Servants brought them strong Turkish coffee and pipes filled with mild but highly aromatic Turkish tobacco. As Simon enjoyed the coffee and Gamba smoked his pipe, the Pasha continued for several minutes to speak with his officers and counsellors seated around him before he turned to Gamba and Simon, when his minions' murmurings ebbed to silence. Smiling broadly, he offered greetings – expressed in Turkish and translated into Greek by his secretary, Gamba translating into English for Simon's benefit - before asking them for an explanation of their incursion into the blockaded Greek waters.

Gamba reiterated his story as told to Zachiriá, adding his lamentations concerning the state of the Morea, 'Such turbulent times, Excellency, making the aspirations of the mere traveller utterly difficult. Bandits and brigands abound throughout the Greek provinces, particularly the Morea, and safety is to be assured only within your Excellency's military oversight.' Gamba finished with a complaint about his capture by Zachiriá 'sailing brazenly alone and taking them so far beyond the line of blockade.' The Pasha, for the most part inscrutable and listening through his interpreter, nodded and appeared mollified with Gamba's additions, satisfied with his explanation, and was seemingly pleased to hear of his captain's exploits.

After a pause the Pasha conversed again with his advisors before turning to Simon and asking, 'What does Sir Thomas Maitland think of the Greek brigands pursuing my corvette upon the rocks of neutral Ithaca and the slaughter of many of its crew including the captain, my nephew? What of the money lost which was onboard and which was to pay my troops? Will Maitland not seek revenge for such an outrage by those pirates?'

Slowly Simon stood up, the somewhat theatrical move allowing him a further few moments with which to formulate his reply. He addressed himself directly to the Pasha, speaking with conviction, 'My name is Ferguson, Excellency. I am physician to the First Lord of His Majesty's Admiralty, Lord Melville... and a Fellow of the Royal Society by virtue of His Majesty's personal nomination... Assuredly, Excellency, His Majesty's Governor, Sir Thomas Maitland...' Simon paused intermittently to allow Gamba to translate into Greek and the Pasha's secretary to translate into Turkish, '... deplores most strongly the incursion of the Greek pirate ships... Speaking personally and without the least authority... it seems likely that His Majesty... through the august offices of his Governor... will make recompense to your Excellency in due course.'

The Pasha nodded gravely, indicating his comprehension and seemingly satisfied with Simon's response, though whether Simon's royal connections were an influence was impossible to determine from his inscrutable face and his immobile demeanour. Eventually he declared, 'We will detain you no longer; your passports will be returned to you; you may continue your travels.'

'We thank you extremely, your Excellency,' declared Simon (through the translators), '... and it is with the heaviest of hearts that we remove ourselves from your illustrious presence.'

The Pasha seemed please and, after an imperial wave of his hand in dismissal, he turned again to his secretary to dictate his orders for their release. Gamba and Simon rose as one and thanked the Pasha, both offering a diplomatic bow before retiring from the room.

'My dear Doctor Ferguson,' said a very grateful Gamba when they were finally outside the Pasha's residence, 'you were most convincing in your statement, and well received it was too; but is such recompense likely to be forthcoming?'

'Oh, I have not the slightest idea, Gamba, yet it would not surprise me. The Governor, Maitland, is reputedly a man of the strictest demeanour and would certainly have been outraged by the Greek incursion on his Imperial coastal periphery. Such minds customarily tend towards rigour and rectitude. Some clever mechanism for recompense may likely emerge from it, given time. Now, what do you say to a perambulation along the coast whilst we are here and awaiting our passports? The marshy nature of the landscape suggests we will find a goodly population of waders... and perhaps raptors too, I dare say.'

'By all means, Doctor Ferguson; I will bring a fowling piece, and I believe I still have a few bottles of porter,' Gamba replied, relief still evident in his voice.

*Saturday 3rd January 1824*                                   *Missilonghi*

*Surprise* anchored that morning three miles off from Missilonghi in the nearest deepwater anchorage. Some little way off were the five Spezziot brigs as had been there during *Surprise's* last visit, but of their crew very few were visible about their decks. Pat himself had gone ashore, rowed in his barge to the town, and they were seated in a small house in which Mavrocordato held court.

'Thank you most kindly for your valued escort of Lord Byron from Cephalonia, Captain O'Connor,' Mavrocordato was volubly grateful for the presence of *Surprise*; 'No doubt it was the appearance of your ship which drove off the Turk frigate, allowing his Lordship to escape.' Pat merely nodded cautiously and Mavrocordato continued, 'I received word from my agents of the encounter. Lord Byron is in Dragomestre, a small port along the coast to the north-west. I have sent a squadron of our gunboats and the brigantine *Leonidas* to fetch him from that place. He will be quite safe in the waters behind the offshore islands. I have asked our fleet to go to sea to find the Turk fleet so that no similar and untoward event can recur. That solitary Turk frigate with Dr Ferguson has returned to Patras. The English consul there, Mr Green, will make the strongest representations for his release. If you will, I would speak with you about our situation in the Morea and also in Candia, where the assistance of your own frigate will now be so beneficial.'

'May I ask, sir, where is the rest of your fleet, the ships that captured the Turk brig on the shore of Ithaca?' asked Pat.

'Sadly, the Hydriots with their nine ships have gone home to Hydra, their month of pay from the government having run out and Lord Byron having declined to provide funds for further months to such mercenary crews. The five Spezziot crews are also ashore for want of pay. Lord Byron possesses of an understandable, if not wholly accurate perception of our mariners, I fear. Whilst it is true that they will not sail without pay in advance, such pay is certainly meagre, and they do not hesitate to place their lives at risk in the service of our embryonic state... though I imagine that the prospect of prizes is not entirely absent from their considerations. The Pasha has already called upon the Ionian government for compensation for his loss of half a million of piastres; in turn the Ionian government has called upon ours, but there is nothing to be done. There is no money. Even were money to be found, doubtless it would never be paid over to the Turks. No, we are now indeed in bad grace with the Ionian government, and the money seized from the Pasha's brig has all gone to Hydra. The Spezziot crews, when their Hydriot compatriots departed, left their five ships anchored out there and came ashore, refusing to continue to serve without further pay being received. My own interventions between them may have prevented a worse debacle, one which would have been to the lasting shame of all Greeks. I find I am now appointed head of the provincial government here and no longer am I a simple volunteer. Our resources remain meagre, our equipment but little, troops few and money nil. This is common knowledge and will certainly find your ear during your stay. I hope that you will not be so dismayed as to leave us too, Captain O'Connor?'

'Your Highness, we are presently well equipped and want for nothing other than direction,' Pat replied, more positively than he felt at that moment; the loss of Simon, for that is how it seemed, was weighing heavy on his spirits. 'My jack tars waited for many months - a year or more - for their pay when fighting Boney, and a bare few months late is of little moment to them. Now that we have our *letter of marque* and can begin seeking Turk prizes, our prospects will surely change for the better.'

'Thank you, that is most heartening. We await the arrival of Lord Byron, which will assuredly also change our circumstances here in Missilonghi for the better, which I believe will be so very favourable for all of Greece.' Mavrocordato continued, 'However our situation in Candia is far from favourable, deteriorating in fact, and I have been asked by my government to convey to you the ever more urgent need for succour for our forces there - in Candia; for they are so very severely oppressed by the Turks. Indeed, we are at our last throw on the island, men and arms dwindling. One more victory for Hussein Pasha there and we are done for. In the matter of interdiction of Turk resupply ships, your frigate could be most profitably engaged. Our commander in Candia is also a Hydriote, Manolis Tombazes, and he has but recently been sore pressed by plentiful Turk reinforcement. It is conceivable that in some very few weeks to come he may require to evacuate his remaining combatants from the island. In this too your ship will be invaluable. Will you therefore, Captain O'Connor, accept our direction for your service as guard ship here until our need becomes greater in Candia, when you will sail to help us there? It will give me grave concern to lose your frigate from here, where it may serve the protection of Missilonghi, our own fleet having left us and the Turk squadron still here in Patras, but the needs of our compatriots in Candia may become more urgent still.'

'We will replenish our water tomorrow, your Highness, and with that we may stand ready to depart on your order for Candia without delay. Are you able to gain any news of Doctor Ferguson and Count Gamba through your sources in Patras?' Pat added, a little anxiously.

'My agents will bring news within a very few days, Captain; of that you can be assured,' replied Mavrocordato as positively as he could put it.

Outside and once again at the quay, a disconsolate Pat stood in the pale winter sunlight, the warmth of the day ebbing with the onset of the early evening, a cooling easterly wind coming off the hills. The prospects for Simon, captured and helpless in the fiercely hostile midst of the plainly untrustworthy foreigners, filled his mind with a chilling dread. He contemplated his immediate plan, standing silently and looking rather distantly across to the distant tops of *Surprise,* moored beyond the shallows of the lagoon. He stared vacantly at nothing in particular, his small band of shipmates standing guard ready about him.

A few more minutes passed by, Pat still absorbed in his private deliberations, until he became aware of his men scrutinising him, when his attention returned to them. 'Mr Pickering, we will allow a rota for crew leave ashore this evening. Not less than half the crew to remain aboard *Surprise* in case of any eventuality. Tomorrow after church we will water the ship, my barge to be used to carry our barrels to and fro. Barton, look about for a clean water supply. I believe I will return to the barky,' Pat concluded.

With half of his crew and officers ashore in Missilonghi, their leave reinforcing Pat's painful awareness of the absence of his close friend, it was all Freeman could do to try to bring some cheer to his captain's gloomy face by ensuring the very first quality of his toad-in-a-hole for supper. He was accompanied by Murphy, bearing a bottle of the finest red that Pat had ever had in his stores, a Romanée-Conti burgundy of 1817, supplies of which had become available in only the tiniest quantities after the demise of Bonaparte. It was a bottle long previously secreted away by Murphy, who had wholly unfounded pretensions of wine knowledge but more real aspirations of usurping Freeman's role as principal butler, the bottle put by for no reason other than his vague and indiscernible feeling that some prime reason would come up. Murphy was sadly disappointed, the savoury aroma of the freshly cooked food and the taste of the exceptional red being scarcely noticed and producing no more than a grunt from Pat who was seated at his table, picking at his food whilst studying his Admiralty charts of the Aegean.

Murphy persevered, 'Well, your honour, now your supper will be a'ruined if it ain't eaten up hot.' As this produced no response from Pat he added, 'Mr Marston is asking of you, and would you care to see him in the cabin this evening?' adding almost as an afterthought, 'sorr.'

The question broke Pat's train of thought. He seemed to welcome the disturbance of his morose mood and looked up, 'Why yes, thankee Murphy. Please pass my compliments to Mr Marston. If he should care for a little music, I am at his service. Freeman, could you kindly bring extra toad-in-a-hole and a glass for him? This is a prime wine, Murphy,' said Pat, noticing the bottle for the first time. 'I collect that you said we had none left... that the rats had got at the corks. Was it in Gibraltar... or in Mahon?'

'Well, it was in the wrong case, in with the sherry,' Murphy explained unconvincingly. 'The extra food and a glass will be here d'reckly... sorr.' Murphy hastened away before he could be asked further questions by his grumpy captain.

A few minutes passed when the chaplain knocked and appeared at the cabin door. Pat sighed, wondering whether he was up to entertaining a guest. 'Ah, Mr Marston, there you are, come in. Please, take a seat, over there near the window; we have still a little light. You have brought your violin... excellent.' Freeman bustled in and set down the glass and toad-in-a-hole for Marston, Murphy hovering at his elbow with cutlery and napkin. 'Allow me to pour you a glass of this most excellent burgundy, near my last one. We are certainly favoured to enjoy it,' said Pat, his voice flat, an audible tone of despair recognisable within it to the tutored ear.

'Thank you, sir, most kind,' Marston was now extremely anxious, wondering if he might somehow stand in bad grace with his captain. He took a large gulp, 'An excellent wine. Never have I tasted better.' A sideways glance afforded him the impression that his captain, who was chewing slowly and repetitively, seemingly deep in thought, was far from contented.

'Murphy there, we will have this bottle's fellow to follow, if you will.' Pat turned to look at his guest, and Marston could plainly see Pat's face betraying his unhappiness; indeed, it was clear that there was a deep undercurrent of dismay, the deepest; but what it was Marston could not tell.

He ventured a tentative exploration, 'Sir, should it be even the smallest concern, I feel sure that the sick bay presents no difficulties at all until such time as Doctor Ferguson returns.'

No answer, and Marston, perceiving that his captain looked distracted, depressed even, remained silent as Pat sipped his wine. A brief pause and Pat picked up his 'cello and began tuning it, a discordant series of brief squeals resulting, which left an attentive Marston wondering whether such was more in tune with his captain's downcast spirits.

'Well, this is the last one,' declared a buoyant Murphy, returning within a few minutes and triumphantly clutching the famous burgundy.

'Thankee, Murphy. Mr Marston, please, the toad-in-a-hole is cooling. This surely is the very finest of wines. You will allow me to refill your glass,' Pat was at last striving to brighten, to observe the civilities. 'Now, what would you care to play, as we lack our viola?'

'Perhaps a little *Vivaldi* might bring some cheering warmth to our playing, sir,' offered Marston in warm voice with a determined effort to help his captain; 'What do you say to the *Four Seasons*? I have oft heard it played in this cabin; *La Primavera*, if you will.'

'An excellent choice, Mr Marston; Dr Ferguson and I do enjoy playing that most wonderful first movement. Why 'tis not more popular these days is a mystery to us all.' With a determined effort to entertain his visitor, the supper and wine having been consumed by both of them, Pat set to with his 'cello, but he played diffidently for a quarter of an hour before setting it down on his knee and looking across towards Marston. His guest had winced at Pat's sometimes flat and occasionally shrill notes, and had become uneasy, but he held his tongue. Pat's playing ended abruptly on a most discordant note. No words were necessary: it was plain that Pat's heart was not in his playing. 'I regret that I am uneasy in my mind,' whispered Pat after a near minute of mutual silence, 'and the music don't answer; indeed, I have failed to find the least proficiency with my instrument... Oh dear.'

Marston had patiently held in check his observations of Pat's errors, his host's gloomy mood so evident despite his best efforts to play and to entertain his visitor, and so the chaplain had doggedly continued, so much wishing to cheer his captain, but all to no avail. 'It is of no moment, sir; it will come back to you tomorrow.'

Pat sat quite still, his 'cello on his lap, his face devoid of any expression, his indeterminate gaze void of any focus, his clenched fist slowly and repetitively tapping on his chair leg. 'I am at a stand,' murmured Pat very quietly.

'Captain O'Connor, sir... it pains me that you may consider me to be presumptuous, yet I find my observations and leanings... that is to say my inclination in our Lord's service... necessitates my enquiry... If I may be so bold, you do have a care-worn air about you...' said Marston gently.

'Nonsense,' declared Pat in wholly unconvincing voice, but he said nothing more and seemed to be reflecting on his answer until he spoke again after a near minute in no more than a whisper, 'Dammit! I am brought by the lee.'

'I beg your pardon, sir; pray tell if you are not equal to company...' Marston persevered after almost a minute of silence; 'Are you oppressed by melancholy thoughts? Are you well?'

'There is no need like the lack of a friend,' mumbled Pat with something akin to despair in his voice. 'Excuse me, I am not quite in my intellects this evening.'

Marston became aware of a growing and conceivably necessary shift in his own position, from shipmate to chaplain. 'Perhaps, sir, I should leave you alone to your deliberations...' he offered very quietly, '... or could I be of some service to you in your hour of... *of distress?* I have some small experience in my capacity as a man of God in... in such difficult times. Will you speak of what is patently weighing hard upon your mind? Pray forgive me if I presume too much.'

'Why, Mr Marston, thank you for your concern.' Pat looked up and peered closely at his companion, 'but never mind me, I beg.' A searching scrutiny from Marston and Pat continued in a whisper, 'To tell you the truth, I am at a stand. I am tolerably uncomfortable since Simon was taken by the Turks. He is the dearest friend a lucky man might possess. Indeed, we have served together since the year 'three and I have loved that man as a brother for so long, *more than twenty years*, that I can scarcely believe what my life would be like were he never to play his

365

viola again in this cabin; indeed, I cannot shake from my mind a feeling of the most acute distress in his absence.'

Marston issued a reassurring murmur, not wishing to break the flow of Pat's thoughts as his captain continued, 'I have fought in many a battle, lost many a fellow crew member... yet never have I felt such a loss - *no, let us say a potential loss* - so personally. Some months ago - you may collect - my new cox'n, Barton, joined us, and he reminded me so powerfully of our loss of his brother in the year 'thirteen. So many years have passed by since then... *yet he is oft still in my thoughts.*'

Marston looked into Pat's troubled face for long moments before replying whilst summoning every shred of the authority he considered vested within him by his calling into his voice, 'It is surely a great compliment to you, sir, that in all your years at sea and... and many other men having been lost serving with you... that you have retained your compassion for your fellow man. Your humanity is plainly preserved, as all can see, and no one could ask more than that; though I am sure that at such times it surely seems a heavy burden.'

'Sure, and I have been contemplating on the fact that scores - *perhaps a hundred or more* - of men have been lost on those vessels I have commanded, Mr Marston.' Pat sighed again. 'It is indeed a burden I am oft reminded of. A sleepless night and some of them are there... in and out of my dreams; old comrades such as Brannan Barton often... and others that are too many to remember; even many of their names I regret I cannot recall.'

'Sir, your mind is conceivably much disturbed by the thought of the possibility - *the mere possibility* - that you may lose more men in this venture. You have gained many victories in His Majesty's service. No more celebrated captain ever commanded any English ship, even Nelson included – *I doubt that anyone would dispute that* – and thanks to you are we not so very much safer in our English homeland - Bonaparte's invasion never having departed? Do we not sleep safer in our beds? Surely so?'

'That is most exceedingly flattering, Mr Marston; and I most certainly do not wish to accuse you of verging on flummery; no indeed...' Pat's social abilities, never exceptional, were severely put to the test in his demoralised state of mind; '... and neither do I care to boast away about my own service; but there are times when I contemplate whether 'tis finally time to tie up for good, the end of my sea-going days, a life ashore...' Pat paused, the strain and distress so evident in his ashen face, and he looked to Marston, 'No more loyal and good men would I lose... Oh dear, I fear my judgement has gone astray, my intellects are oppressed; perhaps I have been in command too long.'

It was the prospect of Simon being lost forever that had brought this despair pressing to the forefront of his captain's mind, Marston realised; and so he determined to persevere, replying softly but with firm conviction in his voice, 'Captain O'Connor, it is plain to the meanest understanding that you are much attached to Dr Ferguson... and, with the greatest personal respect for you, sir, much set back by his capture; but I beg you will consider that he has not been killed in conflict; he was not injured nor taken in the heat of battle... Furthermore, sir... *furthermore...* he is reportedly now in the custody of the most senior officials of the Turk regime in Patras, officials who will certainly accept their diplomatic responsibilities and the requests of British consular officials to see him. He will stand well with the protection of his British passport and the standing of his companion, Count Gamba. I think, therefore... sir, that we may safely place our confidence for his well-being and ultimate return in diplomatic conventions.' Marston looked at a still silent Pat O'Connor and persevered, 'We may most assuredly also place our confidence in our Lord; let us take comfort in the words of Psalm 30... *Weeping may endure for a night, but joy cometh in the morning.* I have not the least doubt that soon we will have news of Doctor Ferguson.'

Pat looked up directly at Marston with an affinity he had never formerly felt for him and said quietly, 'I would never have countenanced a chaplain aboard any of my ships but for the persuasion of Doctor Ferguson. It is he that we both have to thank for you being here. May God set a flower upon your head.' It was all that he felt able to say, but he rose to his feet, seized and shook Marston's hand with an iron grip, a further half minute passing in silence as Pat still held it firm.

Marston stared directly into Pat's eyes, ultimately speaking in firm voice, 'At such times we must draw strength from the Bible... and Isiah's writings speak plain: *Those who hope in the Lord will renew their strength. They will soar on wings like eagles; they will run and not grow weary; they will walk and not be faint.* In such moments as these we must all hold fast to hope... *Hope*; it is the precious mainstay of our spirit.'

A long minute passed in silent reflection until, eventually, Pat spoke again, 'Thank you... you have been most kind... listening to the dreary woes of an old salt... I take comfort from what you have said... I am deeply obliged to you, I am; but now, I beg you will excuse me, I find my mind ails me; I believe I must retire.' Pat released Marston's hand from his enduring grip. 'I bid you good night, Mr Marston. Thank you again. *God and Mary be with you... Father Michael.*'

*Sunday 4ᵗʰ January 1824      aboard Surprise, off Vasiladi island*

'Good morning, Murphy, Freeman,' said Pat in pleasant surprise, gazing at the silver tray as his breakfast was brought in by his stewards, the load a grand plethora of fried bacon of unknown provenance, eggs, mushrooms, tomatoes and toast. Murphy meticulously laid cutlery and clean napkins as if in emphasis.

'Well, it is, to be sure, sorr,' said Murphy before Freeman could speak and noticing his captain's tone of approval, a change very much for the better in contrast with the despairing ambience of the prior evening.

'Pass the word for Mr Pickering and Mr Marston... and my compliments. I will inspect divisions at four bells and we will rig church for six bells,' Pat ordered, 'and Murphy, be so good as to check our stocks in case of any further bottles stored in the wrong cases.' This he added in the lightest of stern tones, the merest hint of a smile on his face.

'Aye aye, sorr, d'reckly,' replied Murphy, his spirits lifting as he felt the improvement in his captain's mood.

At divisions, many a thick head was evident to the experienced eye, the crew having enjoyed a very rare run ashore in the prior evening amidst the best that Missilonghi had to offer.

Yet all were present, which was testimony enough to Pat that he had a prime crew, not a pressed man amongst them. He doubted that any of them would have been other than volunteers even were the press still to be a recruiting force. 'The Press,' he mused as he stepped towards the first division, 'where would his Majesty's fleet have been without it?' And yet on his own ships during the war he seldom employed pressed men. *Tenedos* in particular had long been known as a happy ship and its crew favoured with plentiful prizes, prizes which had substantially enriched those crew from Falmouth and, indeed, the town itself generally. Pickering saluted and the hands removed their hats as Pat began his inspection. 'Dalby, have you had a fall?' asked Pat, looking at a very swollen black eye and heavily bruised cheek. 'What have you to say for yourself?'

'Climbing back on deck, sir,' replied Clumsy Dalby. It was a fiction no one aboard believed, least of all Pat, knowing Dalby's temperament well of old. 'Hmmm,' said Pat, moving on.

'Mr Tizard, are you with us fully this morning?' asked Pat, the ship's carpenter favoured with his title as a non-commissioned officer, as was his rightful due. He was seemingly striving to appear fully awake. Pat did not wait for his reply, but passed on to the crew of *Axeman,* all of whom also seemed considerably worse for wear. 'Hartley, Johnston; do I see you both Bristol-fashion this morning?' he asked pleasantly, although to everyone the answer could hardly be in the affirmative.

'Beg pardon, sir, 'twas the ouzo brandy. They said it should be drunk with plentiful water; but Barton said the water supply wasn't greatly clean... so we left it out,' explained an amiable but somewhat emboldened Hartley, so very obviously to all still suffering from the ouzo.

'I see,' said Pat, concealing his smile as best he could. 'Perhaps you need to see the Doc...' Pat's words tailed off as the recollection of Simon's absence returned to him.

Hartley, with surprising mental agility, quickly redeemed himself, replying with conviction, 'As soon as he is aboard, sir.'

It was a consoling belief that Pat clung to in his thoughts during the remainder of his inspection, much abbreviated due to the evident fatigue of his crew. 'Very good, Mr Pickering,' said

Pat when he had finished; although "very good" it would most certainly not have been described as by any of his peer captains during the French war, nor indeed by Pat himself; but Pat had more important things on his mind, and their status as a *letter of marque* had inexorably changed his perceptions of what was strictly *de rigeur* aboard *Surprise*. The long layoff since his command of *Tenedos* had, even to his own reluctant admission, somewhat taken the edge off his strict insistence upon the traditional service routines of the ship and his crew, but not his expectations of their conduct, nor their adherence to the necessary functions of the ship; and his confidence in his men was diminished not a jot. 'Mr Marston,' he spoke up in affirmative voice, 'I think we will dispense with reading the Articles and we will hold church a little earlier this morning, if you please; I see no need to wait for six bells.' The ship's bell struck five bells. *Surprise* held steady in the very mildest of swell, hardly a breath of wind evident, and the sails, left hanging in case of any urgent necessity to shift, hung loosely from the yards; but still the sharpest of eyes remained at the tops, gazing seawards, a cautious eye always towards the Straits and Patras. The morning was warming with the sun's rising progression towards noon and the day remained dry with not a cloud in sight except over the far peaks of the Morea to the south.

'Are you ready, Mr Marston?' prompted Pat. The crew were all assembled, a degree of indifference not to say boredom visible on many a tired face; but by far the majority stared with a discernible interest, for they were all generally conservative traditionalists by nature, and the Wesleyans of Falmouth most particularly welcomed and strongly approved of the Sunday service; indeed, they insisted upon it whatever the circumstances; and omitting it was likely to lead to discontent, which Pat understood very well.

'I am quite ready, sir.' Marston stepped forward to the capstan customarily used as the pulpit on the deck. He began the service with the reading of the Covenant prayer, *'Christ has many services to be done. Some are easy, others are difficult. Some bring honour, others bring reproach. Some are suitable to our natural inclinations and temporal interests; others are contrary to both...'* Marston paused, a heavy spell of coughing from several men breaking his train of thought. A glare from Pat towards the offenders and the chaplain resumed, *'Put me to what you will, rank me with whom you will; put me to doing, put me to suffering; let me be employed for you or laid aside for you, exalted for you or brought low for you; let me be full, let me be empty...'*

Pat's mind was jarred by these particular words as they slowly registered with him, his thinking a few seconds behind Marston's speaking; and he wondered whether his own feelings of emptiness in the absence of his friend might ever be restored, refilled.

*'... let me have all things, let me have nothing; I freely and wholeheartedly yield all things to your pleasure and disposal.'* Marston concluded by calling on the crew to join him in a hymn, thinking that the more jaded of them might be revived by the singing, but plainly this was not the case, as was evident by the many for whom song remained beyond their powers this morning after the prior evening's indulgences, a most discordant chorus resulting, many men unable to recall the words; and so the chaplain moved swiftly, without the least urging from Pat who was engrossed in his own doubts and fears, to the last piece of the service, his oration. His reference as he commenced to their missing shipmate, the Doctor, did bring about a resurgence of concentration and a shuffling of feet, the torpor sloughing off even the grossly indulgent of the prior evening. It was a remarkable change in the mood on deck generally, a heightening of interest, and it was particularly noticed by Pat, now listening attentively to his chaplain. Eventually, Marston moved on to his conclusion, one on which he had determined as most appropriate to his captain's mind after Pat's confiding in him of the prior evening, 'I will finish our service this morning with words from Psalm 121... *I will lift up mine eyes unto the hills, from whence cometh my help. My help cometh from the Lord, which made heaven and earth...'* Marston paused again, annoyed, a widespread murmuring had become evident within his audience, growing louder every second; he looked up from his Bible in enquiry.

Before Marston could utter a further word there came a loud shout from the lookout on the main mast, 'Ship ahoy, larboard beam!' Instantly all eyes stared directly out to the south-east.

'Murphy, quickly now, my glass!' cried Pat.

'It is a small ship, sir,' declared Pickering. 'She is shifting only with difficulty against the north wind – well, the breeze – with hardly any way on her at all, and it may take her some hours yet to get here.'

Murphy returned with the glass, and Pat continued to study the approaching ship very carefully for some minutes, it being barely visible amidst the haze and the sparkling light refractions over the water. Every man was staring in abject fascination over the bulwarks, chatter louder as time passed. Clarity improved steadily as she gained a mile in the next hour, all aboard *Surprise* gazing at her snail-like approach, Marston's service quite forgotten by all; indeed, the chaplain too was engrossed in watching and, his eyesight indifferent, he listened to every snippet of speculation with the utmost interest.

'My God, could it be? Could it be? It is the bombard! It is Gamba's bombard!' shouted an excited Pat to Tom Pickering, standing alongside him; Pat quite uncharacteristically slapping him on the back, great joy and exhilaration welling within him. 'Barton, go aloft! Quickly now, signal to her,' Pat ordered his cox'n.

'Aye aye, sir,' replied a jubilant Barton, the lingering effects of the previous night falling away in an instant; and he clambered up the ratlines at a speed never exceeded by the fastest of the young midshipmen of all Pat's prior commands. Another half-hour passed but no reply came from the approaching ship in response to Barton's signals. Apart from the men aloft, all aboard *Surprise* were now leaning on the larboard hammock netting, their conversation loud and utterly unconstrained by any custom or regulation, staring intently at the distant vessel, still barely moving and tacking every twenty minutes or so to make the least headway at all, but inexorably closing.

'I think we can be sure she is the bombard, sir,' said Pickering with growing conviction. The vessel was now not more than two miles off and her hull form and details were becoming ever more discernible. The wonderful news was passed to everyone aboard within mere minutes, and shortly thereafter a great hubbub of audible excitement broke out amongst the crew on the deck, loud voices and shouting everywhere, preparations for dinner quite forgotten. The cook was indignant as he emerged from below but he too was soon taken up in the suspense and anticipation, the forgotten dinner burning, ignored by all, as it ruined in the galley as a further hour passed. The bombard, for all were now sure that was what she was, was now barely a mile away, and all could perceive two waving figures on her prow, their identities still obscured. The effects of the haze were already considerably diminished, the sun higher and the late morning much warmer. Pat studied the small ship with his glass, an overpowering feeling of sublime joy in his heart and tears beginning to well from his eyes as it became clear that Simon was one of the two figures waving back vigorously.

'LOOK! 'tis he, 'tis the Doctor! Mr Pickering! Mr Marston! LOOK! 'tis Simon... and Gamba... They are returned to us. Thank God... thank God!' exclaimed Pat with not the least reservation, wiping his eyes on his shirt sleeve as unobtrusively as he could and thinking that it was not good form for his people to see their captain shedding tears. But he could no more staunch the salt stream as fly to the moon; however, all his crew were looking away towards the bombard, every man cheering and waving frantically, shouting and laughing, pointing towards the returnee, joy endemic to all. The exuberant, expectant minutes slipped by so very slowly, but Pat's distress and anxieties swiftly faded from his tormented mind like butter melting in a hot pan to leave a residue of sheer relief, profound and sublime after so long with the worst possible of all fears; indeed, he could not hold back his voluminous tears as the bombard approached, and he was reduced to a frequent and feigned wave of his hat as if striving to dispel the heat in a wholly fruitless bid to conceal the mélange of powerful emotions: joy, tears and relief, all quite untrammelled, wholly outside of his control, and perfectly visible on his face to anyone with the swiftest of glance.

Another half-hour and the bombard came near alongside *Surprise*; her anchor was let go and her jollyboat was lowered.

Simon, with Gamba, was rowed across to *Surprise*, willing and jubilant hands swiftly hauling them up the accommodation ladder without ceremony, Pat standing close by. Royal Navy convention quite forgotten, order become chaos, the crew cheered heartily and pressed forward to greet Simon, a much dishevelled figure; unwashed, unshaven and wearing the grubbiest of clothes; who staggered under the onslaught of much backslapping whilst pushing a few steps at a time through the throng towards Pat, smiling at all, uttering a few words to each man, and accepting every one of scores of profferred handshakes until his hand ached like never before. Eventually he paused, turned about and raised both his arms and shouted out, 'Good day, shipmates; I am most sensible of this prodigious fine welcome!' A hurricane of loud cheering followed immediately.

Without any ado Pat embraced his friend in both arms, hugging him fiercely, finding himself quite unable to speak and finding too that it was ever more impossible to halt the tears of relief that streamed down his face in a flood-tide of joy, now quite unashamedly visible to all. The ensemble of Pat and Simon steadily shuffled through the chaos of the impromptu crew assembly with the aid of Pat's officers clearing a passage towards the cabin. Pickering and Marston led Gamba down to the gun-room, perceiving that Pat would wish some time to speak with Simon alone. After several minutes of pushing through their jubilant throng of shipmates, Pat was able to close the great cabin door behind them, their ears ringing with the continuing cheers of the crew behind them. Not a man had taken the slightest notice of Mower's calls for 'Silence! Silence there!', half-hearted that they were. On deck, the ship's officers now swiftly brought to an end all pretence that the crew inspection was "very good" and a series of commands were barked out by Mower to the excited crew, half going below for a belated and somewhat ruined dinner whilst the others were pressed to the myriad ship housekeeping tasks which they minded not the least, a vibrant chatter endemic.

'Thank God, Mary and Saint Patrick,' uttered Pat in broken voice, seizing his friend's hand. The few words were all that a moved Pat O'Connor could utter, and that he was simply and utterly overwhelmed was plain for Simon to see.

'Pat, hold fast,' said Simon gently; 'You will allow me to say how happy I am to be back aboard the dear *Surprise* with such friends and brothers as I plainly possess. Oh, you are a good-hearted soul. Stand firm, brother.'

Pat was beginning to regain his composure, but still could find no words and simply stood there, gripping Simon's hand in a vice-like embrace, his strength overwhelming any intention Simon may have had to step back. 'How are you?' he said eventually in breaking voice.

'I do admit to the onset of a minor constriction in my larynx,' Simon replied with a smile, 'and a moist eye or two.'

Nearly a minute more passed, Pat searching for the further words to illuminate his relief for the return, the recovery, of his friend, a powerful sense of joy coursing throughout his very being; 'I am so happy, so very happy... overjoyed... to see you alive,' he exclaimed eventually before lapsing into silence as each man gazed at the other, the dangerous separation serving up a profound reminder of their deep mutual feelings for each other.

The status quo was broken by the voice of Murphy, insistent and whining in its usual tone but cheering and warming too by its very familiarity, 'Well, will your Honours want for a tint?'

'Yes, yes, Murphy, thankee,' croaked Pat, finding his voice at last. His eyes remained on Simon, 'I rejoice to see you, old friend. You look quite famished. Come straight to my table. Could you manage a long drink - *you must be mortal parched* - a bite perhaps?'

Oh, indeed; I could manage a number of them. Even the infernal weevil within the biscuit would exhibit an appeal at the present time.'

Pat laughed, relief coursing through him, 'I have asked Wilkins to cook the best of anything that remains in my pantry, and a glass or two of good wine will always answer the case.'

'Well, there is one last bottle been found o' that Roman burgundy, sorr, and will dinner now be convenient?'

'That exquisite elixir? The 'seventeen? Murphy, you are a fine fellow. That is exceedingly handsome in you,' remarked Simon. 'How delightful it is to be in contemplation of a good wine with friends... I am so pleased to see you. For a moment after we were taken, I thought my time had come, *that all hope was lost.* The Turk crew were as hostile as could be, and I collect that we were about to be put in irons - *in irons for all love!* - until - *would you believe it?* - their captain - Zachiria - recognised ours: Valsamarchi; indeed, Valsamarchi had rescued the Turk from shipwreck some fifteen years previously... God moves in mysterious ways...'

'How happy you make me to see you again,' murmured Pat with heartfelt, flowing emotion.

'Hope is a waking dream...' whispered Simon, 'Aristotle.'

Murphy hovered about them, and somehow, miraculously, held his tongue, horrified that he was at the state of Simon's vestments, his dismay exhibited in scowls that were perfectly plain for Pat to see but which Simon did not notice. Eventually Pat waved his steward away, 'Light along, Murphy; please to fetch the wine.'

They settled at Pat's table and Freeman arrived within a very few minutes with a steaming dish of swordfish soup and fresh baked bread – normally a rare delicacy, but the proximity to Argostoli afforded Wilkins welcome scope - and flour - to practise his art. 'Please, Simon, eat up. You look fair clemmed.'

'Thank you, Pat; I am indeed. Rations, though approaching edible at best, have been short and infrequent these past days. At many a meal did I have a hankering for some morsel more nearly resembling food... Though perhaps we are too accustomed to our good fare in these recent times.'

Pat smiled, his customary good spirit returning, and he refilled their glasses. 'We are, sure. I collect the County Clare in that dreadful year 'seventeen; a visit to the Burren to see old acquaintances, no food to be found, nor a potato to be had anywhere... Mrs O'Rafferty's cow killed, nothing to feed it... and her son leaving the land for America, for Boston. Dreadful times they were. Lord, we are well blessed these days, to be sure... though I do not need to tell you that. Here, we have nothing finer than this particular wine on this ship; Murphy has found it out; in the wrong case, so he said; the wicked dog! Will you drink the last bottle with me? Let us drink to our reunion; I can think of no better occasion.'

'Give you joy, brother; it is the noblest of sentiments, and I am as one with your thinking. I confess I have not found as much pleasure as this for many a year... indeed, I wish that our arrival in Heaven proves to be much like this halcyon day.'

Between mouthfuls of bread and spoonfuls of soup Simon recounted the story of his capture and subsequent release. A smiling Freeman brought a huge dish of stewed boar, cooked with plentiful bacon and mushrooms, and accompanied by a mound of steaming rice. Simon resumed his tale between gorging on the food. One incongruous but seemingly important recollection of Simon's which bemused Pat was his days before release studying the wading birds of the coastal marshes: herons, plovers, cormorants and many others being mentioned, and raptors too, including harriers, ospreys and eagles of several variants. It all passed over Pat; he merely nodded with pleasure, spoke but little and contented himself with refilling their glasses, his returned friend's presence giving him immense pleasure; and he called to Freeman for several more bottles as they enjoyed their reunion dinner together.

'We departed at 4 a.m.' said Simon, 'Unfavourable winds held us back until then, and even whilst we sailed they were scarcely less of an impediment. We had waited with a deal of anxiety for our passports as ships arrived from Cephalonia, fearing that Turk agents might speak with the Pasha of our intentions to go to Missilonghi and assist the Greeks... hence, fearing too that we might be detained further. But what news of Lord Byron and Abel Jason?'

'Safely hereabouts... along the coast, and they will be with us presently,' said Pat. 'Pray tell, have you considered further of the Turk fleet?'

Simon hesitated, the question not one for his personal province he thought, a little perplexed. 'Not as often as I might... or perhaps should have done,' he replied cautiously.

'But what Turk ships did you see in their squadron whilst you were there? Did you count frigates, brigs and the like?' Pat raised his voice in emphasis.

'I did not,' Simon replied; 'I am ashamed to say such enquiry was far from my mind, brother... and... I do admit that there are aspects... *lesser elements...* of naval practices with which I am not yet wholly familar. I dare say there were a score or more, all with several masts... guns aplenty... and the associated plethora of sails and nautical accoutrements so familiar to you mariners.'

'What a fellow you are!' exclaimed Pat generously.

'Mind, it was only a general impression; I do not commit myself to the precise number. As to what form of vessels they were, that I cannot say. Sure, there were both frigates and brigs.'

'Simon, 'tis a matter of some interest for our prospects.'

'I dare say, but I never paid it any attention.'

'Can you at least remember the number of vessels?'

'Shall we say a half-dozen of each? Let us not split hairs... for all love; I am not one for exaggeration.'

'Never in life. Did you remark whether they were preparing for sea... canvas let fall aloft and suchlike?'

'Why, as to that, I should have to consider it.'

'Pray do, if you will.'

'I do collect that the Pasha asked me of the prospects for compensation from Maitland for the very considerable specie wrecked on his coast and stolen by the Greeks, and 'twas only the mention of Melville as my patron - *that is to say in a medical capacity* - which secured our release. That seems sure to me.'

'Thanks be that he exerts an influence out here in the distant wilds of the Sultan's provinces,' remarked Pat, his voice an enduring mélange of relief and pleasure.

Tom Pickering looked in to announce that Gamba had gone ashore in the barge, and took the moment to shake Simon's hand again. Two sublime pints of hot coffee followed their dinner until they simply sat back in the deep satisfaction of their mutual company.

It was Marston, a full hour and a half later, that eventually interrupted a quiet reverie that had turned to slumber, knocking persistently and admitting himself to find them both emerging from a semi-sleep state. 'Would the gentlemen wish to join me and play for the crew on deck this evening? Our playing has been requested,' he declared.

'What say you, Simon?' asked Pat.

'With infinite pleasure.' Simon replied with particular satisfaction, looking closely at his friend's wide smile. 'After supper, if that is convenient for the operation of this vessel.'

'Brother...' declared Pat with feeling, 'may the hinges of our friendship never grow rusty.'

Some hours later, Pat and Simon, now more awake, emerged on the quarterdeck with Marston. The crew were sitting patiently along the gangways and on the forecastle, conversing in pleasant banter. The wintry evening was fine and dry, but the temperature was cooling noticeably, and all on deck were dressed for warmth. From far across the lagoon a distant Missilonghi remained dimly visible; the lights from houses were beginning to be more prominent as the sun slowly completed its descent, its low, lingering influence reflecting as weak shimmering ripples on the flat, still water. Pat paused his step and stared across the expanse, quite gripped by the sight, more minutes passing until the near darkness of dusk succeeded the weak twilight, when his friends gave him a gentle nudge. The trio sat on chairs fetched from the cabin by Murphy and began with an old favourite, their own far-ranging adaptation of the third movement of Mozart's *Third Violin Concerto*. Marston's violin lead was echoed by a subdued background from the viola and 'cello, the light and delicate playing accompanied by the crew tapping their heels on the deck, the music now almost as familiar to them as it was to the musicians. As the piece closed a general round of sustained and enthusiastic applause erupted from the crew, and the musicians smiled and nodded their heads in appreciation. Then came music from Bach, Boccherini and Corelli, all played with variations which the composers had never conceived, generally with a lifting of the tempo and with a gesture towards good spirits - as far as they were able to wrest such from their strings - and all was received by increasingly loud applause until they reached their grand finale, the wonderful solo *Caprice No. 24* from Paganini, played by Marston with a joy, an abandon, which was conveyed to all present and in which Pat and Simon marvelled. Although he could not approach the genius of Paganini, never did any of the assembly enjoy hearing a piece so much as they did that evening. The music had been played far into the night with such heartfelt vibrancy and zest; so much so that it was the most memorable of occasions that anyone present could remember; the people were in great heart, the joyous satisfaction of all with Simon's return so obviously endemic. It was plain that the memory of those moments would be cherished by all for the rest of their lives. At the end the crew clapped until their hands were sore and stamped their feet until the officers became concerned for the deck – unwarranted concern as almost all were barefoot. The trio of musicians looked at each other in deep satisfaction, then stood and took their bow, another roar of applause resulting, before they retired in great spirits to the cabin.

'A wonderful day, Simon... simply wonderful,' whispered a very emotional Pat.

*Monday 5<sup>th</sup> January 1824*　　　　　*aboard Surprise, Missilonghi*

In the early hours of the dawn, with thin shafts of light permeating the darkness from behind low cloud, Pat awoke and stepped briskly to his quarterdeck to look about at the sea state, to assess the weather, and to check for any sighting or report of any ships. Far visibility remained obscured by mists arising from the sea surface and *Surprise* rocked gently in the slightest of swell. Pat, bereft of anything save his shirt and breeches, shivered in the cold northerly wind. To his astonishment, anchored a bare fifty yards off from *Surprise*, was the mistico on which Lord Byron and Abel Jason had embarked in Cephalonia and later sailed from Zante. He spoke quietly with a descending watchman who declared that the mistico had arrived, according to their fellows previously atop, at six bells of the first watch, and that no one had thought that its arrival warranted waking their revered captain from his slumbers. The master, Mr Prosser, had been on duty when it arrived and had declared, 'Captain O'Connor needs more his rest than an awakening with news of a vessel scarcely bigger than a fishing boat! Even if it is one on which Lord Byron might or might not be travelling.'

A growing number of Surprises gazed over towards the mistico. Little activity could be seen on her deck until, at seven bells of the morning watch, the mistico's boat sheered off from her side. It was bringing back Abel Jason to *Surprise*. By now many more of *Surprise's* crew had emerged on deck, including Simon, and whilst Jason's welcome could scarcely resemble that displayed for himself, he was nevertheless very warmly greeted by all present as he stepped aboard, particularly by Simon, before being hastened off to the cabin for breakfast with Pat, Simon and Tom Pickering.

As they settled at Pat's table, Jason began his account to an eager audience, 'We had remained three days in Dragomestre after our escape from the Turk frigate... until a Greek gunboat, sent by Mavrocordato from Missilonghi, arrived to take us there. However, his Lordship declined the offer and determined to reach Missilonghi free of obligation and in his own vessel; and so we set off again in the mistico. We later stranded on the Scrofes rocks, his Lordship urging his attendants into the water to push us off whilst the Greek crew did nothing but fluster and lament their ill fortune. Fletcher - his Lordship's valet - and three or four servants struggled valiantly and shamed the Greek crew into assistance until we were off. More Greek gunboats arrived the next morning, and in their company we were beating all the way against the wind until we arrived yesterday evening, too late to navigate the shoals into Missilonghi; but we espied *Surprise* and tied up as near alongside her as we dared in the darkness.' Jason concluded his story but added as an afterthought, 'His Lordship is undaunted by his near capture and demise. He remains in good heart for this venture. I admire him greatly.'

'And rightly so! His Lordship is a pearl amongst a bed of thorns,' Pat opined. 'Are you acquainted with his Lordship's plans, Jason?'

'I believe that he is preparing even now to go ashore, leaving at about ten o'clock.'

'Well,' said Pat, 'we will postpone our own sailing for one day and accompany his Lordship ashore; he is deserving of our escort. Mr Pickering, prepare my barge and its crew, as best dressed as they can muster, if you will. The barge is to be priddied particularly well today... fit for a Lord... for a Lord it is we will be carrying.'

'Aye aye, sir,' said Pickering, nodding, a smile on his face.

'Simon, I trust you are intending to shift your clothes,' declared Pat, staring pointedly at the grubby attire his friend was dressed in; 'for this is a capital occasion, quite exceptional; and we would not wish Lord Byron to think he had fallen in with the coal merchant.' Murphy, grinning from ear to ear, nodded emphatically.

'Oh very well, Pat,' Simon scowled whilst speaking with undisguised asperity, 'For Heaven's sake, I would not care to run foul of such a pedantic perspective... *most disobliging that it is.*'

At 10 a.m. Pat's barge came alongside the mistico, and Barton with great care assisted Lord Byron down the side and into the seat alongside Pat. Simon and Jason sat in the seat ahead of and facing them. The crew had all grasped the great sense of occasion and had plainly done their best: all of the old *Tenedos* hands had donned their preserved, watchet-blue jackets - retrieved from the depths of their dunnage - which had never before been seen on *Surprise*, and they had buffed the brass buttons until they shone brightly. Others without jackets of their own had begged the loan of them from their shipmates. All were attired in clean, starched and pressed white duck trousers, in little shoes highly polished to gleaming black, and all wore low-crowned hats with the customary ribbon with the ship's name to the fore – run up by Whitaker, a mainmast hand who had been a tailor before being pressed in the year 'eleven. The barge crew's long pigtails had plainly all been combed out before being tidily replaited, and a better turned out barge crew Pat had never seen. 'Very creditable, lads! Well done!' he declared, filled with pleasure and reflecting that his crew did justice to the old saying: *You can always tell a ship by her boats.*

Byron himself was smartly attired in a clean and freshly pressed red cloak, undoubtedly of military origin. He was wearing a golden metal helmet resembling something of ancient origin.

'Ancient Greek perhaps,' wondered Simon. He looked closely at Byron for a moment or two before speaking, Byron noticing his gaze. 'My Lord, I am but recently become an admirer, and speaking with the greatest presumption, a friend; for

I hope that is how you may consider of me... and, if you will forgive my remarks, your arrival in this place and your benevolent scheme is of the very deepest significance. Might I say therefore... with infinite respect, that your cloak is most symbolically suited to your purpose this day, though perhaps the helmet less so? We may consider that the Greek need is for modern arms... and such a helmet may strike the observer as a relic; indeed, an excess of embellishment of any message will often diminish the essential content most substantially.'

Byron considered the comment for a few seconds before leaning forward to grasp Simon's hand and replying, 'Thank you, Ferguson; that is a most prescient thought. I venture you are too polite to say what you really meant... that I look like a buffoon. It would please me were you to keep the helmet as some small memento of my friendship for you too, for indeed that is my sincerest perception of you,' and with that he removed the helmet and placed it in the bottom of the barge.

'Welcome, my Lord,' said Pat warmly, marvelling at the spirit and generosity of the man, his humanity so evident, yet preserving a humility that oft escaped others elevated to such heights.

'Thank you, O'Connor,' Byron replied, taking and shaking Pat's hand, smiling all about him. To Pat's scrutinising eye, the barge crew all plainly felt honoured to be there in his presence.

'Barge away, Mr Pickering,' ordered Pat; 'Row dry, Barton!'

The sun was now free of the south-eastern cloud and shining brightly as they rowed across the calm, still waters of the lagoon, the winter day warming as the morning progressed. Byron's arrival had also been observed by the Greek ships anchored outwith the shallows, all of which fired their guns in salute as he passed by within Pat's barge, their decks filled with Greeks waving from their rails. Word had also reached the town itself because the fortress began to echo the gunfire of the ships, booming resonations rippling through the still morning air, distant echoes returned from the hills behind the town. After fifty minutes of the most careful, steady rowing by the crew, none wishing to splash their most honoured passenger ever, the barge grounded on the beach of the town; Pat leaped ashore to help Byron over the prow, when huge cheers broke out from the waiting crowd, which surged around the arrivals. Duncan - Pat was immensely pleased and delighted to see - was standing alongside Mavrocordato, and although he had long claimed complete recovery from his head injury of the summer, the recuperative benefits of a month ashore in relative rest had visibly served him well; for so Pat thought.

Mavrocordato, attired in ceremonial finery, stepped forward to welcome Lord Byron, grasping his hand as the rest of the barge crew scrambled to the beach, when the loud roar of enthusiastic cheering began, a great cacaphony of noise from hundreds of folk and the most glorious of sights, whilst in the background the booming guns of the town opened fire once again with their loud welcome: fully a twenty-one-gun salute.

## GLOSSARY, for pressed shipmates

Bargeman.................weevil (usually in the bread and biscuit)
Blatteroon............... senseless babbler or boaster
Blunties .............Old Scots term for stupid fellows
Boggart................... Mythical creature inhabiting marshes
Boggies....................Irish country folk
Bombard..................Mediterranean two-masted vessel, ketch
Boney...................... Napoleon Bonaparte
Bower......................bow anchor
Boxty........................traditional Irish potato pancake
Breeks.......................Scots term for trousers or breeches
Browster wife...........a landlady of a public house or who brews beer
Bumbo.....................pirates' drink; rum, water, sugar, and nutmeg
Burgoo.....................oatmeal porridge
Capperbar............... theft of government property
*Captains' Thins*........Carr's water crackers, a "refined ship's biscuit"
Caudle.....................thickened, sweetened alcoholic drink like eggnog
Clegs........................Scots term for large, biting flies
Commons (short)..... Short rations
Crabbit.....................ill-tempered, disagreeable, crabby
Crubeens...................boiled pig's feet
Dock (the)............... original name for the navy's Devonport base
Dreich......................Old Scots for cold, wet, miserable weather
Drookit....................Scots term for drenched
Dun..........................Bailiff
Dunnage.................. personal baggage
Etesian.....................strong, dry, summer, Aegean north winds
Felucca....................small sailing boat, one or two sails of lateen rig
Fencibles.................the Sea Fencibles, a naval 'home guard' militia
Flat...........................a person interested only in himself
Flux..........................inflammatory dysentery
Forty Thieves.......... a class of ships subject to dockyard pilfering in build
Frumenty.................a pudding made with boiled wheat, eggs and milk
Galway Hooker....... coastal sailing craft (fishing) of western Ireland
Golden Horn (the).... the harbour of Constantinople
Gomerel...................a stupid or foolish person
Groyne (The)...........La Coruña in north-west Spain
Gull..........................to deceive
Hallion.....................a scoundrel
Hazing (& starting).. harassment of crew by officers (with canes)
Hockogrockle, Marthambles and Moonpall ... Tufts fictional diseases
Hoy..........................small (e.g. London-Margate passengers) vessel
Jollies......................Royal Marines
Jollux.......................a fat person
Kedgeree..................a dish of flaked fish, rice and eggs
Kentledge.................56lb ingots of pig iron for ship's ballast
Laidron....................loutish, lazy rascal

*Letter of marque*..... an official (legal) document (and ship) to differentiate from pirates

Larbowlin (and Starbowlin) those of the crew who attended the larboard side (and starboard)

Laudanum................a liquid opiate, used for medicinal purposes in the Blue pill

Lobscouse................beef stew, north German in origin

Marchpane................marzipan

Mark of mouth.........from aged eight a horse's teeth no longer indicate its age

Marshalsea...............19th century London debtors' prison (another London prison was the Fleet prison)

Mauk........................Scottish for maggot

Meltemi....................Greek and Turkish name for the Etesian wind

Millers......................shipboard rats

Mistico.....................similar to the Felucca sailing vessel

Negus.......................a hot drink of port, sugar, lemon, and spice

Nibby........................ship's biscuit

Pinchfart...................miser, withholding to the detriment of others

Popinjay....................a vain or conceited person

Porte (the Sublime).. The government in Constantinople (actually the Sultan)

Press (the) ............... the Press Gang service to seize unwilling navy recruits

Puling.......................whining in self pity

Rapparee ................. a bandit or irregular soldier in Ireland in the 17th century

Receiving Ship........ where new navy entrants were received

Scrovies    .................worthless, pressed men

Seventy-four.............a 74-gun ship (a 3rd rate in the hierarchy of warships)

Sick and Hurt (Board).... the governing medical authority of the Royal Navy

Sillery................. a still, dry white wine of NE France

Skillygalee............... a gruel made with oatmeal

Solomongundy..........a stew of leftover meats

Snotties....................midshipmen

Stingo.......................strong ale

Strategic Chess......... Strategichess, 14x14 squares (multiple) chessboard(s) (game available from the author)

Treacle-dowdy...........a covered pudding of treacle and fruit

Trubs..........................truffles

Truckle...................... interfere with

Whoreson...................an unpleasant or greatly disliked person

Yellow jack................Yellow fever (or flag signifying outbreak)

Xebec........................ A fore and aft rigged sailing vessel with (galley-like) oars

## AFTERWORD - PTSD

If you are a serving military person or a veteran (or a friend or family member of either) who is in difficulty or affected by any form of distress, turmoil or anxiety, don't hesitate to seek help:

### in the UK, contact SSAFA

the Armed Forces Charity

www.ssafa.org.uk/help-you/veterans

or

### Combat Stress for veterans' mental health

www.combatstress.org.uk/helpline

email: helpline@combatstress.org.uk

The free telephone helpline is open 24 hours a day,

365 days a year

0800 138 1619 (veterans and families)

0800 323 4444 (serving personnel and families)


### in the US, contact the Department of Veteran's Affairs
### The National Centre for PTSD

www.ptsd.va.gov

call 1-800-273-8255

email: ncptsd@va.gov

**Elsewhere**, search the web and find your country's help providers.


Please do bear in mind that trained, courteous, caring people are standing by to help. There is nothing at all to be lost by calling. There is not the least shame in seeking help. There is no need to struggle on alone with PTSD difficulties. Call: you are not alone.

This extended and enhanced edition of **The Massacre of Innocents** has been written in response to reader comments about the first two editions (more so the first one), and I hope it will now satisfy (indeed delight) the most critical of readers.

Together, all editions have been ten years and many thousands of hours in the making: from meticulous historical research at the outset (and ongoing) to first draft, second draft and probably ninety-seventh draft *etc* (you get the idea), through interminable days of editing, and then to the tedium of page setting, until ultimately the tricky and precise task of full colour cover production.

This edition contains some 30% more than the second edition.

If you have enjoyed the book, I would be most grateful if you would post an Amazon review and also mention it on the social media sites which you enjoy using; other fans of historical (and particularly nautical) fiction may then discover it for their own pleasure.

Thank you in anticipation; a glass with you!

Alan Lawrence          Devon, June 2022